"What a gorgeous debut novel! The writing is witty, breezy, and sophisticated. Each character is fully developed and seems as if they've been plucked from our very own circle of friends and lovers. A *Love Noire* is the perfect book to snuggle up with."

—Yolanda Joe, *The Hatwearer's Lesson*

"Sizzling and sophisticated, A *Love Noire* is more than just a promising debut. It's a provocative, thoughtful love story that resonates with complexity and grace, and marks the arrival of a fresh and original voice. A gem."

—Travis Hunter, author of *Trouble Man*

"A *Love Noire* pulsates with depth and consciousness. Turnipseed has crafted a story of love that spans the African diaspora and skillfully reveals the complexities and the power of true love and intimacy."

—Tracy Price-Thompson, author of *Chocolate Sangria*

"A *Love Noire* is a refreshing glimpse of love in all its glorious shades of blackness. Turnipseed has written a smart, sexy, impressive debut."

—Lori Bryant-Woolridge, author of
Read Between the Lies and *Hitts & Mrs.*

"A *Love Noire* is a prayer answered for all of us black girls dying for contemporary fiction to offer us 3-D reflections of our admittedly complex but fabulous, textured, and sexy lives. Turnipseed's debut novel offers all of the above in page-turning prose as lush as cashmere sweats and as titillating as your favorite stilettos."

—Joan Morgan, author of
When Chickenheads Come Home to Roost

"A *Love Noire* is a captivating love story with provocative characters who blend passion, race, and class on three continents. Erica Simone Turnipseed has given us a first-class novel that pushes all the right buttons. A great read!"

—Lawrence Otis Graham, author of *Our Kind
of People: Inside America's Black Upper Class*

Erica Simone Turnipseed was born in 1971 and has a B.A. from Yale University and an M.A. from Columbia University, both in anthropology. She has been published in the anthology *Children of the Dream: Our Own Stories of Growing Up Black in America*. Erica is Director of Development at The Twenty-First Century Foundation, a national public foundation that promotes black philanthropy and supports African American community-empowerment organizations. She will donate a portion of the proceeds from *A Love Noire* to the foundation. Erica is a member of the board of directors for the Black Ivy Alumni League and the founder and co-chair of the "Five Years for the House Initiative," a fund-raising drive for the Afro-American Cultural Center at Yale. She lives in Brooklyn, New York. *A Love Noire* is her first novel.

ERICA SIMONE TURNIPSEED

A
Love
Noire

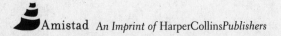 Amistad *An Imprint of* HarperCollins*Publishers*

A hardcover edition of this book was published in 2003 by Amistad, an imprint of HarperCollins Publishers.

HarperCollins books may be purchased for educational, business, or sales promotional use. For information, please write: Special Markets Department, HarperCollins Publishers Inc., 10 East 53rd Street, New York, NY 10022.

FIRST AMISTAD PAPERBACK EDITION 2004

Designed by Kate Nichols

Printed on acid-free paper

The Library of Congress has catalogued the hardcover edition as follows:
Turnipseed, Erica Simone.
A love noire : a novel / Erica Simone Turnipseed.—1st ed.
    p. cm.
ISBN 0-06-053679-9 (acid-free paper)
1. African-Americans—Fiction. 2. New York (N.Y.)—Fiction. I. Title.
PS3620.U767L68   2003
813'.6—dc21   2003040382
ISBN 0-06-053680-2 (pbk.)

04 05 06 07 08 ❖/RRD 10 9 8 7 6 5 4 3 2 1

For my sista-spirits . . .

and for Grace Ayodele Webb,

Mommy's special angel

Acknowledgments

Though the act of writing is a solitary one, it finds a home in community. And so, I send out innumerable winks, kisses, hugs, tickles, and tremendous gratitude to my circle of love and support. You offered me information and inspiration without reserve, and kindness and prayers all the way through.

For my partner in life and love: Kevin Webb. Thank you for championing my successes, accepting my shortcomings, and always encouraging me to share my best self according to God's plan.

For nurturing in me wonder, wisdom, and faith, my family: the world's best older bro Dougie (Alfred Jr.), who always wanted a baby sister, and proved it by always loving me and keeping me giggling. And younger bro, Tyrone Gabriel, "the brother formerly known as . . .' for showing me that we can write our own script. You inspire us all. And to the 'rents, Juanita and Alfred Sr.— "Mommy" and "Daddy" for short. Thank you for cultivating in me kindness, forgiveness, and good humor, and for giving me the tools to live a life that is sweet. (And Mommy, I'm not the only one who calls you "Triple Cute"!) Also, special smooches to Tanya Ruff-Gure, my sister who God gave me in college.

Love also to Evelyn "Big Mama" Turnipseed, special auntie Barbara Ferguson, godmother Sharon Handy, cool cousins Karen DeGrasse-Mitchell and Parris Andrews, Catherine and Doretha Webb, and the families that form the threads of my past, present, and future. I am encouraged by the hearts and spirits of our ancestors who span across time and space.

Much love to my agent and friend, Nicholas Roman Lewis, who told me in our freshman English class that I had a gift; I say the same to you because you've helped me to share mine. Many props to my editor, Kelli Martin: thanks for still "crying at the end"; your keen eye is only out-weighed by your passion. Thanks to you, Dawn Davis, and the entire Amistad team for believing in the bigness and beauty of this story and for knowing that "the whole story is ours to tell."

Enormous gratitude to all of the generous spirits who read and reread, fielded midnight phone calls, served as enthusiastic cheerleaders, and readily offered me insights and gems of authenticity all throughout; this one's for you: Ben Agyeman, Yaw Agyeman, Donia Allen, Nsenga Farrell, Clare Garfield, Quentin Messer, Steve Nelson, Bambi Oladapo-Johnson, Greg Thomson, Sean White, and Kimberly Wright.

And to the sages, diviners, and gurus who tended to my spirit; your love and wise counsel is more than I could have hoped for: Victor Chears, Debbie Cook, Jamal Gure, Yma Gordon, Lisa Jones, Peter Kavuma, Kensika Monshengwo, Patrice Rankine, M'B Singley, and Ryan Smith. Special thanks as well to Cherise Grant for your professional encourage-ment at a very early point in this, and to my incredible high school English teachers: Frank Ingargiola, Sharon Lustbader, and Steve Zwisohn.

To my colleagues who form The Twenty-First Century Foundation cheering section: Erica Hunt, LaQuanda Norman, David Roberts, Alexandra Rojas, Pat Terry, and the board of directors. It's indeed a gift to work with people who encourage personal fulfillment alongside com-munity empowerment. Thanks for your support and understanding.

To all of you who have wished me well, inspired my voice, and called me a writer before I did, I am indeed humbled.

Part I

Début

Chapter 1

See No Evil . . .

Noire was in the wrong place at the wrong time, an Afro in a sea of perms. Regretting her decision to wear a thong that rubbed her cheeks like industrial-strength dental floss, she adjusted herself surreptitiously and cut her eyes at her lacquered, perfumed, and coiffed business-casual brethren and sistren at Brown Betty Books clutching copies of Marcus Gordon's bible on black folks and finance.

First, Jayna lied. Second, Jayna was late. Noire rammed her hand into the pocket of her waterlogged overcoat, crumpling the copy of Jayna's e-mail message that disingenuously proclaimed the evening to be about black empowerment and a magnet for progressive brothas. Instead, she was stuck trying to amuse herself amid a swarm of coffee-colored men whose tailored trousers and five-hundred-dollar shoes attracted equally well-heeled women with hungry eyes. Noire hated the pose.

Even Brown Betty herself—her head a cascade of golden dreadlocks and her body awash with purple fabric and musk-scented cowrie shells and crystals—looked at, through, and past Noire in the time it took her to say hi. Clearly, her hair was *not* political tonight.

Her disdain mounting, Noire railed against the ready display of brand-name degrees, six-figure salaries, and gentrified addresses that smacked of a latter-day slave auction. Was this what the Civil Rights Movement was all about?

"Don't hate, congratulate!" she heard one of her sistas tell an empathetic friend. She imagined they were corporate lawyers.

Noire made a plastic cup of white wine her temporary companion. She sipped it too fast and scanned the bookshelves lining the walls. Her eyes flitting over the haphazardly stacked volumes, she consoled herself with the presence of books by Maya Angelou, Ben Okri, Toni Morrison, and Edwidge Danticat. She jotted down a few titles in her Filofax, crammed it into her mini-backpack, and refilled her cup with seltzer before reclaiming her mantle of righteous indignation at the scene. Measuring the smugness of those around her with the yardstick of her own discomfort, Noire wondered about Jayna. Where *was* homegirl?

Jayna was straight-up wrong. She just was. Fifteen years of friendship with Noire should have taught her that, at twenty-eight years old, Noire had no time or interest in the self-congratulatory games of "name-that-Negro" that the newest generation of the talented tenth had a particular fondness for. Wasn't the biggest argument that Jayna and Noire ever had over love and money? Then high school seniors, they had fanatical obsessions with Terrence Trent D'Arby (Noire), Blair Underwood (Jayna), LL Cool J (both), and half the boys in their Queens neighborhood. At seventeen, Jayna was then a recent nonvirgin and reflective.

"Sex is no big deal. Mama says it's as easy to love a rich man as a poor man. I plan to marry rich!"

"Jayna: Sold to the highest bidder!"

"Let's hear you say that when you're shacked up on skid row!"

"Fuck you!"

"At least someone *does* want to fuck me! And, Nicholas is going to Stanford, too! I suggest you check your *attitude*."

Noire remembered the sting of Jayna's words. She had masked her hurt with anger over the Jayna-Nicholas hookup; she would have done anything for just a *kiss* from him. Shrugging off her thoughts, Noire became annoyed with her unplanned solitude at the bookstore and resolved to pass the time near a ripe discussion between Brown Betty's yards of purple fabric and a buppie poster boy. Amusing herself with her role of infiltrator, Noire nodded at both parties who, as recent Harlem residents themselves, vigorously debated the effects of the latest wave of multicultural homeowners into "their neighborhood." Her interjected comment about the displacement of longtime Harlemites because of the steep increase in rents received a cool glance from Buppie Poster Boy and a huff from Brown Betty. She wondered if they bought their groceries in lower Westchester.

Jayna was still missing in action when, at seven-thirty, Brown Betty asked everyone to sit for the start of the reading. Buppie Poster Boy glared at Noire before revealing himself to be the center of attention by propping himself against a stool at the front of the room and holding a much book-marked copy of his tome. His face looked important and solemn, his thirty-two privileged years filling the air. Five rows of mismatched chairs ringed him in a tight arc. Noire claimed a place toward the back of the store and attempted to hold the aisle seat to her right for Jayna. She figured that Jayna was trying to be slick, timing her arrival so as to miss the start of the reading and thus the brunt of Noire's venomous response to her. Planting her bag on the chair, Noire surveyed the assemblage of about forty-five people and caught the eye of Jayna's friend Alan. He was too far away to say anything so she mouthed a tepid hello.

Marcus Gordon had already shared five of his ten commandments of creating wealth in the black community when someone approached Noire. "Is this seat taken?" he whispered, handing Noire's bag back to her and lowering himself into the chair. He raised his right fist in an abbreviated black-man salute to the pontificating Marcus and settled into immediate concentration upon his words.

Arrogant, she thought, settling her bag onto the floor in front of her. She stared ahead but noticed his well-defined profile in her peripheral vision. *Probably full of himself.*

"Number Five is 'Own instead of rent.' Too many of us have spent too much money on our sound system, our silk sheets, and our summer vacation without first investing in our futures. If you don't own your spot, you're just making someone else rich."

Noire thought about the late rent check she had put in today's mail and the vacation she and Jayna were taking to New Orleans in a couple of days. *Maybe Marcus is my landlord.*

"Number Four is 'A penny invested is a penny earned.' Checking and savings accounts are cute, but in today's economy they're not enough. With interest rates barely outpacing the rate of inflation, that's as bad as hiding money in your mattress. And at that rate, your golden years will be spent flipping hamburgers under the golden arches. Invest in your company's retirement plan and make your own plans as well."

Maybe he can be my sugar daddy! Noire mused, trying to mask her discomfort about her own grim graduate school finances. Her mind unwillingly fast-forwarded through her prospects of five more years of student-induced poverty as Marcus shared his financial wisdom.

" . . . But most of all, you must follow the first commandment if you are to realize your own potential. 'Remove all people and barriers that stand in the way of your success.' I'm going to repeat that one. 'Remove *all* people and barriers that stand in the way of your success.' This is the one that always confuses people. They say, 'What about my family and my friends from back in the day? I can't just cut them off like that.' My response to that is simple: Cut them off or suffer from excess baggage. Last time I checked, we only had one life to live and a finite time in which to live it. So you better seek to thrive and not simply survive. Trying to hang on to all the folks who ever passed through your life 'just because' can strain your limited personal resources—whether that's your time, your money, or your emotions. People who impede progress will cause you to digress and ultimately regress. You can't afford that. So if you have family and friends who are messing up your program, they've got to go. If folks are distractions to you, kick them to the curb and don't look back. A person without direction is dangerous. But more dangerous is a person who is heading in the opposite direction from you. Because if you're trying to go forward and they want you to follow them, that means you're going backward—plain and simple. People like to make this a more complicated issue than it is. But folks—and black folks in particular—need to grip this reality if they really want to attain success and financial stability."

Mom, Dad, thanks for the memories. Noire almost laughed out loud but silenced herself amid the appreciative audience. Their clapping was enthusiastic. Her eyes rested on the still hands of her neighbor. Shifting in her chair, she noticed that his eyes were cast on the page emblazoned with Marcus's first commandment. He fingered the page, then folded down its corner before snapping the book shut.

Marcus fielded questions for fifteen minutes before encouraging people to purchase the book and get it signed. Noire's seatmate still sat. He clutched his copy in both hands. She looked at the cover and noted that Marcus's name was in larger type than the book's title.

"Mr. Gordon seems to think a lot of himself," she said, pointing to the book cover.

He turned to face her. "I suppose that when you're a part of the Gordon family, you want people to stand up and take notice. He's my boy from b-school. We went to Columbia Business School together. He's good people." *He has an accent.*

Noire feared expelling all the contents in her stomach. *THE Gordon family?!* "Oh." She tried to look indifferent.

"Why are you here?" her handsome companion looked at her blankly.

"I was meeting a friend."

"Tell your friend thanks for the seat."

"Something came up." Noire shot out of her seat, seeking to reclaim her dignity.

"I'm Innocent." He extended his hand.

"Noire." She shook it belatedly. "Interesting name."

"As is yours. You'll have to tell me where it comes from," he said before getting up. "Let me just get Marcus to sign my book. I haven't seen him in quite a while."

Noire marched toward Alan, wanting to move before Innocent did.

"Hey, Noire, happy you could come." Alan blew warm air onto her cheek and introduced her to his friend Nate.

Shaking Nate's hand, she said, "Apparently Jayna was looking for an inventive way to break friends with me, inviting me to something like this."

"I went to Morehouse with Marcus." Alan looked at Noire as though all of her teeth had fallen out of her mouth. He sighed and continued, "Jayna asked me to tell you that she's really sorry but she got caught up in this oral surgery project she's working on with some folks. More dental school hazing . . . Anyway, her group's test subject rescheduled for six-thirty tonight. The first draft of the project is due tomorrow, you know."

"Mmm." Noire warbled and thought about her own late paper languishing in the bowels of her laptop. "Yes . . . well, OK, Alan, good to see you again. Nice to meet you, Nate."

Alan blew cool air on her cheek this time and Nate winked. Seeing the sparkle in his eye, she couldn't imagine his familiar expression had been for her. When Alan winked in return, her question was answered.

Noire turned away from them, measuring the steps it would take her to get to her coat and umbrella, when Innocent approached her. She was blinded by the whiteness of beautiful teeth flashing between welcoming, full lips. He said something to her. His velvety dark skin warmed the harsh overhead lighting. He was probably in his early thirties, a shade under six feet and of a medium, athletic build. His custom-tailored Shaka King suit was complemented by a tie a bit too risqué for the corporate America he inhabited and cufflinks that were understated works of art. But he carried off his look with such finesse—from his nearly bald head to his highly polished shoes to—

He touched her elbow and she realized that he was waiting for a reply to whatever he had said. She didn't know what he had said. So she figured she'd ask a question of her own. "Yes, so, why the French pronunciation . . . for your name?"

His eyes held a hint of confusion before he answered, "Because I'm from Côte d'Ivoire in West Africa."

"I'm familiar with it." She made her face subdued.

"But Noire is pronounced with an American accent."

"That's because I'm from Queens."

"That seems appropriate." Innocent's looks were clouded with unknowable thoughts. Noire met them with question marks and points of ellipsis. His next statement reminded her who he was and why she didn't like him. "So, did you enjoy the reading?"

"I'm not Marcus's target audience." She narrowed her eyes and recovered her former righteousness.

"Well, Ms. Noire from Queens, I'm happy to have made your acquaintance. If you don't mind, I'd like to give you my card. Maybe we can get together . . . to talk shop."

She restrained her surprise. "Take mine instead," she said, remembering the flimsy cards she had printed in the computer lab for the symposium she attended last month.

"OK."

She fished around her overstuffed wallet to find one that didn't have information already scrawled on the back of it. Retrieving a slightly dog-eared card, she presented it to him with a hint of a flourish.

"'Noire Demain, Ph.D. Candidate, Comparative Literature, New York University.' Mmm. So what exactly does that mean you're doing?"

"Ask me later if you really want to know." Noire slid him a coy smile, and Innocent gave a surprised laugh.

"Oh, it's like *that*?"

"Yes, it's like that."

Noire departed gracefully before letting her warring thoughts draw lines of confusion across her face. She walked through the bone-chilling rain toward the subway. She couldn't wait to talk to Jayna.

Fingering Noire's tattered business card, Innocent felt tingly. Her energy had put him off balance. He ruminated on her bohemian good looks: five-feet-eight womanly build, burnished brown skin, retro cat-eye glasses. Her lips were pouty and small, but her voice was rich and her expressions quirky. *Noire.* Her name delighted Innocent's tongue. He wanted to know more about her.

Slipping her card into his own slim cardholder, he returned it to his breast pocket and rejoined the dwindling crowd around Marcus. "This was nice, man. Really nice."

"I'm just happy you made it, man," Marcus said, shifting his attention to Innocent. They had become "boys" at business school, but their hectic professional schedules and personal lives prevented them from seeing much of each other in the four years since graduation.

"Yeah. Look, do you want to get a drink? I'm never out of work this early; it's like lunchtime for me." Innocent snickered.

"Sounds good. But I can only have one because Lydia has the flu. I don't want to leave her alone with Nile for too long."

"How are she and the little guy doing? How old is he now?"

"He'll be two on April 1. Look, just give me a second to wrap things up in here."

"Sure." Innocent watched Marcus clap people on their arms and gesture expressively in response to their questions. People have always loved Marcus. He was from a family firmly entrenched in the business world and well known for its support of black philanthropic causes. He always joked that his family was a part of the black bourgeoisie *for real*, but Marcus was down; he was good people.

"Alright, man, let's push out." Marcus had his coat on and his fedora between his fingers. Innocent slipped on his trench and grabbed his umbrella from the stand by the door. They dashed out into the steady March rain and ducked into Sublime.

Innocent ordered a Black and Tan, and Marcus a vodka tonic.

"Here's to you and what is sure to be only the first of many books that will get black folks to see a rosy financial future. Cheers!"

"Here, here." They toasted and had their first gulp.

"So what's up, man, what the hell is goin' on?" Marcus started off.

"Well, work is kickin' my God-given ass is what's up. The bank is unrelenting."

"That's why I don't work for the proverbial 'man.' I've got to *be* the man!"

"Easier said than done, Marcus. Easier said than done."

"You've got an M.B.A., money in the bank, and me. What more do you need?" His face held no hint of facetiousness.

"Man, I haven't even seen you in two years!"

"Then consider this the first day of the rest of your life." Marcus clinked his glass against Innocent's a little too hard and took another swallow.

• • •

"Jayna?!"

"Hello? Oh, hey, Noire. Sorry I missed you earlier. Did Alan tell you about my project?"

"I figured you just couldn't face up to your lie." Noire struggled out of her rain-soaked coat without dropping the phone. "Actually, I'm happy you didn't come; it would've been ugly."

"Damn, Noire."

"Don't tell me you didn't know it would be an incognegro scene!"

"I didn't know."

"Bullshit, Jayna!"

"For godsakes, Noire, are you saying that you can't hang in that crowd for two hours?"

"What's that supposed to mean?"

"It means, get off your fucking high horse. We need for *some* black folks to make money and God knows it sure ain't gonna be you!"

"There is *no* reason for you to go there, Jayna." Noire frowned at the phone.

"What ever happened to your ugly LIVE AND LET LIVE T-shirt, Noire? If I recall, you wore that damn thing so often in undergrad that I had to steal it from your room just to wash it. That slogan should have been practically tattooed to your breasts. What happened to all of that liberalism?"

"I'm just not into all that bourgie bullshit. That's all."

"My dear, foolish friend, bullshit comes in many forms. *Trust.* So now what? I'd like to see you put your hundred-thousand-dollar Amherst degree in the shredder."

"We're not talking about my degree; we're talking about the book signing." Noire laughed, signaling her defeat.

"Love-15. Venus and Serena have nothin' on us! Your serve, Ms. I'm-Getting-My-Ph.D.-But-I'm-A-*Righteous*-No-Money-Havin'-Nubian-Sista."

"Remind me why I like you!"

• • •

"So, where's the money at on the continent, son?" Marcus sipped his drink. "Dad wants to see me get into some more Latin America stuff, but I really want to explore some opportunities in Africa. You're gonna have to drop some knowledge on a brotha."

Innocent laughed. Even after six years he still couldn't get used to that African Americanism, "the continent." It was cute. "Well, it depends on what you want to do. Of course there's South Africa, but if you want to create your own thing, and potentially get a really big return on your investment, you should look to the West—Ghana, Nigeria, Côte d'Ivoire, and Senegal especially."

"Man, I don't know about Nigeria. Folks are getting swallowed whole over there."

"Mmm."

They chatted, Marcus filling him in on the most recent Gordon family dramas. Despite his hemming and hawing, Marcus was equally invested in being a Gordon, with all of the rights and responsibilities it afforded him.

"So, man, tell me about the other you." Marcus gulped his drink. "What honeys have you got lined up? Give me the details. Since I'm a one-woman man in front of God and everybody, I've got to live vicariously through a smooth African brotha such as yourself."

"You are so full of shit!" with a laugh. "Look, the waters are not being stirred."

"Well, you know what they say, 'Still waters run deep'!"

"Well, then I'm a deep muthafucka right about now."

"That's alright, man; the year is young. Just don't forget how to play ball."

"I'm sure I won't."

"I saw you speaking to Afro before. Don't trip. Believe me, she was there by accident. Probably looking for an incense-making class . . ." He scoffed and put his drink up to his mouth.

"She seems alright."

"Alright in the don't-fuck-with-me-unless-you're-a-revolutionary kind of way, yeah!"

"Why all that?" Innocent finished his drink prematurely and ordered another.

"I met her before the signing. She's trying to hate, man. What she doesn't know is that *I'm* not her enemy."

"Did something happen?"

"That's not the issue. What's important is the fact that you're my boy and I want you to handle your business in a large way. She's going in a different direction from you, Innocent. Plain and simple. Sure, she's pretty to look at, but New York City is full of pretty women. And believe me, most of them would be happy to suck your six-figure African dick."

"Damn, Marcus!"

"Oh, you can handle that, black man. The thing is, am I lying?"

Peeling her cold and wet tights off of her legs, Noire announced, "Well then, you'll be happy to know that I gave a guy my number. One of *your* kinda people. I was holding a seat for you and he came and sat in it. He's Ivoirian."

"Ivoirian?"

"Just a second." Noire tussled with her velvet blouse. Slipping it over her head, she put on her ten-year-old AMHERST sweatshirt. Bringing the handset back up to her head, she cradled it between her right ear and a hunched shoulder as she hung her clothes up to dry. "He's from Côte d'Ivoire. Corporate but with sort of an artsy thing happening."

"So you're not holding his salary against him?" Jayna sounded incredulous.

Noire ignored the statement. "*Anyway.* His name is 'ē-nō-sah.'" She said his name phonetically, enjoying the novelty of it. "He was wearing a salmon-and-blue-striped tie with a gray wool pinstripe jammie." She was now cross-legged on her bed.

"Noire, you're speaking to me in codes! Tell me what happened in plain English. And fill in the details."

"OK, but wait. Let me just get some orange juice." Noire uncrossed her legs and scooted herself to the edge of the bed. Walking with the receiver nestled in the crook of her neck and the base in her hand, she laughed at her friend's expressions of impatience on the other end.

"Girl, I know you can talk and walk at the same time. It's not a cordless but I know that shit's got a long-ass cord!"

"OK, Jayna." Noire began to unwind her tale, embellishing her descriptions of Marcus, Brown Betty, and all the man-hunting women and posers in order to elicit the right reaction. Making a pit stop at the bathroom, she found her way to the kitchen.

The light from the refrigerator illuminated a triangle on her tiny square of yellow linoleum flooring. She gulped her first glass of orange juice with the door still open and then filled the glass again before returning the carton to its chilly home and kicking the door closed.

"So basically I told him to keep his business card and I gave him mine instead." Noire walked into the living room, dodging the pile of books strewn on the floor around her desk, and plopped down in front of her computer.

"Well what'd you do that for? Now you don't even know his last name or where he works! How you gonna run a check on Negro?"

They polished off their drinks and Marcus offered to settle the bill. "Look, it's pushing ten o'clock. I better get outta here."

They walked out of the bar and stood on the sidewalk saying their good-byes in the now misty rain. Marcus tried flagging down a cab. Three zipped by him until one finally slowed to a stop. "Thanks, brotha," he said to the driver. "Looked like nobody was trying to stop for a homeboy in the rain. Not even a homeboy in an Everett Hall suit!"

Then to Innocent, "Don't be a stranger. Give me a call sometime." He handed him his newest business card. "Better yet, Lydia and I will have you up soon, around Nile's birthday. You know we bought a brownstone up in Harlem?"

"No, I didn't know."

"Yeah, it's great. Huge spot in Sugar Hill, and I got it for a *great* price."

"More power to you, then."

"Yeah. Listen, take it easy. And tell the man to take his foot out your ass."

"I'll remember to tell him that tomorrow." They embraced like the old friends they were. Innocent closed the taxi door for Marcus and watched the cab pull off before he began to walk toward home. He lived about twelve blocks away, in the heart of SoHo, and thought the walk would give him more time to think about the mysterious Noire.

"Well, Noire, it definitely sounds exciting. A 'corporate Cudjoe'!" She snickered. "Just don't be too cute for your own good. Let me know if he contacts you."

"*When.*" She tapped her laptop's ON button.

"Right, when. Look, I'd love to tell you about my glamorous evening full of saliva and halitosis, but schoolwork calls."

"Yeah, I have a paper that I need to hand in by Wednesday. It's over-due."

"Well, good luck then. E me."

"Remember, the revolution will not be televised."

"I know. It'll be on the Internet. Good night, Ms. Thang."

Noire's neighbor's coo-coo clock announced the hour: 10:00 P.M. Her unfinished paper screamed her first and last name from the laptop. She stared through the screen saver that danced before her and envisioned Innocent's facial expression as he said, "Oh, it's like *that.*" What a curious expression it was—surprised, reserved, engaged. She replayed in her mind him taking her card, reading it, smiling. *I think he likes me.* Or was he just flexing his charm at her expense like so many homeboys? *I hope he's different.* Noire sighed. Her relationship with Cudjoe when she was twenty-one was the last one of real significance. The intervening seven years of dating were a hodgepodge of high drama, insecurity, immaturity, and the tired formula of three dates plus good sex equals no relationship. Her threshold for game playing was at an all-time low, her emotions a house of cards atop a fragile ego. Touching the mouse, Noire resolved not to think about Innocent for at least the next twenty minutes. After all, she was a woman of discipline.

Chapter 2

Stop at "Go"

SUBJECT: Comparing literature
DATE: March 9, 1999, 6:26 P.M.
TO: Noire@nyu.edu
FROM: IPokou@wright_richards.com

Ms. Noire from Queens,
  I figured you'd be the best person with whom to "compare literature." I've read the Bible, *Native Son*, *Another Country*, *Une Vie de Boy*, and *Texaco* among others. Would love to compare my list with yours. Does that interest you?

Innocent

Innocent pressed SEND. *I hope that I don't seem too eager, firing off an e-mail only twenty-two hours after meeting someone. What's even the proper e-mail etiquette on that sort of thing?*
  The drizzle that clung to his office window made it an opaque rectangle of darkness. He stared at his tired face reflected in the glass . . . wondered how many tired

faces were staring out of the thousands of offices in the World Trade Center. 6:28. *Maybe I'll call it a night in two hours*. He dialed the phone number of Two Towers Deli eighty-five flights below and ordered a number ten with everything but pickles.

"This is *not* cool," Innocent mumbled to his computer screen, staring at the sign that declared, PROPERTY OF WRIGHT RICHARDS. DO NOT REMOVE. He was only one of the investment bank's hundreds of vice presidents and thousands of employees throughout the world, just a cog in the wheel. Here it was only Tuesday and his patience for the workweek was already wearing thin. *Working the whole damn weekend has already made it a nine-day week for me!* His frown reactivated a headache from the morning.

As he scrolled through his daily call list, Innocent's eyes locked on "Marie," his mother's namesake. His thoughts tumbled back to last Christmas when he broke the news to Maman that he would not come home for the holiday. It had become a painful memory affixed to his unconscious; the recollection sneaked up on him with little warning. His mother's caustic words were still harsh French barbs in his ears.

"Have you become *so* addicted to blond girls and dollar bills? Is *that* it?!"

Innocent winced. He knew his mother didn't want an answer, so he didn't give one.

"There are good women right *here*. Women from respected families who will bear children who live up to the Pokou name."

"Maman, I'm not dating anyone seriously."

"If you were here, you'd be married. Must I go to my *grave* without knowing my own son's child?!"

"I'm sorry, Maman. But this is not about you."

"As an African man, your life is *always* about your family!"

Shamed, Innocent shrunk in his office chair, thankful that he could not see his mother's eyes narrowed at him in anger and regret.

"Son, Americans covet money like a young whore and worship it like it's the body of Christ. 'In God we trust!' It's blasphemy, Innocent. Has that country corrupted you?" She lowered her voice to a searing whisper. "Innocent, what good is *any* of it if you can only enjoy it selfishly? Sometimes you need to choose the people you love over the people you work for. They are not the ones who will cry at your funeral."

Innocent stood up at his desk. "Maman, this is not about sacrilege or disrespecting my family or culture, or lusting after money and blond women! It's not any of it! It's that I *just* made vice president; I can't afford to take off the time from work right now!"

"Innocent, please don't tell me what you can't *afford* to do. Your father, sister, and grandmother will miss you."

They tried to recover the conversation with the half-hearted pleasantries that should always be said between a mother and son, but Innocent's tear-streaked thoughts prevented him from voicing his usual expressions of love. Maman had succeeded in making him feel like a sellout. They hung up, and Innocent's heart pounded out the pain he could not express.

How can I explain to Maman that coming home is the problem? That returning for a week or two only to turn around and leave makes me schizophrenic?

Sometimes it was easier just to save himself the stress of the five-thousand-mile trip. When he returned to Côte d'Ivoire he wanted to relax, but he couldn't. Instead he was subjected to the unwelcome comments from the Pokou family inner circle, who quizzed him on his prospects for a wife and children. Of course he relished the nearness of his eighteen-year-old sister, his eighty-year-old grandmother, and his parents, but he *ached* when he had to leave them. It seemed like God's cruel joke. How other people did it, Innocent did not know.

"*Mr. Pokou, the Two Towers deliveryman is here.*"

Fumbling unsuccessfully with his phone's intercom, Innocent knocked it to the floor, then yelled toward his feet, "Thanks, Ralph!" He grabbed his wallet and left his office with more urgency than was called for, as if to put physical distance between himself and his thoughts of home. Walking down the hall, Innocent heard the muffled cacophony of multiple conversations behind closed office doors. Entering the reception area, Innocent gave the Two Towers deliveryman a ten-dollar bill for his seven-dollar order.

"OK, thanks, boss! My name is Joseph. I work every weekday at this time. Just ask for me next time."

"Alright, chief. Have a good night."

"Oh, I will!" The deliveryman strode out of the office with a buoyant step.

"Ralph, do you know if Alexander is still here?"

"Yes, he came back from the men's room a little while ago."

"OK." Innocent veered toward the cluster of cubicles at the back of the floor. As he got closer, he was assailed with Alexander's foulmouthed agitation.

"What the fuck do you mean 'we'? I brought in the fucking account. You didn't do jack shit but hear about it! I don't see any 'we' in it, asshole!" He slammed down the phone.

"This is bullshit, man!" Alexander said in greeting to Innocent, who now stood at the entrance of his cubicle.

"What's bullshit?" he asked, lowering himself into the lone empty chair within Alexander's three and a half walls. Unwrapping his sandwich, Innocent looked at Alexander's framed M.B.A. degree that was the sole adornment in the space.

"This turkey Wilson trying to stomp me is the bullshit. Remember that urban platform radio station that I just set up as a client? Well, this asshole is trying to get a piece of the deal just because I asked him some questions about it! What kind of bullshit is *that*? I shouldn't have asked his ass a damn thing!" Alexander shook his head more in anger than in remorse.

"Why didn't you ask me?"

Alexander rolled his eyes.

"Look, that's fucked up, but he really doesn't have a leg to stand on. Why don't you take it up with Renée tomorrow morning? I'm sure she'll see things your way."

"Yeah, she's the only managing director around here who's even worth her weight in *dust*!"

"You know that she looks out, man."

"Yeah." Remembering Innocent's first question—"And your black ass wasn't around for me to ask you anything!"

"I'd prefer it if you didn't color-code my anatomy in the office." He raised his eyebrow to make his meaning clear.

"Shit, man, I'm sorry. Just can't get the 'hood out of the homeboy sometimes."

"Mmm." Innocent plowed into his sandwich. Motioning to the degree on the wall, Innocent asked, "So how was Howard?"

"What? Oh yeah, it was cool. It's nice to be a black man at Howard. Folks at least respect that much. But it's got its share of uppity Negroes."

"Guess that's the case everywhere."

"Yeah . . . May will make a year since graduation. I do sort of miss it, especially those bodacious shorties. Damn!" He shifted in his seat, his body gripped with memory. "What about Columbia?"

"You know, it was alright. No shortage of beautiful women, met good people, and of course it landed me a plum job in this hellhole." They laughed boisterously before Innocent continued: "I sometimes wonder what it would have been like to experience a black school."

"Man, you from Africa! What kind of school did you go to when you were there?"

"Alexander, that's not what I mean. I'm talking about in the U.S. Coming from somewhere else, there's some novelty attached to the thought of attending a predominately black university."

"So why didn't you?"

"Well, I wanted to be in New York City and I got into Columbia. It chose me, man."

"Yeah, I guess that's cool." He took a swig of his Gatorade. "Where'd you go for undergrad?"

"The Sorbonne."

"Damn." Alexander eyed Innocent as he took another bite out of his sandwich and spit out a pickle.

"Damn pickles," he muttered, and pulled out more. "I *hate* pickles."

"That's too bad." Alexander laughed and shook his head. "So how long are you staying tonight?"

"It's going to take me at least two hours to clear my desk, but I think I might try to leave sooner, probably around eight-thirty."

"Shit, you livin' the life. Midnight is going to meet and greet my new associate ass right here in this fucking office!"

"Sucks to be you."

"Yeah."

"Look, don't forget to talk to Renée first thing in the morning about the Wilson bullshit. And let me know what comes of that conversation. If need be, maybe I can talk to her. I'll tell her that we talked about the deal too and I'm not looking for a cut. Stick a copy of your proposal under my door so I can be up on it."

"Alright. Thanks, man."

"Easy, Alexander."

Sitting down to his computer, Innocent noticed he had a new e-mail message.

SUBJECT: Re: Comparing literature
DATE: March 9, 1999, 6:53 P.M.
TO: IPokou@wright_richards.com
FROM: Noire@nyu.edu

Mr. Pokou,
Rather an eclectic mix, your literature collection. Comparing lists could be fun. But you didn't suggest a time or a place. I'm on self-imposed lock-down till Thursday. But Friday could work for a drink or something.

RSVP,
Noire

Innocent smiled at Noire's words. *She's cute.* Resisting the urge to hit REPLY, Innocent instead savored his mounting curiosity. He could hardly figure her out from five sentences, but he nevertheless read and reread her words, trying to hear the inflection in her voice as if she had spoken to him.

Noire stared at her sent message, a half-grin pulled across her face. She had hesitated in responding only as long as it took to rationalize that talking books didn't mean anything. *A prompt message deserves a prompt response*, she reasoned, and kept her expectations low.

Noire was still struggling with her paper. She cupped her head in her hands and massaged her bloodshot eyes, now blurred before the computer screen. Twelve hours. She could have flown to the South Pole, but instead she stared at the same eight pages of her overdue twenty-page paper for Professor Fuentes. She grabbed a fistful of plantain chips and chewed violently. And what about Fuentes? Noire had hoped that she would so impress her that Professor Fuentes would want to be her faculty adviser, but the chance of that happening now looked slim. *She'll never want to help me if I can't even write one damn paper for her class!*

Uttering timid incantations to God and everybody else, Noire weighed her options. *Would it be really bad if I called Professor Fuentes to explain my predicament?* Two more minutes of rubbing her eyes helped her make up her mind. Opening her loose-leaf binder, Noire found a battered copy of the course's syllabus. Professor Fuentes had only listed her office number. *Shit.* Figuring she had nothing to lose by leaving a message, Noire stuffed her mouth with more plantain chips and dialed the number.

"*Halo?*" She picked up on the first ring.

"Oh *shit!*" Noire hastily pushed the moistened chips to the corners of her mouth and swallowed a few prematurely before she continued. "Shit! Sorry! Sorry!" She forced more chips down her throat and coughed. "Um, this is Noire Demain. I'm in your Women Write Diaspora Fiction class?" she asked rather than told. She got up to get water.

"Yes, Noire, I know who you are. I received your e-mail message yesterday."

An excuse for her paper's lateness, and a bad excuse at that. "Yes, right. Well, I'm actually calling to follow up on that e-mail."

Silence.

"Well, as you probably figured out, I'm having a hard time writing my paper. I mean, I understand my topic—I know I want to argue that writing in Caribbean dialects and pidgins is a political statement that questions what is considered a culturally authentic 'voice of the people.' But I don't feel like I can say anything more about it than the most basic things."

"What kinds of 'basic' things?"

Noire rattled off observations and connected disparate texts but prefaced her statements with qualifiers like "this is really obvious but . . ."

"Noire, you are a first year in the Ph.D. program, no? The first thing you need to learn is to be confident in what you have to say. The observations you just made are far from obvious, especially when you draw in the examples from the texts that you cited. If you develop a thesis statement around those observations you will make a very compelling argument."

She continued before Noire could interject. "As you move through this Ph.D. process, Noire, and progress throughout your academic career, you will see how important it is to begin from a position of arrogance. You are already making a contribution to the discipline just by being a part of it. There will be many people who will seek to undercut your voice, and some may even succeed temporarily, but you must continue to assert your position. Accept criticism, but don't compromise yourself just because someone else doesn't agree with you."

Listening to Professor Fuentes, Noire felt as though she were an eleven-year-old again. She thanked her for her time and opinion, and they hung up. Graduate school was as much about endurance as it was about intelligence, just like the rest of life. She would have to remember that.

Noire typed, edited, and reread twenty-three pages of her impassioned arguments and hard-nosed research before falling asleep to a modest sunrise.

SUBJECT: . . . or something
DATE: March 10, 1999, 7:48 A.M.
TO: Noire@nyu.edu
FROM: IPokou@wright_richards.com

Mlle. Noire,
I liked the "or something" part of your suggestion for a drink on Friday. It certainly sounds promising. I do love openness and a hint of spontaneity. What do you love?

Innocent

SUBJECT: Noire loves . . .
DATE: March 10, 1999, 10:36 A.M.
TO: IPokou@wright_richards.com
FROM: Noire@nyu.edu

. . . loud music on a rainy afternoon, cashmere, spicy food, provocative conversation, french kisses, and drinks "or something" on Friday evenings with attractive men with mysterious names. How's 7:30 at The Llama? Call me this evening. Don't forget the 718. I am "Manhattan-challenged," you recall.

Noire

She wanted to see if Innocent could be as quick on his feet when they talked as he was over e-mail. As Noire prepared to log off of her e-mail account, a message flashed across the screen from "The Innocent One."

SUBJECT: It's me
DATE: March 10, 1999, 10:45 A.M.
TO: Noire@nyu.edu
FROM: theINNOCENTone@mymail.com

It's me, Noire. After reading what you love, thought I'd do well to give you my personal e-mail address. I wouldn't want the people in our information technology department to have too much fun reading my messages! I usually check this account two or three times a day.

I'll call you tonight,
Innocent

Two or three times a day! Well, she would look forward to his call.

The phone rang at eight-thirty. Noire stood a foot from it and watched it quiver two more times. She picked it up on the third ring.

"Hello?" delivered in a sexy silkiness that could melt the polar ice cap.

"Girl, it's me!" Jayna shouted into the phone.

"Oh! I thought you'd be Innocent." Noire did neck rolls.

"Well, obviously you weren't dripping sexuality for me. He hasn't called yet?"

"No. Why is there so much noise in the background? Where are you calling me from?"

"I'm at Alan's place. He and Nate are throwing a little Wednesday night groove for no reason. Just because we finished round one of our projects, I guess."

"What's up with him and Nate? My gaydar was going off when I saw them in the bookstore."

"Yeah, girl, you know they are too cute to be straight!" She chuckled. "Anyway, it's cool. There are about fifteen people here. Folks are scheming on each other and acting hard-up though. I might even get some tonight!" Noire and Jayna squealed at the thought.

"Just a minute, Jayna. I have another call," she said, her voice full of giggles. "Hello!"

"Whoa!" He pulled his ear back from the phone. "Hi, this is Innocent."

"Oh gosh . . . sorry! It's just that I'm on the other line," Noire explained.

"OK? Well, do you want me to call back?"

"Oh no." Noire tried to sound more sultry. "I can get off the other line." She added, "I've been on the call for a while."

"Alright."

"Just a second." She clicked back over to Jayna who, was singing into the phone. "Jayna, it's him. It's Innocent. I just yelled in his ear by mistake."

"Oops. Well, you go ahead and take it then. I'll catch you later."

"OK, bye. And say hello to Alan *and* Nate."

"Will do."

Noire clicked back over to Innocent. "Sorry about that. I was just talking to my friend Jayna. She was calling from a party."

Innocent laughed. "Do you guys usually call each other to have heart-to-hearts when you're at parties?"

This time, Noire laughed. He caught her. "Well, you know, some-times parties are the best place for heart-to-hearts. If you've been drink-ing you're less inhibited and will say anything. And since the music is so loud, nobody will hear you!"

"Good recovery. So, how are you?"

"I'm pretty great now that I've finished my paper. I had been labor-ing over it for nearly two weeks. It was due the day I met you but I handed it in today."

"Well, congratulations."

"The rest of the week is pretty smooth sailing. Two classes tomor-row and nothing on Friday."

"I wish I could say the same. I have a big project that's due tomor-row. So I think I'll be here all night."

"You're calling from work?"

"Definitely. The night is young, Noire."

"My God, won't you get tired, hungry?"

"Tired is a state of mind and hunger is easily remedied by a call to our friendly neighborhood twenty-four-hour deli. If push comes to shove, I have a fresh shirt and some necessities in the office. Hopefully I'll be able to go home and catch a few winks, though."

"That's absurd."

"All in a day's work."

"Sounds more like forty days and forty nights!"

"Mmm." Innocent changed the subject. "So what part of Brooklyn do you live in?"

"Clinton Hill. Actually I'm on the border of Clinton Hill and Fort Greene."

"Sure. There are some very pretty brownstones around there. One of my coworkers has a place in Fort Greene, around the park somewhere."

"And where in the City do you lay your head?"

"I like to call SoHo home."

"*SoHo?*"

"Yes. Why do you say it like that? Do you not like the area?"

"No, I *love* the area to hang out in. But I've never known anyone to actually *live* there. It's like saying you live by Lincoln Center or in Trump Tower. Who lives there?" *Who can afford to?*

"Plenty of people."

"Yes, it's just—I don't know. So, how long have you lived in *So-Ho?*" She emphasized each syllable separately to elicit a laugh. It worked.

"I moved there a month after I graduated from b-school. This woman who was a classmate of mine bought the place when she started school but then ended up taking a job in France. So she rented it out to me, and last year I bought it. It's actually a really nice space. Doesn't look like anything from the outside, but there are very high ceilings and lots of light. It's a loft."

"Sounds nice. Do you have it all fixed up?"

"Actually, I've done very little with the space. I have a few masks and my best friend's watercolor hanging up, but that's about it. It's unfortunate that I hardly ever get to see it during daylight hours. One of the biggest selling points of the place is the sunlight." This time his laugh was tinged with a bitterness that Noire couldn't place.

"Well, I have a sort of cozy one-bedroom that's overrun with books, magazines, and other things that I can't seem to get rid of. But it's fine, comfortable for me. No great view but the neighborhood is cool. And I'm only twenty minutes away from school by train. That's a real plus when I have to beat it back home at night."

"You take the train when it's *late?*"

"That's all I can afford on my grad student budget." She frowned.

"Mmm . . . Well, Noire, I would love to talk a bit more but—"

"Oh no, you have a whole night ahead of you. You can e-mail me if you get a chance, but we'll see each other soon enough."

"OK, Noire. I look forward to Friday; it's the only thing that will get me through the next forty-eight hours of hell."

That was sweet. "Thank you, Innocent."

"*Bon soir*, Noire."

"Good night, Innocent."

Innocent got off the phone feeling good. He didn't know what it was about Noire, but she ignited his imagination. She wasn't sweet but she was real—he appreciated that. Shaking the mouse on his computer, Innocent felt a smile linger on his lips as he began to type.

Noire was experiencing her own minor jubilation despite herself, his sumptuous accented voice ricocheting off of every nerve in her body.

Closing her eyes, she pictured Innocent sitting at his desk in his sterile box of an office, the fluorescent lights raining cold light down on him. And yet, he seemed composed, relaxed almost, even though he had pressing deadlines weighing on him. Noire marveled at this trait, then reminded herself that she barely liked him when she met him (though she conceded that he was charming). A couple of e-mails and a phone call couldn't change all that . . . or could it? She'd know on Friday. Noire felt horny and hopeful.

Chapter 3

Speaking in Tongues

Lying naked in the warm darkness of the NYU gym's sauna, Noire was transported. Her spent muscles grew slack and long, her mind a murky stream of slow-moving thoughts. She mused at the woman on the front bench with her head between her knees, then dismissed her. She batted her eyes heavily in the haze. Silently counted the number of blinks. *One . . . two . . . three . . .* She thought about her last official "date" three months ago. *Four . . . five . . .* Her unintentional dating dry spell. *Six . . .* No sex, though she's been horny. *Seven . . . eight . . .* That pretentious history Ph.D. student. *Nine . . .* Asshole. *Ten . . . eleven . . . twelve . . . thirteen . . .* Had to purge herself of his bad karma. *Thirteen?* No, *fourteen . . . fifteen . . .* He thought he could finish her sentences, order her food, and make her jerk him off under the table in the restaurant. *Sixteen.* Instead, she squeezed his penis till he screamed and left. Noire smiled. Stopped counting.

She was studying her beads of perspiration when Arikè walked in with her towel wrapped around her head. Her taut body was dewy and the blood that had rushed to the surface of her skin from their workout made her look like an overripe peach. She kissed Noire's forehead, then lay out on the bench beside her, their feet nearly touching. "You played well today."

"Just not as well as you." Noire raised her arm in a lethargic racquetball swing. "So when did you pierce your navel?" She eyed the ring of silver in the dimness.

"December, right before I left for Trinidad."

"Oh, is that where you went? Do you have family there?"

"Well, Dennis does. His mom and everyone. I spent Christmas with them. It was really nice!" She giggled.

"Wow, Arikè, I had no idea you guys were *that* tight!"

"Yeah, well I didn't either until Dennis asked me in November to go home with him for the holidays."

"That must have been *so* nice." Noire let the idea of it sink in before she continued. "So how are you guys doing anyway?"

"So far so good, thank God. It'll make a year in April! April 17."

"See, black love isn't dead."

"Girl, it's really not!"

"You know, I have a date tonight!"

"Whaaat! With that Dashiki Brown?" Arikè grunted.

Noire's libido somersaulted as she ruminated on what it was like to run her fingers through his 'fro as he ran his fingers through hers in the control booth of NYU's film center. His twenty-three-minute film short was playing to a full house for the sixth time during the university-wide Radical Reels Film Festival last month as they stood behind it in the seven-by-twelve black box. She licked her middle finger and ran it around the ring of exposed skin between his unbelted jeans and his shrunken Blackfilm.com T-shirt. He fondled her earlobes with his tongue before whispering, "I'm living with someone." She slipped her hand up her blouse and whispered back, "Fuck you, Dashiki."

"No, he's got a girlfriend." Noire swallowed. Hard. "His name is Innocent. I met him at a book signing on Monday."

"Ooh! Gotta love those literary brothas!" She nodded in approval. "Innocent? Where's he from?"

She crash-landed her thoughts back into the present. "Um, Côte d'Ivoire."

"See what I'm sayin'. Homeboys from the continent are the *bomb*! My mom said Dad convinced her that African men really are the best lovers!" Arikè chuckled at the indiscretion.

Noire's laughter was more in surprise than agreement; Arikè had never mentioned her parents' relationship. Their five-month-old friendship began when Arikè invited Noire to be her replacement racquetball partner after hers—a fellow classmate—quit NYU Law School and moved to Las Vegas. Noire's ineptitude notwithstanding, she became her weekly gym buddy that grew to include the sauna and eventually a shared love for university lectures on progressive politics and parties featuring African pop music.

"Where'd your parents meet?" Noire tapped her with her toe.

"University of London. Mom was a student tour guide and Dad was on her tour. He had some sort of commonwealth scholarship . . . an apology for colonialism, Nigerian style. They got lots of flack. Folks called her confused and him a sellout. But Mom says you can't stop fate."

"Maybe."

They were silent, momentarily lulled by the arid heat and the darkness.

Arikè propped herself up on her elbows, wrapped her legs under her body, and then kneeled over Noire.

"So, what are you going to *wear*? I'm sure you're tryin' to be diva."

"Seriously, I can't figure it out!" Noire struggled to a seated position.

Arikè contemplated her naked body. "Emphasize your breasts. And your waist."

Noire's cheeks flushed hotter under the weight of Arikè's bold gaze. "I wore a tight-fitting blouse on Monday."

"And you think once is enough? Don't let your attributes be a *memory* for him, Noire. You've got to continue to accentuate the positive!" she said, shaking her own perky breasts.

"Girl, you know you need to *stop*!" Noire blushed, darting her eyes across Arikè's figure. "Maybe my new Exodus Industrial navy V-neck would work."

"And wear a long necklace that kind of dangles right there." Arikè touched a point between Noire's breasts. "That way, you'll keep his eye drawn to them."

"Damn, Arikè!"

"Noire, we're the only two in here! I guess we were too loud for Ms. Thang over there!"

"*You* were too loud!" Noire teased.

"You have a very pretty body, Noire, and you should be proud of it. Black women are so self-conscious sometimes."

"Well, I can't help it."

"You can be modest without being self-conscious, you know."

"And of course you're neither!" They both laughed at that, Arikè in simple agreement and Noire in relief that they finally ended that conversation.

"Girl, let's get out of here. *You* need to get home and pick out a killer outfit!"

"So what language do you speak?" Noire asked Innocent. They sat huddled on squat chairs around a low square table at The Llama, a windowless den lit by votive candles and lava lamps.

"Well, it looks to me like I 'speak' pretty good English." His voice was tight.

"Yes. Obviously. But I mean, what *indigenous* language do you speak, Innocent?"

"French is my native language, Noire. Can't say it's 'indigenous' to Côte d'Ivoire, but it's indigenous to me."

Silence.

Innocent knew that her questions were merely naive, not malintentioned. He sighed. "Look, my parents are from different ethnic groups—my mother's Abure and Papa is Baoule—so they just always spoke French to each other and to us. And at my boarding school, everything was in French. I know a smattering of Abure and Baoule here and there, and I could follow a traditional naming ceremony if push came to shove, but French has been my lingua franca. We're pretty 'bourgie' African folk, in case you were wondering."

"Oh." She spread her fingers out on the table and listened to the bawdy conversations of the crowd gathering at the bar. "It's just that I'm really into languages—I'm fluent in Spanish and I understand French and I'm trying to learn Haitian Kreyòl and Papiamentu—" Noire stopped herself short. She had been looking down the whole time, embarrassed and defensive, but when she glanced up, she met Innocent's smiling eyes.

"Yes, Noire, I get it. You don't have to run down your entire résumé just yet." He laughed. "But, you should know that for better or worse, there are lots of folks like me all throughout Africa. Colonialism runs deep, and being cosmopolitan doesn't help matters."

Noire looked at the richness of his dark skin, the unquestionably African planes of his face. He was a black man; she knew he didn't deny it. She squeezed her brain into a tight ball, then let it go slack. She tried to understand Innocent's words within the context of his African sensibility. She imagined it to be broader than her own American thinking, which always grouped race with struggle. "But don't you feel bad that you don't know any of the languages indigenous to the continent?"

He smiled at that reference to "the continent" but didn't answer.

Noire continued: "I mean, when I spent a semester abroad at the University of Ghana as an undergrad, I marveled at people's ability to move from Twi to English to the English-based Creole. It made me proud and jealous all at the same time. You know, I tried to learn a bit of Twi while I was there, but people would never help me with it. Beyond the standard greetings, it was totally a lost cause. One guy at the university even said I was crazy to try and learn it. He said, 'What's the point of learning to speak a language that perhaps ten million people speak? That's little more than the number of people who live in New York City alone. The language of commerce is English and that's all you need to know.'"

Innocent fondled the votive candle on the table and watched the flame flicker like golden tears in Noire's brown eyes.

"But he was so wrong. It's like he totally discounted his own language. He didn't see the beauty in it or the history or the cultural significance. So many African Americans yearn for that kind of connection to the continent. They would love to be able to *identify* a culture and a language group that their ancestors originate from. And yet it can mean nothing to a person who already possesses all that."

Her passion was beguiling. "Noire, for many of us, language is not about beauty, it's about economic access. And in modern-day Africa, a lot of us find ourselves on the wrong side of the world's economic equation.

"When I was younger, my grandmother used to struggle to speak to me in broken French. She insisted that if I could speak French as well as any Frenchman, I would 'never have to worry' because I'd have access to money, power, and education." He grinned at her frown, tried to guess the degree of her displeasure.

"You sound like Fanon in *Black Skin, White Masks.*" Noire referenced the Martinican writer. She pursed her lips.

"Yes, well I guess it happened to me by default because of my parents and my education—first at an elite boarding school and then at the Sorbonne."

Noire's body glowed red. She felt like those old men who play chess in Washington Square Park and whose faces filled with race pride when they saw self-possessed black students clutching schoolbooks on their way to class at NYU. Black people could take pleasure in the accomplishments and uncommon experiences of other black people and be linked through a common ancestry even amid a vastly different present. And so, in that way she was proud of Innocent. He knew a life that most Americans didn't experience and fewer realized exists in Africa. He made no apologies and felt no contradictions about who he was. Remembering the twin experience of indelible cultural heritage and amazing ordinariness that characterized being black in Ghana, Noire made an effort to relax. She reminded herself that these differences in outlook, experience, and expectation were what drove her to pursue her Ph.D.; she *loved* the creative and ideological tensions around cultural authenticity. *Isn't that what I like about Innocent?* Her fire became a smoldering flame.

"What was the Sorbonne like?" Noire offered her prettiest smile.

"It was incredible. It really was. The people I met were such an eclectic group—from all over the world—and they really challenged me to rethink what I believed. And Paris is a city that was made for learning, you know. Even though I studied economics, I was always exposed to art and music and politics. The city is a mecca for all that. Of course the French are arrogant enough to think they've cornered the market on haute couture, but even that can be fun!"

He took a sip of his mango martini. "I certainly feel like I became a man in France, you know."

"That's a strong claim." She remembered her smile and flashed it again.

"I mean, I have always been a very self-reliant person, but it was the first time that I was among so many people who were so different from me. When I was in boarding school, most of the other students were from backgrounds similar to mine—parents educated abroad, had status and means—so it felt natural. But at the Sorbonne, it was *completely* unnatural. Sure there were Africans there, but they were from Senegal, Morocco, Algeria, Zaire—sorry, the Democratic Republic of Congo now, I guess." He popped a tapas olive in his mouth. "But we were still very different. Our Africanness did bring us together on some level, but the common denominators were sometimes hard to find. And since I'm not Muslim, that set me apart from many of the others.

"Interestingly, some of the white French students I met knew more about Côte d'Ivoire than some of the other West Africans did. People would come up to me and say, 'Oh you know, my family has traveled to Abidjan on vacation,' and then they'd list all of the sights they remember seeing."

"Well, *that's* a mess." Noire crunched a tiny round of bruschetta.

"Yes and no. Sometimes people did just want to pick my brain for their own purposes, but when you're far from home for the first time it can be comforting to find people who know that place, no matter how superficially. I didn't always process their statements politically." Innocent watched her quell her reaction to his provocation before she would respond. He kept his own features unreadable and waited.

"Yeah, I guess so." Noire was unconvinced. She took a sip of her sherry.

"You know, Noire, you are a very passionate woman. And passion makes me hungry. Would you like to continue our conversation over dinner?"

Is he trying to patronize me? Noire stared at him knowingly. He returned her stare with slightly shaken confidence. She smiled. "How can I say no to such an earnest offer?"

He stood up, bending forward slightly in an abbreviated bow. Amused, Noire got up and allowed him to help her with her coat. Innocent kissed her cheek and she blushed.

They were on the subway heading uptown. At eight-thirty, the train was only moderately crowded, but Noire took the opportunity to stand close to Innocent. She liked how it felt and relished the rough ride for the ample opportunities it offered to "bump into" him. He had braced himself against the door and Noire held the pole and stood in front of him close enough so that she needed to look up to his six-foot frame. Noire was five-eight on a good day, and her shoes provided her with an extra inch of lift, which gave her the perfect position from which to adore his chiseled features and sensuous lips. She did just that.

Jumping off the train at West 116th Street, Innocent and Noire found themselves face to face with West African Harlem. Street vendors who had long since packed their wares still lingered in the chilly evening air to catch up with their compatriots on the news from back home. Wolof mixed with Fanti and Bambara in the night breezes. Catching the eye of one man still patiently trying to sell purses and knapsacks, Innocent greeted him in Baoule.

"*Ohonti-kpa?* And how is work?"

"All is well, thank God. Keep good, eh. And your lady too." He offered a sly smile to emphasize his admiration of Noire.

Noire smiled as well, not from explicit understanding of the words around her, but because she felt as though she were part of something.

Innocent walked by Noire's side, buffering her from the street and negotiating her through the clutches of people milling about on the sidewalk. She thought it a bit too chivalrous, then remembered that he was being kind and decided to enjoy his "gentlemanliness."

"Here's the place I was thinking about." Noire pointed to Africa #1, the Senegalese restaurant that had been her recommendation.

Stepping into the vestibule together, Innocent and Noire found themselves in a telephone booth–sized space. A thick, dark curtain sep-arated them from the restaurant's main room.

"To keep out the draft," Noire mumbled in explanation, momen-tarily flustered by her unexpected closeness to Innocent.

He pulled back the curtain, displaying a dim interior draped with an array of traditional Senegalese fabrics. Its coziness suggested an after-hours lounge, but the sight of children eating and tussling with siblings revealed its purpose.

The waitress seated them at a table in the corner next to a couple with a screaming baby and then left. Though the father had lifted the baby onto his lap, the child would not be consoled. Noire giggled in spite of herself.

A grin crept across Innocent's face. "I'm having a nice time with you, Noire."

"Must mean you're bringing out my good side. That's a great sign!" Noire winked before ducking her head into the menu.

They ordered—the Senegalese national dish of *chebu jeune*, or sea-soned rice and fish, for Innocent, and *ganaar maafe*, chicken in a tomato-based peanut sauce, for Noire—then sipped sorrel drinks as they settled into conversation.

"You know when I was at the Sorbonne, my best friend was a Wolof guy named Mamadou. We're still close. Anyway, by the time I met him in our first year, he had already been living in Paris for about six years. He knew every Senegalese haunt there was. One of our favorite pas-times was going to this one very homegrown spot in the nineteenth arrondissement on Thursday nights before heading into town to a great dancing place frequented by the entire French-speaking African 'dias-pora' in France." He made quotes with his fingers.

"Mamadou had something going on with one of the waitresses there, but he would never talk about it because he's what he called 'a modest Muslim.' But she always brought us free appetizers and extra tea. That was a really good time!" Innocent shook his head at the memory.

"Sounds like there's more to know."

"I guess there always is."

"So, you like to shake your thing?"

"I'm a black man!"

"Innocent!" Noire laughed.

"Yeah, I've been told I have a few moves up my sleeve."

"Well, if you have just a few, then perhaps I can help you add to your repertoire."

"I eagerly await my first lesson."

"Just make sure you're warmed up."

"Maybe you'll help me with that as well."

Noire did her best to indulge Innocent's interest in her. She wove a vibrant and textured tapestry of storytelling, setting a tone that favored the spectacular over the mundane, and the amusing over the painful. Her early fascination with languages became a curiosity about the Spanish exchanges of her childhood best friend's parents, who remembered Puerto Rico in the soft hues of sentimentality; the lilting Louisiana French of her father's mother; and the anxious words of a French boy with whom she stole a kiss in the bathroom of the Louvre during her high school trip to France. She did not mention the cruelties spat out in French by her cousins during those prepubescent summers in New Orleans that made her ache with ignorance and exclusion.

"So, Noire, I know you're this fabulous Ph.D.-to-be from Queens, New York—"

"And you want to know how I got to be so fabulous?"

"Exactly."

She revealed to him her freshman year at Amherst that was anchored by her cosmopolitan attitude, short-lived half-a-pack smoking habit, and vintage camera that hung around her neck like jewelry.

"You sound like quite the *artiste*."

"Tell that to my first-year photography professor. She hated my stuff—thought my subjects were too posed and stiff. About two months into the class I just burst out, 'I *like* to photograph black people, and the black people I know don't let you take pictures of their crotch and their grandmothers' naked breasts like some white people will. Just because every picture I take isn't homoerotic or borderline pornographic doesn't mean it's not art!'

"She got really offended by what she called my 'implication that she's a racist,' and she said that I needed to 'confront my heterosexism.' I told her she was full of shit and I dropped the class. I'm kind of sorry that I never took any other photography classes, because I really liked it. Of course she probably blacklisted me in the entire Fine Arts Department. That professor was *truly* full of shit!"

Noire's last syllable rang out in an unexpected lull in the conversations and clanking dishes. The approaching waitress, laden with their heaping plates of rice and bowls of stew, flinched. "Sorry," Noire said sheepishly as Innocent helped the waitress rebalance the plates resting precariously on her wrists. Setting the food down on the table, she made a hasty exit.

Noire continued. "Anyway, that ended my photography career. I found myself back at Spanish as a major by default. It was what I was good at and it gave me the most flexibility with my schedule so that I could travel to Ghana."

They exchanged bite-sized portions of their entrées and inquisitive glances, the silence full of cutting and chewing and swallowing. He mumbled questions and she garbled answers between mouthfuls, weaving intricate patterns both decorative and functional. Sitting his fork down for a break, Innocent took a sip of his sorrel and then asked another question: "And what followed college?"

"Do you really want to hear the long sordid story?"

"The abridged sordid story is fine."

Noire giggled. "Well"—she gulped her sorrel—"let's say that my life happened to me after college."

Innocent knit his eyebrows together in response but remained silent.

"See, I've always considered myself to be different from folks, so I figured that, rather than map out my life like some folks did, I'd take the more *organic* approach. So, basically, I graduated with no prospects of a job and without a plan. I ferried myself back to my mom's apartment in Queens, where she promptly told me that a B.A. from Amherst meant that I had a license to earn a living and I needed to start earning it.

"My luck has always been pretty good, and I got a job with a student travel organization that needed another chaperone for an eight-week trip to Spain and France. It was harrowing but terrific, and they kept me on as a casual employee for a couple of months. One of the counselors there tipped me off to a generously funded independent-research project in the Spanish-speaking Caribbean and Central and Latin America. She coached me through the entire application process, and I won an eight-month grant to study the relationship between African and indigenous Indian cultural forms in Cuba, Venezuela, and Panama. I learned a lot about New World diaspora cultures, and it started me thinking about the possibility of doing graduate-level work on some of these issues.

"But when I came back home, I was nearly twenty-four years old and I wasn't ready to plunge myself back into the academic scene at all. I also had less than no money. My Spanish was fluent by that time and I figured that that was one of the biggest selling points I had. So I scoured the Spanish-language newspapers, and after two months finally lined up what sounded like a dream job working in Madrid as a representative from the Americas for one of Spain's leading cosmetics companies. It was trying to break into the Latin, Caribbean, and American markets.

"I loved the job for about a week and a half and then tolerated it for the next seven months. It was at that point that I realized I was tired of being away from home and in a country that doesn't know if it loves or hates black people."

Noire compared her half-eaten entrée to Innocent's clean plate and decided that she had been talking too much. She said so but Innocent came back with, "But I asked, Noire. And it's all interesting. Besides, now that you've brought me this far, you'll have to tell me what you did after leaving Spain."

Noire gave up on her meal when she realized she was no longer hungry. She asked for a doggy bag and graciously allowed Innocent to pay the bill before they made their exit. Deciding to extend the date still further, they boarded a downtown subway headed for an unnamed joint in the East Village that Innocent contended was a lounge.

At Innocent's insistence, Noire concluded her story in broad brushstrokes. Returning to the U.S., she became the manager of health, safety, and travel advice at a New York City youth hostel in January

1996. "And with the blessing of my mother, I moved out of her apartment and got my own, the same place I'm living in now." The job paid her bills and kept her language skills sharp, but after one and a half years, she realized she needed something more intellectually stimulating. Jayna's second year in dental school encouraged Noire to have grad school "on the brain," and she settled on comparative literature, given her love for languages, cultures, and reading. "So I applied to a couple of places between Boston and D.C. and ended up at NYU in September of '98. And then I met you."

Noire was eager to get the spotlight off of her. She had said a lot, perhaps too much for a first date. She had startled Innocent with her comment, she could tell. So when she jumped out of her seat, he continued to sit and look confused.

"It's our stop, Innocent," Noire said, standing in the open train doors.

"Oh." He dashed out behind her. They exited the station and walked along the noisy street in silence. Innocent ventured to hold Noire's hand, and she did not refuse. He was taken by his own boldness, taken by Noire and the overwhelming nature of the evening. He worked diligently to try to organize his emotions when Noire burst in with:

"A penny for your thoughts."

Innocent's words were tentative. "I guess I was just thinking that our meeting was an accident. Um . . . I mean, I almost didn't make it out of work in time to get to the book signing. It's just that Marcus is my boy . . . but tonight was good. Um, yes, definitely good . . ." He trailed off, aware that his utterances were only tangentially connected to one another, and shook his head.

"Sometimes accidents are the best surprises."

Innocent stopped walking and faced Noire, her hand still in his. "This is not an accident." He kissed her lips and found them disarmingly receptive. They shuddered in the cool night air.

Innocent put Noire in a taxi home at three A.M. but not before offering her his lips as a small token of his affection. The nocturnal breezes circled him as he flagged down his own cab. His mind was full of premature thoughts that he chose to let pass without further contemplation.

He climbed into the backseat of the cab, then simply focused on the empty streets that whizzed by and allowed his body to be tossed around by the cab driver's aggressive driving.

Four blocks into his trip, the taxi screeched to a halt at a red light at 2nd Avenue and Houston. "This is fine. I'll walk the rest of the way." Innocent felt like melting ice cream. He gave the driver a five and spilled out of the cab before the receipt finished printing. After regaining his footing, he began to walk, his steps punctuating the thoughts in his head.

Suddenly thirsty, he stopped at two delis and a bodega before finding the Dr Pepper he wanted. Innocent ignored the brisk air and claimed a seat on the plastic lawn chair that was the match to the bodega owner's own. They sat side by side silently, long after Innocent drained the contents of his can. Catching the sight of jerking bodies to his right, Innocent focused on the hurried activities of public sex in an adjacent alleyway. Their animation made them appear like a video in fast-forward. Looking Innocent in the eye, the woman exhaled loudly, then planted a hard kiss on top of her partner's head. Innocent averted his eyes, resisting being drawn in. He looked at the bodega owner—who was staring at the couple—and said good night first, then good morning, before getting up to leave.

His body full of caffeine and adrenaline, Innocent finally turned onto Greene Street at 3:54 A.M. His keys still in his front door, he heard the balance of Noire's answering machine message: ". . . myself very much. I just feel like I did a lot of talking. But it was nice of you to listen. Have a good night, Innocent. I'll speak to you tomorrow." She hung up but her voice still clung to the damp air of the loft. Walking across the large room, he pressed PLAY on the answering machine and sat on his desk chair to listen to the message in its entirety. It was delicious, her tone buoyant and unrehearsed, her sentences punctuated by audible exclamation points.

The streetlamps provided ghostly light to the otherwise dark apartment. Undressing, he recognized his own expressions of excitement. He brushed his teeth before descending upon his queen-size bed. Acknowledging the end of another day, he included Noire among his special intentions. Then he fell asleep.

Chapter 4

Happenstance

Noire turned her full laundry basket out onto her couch and thought of Innocent. She got her carton of orange juice, turned it up to her mouth, and thought of Innocent. She put it back. Thought of Innocent. She had had a good date. A *really* good date. He was witty and ridiculously handsome and well traveled and attentive. And a banker. And hadn't he called his family "bourgie"? How many people do that? Isn't that a sign of some sort of superiority complex? Noire made a face. Well, maybe not, but he definitely seemed accustomed to things. But, she reminded herself, he's a man, first and foremost. And a black man at that. She decided to write his name on a piece of paper so that she could stop thinking about him. She had things to do.

Noire pulled underwear out of her heap of newly cleaned clothes and folded them into five small piles on her couch: traveling panties (to be taken on Monday's trip to New Orleans), sexy panties (she only had two), everyday panties, and super-elasticized-time-of-the-month panties that kept even the bulkiest pad in place. And then there was the pink panty pile: the six pairs of pink cotton briefs that had been a gift from her brother. Last Christmas, Noire requested underwear; it was a mistake. She imagined her ex-stepmother, Celine, pulling nine-year-old Jabari through women's lingerie and picking out the most girlie, most chaste assortment she could find. Men and vacations were two good reasons to buy new bras and panties, Noire reasoned, her mind bouncing between Innocent and the spring break trip. Cursing the motley collection still warm and smelling of fabric softener, she proclaimed, "I must buy matching underwear!"

She'd be seeing Celine and Jabari in just a couple of days; she and Jayna were staying with them in New Orleans. She wondered again, for the tenth time since she called Celine six days ago, whether it was a good idea to stay there. But Grand-mère's house held too many memories of childhood summers full of being teased by her cousins, and weekly burns on her ears and neck by the hot comb her grandmother bought and used to make her "black" granddaughter look presentable for church every Sunday. Celine was the lesser of two evils.

Jayna's standard Saturday-morning call was overdue, so Noire checked her e-mail. The first was from Professor Fuentes.

SUBJECT: Re: my [late] paper
DATE: March 12, 1999, 8:48 P.M.
TO: Noire@nyu.edu
FROM: Fuentes@faculty.nyu.edu

Noire,
I may have my next protégée on my hands . . . this is a good paper. Come to my office the Tuesday after you get back, the 23rd. 4:00 P.M. I've blocked out an hour.

Enjoy your spring break,
B. Fuentes

The second was from Jayna.

SUBJECT: Mama's dramas
DATE: March 13, 1999, 7:53 A.M.
TO: Noire@nyu.edu
FROM: Jayna@dental.columbia.edu

Black (you know my French was never good!)—
Of course I couldn't make it outta here without a little bit of drama. Remember I told you that I was supposed to meet up with Mama to pick up the airline vouchers yesterday evening? Well, she canceled on me at the last minute because some no-good Negro that she's currently liking invited her to a basketball game. So, now I have to beat it up to the Bronx to get them. Apparently, homegirl will be "busy" for the balance of the weekend. Oh, she said we should try to take the 2:00 P.M. flight on Monday because less people are likely to be traveling then.

After my dear mother, I'm headed out to Flushing to say hey to Nana and Papi. I haven't seen them since President's Day and you know how they get before I travel. Anyway, we should talk tomorrow about where to meet at the airport. Then you can tell me all about the date. But you should definitely e-mail to at least say if it was good or not.

Catch you—
Jayna

Noire hit REPLY and typed quickly, *"Girl, it was GOOD! You're gonna scream . . . Noire."*

She disconnected from the Internet and noticed the time. Ten forty-five A.M. She memorized Innocent's number written on the chalkboard above her desk and dialed.

After two and a half rings she was greeted with *"Bonjour!"*

"Ooh! *Bonjour,* Innocent. Did you know it was me?"

"Of course."

"Are you up?"

"Sort of. I was reading in bed. *Invisible Man.* I couldn't finish it the first time."

"My dad said that when he first read it, he couldn't talk to anyone for a week. He still reads it once a year."

"I just hope I finish it this time." Innocent measured coffee into his espresso machine.

"You will . . . hey, I guess we never did 'compare literature' last night, did we!" Noire flopped on her couch and scrunched her panty piles with her toes. "Tell me, who is Mr. Marcus Gordon's literary inspiration?"

"I detect sarcasm."

"He's preachy."

"Then he's in good company."

"With who?"

"Ask your academic colleagues."

Noire raised her eyebrows.

"Pretension is not profession-specific. Marcus is a good guy, Noire."

"He's your friend."

Innocent egged her on. "*And* he's the reason we met."

"Well, there you go." Noire let it rest.

"Noire, you never told me about the origins of your name." He sipped his espresso and thumbed through his latest issue of *Untold* magazine, his eyes scanning a review of London's Manjaro Bar & Kitchen.

"It means 'black' in French," Noire teased. "No, seriously, my parents named me Noire because I'm their black love child. And also to get back at my grandmother in Louisiana who happily refers to herself as a 'quadroon.'"

"I think you'll have to back up and come again, Noire." He closed the magazine.

"Basically, my parents met at a Black Pride rally in '70 in Washington, D.C. My mom had just finished college a few weeks before and was working for a black radio station. And Dad was passing through on his way to find his new black identity in New York City. I was conceived on their first date."

Innocent was slow to respond, processing the meaning of Noire's story and the matter-of-factness with which she told it.

"Do you have a problem with that?" Her tone was softer than her words. She walked into the kitchen and leaned heavily against the sink, her mind regurgitating her father's misguided revelation two years ago that her mom got pregnant after they did speed at a party. She wondered, if not for the drugs, would she even be here?

"No. I mean, I guess it wasn't what I expected. Not that I knew what I expected." He feared sounding judgmental.

"Yeah, I wasn't what they expected either. But here I am!" She tittered and waited for his response.

"Well, then I will happily embrace the unexpected, Noire." His delivery was gentle and serious. Noire was touched.

"And you? Tell me about your adjective of a name."

"It is an adjective, isn't it? And a noun too, like yours. My parents were going for something that had the flavor of Christianity and Frenchness all rolled into one. And they weren't alone. There are quite a few of us Ivoirian Innocents walking around."

Noire smiled, then looked at the inside of her thoughts. "Well, our names together make up a phrase more curious than the sum of its parts."

"A wise woman once told me that 'sometimes accidents are the best surprises.'"

"A wise woman." They sat in silence on the phone, letting their feelings float in the air. Innocent ran his hand along his chest.

Noire broke the news of her impending trip to New Orleans for spring break. "Jayna and I are going to stay with my ex-stepmom and my brother, Jabari. He's almost ten."

"But your dad doesn't live down there?"

"No, they're not together." Noire answered the question Innocent was too polite to ask. "They called it quits after three years of marriage. Apparently Dad doesn't know how to be friends with his wife or married to his friends. He and Mom lived together for eighteen months— including the first ten months of my life—and even after raising me, they still talk on the phone at least two or three times a week."

Innocent sipped his second cup of espresso; Noire scrambled eggs.

"I'm sure to have a hell of a time." Changing the subject, she asked him when he last visited his family. He offered a perfunctory description of his parents, sister, and grandmother in Côte d'Ivoire, and a sister in France; of last Christmas spent alone at a French Catholic Church on

West 23rd Street; and of his twice-monthly call home, planned for tomorrow evening. Turning on the shower, he told her of his squash date at eleven-fifteen.

"The memory of your kiss will give me strength," he said over the spattering in his bathroom.

"Ooh la la!" Noire licked her lips audibly. "You could catch a woman with a line like that!"

"Then I'll remember to say it often." Innocent's stomach danced the hokey-pokey.

Jayna held Noire's right hand with her left and gripped the arm of the plane chair with the other. Her closed eyes and moving lips told Noire that Jayna was praying. She squeezed her hand for reassurance before focusing on the rapidly disappearing airport below. Clouds anointed lampposts and treetops, draping the earth in a dreamy haze. Noire wanted to capture its surreal beauty in a photograph, but Jayna's death clutch prevented any sudden movements.

Noire turned back to her once they reached cruising altitude. "Hey, don't worry. We have great weather for the trip." She made her voice comforting as she massaged life back into the hand Jayna had finally released.

Jayna's face was set in a frown.

"Hey, what's wrong?"

"Well, it's just that—I slept with this guy, this *white* guy. Spencer. He's a third-year too."

Noire stared in astonishment. "Are you serious? How?"

"What the fuck kind of question is that, Noire?"

"What *else* am I supposed to ask, Jayna?"

"You could ask me how I feel. Do I seem happy?" She blew her nose expressively.

"Jayna, I'm sorry. Damn . . . What happened?"

Jayna launched into a story, none of which Noire had heard before. She explained that Spencer was on her oral surgery rotation. He was quiet and intense, and he *always* knew every answer to every question. He came from a long line of dentists. So, Jayna sought him out at every turn to get added assistance on her work. He was encouraging and help-ful. In fact, he seemed to enjoy the extra review with Jayna and began to seek her out as well.

They went from hallway discussions to meetings for nightcaps before she knew what hit her. Jayna kissed him first, on a dare. She wanted to see if she could really kiss a white man. But she had mis-judged her own blossoming feelings to think they'd sense his race through their kiss. Or maybe she didn't really care about his race. All she felt was unmitigated desire. In those draining weeks of her rotation, Jayna had come to rely on Spencer. She wasn't sure when it became sexual.

Given the fits and starts of their time spent together, there seemed no good way to "pace things," she explained. So they volleyed over hur-dles with little forethought and less reflection. Then, last night, as Jayna pulled off Spencer's T-shirt in her apartment, it became apparent that they were fast approaching another hurdle. And they had enough height to clear it.

She and Spencer progressed through sex with more urgency than finesse; it was all sensory, and her neglected body responded forcefully. But as her body was awash in postorgasm sensitivity, she looked at his creamy pinkness against her deep mahogany and balked. In college, Jayna used to say, only half-jokingly, that she was going to get a T-shirt that read FUCK ME, WHITE BOY to scare off all of the liberal Amherst College coeds who felt "ready" to experience the interracial thing. And so she cajoled Spencer out of her bed without even the minimum grace time required to be courteous.

Jayna stopped her story before Noire thought it was over, and looked to Noire for a reaction.

"Damn . . ." Noire's thoughts were in a jumble around her head. She pulled at words and strung them together in her mind before offering them to Jayna as fodder. "I mean, Spencer is not every twenty-year-old white boy at Amherst with an acute case of jungle fever." Her response was weak; she knew it. She shrugged.

Jayna rolled her eyes. "Noire, you don't know shit about him."

"You know, you're right. But what am I supposed to say? I mean, you're OK, right? He didn't hurt you?"

"See, I shouldn't have told you!"

"Well, if you won't let me help you—"

"Help me what, Noire? *Un*-fuck him? I was just telling you about my last twenty-four hours. Damn."

The flight attendant gave Jayna and Noire a horrified look as he approached them with the lunch cart. They glared at him in response. He blushed, then handed them trays of mini chicken sandwiches, pint-sized cups of water, and tiny bowls of Jell-O in silence. One mini banana lay at the edge of the tray.

Noire looked at Jayna, who was ripping open her Jell-O. "OK, this conversation has officially become crazy."

"I know." She smirked and started eating.

Noire pulled the chicken out from between the bread and cut it into eight bite-sized cubes, which she chewed unsuccessfully. Setting it aside, she peeled her banana and ate it in two quick mouthfuls and washed it down with her taste of water. Unsatisfied, she forced herself through her bowl of Jell-O. Jayna was adding salt to every bite of her sandwich.

"You know that I lived with Mama when I was little, right?" Jayna said between mouthfuls.

She didn't follow the shift in conversation. Looking at Jayna quizzically, she answered, "No." Noire had never thought about it. When she first met Jayna, she was wearing braces and had a white lacquered Holly Hobby bedroom set, a black Cabbage Patch Kid, her own twelve-inch black-and-white TV, and her walls plastered with New Edition posters. Noire was jealous because her grandmother let Jayna have sleepovers during the week and wear fingernail polish to school.

"Well, I moved to Nana and Papi's when I was six. Mama was with yet another of her fucked-up boyfriends, this white guy named Joe. They had this really, like, manic relationship, either fighting or fucking. Seemed like half the time it was all the same. Anyway, I hated Joe and so did Nana and Papi. Joe seemed to hate everyone, including Mama. So, when he moved in, I moved out. That was the end of it. Mama never said anything and no one ever asked me if I wanted to move, or explained why. It just happened. But I didn't mind because my grandparents spent more time with me than Mama did, and since they had a house, I was allowed to have outdoor parties with my friends. Mama came over to see me all of the time, and after a while, I did make weekend visits with her. She never told me what happened to Joe and I didn't ask.

"Mama's still up to that same bullshit, dating the hellified flavor of the month." Jayna speared her last bite of chicken, sparing the bun. "I just can't believe I could fuck a white man."

Noire wrinkled her face in confusion.

Jayna frowned in return.

"Noire, I know you're gonna suggest therapy. But I really don't have the time, money, or inclination to deal with that. I don't know if it even works. I mean, what's the point in telling a stranger all the fucked-up things that happened when you were a child? Everyone has a fucked-up childhood!"

Noire winced. Jayna's question seemed not to seek an answer, but she tried to offer one. "It can't hurt."

Jayna massaged her temple with her right hand. "I guess I could say the same to you."

"Are you being mean?"

"No, Noire." Her face grew serious. I'm wondering how you're feeling, how you're *really* feeling about seeing Celine and everyone."

Tension pulled Noire's eyes together like a drawstring. "I don't know."

"Of course you do." Her voice was soothing. This was Jayna at her best. The spotlight was off of her and she could approach Noire's own sore points with kindness and generosity.

"I don't, Jay. I don't know how to be a long-distance sister to Jabari or granddaughter to light, bright, damn-near-white Grand-mère." She rolled her eyes. "And I don't even know *what* I am to Celine."

"Don't be anything but yourself. It's that simple."

"It's not. They're my family. My color-obsessed—and otherwise dysfunctional, I might add—family. That makes it different."

Jayna shrugged her shoulders. "Well, you're a beautiful black and proud woman. So the color drama shouldn't be an issue."

"It's not. It's just—"

"There's no 'just,' Noire."

"Yeah, I guess."

"There you go. And about the big-sister thing, it's not that hard. When I first met Jabari six years ago, he was a four-year-old kid from a place I had never visited and with an accent I had never heard. I didn't know how to be *anything* to him. So, I didn't try. I just talked to him, on his level."

"You have a gift, Jayna."

"Maybe I do. But who's to say that you don't?"

"Mmm."

"He's like a little buddy, you know. Don't sweat it."

"But he's *not* my buddy, he's my little brother. He must think I suck as a sister. I mean, I barely call the boy, and I only see him, like, once every two years. And the birthday presents I buy him I bet he can buy for himself!" Throbbing pain claimed her head.

"Just be yourself with him—"

"The accidental older sister—"

"And make yourself *available*. In big and small ways, Noire. But most of all, love him. And let him love *you* for that."

"Spoken like a sage."

"That's because I love ya, chick." Jayna chuckled and stroked her friend's hand.

"Thanks." She gave a weak smile.

They sat, the silence confirmation that their fifteen-year friendship bond had made them closer to being sisters. They didn't always agree, but it didn't matter. They loved each other; they always would.

"And now, you *must* tell me about the d-a-t-e. You said it was good."

"We have all week for that." Noire's feigned lighthearted laugh stuck in her throat and came out sounding like a cough.

Chapter 5

Single Consciousness

Jabari hugged Jayna and slapped Noire five. Jayna placed enthusiastic kisses on his awaiting cheeks while Celine pressed her cheek against Noire's ear. Noire felt like a stranger.

Claiming the backseat of Celine's 1989 Volkswagen Rabbit, Jabari and Jayna launched into an earnest conversation that only a nine-year-old boy and a twenty-eight-year-old woman could have. Jabari told Jayna about his skateboard collection and asked her for her favorite skateboard colors. He mentioned that most girls in his class were yucky except for one nice girl who looked like Jayna. He explained that a really stupid boy named Lenny picked a fight with his best friend, Hector, yesterday, but Hector tripped him and Lenny chipped his front tooth. Jayna talked about how cranky she becomes when she doesn't get enough sleep. She told Jabari about her hardest classes in dental school and that she's still scared of airplanes and lightning storms. They were rapt with each other, asking and patiently answering questions, giving advice only when the other seemed to seek it.

Noire listened and measured car lengths uneasily with her eyes. Her right foot pushed into the floor of the car, she regulated Celine's aggressive driving through the narrow New Orleans streets and tried to keep her mounting nausea at bay. Turning around to face them, she readied herself to add something insightful to their discussion of Jabari's reading tutor. Celine wrenched the car into the opposing lane and accelerated to pass a truck. Noire choked her airplane lunch back down her throat.

"Jabari, lower your voice. You are giving me a headache." She glanced in her rearview mirror and made a mad mommy face.

"But I'm telling Jayna about the exercise that I was doing with Miss Arnold!"

"It sounds really fascinating." Noire seized the chance to undermine Celine's protestation. "Jabari, I'm so proud of you. It seems like you've made a lot of progress."

Jabari's face was aglow.

"With all the money I'm spending on that tutor, there needs to be *progress*. Tell Jabari's dad he can increase his contributions to *that*. He knows how expensive a good education is for one's child." She gnashed her teeth and accelerated.

Noire scoffed at Celine's veiled criticism of her father's financial support of her while she was in college. Celine had accused him of taking food out of Jabari's newborn mouth.

"Tell him yourself. And *not* in present company." Noire's clenched mouth spat her words out like daggers and forced Celine's silence for the balance of the ride. At forty-one to Noire's twenty-eight, Celine was barely old enough to be Noire's elder, and Noire never respected her role as stepmother even during the three years when the title had been official. She was her brother's mother, so she remained civil. But Celine was pretentious and self-righteous, shouldering Jabari's dyslexia like her own personal tragedy.

After arriving at the house, Celine showed Jayna and Noire where they'd be sleeping. "This couch opens up into a full-size bed. It's lumpy, so sleep diagonally. You can use the dressing room in the corner to store your bags and clothes. And it's big enough for changing. Jabari, please go and get two towel-and-washcloth sets for Noire and Jayna. The air conditioning in our bedrooms won't reach the living room at night, so I've set out a fan. That should cool things off well enough."

Their thank-yous ricocheted off the back of her head. Jayna went to unpack and Noire sat on the couch with Jabari.

"It's great to see you, Jabbo!" Noire planted a kiss on his nose. "You are getting so tall, you know. I think you'll end up taller than Dad."

"That won't be too hard."

"Yeah, I guess it won't. You know, I meant what I said earlier—I'm really proud of you. I'd love it if you would read something to me."

"Sure. I'll read the letter that Jayna sent me!" He raced out of the room to retrieve it. Noire felt a tug at a corner of her heart. She called Jabari twice a month, but she rarely wrote him or even e-mailed. But that would probably help him improve his reading skills. She'd have to remember that.

Jayna emerged from the dressing room just as Jabari ran back in, her letter flapping behind him like a flag. "I received it on Friday, Jayna. I read it three times already."

"You're making me blush. You act like I'm a celebrity!" she teased.

Jabari's beige cheeks flushed pink. *"Dear Jabari."* He cleared his throat. *"I can't wait to see you next week! It will be such fun to spend time together. The weather has been terrible here—cold and rainy. I would prefer snow to rain because at least it is pretty. The rain just makes me want to stay in my bed and eat cookies all day."* Jabari giggled at the thought.

"Noire and I have been very busy with school these past few months. For me, I've been doing something called rotations. Basically that means that I have been learning different aspects of dentistry by working closely with dentists and other students. It's fun but very tiring at times. Well Jabari, we can talk once I see you. Tell your mommy I said hello! Love, Jayna." He looked up expectantly.

"That was lovely reading, Jabari. And that was a really nice letter, Jayna." She offered a heartfelt smile to her friend, who loved Jabari like her own brother.

Time had made Grand-mère's house a dilapidated relic of what lived in Noire's childhood memory. Propped on a corner in New Orleans's

Faubourg Tremé district, renowned as the country's oldest continuous neighborhood of "free people of color," the Creole cottage looked like the elder at a nursing-home block party. The filigreed woodwork was moldy from years of damp mornings and sultry evenings. Drooping steps struggled to reach the barely green floorboards of the leaning porch. Noire opened the screen door and knocked tentatively while Jayna tottered in the fragile rocker at the far end of the porch.

The house was still, sagging in the unseasonable spring heat wave, but Noire sensed movement inside. She was mopping her hairline with a damp backhand when her grandmother inched open the door. *"Grand-mère, c'est Noire"* confirmed her positive identification of her first granddaughter. She used her whole body to open the door fully.

"Mon dieu, ma petite-fille!" was succeeded by a series of Louisiana French incantations of which Noire had never learned the meaning. Natalie Demain hugged her granddaughter with all of the power left in her seventy-eight-year-old shrunken frame. Extending her right arm up to meet Noire's head that stood six inches above hers, she patted Noire's free-form tendrils that danced the jitterbug across her head. With thinly veiled disapproval, she commented, "I see you're trying something different." Her own hair lay in two neat braids that criss-crossed her head like reinforced cables secured by bobby pins. Noire's father had once told her, with a bitter laugh, that his mother used to say the family had "come to Jesus" hair because the phrase could be sung languidly while pulling a fine horsehair brush through their locks. This was in contrast to the unfortunate others whose shorter, coarser hair warranted a quick work song or nothing at all. Noire had learned that she was among the unfortunate.

"Ooo, ma petite-fille," she cooed, hugging her again, this time in sympathy.

"Grand-mère, you remember Jayna?" She motioned for Jayna to step forward from her safe observation point a few feet in front of the rocker.

"Mais oui!" she exclaimed as she hugged Jayna's petite frame to her own. Instinctively she caressed Jayna's relaxed, carefully coiffed head, then stopped short when she remembered that Jayna was not techni-cally family. "Long time, long time," she repeated in greeting.

Smoothing her own hair in reaction, Jayna agreed, "Yes, since college. It's a pleasure to see you again, Mrs. Demain.".

"Well, come inside." She unhanded Jayna and turned quickly. Jayna and Noire followed her into the relative cool of the dark house. "On hot days like today," Natalie explained, "I just keep the lights off and take it easy. I'm too old to try and break a sweat." She chuckled at her use of the turn of phrase.

"Oh, I know what you mean, Mrs. Demain," Jayna chirped.

"Please, *ma cherie,* 'Madame Natalie' is fine. I haven't been Mrs. Demain since he died over ten years ago, God rest his soul." She motioned toward the black-and-white picture in a tarnished silver frame with an engraved placard that read: 16ÈME MAI 1939. A thirty-year-old Benoit Demain held his eighteen-year-old bride's elbow with all the gallantry required of the occasion.

Noire raised her eyebrow at the belated disclosure.

"He was an octoroon, you know. Wasn't common for an octoroon to marry a quadroon like me, especially back in those days." The fondness of the memory was evident in her smile.

Jayna looked worried as Noire rolled her eyes and said, "Funny that the slave mentality has so brainwashed black people that we celebrate disparaging and exclusionary terms like 'quadroon' and 'octoroon.' What does it even mean to be a quarter or an eighth black?"

Madame Natalie took Noire's criticism as no indictment of her. "I was pretty too, in my day. Thick black hair down to my twenty-two-inch waist, a complexion as fair as fresh butter cream. But everyone agreed that Benoit was handsome, by colored *and* white standards. His gray eyes caught fire in the morning sunlight and smoldered in the haze of dusk."

Noire flushed hot and cold.

"Madame Natalie, do you have something to drink? I'm feeling a bit overcome." Jayna glanced at Noire and winked.

"Thank you," Noire mouthed surreptitiously. She could count on her friend to steer the conversation away from the issue that caused Noire untold grief during her childhood summers spent with Grand-mère and the rest of the color-conscious Demain extended family.

"Of course, *cherie*. There's fresh tea in the icebox."

"I'll get it." Noire exited the room, her heart full of remembered pain.

"And I'm going to the bathroom," Jayna proclaimed as her eyes caught sight of a toilet bowl peeking from behind a door in the hallway.

Noire took her time preparing the drinks. She retrieved three dull mismatched glasses and a heavy serving tray that she imagined Grand-mère had once used for entertaining. She reminded herself that she was far from being a gangly twelve-year-old helpless to her cousins' taunts, and her pain morphed into sadness and exasperation. Filling the glasses, she told herself that she couldn't alter beliefs that Grand-mère had held all of her life. So she changed tactics.

"Grand-mère"—Noire's voice preceded her reappearance in the parlor—"I've met a nice man, a banker." She looked her grandmother in the eye. "He was schooled at the Sorbonne and Columbia."

"Ah, is he French, *ma cherie?*" Her eyes were hopeful.

"He's French-speaking. From Côte d'Ivoire. In Africa."

Natalie grimaced. "Africa . . ."

Noire followed her grandmother's roving eyes with smug satisfaction as they surveyed her: her curly-kinky hair more sculpted than floppy, her skin the color of her strong iced tea. "Yes, well he sounds successful, Noire."

Noire was winded. She had been prepared to contest her grandmother but now she had taken that opportunity away from her. And she had called her by her own name. Grand-mère seldom called her "Noire" because of its bold proclamation of blackness. But here she had used it without hesitation. She stared into her grandmother's hazel eyes and registered an implacable complacency. Her own eyes reflected shame.

Returning to the room, Jayna added, "Madame Natalie, did you know I'm in dental school? This is my third year." Jayna flashed a quick smile.

"How wonderful! The things that a lady can do nowadays . . ." Her voice trailed off. "If I had to do it again, I would have been an interior decorator. I always loved to decorate, but it made no difference to Benoit. He would have been happy to live in a cardboard box."

Noire stared at her grandmother in amazement. She had never

known Grand-mère to have a career aspiration; she never even considered it. And she tried to reconcile her grandmother's revelation with the weather-eaten façade and gloomy interior of the house.

"But I can't anymore. Can't be bothered to fix things up, to make appearances. Every night I expect my covers to be my winding sheet and my bed to be my coffin. But God won't call me home." She took a sip of the syrupy-sweet iced tea. "I'll be ready when He does."

Noire tried to imagine Grand-mère's body lifeless, her voice silenced forever. It made her sick. She was her *grandmother*, after all, and the only living grandparent she had. Grand-père had been a hands-off authoritarian who only poked his head above his French Creole newspapers and books of crossword puzzles long enough to send Noire to the store for a hand-rolled cigar. In their longest conversation—when she was eleven—he told her that he never had patience for girls, and he certainly didn't know what to do with Northern black city girls like her.

But Grand-mère knew what to do. She taught her how to cook crawfish, and make dainty mint julep drinks for her bridge-playing friends on Thursday afternoons. She showed her how to cross her legs when she wore dresses, to use a handkerchief to keep herself fresh on hot days, and to say special prayers in French to all the Catholic saints who could ask God to help you to find things that you lost, or keep from sinning, or have a baby if you wanted one.

By contrast, her Big Mama on her mother's side—who had been a powerhouse in her young years—was a crumpled woman wracked with "feminine illnesses" for as long as Noire could remember. For Noire, she had always been small and frail; as a little girl, she never understood why she was "*Big* Mama." When she died the year Noire turned twenty-one, Big Mama had spent the last twenty years of her downsized life in the confines of her twelve-by-twelve bedroom at Cousin Nandi's Baltimore house.

Noire looked at her grandmother. She saw that her face was stamped with a peculiar American history. Her voice, clothing, and outlook on life marked her as a colored Southern gentlewoman, and she held the position with all the dignity and pomposity of the best of her generation. Natalie was as much a product of her history as Noire was a product of hers.

She decided to try and set aside her issues with her grandmother so that she could relax and ask about the family; Grand-mère tracked the most minute details in the lives of children and grandchildren, aunts, uncles, cousins, and ambiguous relations scattered throughout southern Louisiana, Los Angeles, East St. Louis, and Chicago. Her father had been the renegade when he charted his path through Washington, D.C., long enough to father her. Her parents traveled to New York City apart and together, their commitment to coparenting stronger than their premature commitment to each other.

Jayna had abandoned the conversation for her own thoughts. Noire wanted to reengage her. "You know, Grand-mère, Jayna's really great with kids. She and Jabari get on like old pals." Jayna looked startled.

"I haven't seen that child in ages—"

"You should be a pediatric dentist, Jayna; you'd be terrific!" She nodded approvingly at her friend.

"Yeah, I've thought about that. Maybe—"

"Do you have a boyfriend, Jayna?"

"No."

"Well, isn't there anyone you *like?*"

Noire cringed at her grandmother's question.

"I'm not sure how I feel about him." Jayna gave a tepid smile.

"Maybe you need to figure out who likes you. You're a pretty girl. Twenty-eight is old enough to be married, you know."

"Grand-mère!"

"Time waits for no man *or* woman, *ma cherie.* A girl shouldn't be so independent that she bites off her nose to spite her face." She sucked her teeth for emphasis.

The dim parlor grew hazy with the approach of evening. Each woman sat in her own thoughts. Noire felt frustrated. Why did women always feel so comfortable admonishing other women on winning the affections—and engagement ring—of a man?

"*Ma cherie,* Jayna looks like she just lost her best friend. Please take this child somewhere and cheer her up."

Natalie pushed herself to standing and patted moisture from her upper lip. "Feels like the devil's in town!"

"Maybe she is!" Noire said with a laugh.

"*Cette fille n'a aucune classe,*" Grand-mère humphed.

Noire turned to Jayna. "She just said I don't have any class."

Giggling along with Noire, Jayna got up and kissed Noire's grand-mother on the cheek. "It was good to see you again, Madame Natalie. You look well."

"It's no small feat, *cherie*. Noire, give your Grand-mère a kiss good-bye. And a hug in case I don't see you for a while. I'm proud of you," she said as if passing a decree.

"Thank you." She kissed both her cheeks and hugged her tightly. "Dad sends his love."

"Tell him to visit me. I haven't seen him since Thanksgiving." Her tone suggested that the holiday had last been celebrated five years ago.

Noire smiled.

"Say a prayer for your grand-mère, now. Don't forget me."

"I could never forget you." She turned to go, the image of her grand-mother leaning heavily on the front door her parting glance. As she and Jayna rounded the corner, she turned back and was surprised to find her still there. Her eyes cloudy, Noire said a quick French prayer to one of Grand-mère's favorite saints.

Innocent's fingers danced across the computer keyboard. He was under the gun, trying to produce a pitch book for Renée, his managing direc-tor, before she left for San Francisco.

At 4:45 she walked into his office announcing that the business trip had just been pushed up by a day due to the client's scheduling con-flicts; she needed a finished product in four hours. Standing in the doorway, she added, "Sorry for the added pressure," and left.

Innocent buzzed his assistant, Amy. She appeared, her trench coat and sneakers announcing her imminent dash to the baby-sitter's house to pick up her daughter.

"Yes."

"You have yet another opportunity to save my life. Can you please just get me two cans of Dr Pepper before you leave?"

"I think that two cans of Dr Pepper may actually kill you."

"Just as long as I stay alive until nine o'clock."

"Nothing like sugar and caffeine for a quick high." She sighed and took the two bills from his hand unceremoniously. "Aromatherapy is healthier and more effective."

"I'll sniff the can." Innocent started to write an e-mail:

SUBJECT: that sinking feeling
DATE: March 15, 1999, 5:04 P.M.
TO: Noire@nyu.edu
FROM: theINNOCENTone@mymail.com

Once again I find myself plunged into the cold waters of everyone else's whims and time pressures. Sometimes I feel like I'm

Innocent stopped himself short. *I can't send this to her.* He pressed DELETE.

"Soda is not a meal." Amy dropped two dimes on his desk and the two cans of soda. "Good night, Innocent."

"I'll see you tomorrow."

"Remember, I'll be in late; Jody has a pediatrician's appointment at nine o'clock."

Did I know that? "Oh."

She walked out of his office, her mind already out the door, focused on the rest of her life. The more important things.

He wrote a new, benign message and pressed SEND. The e-mail launched into cyberspace, he flicked the tab on his soda with his thumb and took a gulp. He had four hours to do twelve hours of work.

Innocent was in "the zone" fueled by Dr Pepper, adrenaline, and sleep deprivation. His tie a bandana and his shirtsleeves crumpled at the forearm, he smelled of hard work and carbonated beverages. The sun had risen in the rectangle of his office window this morning; he would watch it from his bed tomorrow.

Nine o'clock beckoned. Analysts rushed into his office awaiting modified assignments and e-mailed him their rerun financials and more sophisticated pie graphs on the half hour. He printed out a new draft of the document at forty minutes after every hour, popped open a can of

Dr Pepper, and edited for twenty minutes. Then he would start again. His brain saturated with reams of detail, he distilled thirty cumbersome pages into twelve pages of crisp, highly functional bullet points, graphs, charts, models, and answers to anticipated questions.

Renée stepped into his office at 8:53, a trim overnight bag rolling behind her.

"Voilà." Innocent placed five bound copies of her pitch book in her hands.

"It looks wonderful, Innocent." She flipped through it, perused the graphs, skimmed the conclusion. "I didn't think you could do it."

"Is that why you asked me?" He watched her face turn red, then cast his eyes downward, mindlessly scanning his desk until she left. She forgot to say thank you.

Morning set the New Orleans living room ablaze. Noire propped herself up on the sofabed and caught a glimpse of Celine in the kitchen making coffee. Her flimsy nightgown revealed a mother's graceful breasts and luxuriant belly. Her skin looked like fresh saltwater taffy. Noire wondered why she and her father didn't invite her to their wedding ten years ago and whether she would have attended if they had. They met the year that Grand-père died, and Dad was back in New Orleans helping Grand-mère to settle his affairs when he met Celine in the fifth month of what was to be a six-month stay. Celine had been thirty to her father's forty-five. Noire was nearly eighteen. Jabari came along eight months later.

Her father had become a father to the child who some thought was his grandchild with the wife who some thought was his daughter. Noire's eighteen-year-old wisdom concluded that he was going through a midlife crisis, with Celine as the unwarranted object of his affections and Jabari the unwitting victim.

She had said as much to her mother, expecting an ally.

"When I was thirty-one years old, I had a nine-year-old child. I knew that I was an adult, by anyone's standards. Celine is an adult, and so is Paul. They've made a decision and they have a responsibility to live with it. Neither of us can say much about it, nor do much about it, and we shouldn't because it's not about us. It's about them trying to live their lives."

"Well, Mom, it may not be about you but it has everything to do with me. He's *my* father, for godsakes. I mean, don't I have any say in this?!"

"Ask Jabari. Paul is his father too. Noire, I know this is awkward for you, but your feelings are not the only ones to be considered here. People—including those we love—make decisions all the time that we may not agree with. But it doesn't necessarily mean they were wrong or intended to hurt us. Paul has been a great father to you. He's not going to stop. But he's more than just your father. He's a man. Just pray for the best and keep loving him and letting him love you."

Noire was quieted but not convinced. Why did he marry Celine but not *her* mother? She looked at the face she knew better than her own and was certain she wondered the same thing.

Celine had her own set of sensitivities. Noire stepped off of the plane and into her life, her New York–savvy eighteen-year-old step-daughter produced just in time for Thanksgiving. She offered her a smile without teeth. Noire's mouth hung open, resisting any discernable shape.

Paul was tan. His new fatherhood radiated on his skin and sparkled in his eyes. He hugged Noire meaningfully. She reciprocated but was unsure if she was the source of his joy.

"This is Celine and your new little brother, Jabari." His voice was a trumpet at revelry.

Noire shuddered. She played a stingy game of dodge ball with Celine's eyes before stepping forward.

"Nice to meet you, Noire. I hope you had a good flight." Celine turned Jabari's face toward Noire in greeting, but held him close.

"Oh, he's beautiful," Noire breathed, overwhelmed by his miniature perfection.

Celine's back slackened.

"Would you like to hold him?" Paul still spoke too loud.

"I must be dirty or something."

"Just throw this little towel over your shoulder"—he adjusted it on her right shoulder as he talked—"and you'll be fine."

Celine handed her the nine-pound bundle. She looked at the face of her two-month-old brother and tried to discern their shared parentage in his baby features. His skin was new and unspoiled, and he smelled of baby and mother's milk. She thought of her mom's comment: *"Ask Jabari."* Her love for him was unqualified and complete in that instant. But her feelings for Celine were more complex.

Her thoughts returning to the present, Noire squinted into the morning sunlight.

Jayna rolled over onto Noire and woke herself up. "Aaah! Oh, hey." Jayna shielded her eyes from the yellow light.

"Hey."

"So you're awake." Celine peeked out from the kitchen. "Do you drink coffee?"

Jayna retied her headscarf over her eyes and grunted.

"I do. Thanks." Noire made her face and breath presentable in the bathroom, then joined Celine in the kitchen.

"What time does Jabari wake up?"

"Seven forty-five. I like to let him sleep as long as possible. And he can get ready in about forty minutes. His school is only five minutes away." Her head was resting against the wall and she clasped her coffee cup in both hands as though it were too heavy for her. Her left leg was crossed over the right and bounced about showing off a butterfly tattoo at the ankle and chipped hot pink toenail polish.

"Celine, do you have orange juice?" Jayna queried from the sofabed.

"There's pink grapefruit juice in the fridge."

"Thanks." She dangled her feet over the edge of the bed and blew her nose.

Jabari rushed across the kitchen and hugged his mother's seated frame at the waist.

"Oh buddy!" Noire rescued Celine's coffee cup. She hugged him back. "You're up early."

"Everyone else is up . . . I couldn't help it!" Jabari imparted kisses and hugs to Jayna and Noire with great ceremony.

"Would you like Cheerios, Raisin Bran, or oatmeal?"

"I'd like Cocoa Puffs please?" His expression was angelic.

"We don't have Cocoa Puffs, Jabari. We *never* do."

"But you can buy them at the store." He craned his neck and pushed his chin out in supplication. His eyes were tightly closed.

"I will not be accused of feeding my child dessert for breakfast."

Letting out a sigh that Noire feared would get him slapped, he conceded, "I'll have Raisin Bran."

Noire watched old episodes of *The Cosby Show* and stayed out of Celine and Jabari's way. Together they played a well-rehearsed jazz duet: the beginning melody and driving bass to keep them steady, but full of improvisation, chord changes, and the occasional solo. She noticed Celine's very different parenting style from her mother. She was a time-keeper and taskmaster with Jabari where her mother had been an omniscient observer. Her stern voice repeated, verbatim, the items on Jabari's dwindling list of to-dos every five minutes. Initially Noire bristled, but when she saw a scurrying Jabari mouthing his mother's words as she spoke them, she realized that their system was one of repetition and reinforcement. By restating the theme, Celine kept their song going. And even when Jabari strayed into a wild improvisation, he still heard the melody in his head.

Jayna pulled herself off of the floor, where she had been doing sets of crunches, just in time to avoid being trampled by Jabari, who dived onto the sofabed to give Noire a good-bye kiss. Then he latched onto Jayna, who counted the number of times she rocked him back and forth in her arms—six—before his mother restated the last thing on his list: "Put your homework in your knapsack so we can *leave!*"

"OK, good-bye, Jayna and Noire!" he sang with gusto. He stuffed his homework—which had been checked and signed by his mother and sat on the entrance hall table—into his child-sized Dillard University book-bag and plopped a Xavier University cap on his head. "I'm ready, Mama!" he shouted.

"OK, buddy, good job today." She turned to Noire from where she stood. "OK, Noire, don't forget to take the key on the front table. We'll be home around six o'clock."

"Alright. Bye, Celine. Have a good day. See ya later alligator!" she added for Jabari's benefit.

"After a while crocodile!" And the door slammed shut.

"Finally I can get into the bathroom!" Jayna ran out of the room.

Noire smiled to herself. Celine's style was different but no less effective. Chuckling at Jabari's collegiate gear, she remembered her father's story about the flack he received for refusing to go to Xavier, the historically black Catholic university that the Demain family has attended since it opened in 1915, and instead opting for Dillard, which he claimed had a greater "black consciousness." After he married Celine, a Xavier graduate, he softened his stance against the school and even came to admit that Xavier—which graduates a quarter of all black pharmacists in the U.S.—was as committed to serving the black community as his alma mater. But, he added, Dillard always had better parties, and it cultivated his activism in the Civil Rights Movement, participating in sit-ins and demonstrations during his time there from 1961 to 1965.

Jayna returned to the room freshly showered, oiled, and clad in a camisole and tap pants. She looked at Noire. "Why the smile?" She untied her carefully wrapped hair and fingered it into the day's style.

"Just thinking about my family. They're a funny bunch, you know." She snickered.

"They're not perfect, but they are good people. Be thankful for that."

"I am."

Chapter 6

Virtual Reality

Noire had twenty-six e-mail messages. She sipped her café au lait and deleted seven. A battered copy of *New Orleans Living* held Jayna's seat. She returned and unburdened herself of her scone, Italian soda, and Noire's crumb cake.

"How many from the man himself?"

"Three." Noire responded to her mother's message and then her dad's.

SUBJECT: RE: How're things?
DATE: March 17, 1999, 3:26 P.M.
TO: BlackPower#1@everyonesblack.com
FROM: Noire@nyu.edu

Mon père extraordinaire,
Things are just fine in N'awlins. Jabari is getting tall and really talkative, and Celine is acting decent. Grand-mère reminisced on Grand-père's octoroon past . . . she's

so affected! But it was good to see her. Anyway, she can't wait till your next visit. Same with Jabari. What should I tell them?

Later,
Black Power's #1 Daughter

She pressed SEND and then read Innocent's first message.

SUBJECT: c'est la vie
DATE: March 15, 1999, 5:06 P.M.
TO: Noire@nyu.edu
FROM: theINNOCENTone@mymail.com

Hope that you arrived in New Orleans safely and that you, Jayna, and the rest of the crew are having a grand time together. For my part, I'm chained to my desk for the next four hours and then will probably just go home and crash. Such is the life of a promising VP at an I-bank!

I'm thinking of you, Noire,
Innocent

"How odd."

"What?" Jayna looked up.

"Innocent makes this sarcastic remark about being chained to his desk and being a 'promising VP.'"

Jayna made her hands look like flashing headlines. "Investment banking: the new slavery."

"Seriously?" Noire looked worried.

"Girl, no! If I were making six-figure bank, I'd be feeling more than a little bit cute!"

"Not if you were working a hundred hours a week!"

"Trust me, I *am*. But the difference is, I'm paying Columbia dental school for the privilege instead of the other way around!"

"True." Noire clicked on the next message.

SUBJECT: *done*
DATE: March 16, 1999, 10:43 A.M.
TO: Noire@nyu.edu
FROM: theINNOCENTone@mymail.com

Noire,

I made it. Finished the project and lived to tell about it. Some would call this success; I call it survival . . . Hope you've been making the most of the heat and humidity. You must look like a copper Venus.

A bientôt,
Innocent

Noire opened the next.

SUBJECT: interested? let me know asap
DATE: March 17, 1999, 2:43 P.M.
TO: Noire@nyu.edu
FROM: theINNOCENTone@mymail.com

Hi Noire,

My coworker just made me buy two tickets off of him since he won't be able to use them. They're to see a Brazilian dance troupe on Saturday the 27th. I'm hoping you'd like to join me; it's a matinee. We could have dinner afterward.

Sound good?
Innocent

Noire began typing her gracious acceptance and announced over her shoulder, "He invited me on another date." Her voice calm, she tried not to get too excited.

But Jayna called her bluff. "Aw sookie, sookie now!"

"Marcus!"
"Hello?!"

"Man, it's Innocent. How many brothas with French accents do you know?" Innocent's voice was full of laughter.

"You hadn't even said anything!" Marcus made chewing noises into the phone. "We're just finishing up with dinner. So, what's up with you?"

Innocent reclined in his office chair and perched his feet on the edge of his desk, his legs at sharp angles. "I'm alright—good in some respects."

"Yeah? Work is good then?"

Innocent could hear his wife and child having a baby-talk conversation in the background. "No. I mean, it's OK, not great. But I'm talking about the woman I met at your book signing."

"Afro?"

"What? . . . Oh yeah. We got together last Friday. She's nice, man."

"I guess she has bohemian appeal." His voice was flat.

Silence.

"Look, I'm not tryin' to hate." Marcus snorted.

"Yeah . . . well, I was calling to say that we should hang soon."

"No doubt. I'm gonna roll with some brothas tomorrow. You're welcome to join us. Or are you gonna kick it with—"

"Noire? No, she's away this week. Where are you meeting?"

"At Dub. Around eight-thirty, nine. OK?"

"I'll see you then, then."

"Stay black."

"Easy."

Innocent hung up the phone and looked at his watch. Sipping a warm Dr Pepper, he considered whether to order from Two Towers Deli now or have Indian take-out at home. Opting for the latter, he struggled through his last hour of work.

He visualized Marcus at home having dinner with his wife and child. Innocent rode his finger over his card, feeling the embossed lettering state his subsidiary to the Gordon family business. When did Marcus know he would marry Lydia? He fantasized about sharing dinner with his own Lydia, making love to her four nights a week at ten-thirty, and going to sleep. His elbows on his desk, he smoothed his hands over his nearly bald head and held the pose as if willing himself to think about something else. He looked at the work in front of him, stood up, and left.

Noire didn't want to argue, but Celine was being unreasonable. "Jabari won't become a juvenile delinquent from missing three hours of school tomorrow."

"It sends the wrong message."

"It *is* educational." She handed her the tri-fold brochure for the New Orleans African American Museum of Art, Culture and History.

"He went there last year, on a class trip."

"There's a new exhibit." Noire paused. "Look," she continued, "we're only here until Sunday. And you can't even count Sunday because our flight leaves at like eight A.M. And you were the one who made his orthodontics appointment for Saturday."

"That was the only available day, Noire. I couldn't just stop the world—" Celine aborted her thought but its unarticulated meaning hung in the air.

Noire squinted her eyes and Jayna jumped in. She appealed to Celine's self-interest: complimenting her pretty but neglected feet, Jayna suggested she play hooky herself on Friday and opt for a day of beauty with no responsibility to Jabari. They would ferry him to school, pick him up, feed and entertain him. Noire looked at Jayna gratefully.

Celine decompressed her lips, which had been a thin pink line across the bottom of her face. "Well, let me explain it to Jabari and I'll write a note to his teacher." She smirked.

Noire's smile was full. She stood up, grabbed her backpack, and beckoned at Jayna, who had been her only witness. "Thanks, Celine. It'll be fine. Thanks!" She reached out to give her arm a tentative squeeze. Celine's eyes glistened.

Thursday night dragged into the wee hours of Friday morning. Jayna and Noire stood at the periphery of the human tidal wave on Bourbon Street in the heart of the French Quarter. The spring break crowd swarmed in packs of eight to guarantee support for every drunken excess and display of public nudity they could manage to perform. It was as if all seemed to realize that their coveted week of decadence was quickly drawing to a close and they had to make up for lost time.

Noire scanned the crowd of the barely legal, bypassing the beer-guzzling frat boys and jocks for the more quirky and less physically intimidating guys who sipped oversized mixed drinks through a straw. Her gaze landing on an ideal temporary object of interest, she mused, *He's too young to love but old enough to fuck.* She watched him twirl his rude-boy dreadlocks around his fingers. His jeans sagged low enough to irk the sensibilities of the parents he probably still lived with on university holidays.

She pointed out her curiosity to Jayna and steered them into his path.

"Girl, he's a baby-thug!"

"Only young . . ." Noire thrust herself into his line of vision and smiled. She enjoyed his walk as he came closer.

"Too young," Jayna hissed.

"For what?"

"Hello." His voice was embarrassed. He dropped his head to study the stray Mardi Gras beads that rolled around the ground, and his hair draped his face like a cape.

"Let me see your face," she ordered. He looked up and stared over her left shoulder. "I'm Noire." She bent forward and let him kiss her cheek.

"Kamau." He shifted about like a fifteen-year-old hoping he wouldn't get a hard-on during a slow song.

"Nice." She looked at Jayna glaring at Kamau and decided not to introduce her. "Where are you from, Kamau?" She watched his eyes follow her tongue as it circled her lips.

"Atlanta." His voice cracked.

"I wish I were from Atlanta too." Noire smiled and allowed him not to answer. He looked relieved. "Join us for a drink . . ."—she registered fear in his eyes—". . . or not."

Overcome, he stepped in to kiss her, but she placed her finger across her lips. "Fantasy can be better than reality. Good-bye, Kamau."

She walked away, forcing Jayna to follow.

"I thought you were trying to *hit* that!"

She ignored the disapproval in her voice. "Yeah, I thought so too . . ."

• • •

By four A.M., the thinning crowd had moved from being festive to desperate, their flamboyant flirtations becoming propositions from horny coeds whose top spring break priority was wanton sex. Noire slid her eyes around, watching clutches of baby-faced college women whose lopsided breasts under skimpy halter tops and multiple strings of Mardi Gras beads suggested that they had been exposing themselves to men all night long. Equally wasted guys—their faces flushed and voices loud—nursed warm beers and scoped the remaining women.

Sobriety and fatigue made Noire reflective. "Jayna, were we *ever* this ridiculous?"

"Never."

His tired eyes stared back at him in the taxi driver's rearview mirror. Innocent threw a mint into his mouth and patted and pinched his face in a hasty massage. He was trying to get into the party mood. "Long fucking week."

"Yeah." The driver's eyes met his in the mirror and then lost interest.

Adjusting his gaze, Innocent read the name placard displayed in the cab's partition. "You're from Guinea?"

This time the driver's eyes befriended his. "How do you know?"

"I'm from Côte d'Ivoire, but I know people from Guinea." He left out that he had met them at the Sorbonne and that they hadn't been friends.

"When was the last time you were home?" The driver said this in West African French.

"Over a year. You?"

"Four years. I haven't been back since I got here. I want to send for my wife and daughter."

He shook his head. "How old is she?"

"Six. We were trying to have a son before I left, but my wife doesn't get pregnant easily. But I have a son here, with a Haitian girl."

"Oh." Innocent didn't have a quick response.

"She's nice. Loves me good. And she's pretty. But I would never marry her though. She just doesn't understand a lot. I want to go back home in a few years, but she says America is God's own country. I think God lives in Guinea!" He snickered.

Innocent wondered if his wife knew about his Haitian-Guinean-American son. "To each his own, I guess."

"My wife understands. She wasn't too happy to know about Claude, but . . ." He shrugged. "Actually, she found out she was pregnant soon after I came here but she lost the baby. It was a girl though."

Innocent kept his suspicions private. "Sorry about that, man. Look, just let me off at the corner of 8th Street."

"OK."

"And good luck with everything. Your wife and your daughter *and* son—and everything." Innocent thought he knew too much.

As he handed the driver a ten-dollar bill, they shook hands and snapped as men often did back home. Then he left.

Dub smelled like men. The scent of beer-stained wooden floors and stale cigarettes and postworkout, postworkweek men filled his nostrils as he descended the stairs into the bar. The air was stagnant and full of thumping rockers and dancehall interspersed with some more righteous reggae from Bob Marley and Black Uhuru.

As his eyes adjusted to the dank haze, he was greeted by a woman whose breasts were barely restrained by a gauzy handkerchief of material. Her shiny, plum-colored lips moved vigorously as she chewed what must have been a wad of gum. She was a strawberry blonde, at least for the night, and her assured stride demonstrated her conviction that her taut and dewy body could elicit at least momentary excitement from any man she passed. Her thick legs leapt out from under a scant leather skirt with each step. She brushed Innocent with her breasts as she walked by him. He quieted himself before proceeding further.

Men outnumbered women at least ten to one. They were slung over their drinks in sport jackets and tailored trousers. But their hips were loose and they had thrown off their corporate lexicon and manners in lieu of a more user-friendly Caribbean cadence, down-home southern drawl, or inner-city staccato. The women's dress was decidedly more decorative and appealed to the common denominator of sexual allure.

Large or small, the women joyously displayed what they thought attractive about themselves. And judging from their exhibitionism, the women at Dub considered themselves to be highly attractive.

Innocent spotted Marcus at the end of the bar with two other guys. They were the perfect triumvirate, Marcus in his penny loafers, gray slacks, and monogrammed blue-and-white-striped shirt, the guy to the right in a proper Englishman's suit, and the guy to the left in a blue blazer, white button-down, and beige khakis.

Marcus reached up to hug Innocent around the neck with his left arm as he introduced him to Jordan and Khalib. "Let's pull these stools over to this table. Innocent, what are you drinking?"

"Dragon Stout!" He sounded convincing.

"See, this muthafucka knows it's the weekend!"

They settled into their corner of Dub. Khalib pulled a finely crafted cigar from the breast pocket of his suit jacket and then produced a cigar cutter from another pocket. He brandished it like a weapon and then clipped the end with practiced nonchalance.

"I should have let you circumcise my son!" Marcus laughed mightily.

Jordan clapped Marcus on the arm. "Man, you'd entrust him with the family jewels? I don't know about you, but my shit is sacred. I wouldn't let just anybody deal with 'em."

"And I'm just anybody?" Khalib feigned offense as he took his first drag on the now lighted cigar. Innocent gulped his stout.

"Marcus said you're at Wright Richards? I hear it's a tight place to be. How long you been there?" Jordan questioned.

"It's OK. Four years. Since b-school."

"So you're a VP?"

"Yeah."

"Man, well more power to you. I couldn't hang with the slave driving when I was at Calhoun. That shit was drivin' me to drink!" Jordan took another sip of his high-baller.

"More like drivin' you to fuck! We were concerned that Jordan's dick was just gonna fall off one day, he was being so random. Jordan, you're a lucky muthafucka. Especially that Michelle. She musta really been able to give head 'cause she sure as hell looked tore up!" Khalib shook his head at his friend.

"Well, when you don't have live-in pussy, sometimes you gotta make compromises. At least that's what they tell me. Right, Innocent?" Marcus shot a glance at Innocent before putting his head back into his gin and tonic.

What the fuck is that supposed to mean? He cut his eyes at him, then traded glances with Khalib and Jordan. "Marcus forgets that I witnessed his pimp-daddy days during b-school."

"I thought you said you were with Lydia ever since college," Jordan inquired.

Marcus returned Innocent's glare. "I was. But you know, it's all possible until you jump the broom! Innocent, lighten the fuck up! Look, I say, if she can suck you off and you can talk to her too, you're ahead of the game. It don't matter what anyone else says. Unless she's suckin' their dick too!" Marcus laughed and the others joined him in an attempt to make things comfortable.

He continued, "Innocent met a very nice woman just last week, at my book signing. A little avant-garde for my taste, but hey, Innocent has always been a more cosmopolitan kinda brotha than I am. I mean, he can hang in all kinds of atmospheres, no sweat. You know I'm just one of these highfalutin Negroes. But hey, aren't we happy I own my house on Martha's Vineyard instead of just renting? But it's all good man, really." He flashed his winning smile.

"Pretension often seems to win out over graciousness. You can't help it." Satisfied, Innocent didn't look back at that part of the conversation. "How do you guys know each other?"

Khalib spoke first. "Marcus and I went to Morehouse together, and I met Jordan when he was at b-school at Kellogg and I was in journalism school. Northwestern."

"Yeah, yeah." Innocent shook his head in acknowledgment.

"And, as it turned out," Khalib continued, "Jordan had dated my cousin for a bit when he was at Fisk."

"Small black world," Marcus offered.

"That's why you can't piss folks off with impunity. Everyone knows someone who knows you." Innocent drained his bottle and called the waitress to replenish their drinks.

"That's the *truth*." Jordan raised his empty glass in the air.

• • •

By the third round, Innocent had forgotten any gripe he may have had with Marcus, and Jordan and Khalib had graduated to being his boys. They were talkin' shit and enjoying the grubbiness of Dub. The strawberry blonde from earlier joined them at the table, sitting on Jordan's lap and leaning breasts-first toward Innocent. His pants became tight at the crotch. He eased himself to the edge of his chair to relieve the pressure. Khalib bought her a rum and coke, and she told them that her name was Patricia but she often went by "Butta," "because of my smooth skin." She was twenty-one years old and worked as an entertainer to put herself through school.

"Who do you entertain, Miss Butta?" Khalib asked, his eyes fondling her nubile breasts.

"Oh, men mostly. Sometimes women. At clubs and stuff. I dance." She made her expression pouty and seductive. Marcus removed a waft of misplaced blond hair from in front of Butta's face and then returned his hands to his lap.

Jordan's voice was throaty. "Do you lap dance?"

Butta's ripe and full behind, which had been mostly still in Jordan's lap, now rose slightly. She straddled him, her back still to him, and began pumping against his crotch. Her movements were controlled and followed the rhythm of the heavy dance-hall bass, her nearly naked ass meeting his crotch on the downbeat. Butta hiked up her skirt to increase her range of motion and her freed behind undulated knowingly. Jordan hooked his thumbs into her thong at either hip and he closed his eyes. The table was quiet, their eyes transfixed on Jordan and Butta. Sensing the mounting excitement of Jordan and her audience of three, Butta arched her back further. Her head nearly rested on Jordan's shoulder and the bottom of her breasts revealed themselves at intervals. Innocent felt himself pulse involuntarily.

Jordan's hands began to travel up across her taut stomach and toward her barely restrained breasts. She grabbed his hands in her own and allowed him one squeeze before announcing, "I'm the only one allowed to touch." She got up and turned toward Jordan, whose eyes were large and lustful. "Here's my card." She pulled a crumpled card from her skirt pocket.

Jordan didn't trust himself to speak but Marcus offered, "Um, Butta, here's a little something . . . toward your education." He peeled off a 50 and three 20s, rolled them in his palm, and handed them to her. His expression was reverent. "Thanks." Butta walked the long way round the table and touched Innocent's thigh as she departed. He flinched, his loins aflame. Jordan made a hasty trip to the men's room.

"Damn. I could part that ass in a second, yo." Khalib was the voice of reason.

"Pull up to the bumper, baby," Marcus sang saucily, then laughed.

Innocent regulated his breathing. He envied Marcus. *I guess that's what he means by the benefits of live-in pussy. I've only got my own hand to go home to tonight.*

Jordan returned from the men's room looking relaxed. He ordered another round of drinks for everyone, making his a double.

Chapter 7

Cultural Idioms

Innocent's mind was waging a bitter battle with his body. At four o'clock in the afternoon, he still struggled to hold on to his Dragon Stout dinner from the night before and his predawn breakfast of blueberry pancakes and turkey sausage.

Realizing that he wouldn't make it into the office for his usual three-hour Saturday stint, he brought his laptop to bed and signed on to his e-mail. He had eight new messages but opened up his sister's from the other day.

SUBJECT: Hi!
DATE: March 18, 1999, 10:54 P.M.
TO: theINNOCENTone@mymail.com
FROM: Mireille@cotedivoire.net

Dearest Brother,
How are you? I hope you are well. I'm missing you now as I am always missing you, but I am happy to write you again. Maman, Papa, and Grand-mère are doing fine.

I have much news to share for you. First, Maman and Papa will visit in Senegal next month for a month. It is for holiday and for work too. Maman will research for her next book on recent migrations into Côte d'Ivoire. Papa will meet with some possible clients. I wanted to go too, but I cannot go because I have more school. They will see l'île de Gorée and the slaving areas. I want to see them too. It is important to know, especially in Africa.

I have a beau. His name is Abdul. He is twenty-three and an engineering student at university here. He says he loves me very much. I think I love him too, but only a little bit. He is handsome. Do you know the Doumbia family? He is a relation from the mother's family. They are from the North. He is Muslim. Papa does not like it, I think. But he is nice to him.

Abdul does not support my wish to study in the U.S. He says the university here is good enough. He also says when Africans leave Africa for school, they never come back. He is right. From all of the people who are your agemates, no one comes back yet. But when people leave, they say to their family "I will be back."

I will come back to Côte d'Ivoire. I am sorry, Innocent. I talk like I do not understand why people never come back. But I understand. France has many opportunities. I am sure that the U.S. has good things too. It is hard to leave a comfortable life. I want to see the U.S. and meet new people and experience the good things too. But I want to give birth to my children in our country for them to know it is their country. They can visit everywhere, but they will know that Côte d'Ivoire is home.

I tried to visit Howard University on the Internet but I cannot connect to their website because my computer stops working. There was a problem here and the electricity was cut for two days. Papa did not let me use the computer until today because the generator was working too hard. He wanted to make it rest. We went to bed early; there was nothing to do. Innocent, please can you get the information for me? Thank you.

Charlotte is pregnant. The baby will come on the 18th of September. Maman is not happy because her first grandchild will be French. But she is happy about the baby. He will be half white. I wonder what the baby will think about his family here in Côte d'Ivoire. Do you like Michel? I think he will be a good father. I hope he loves Charlotte a lot. Maman will travel to France in September and visit them. I am happy. Charlotte said that it was hard to get pregnant. She was very sick. She was scared she would lose the baby again like last time. I will be an auntie and you will be an uncle.

Innocent, there is not any more to say. I hope to read your response soon.

J t'embrasse,
Mireille

Innocent saw in Mireille's words the image of a woman he only partially recognized to be his little sister. Telltale signs of growing maturity and reflection laced her imperfect English to form sentences that meant more than they said. He wondered, had he grown in as much wisdom as she had since they last saw each other more than a year ago? What life lessons had Mireille opened herself to?

As Innocent crafted the beginning of a response to his sister in his mind, his thoughts became a gaggle of existential questions that exacerbated his hung-over headache. *Does idealism die with age? Must life experience shrink conviction? Is this the birth of wisdom or is it defeat? Is wisdom the dignified acceptance of defeat?* He began his response to his sister:

SUBJECT: Re: Hi!
DATE: March 20, 1999, 4:27 P.M.
TO: Mireille@cotedivoire.net
FROM: theINNOCENTone@mymail.com

My dear Mireille,
Your message caused me to reflect on a lot of things, namely the question of when I will come back to Côte d'Ivoire. You're right, many people say they will return but don't because the pull of the "Western world" is so great, and they've just become complacent. But for some, the reasons are more complex. They stay because they've created lives there. They've gotten married, had children, built careers, and they just can't uproot themselves and everyone around them. So the decision to stay in the States or in Europe is not always a selfish one. For myself, I sometimes feel torn. Every year that I stay, there are more things that tie me here and the deci-

sion becomes more difficult. But I can't leave yet because there's more yet to do. And, truth be told, I don't know if I could live in Côte d'Ivoire again on a full-time basis. Mireille, understand what I'm saying to you. I love our family and I love our country. But if I were to return now, I would feel tremendous pressure to become Papa's protégé in his business. I don't want that. I want to do other things and create my own name, but in Côte d'Ivoire our name is already made. Do you see what I mean?

It is more than I can even understand myself. I miss you and Maman and Papa and Grand-mère more than anyone knows. And Charlotte, it's almost like I don't know her anymore. The last time I was in Paris on business, she and Michel had traveled to Italy on holiday. Do you keep up with her via e-mail? Maybe I can write her to congratulate her on her pregnancy. Will you send me her e-mail address?

Enough about all of that, Mireille. You've given me quite a bit of information about Abdul. Is there any other reason that Papa doesn't care for him besides his religion? Mireille, I know you are a young woman and can make decisions for yourself, but I also know how 23-year-old men can be. Please make sure you are being treated well and that he respects you. And believe me, if you take your time with things, he may whine about it, but he'll love you more in the end. If he threatens to leave you, let him. There are more where he came from.

About Howard, I have sent for information and I should receive it within the next week or so. Once I get it, I will express-mail it to you. I have a coworker who went there for business school and he enjoyed it. He is helping me to find a West African woman who is at the school and maybe you can e-mail her some of your questions.

Mireille, I wish I could write more but I'm feeling quite ill right now. (Don't worry, I'm not sick, I just ate and drank the wrong things and now I'm paying for it. Your brother is getting old!) Please give my love to the family and tell them I will call tomorrow evening.

Bisous,
Innocent

Innocent sent the message and looked for a new message from Noire. Seeing one from her little brother's account, he opened it.

SUBJECT: *C'est moi!*
DATE: March 20, 1999, 10:43 A.M.
TO: theINNOCENTone@mymail.com
FROM: Jabari1989@mymail.com

Hey Innocent, it's me! Jabari let me e-mail from his computer but he's standing right next to me and reading as I type so this'll be quick!

The week was good. Jabari, Jayna, and I went to the New Orleans African American Museum of Art, Culture and History yesterday and then loaded up on fat and salt at Two Sisters Kitchen, and sugar at this little praline shop at the French Market. We figured that since Jabari was getting braces today we might as well coat our teeth with every terrible thing we could. Jayna brushed her teeth a million times last night!

Anyway, we're flying out at 8:00 A.M. New Orleans time so I should be home by noon at the latest. I'll call you.

Hope you're having a good weekend,
Noire

Just the idea of salt, fat, and sugar made Innocent wretch. He bounded into the bathroom. Apparently his body had conquered him after all.

Monday morning seemed to catch everyone off guard. Because he had only gone into the office for two hours on Sunday, Innocent was far behind and needed to bring himself up to speed on Tuesday's satellite conference with clients in Düsseldorf. Noire realized she hadn't given any thought to what she would discuss with Professor Fuentes during their meeting on Tuesday afternoon, and she was trying to gather her thoughts. And it seemed that Jayna hadn't figured out a good strategy for dealing with her drive-by sex with Spencer. She and Noire had agreed that she needed to be cordial and avoid any one-on-one time with him until she knew what she wanted to say and do. But despite Noire's coaxing, Jayna resisted the idea of speaking to anyone about her issues with men—especially white men—and her mom's history of messy behavior. Her tone was adamant, her reasoning illogical.

"Noire, I don't need somebody up in my business, looking at me as just another fucked-up black girl with no daddy and a slap-happy mama who fucked every man who winked at her."

Noire cringed but fought to keep her face placid. "Therapists hear all kinds of stories all the time."

"Well, then they don't need to hear mine. And for money too . . . shit!"

"For a woman who's dedicating her life to helping people on a fee-basis, you sure have a jacked-up way of looking at this!"

"Difference is, I try to help folks fix problems they can't fix themselves. I don't need for anyone to tell me that I need to forgive my fucked-up mama and get over my white-boy issues. I'm a twenty-eight-year-old woman. At this point I've just got to live my life the best way I know how."

"Jayna, I don't know what else to say. I mean, you're not eighty-eight! You've got a whole life ahead of you. And who knows, maybe your future husband is a white man! It does happen." Noire shook her head.

"Are you wishing one on me? Look, thanks for all the sista love, but I need to deal with my own shit in my own way and my own time. OK?" There was a note of finality in the statement and Noire let it drop with an acquiescent shrug of the shoulders. After nearly fifteen years of friendship, she knew better than to force the issue; Jayna seldom took Noire's advice about anything.

At ten-thirty on Sunday night, Noire left an uninspired message on Jayna's answering machine to check in, jumped on her bed with three books and her vibrator, and dialed Innocent's number. He answered on the first ring. Noire digested the sound of his voice and curled her pubic hair around her finger. Flicking her vibrator on, she ran it along the base of her stomach and considered renaming it Innocent.

"Also, my sister Charlotte—she lives in Paris—is three months pregnant. My mother is planning to visit her in September right before the baby is due."

"That's great. Is this her first?" Noire wiggled out of her panties.

"Yes. She miscarried at five months about a year ago."

"Oh my God." She turned off the vibrator. "How old is she?"

"Thirty."

"And your other sister?"

"Eighteen."

"Wow. Your parents waited a while."

"Well . . . there was another—my brother. He died, was killed when he was fourteen. Serge and Charlotte were twins."

Noire grew twenty degrees colder. She wrapped herself in her blanket. "I'm so sorry."

"We were traveling to the birthday party of one of our neighbors, my girlfriend at the time. Her brother had offered to let my brother ride on the back of his motorcycle with him since I couldn't. I was in their father's car, holding the birthday cake. They skidded on some loose gravel and because my brother was so light, he flew over the handlebars and into the path of an oncoming car. The other guy lacerated his leg."

"My God, Innocent . . . gosh, I didn't mean to bring it up. I mean—" Her stomach thumped and churned. The vibrator fell to the floor and turned itself on. She grabbed it and slapped it off.

"Noire, I know. You couldn't have known before I told you. It happened sixteen years ago. We were really close . . . Hey, um—" His voice cracked. "I'll tell you more about him, about the family, at another time."

"OK," Noire whispered.

"Let me tell you something good."

"Yes . . . please." She released a full breath and pulled her panties back on.

"We're invited to Marcus's place for dinner on Saturday."

"What about our plans?"

"Oh, the Brazilian thing should end by five-thirty at the latest. I told him we had plans but that I'd get back to him. They're having a party that afternoon for their son, but he and Lydia, that's his wife, are planning a mellow evening with friends."

"Surprised I made the cut." She looked at her vibrator and mouthed "Marcus," then returned it to her nightstand.

"Noire, if you don't want to, that's fine. It's just that I haven't seen

Lydia since their wedding and I've never met Nile. But it's up to you."

Up to me? No, Innocent, I'd rather not spend our next date around the card-carrying black bourgeoisie who summer on "the Island" or "the Vineyard" and support causes with the highest profile and tax deduction . . . A momentary flashback to how they arrived here in the conversation robbed her tongue of its venom, leaving it parched. She choked, "Fine."

"Wonderful. And I'd love to fit in a midweek date, Noire. Maybe lunch on Thursday?"

They made plans for a late lunch rendezvous in Wright Richards's swank corporate dining room and ended the call. Noire retrieved her vibrator, named him Shaft, and turned him on.

Not knowing what to say to Professor Fuentes, Noire told her everything: how she came to love languages, what her travel and work experiences had been like, why she wanted to study comparative literature and Creole languages in particular. Her hands slicing the air and her gaze cast into her own lap, she deluged Professor Fuentes with fifteen minutes of relevant and irrelevant information. Raising her eyes, Noire looked into her poker face and stopped abruptly.

Professor Fuentes tore a piece of paper from her notepad and jotted something. She held it up. FIND YOUR ALLIES, it read in curly red script. She lit a cigarette and took a deep drag. Her face had the temporary haze of a drug addict when she first feels her poison of choice course through her veins.

Her eyes unfocused slits, when she reopened them they became laser beams on Noire's face. "I'd like to be your ally. This is a hard environment. You're trying to study languages that the discipline doesn't recognize. And even the people who speak them have problems with them. Some don't think they're languages at all. They are invisible, below the radar. I don't want you to be invisible too."

Cigarette ash collected on her desk. She pushed a newsletter at Noire from the American Comparative Literature Association. It was opened to the page describing their upcoming annual convention in Montreal at the end of April.

"I want you to attend with me." She tucked her cigarette into the corner of her mouth.

"But I don't have any money."

"If you can pay for your own food, you can drive up with me and stay in my hotel room. I got a double. Don't worry, I don't bite." Her smile was peculiar.

"Thanks, but—"

"It'll be a good chance for you to explore the discipline. See the people with whom you are choosing to become lifelong colleagues. Academia is not a job; it's a vocation. You need to see if you like the cult or not!" Her laugh was caustic, almost bitter. "I don't mean to scare you, Noire. There are people doing very meaningful work. I want you to look at them. Listen to how they speak to one another, how they describe their projects, how they socialize. As with any other field, academia has its social climbers too."

"I'll see what I can do."

"Good. Tell me by next Friday."

Noire stood up to leave and Professor Fuentes held up her sign again. *Find your allies* reverberated through her head as she walked out of the building and into the damp cold of the early spring evening.

The Brazilian dancers' unrestrained breasts bounced on the downbeat. Their countless strings of wooden beads created a shimmer of percussion and, together with the drums, stirred a cauldron of sound. Innocent felt his loins ignite right in the middle of the dance hall. He traced the knuckles of Noire's hand to provide focus for his burst of energy.

"They're good." Her words were a quick, hot breath whispered against his ear. His groin flinched before he eked out, "Very good."

Curious about his restraint in the company of bare-breasted women, Noire let her eyes rest in Innocent's lap. Noting his excitement, she slipped her left hand from under his and carelessly skimmed his upper thigh before stilling it at the crease of his leg. Turning to look at Noire, Innocent saw a brazen playfulness rim her eyes like eyelashes. She was teasing him!

The balance of the show was spent in a sensual participatory dance, the Brazilians on the stage and Innocent and Noire on the floor. Their movements—though more reserved—were no less intricate, with fingers and high heels playing an erotic game of hide-and-go-seek. Innocent's baritone purring tangled Noire's mind in lust.

Noire felt frisky in the taxicab headed uptown to Marcus's house. "Perhaps I'll try out for that dance troupe. Will you teach me a move or two . . . for practice?" She rolled Innocent's left earlobe between her thumb and forefinger.

"Oh, I don't know," he responded absentmindedly.

Noire turned to face him, her expression quizzical. "What's there not to know?"

"Oh . . . nothing." He kissed her on the cheek. "Guess I was just thinking about the birthday party."

"Mmm." She rested her hand in its place at the crook of his neck. "By the way, how old is—"

"Nile? He's two . . . Oh, Noire!" His voice was an exclamation point. "Guess what I got him!" He patted a bag the size of a box of cereal.

Noire stared at the shiny red gift bag that hinted at nothing. "I don't know . . . what is it?"

"Three guesses." He sparkled with expectation.

"I can't even imagine." Tickled by his enthusiasm, she eyed the bag again. "A race car."

He shook his head.

"Some of those, you know, kids' board books."

"Think creatively, Noire." He teased her.

"Finger paints! I loved to finger paint when I was little." She beamed and awaited the revelation.

"Not even close!" He laughed. "It's an incredible toy, a collector's item actually." Innocent edged something out of the gift bag and carefully unwound decorative FAO Schwarz tissue paper from around the box.

"Did you ever have an Etch A Sketch when you were young?" he asked as he handed Noire the gift. Her puzzled smile evaporated on her face before it had fully arrived. Innocent continued. "Well, this one is a limited-edition Swarovski Crystals Etch A Sketch! It's lovely! It has over fourteen thousand hand-set Austrian crystals and was designed by a well-known handbag designer. FAO Schwarz produced only twelve. It was a *coup* to be able to get one!" Innocent's smile was triumphant.

Noire's stomach churned and her mind reeled in disbelief. She ran her fingers along the fourteen thousand crystals that looked like a crust of diamonds. "How much was this toy, Innocent?"

Innocent bobbed his head. "It was a little more than I planned to spend!" He tittered. "But it's a collector's item. Who knows, it may be worth *thousands* more by the time Nile turns eighteen."

"What did you *pay* for it, Innocent?"

He registered the edge in her voice and frowned. "Fourteen hundred fifty dollars."

"*Please* tell me you are *lying* to me!" She tried unsuccessfully to lower her voice. "That's the better part of two months' rent for me, and you spent that on an *Etch A Sketch* for a two-year-old child! He'll probably break the knobs off of the damn thing and then throw it into his toy heap before the end of the week!"

Noire handed the gift back to Innocent. She wound her legs around each other and crossed her arms over her chest. Her brow was a knot on her face. She glanced at him, then rested her head against the backseat, her eyes staring straight ahead. "I can't believe you."

"It's a *collector's* item, Noire. Nile may *never* use it. That's not even the *point*." He turned away from her. "Man, why'd you get on this?" Innocent's annoyed voice took aim at the front of the cab. "Didn't you know there was construction?" Their taxi was a part of a vehicular tapestry sprawling out along the length of the West Side Highway. Weekend roadway construction meant headaches and hefty tabs for those in metered cabs.

The driver's Indian English staccato deflected Innocent. "This is New York City. There's construction everywhere."

Noire stared at the back of Innocent's head in disgust. Why did they have to ruin a perfectly good date with the addition of this dog-and-pony show of conspicuous consumption with Marcus as head Negro in charge?

"So, this is how you and your mad-tight homeboys do it? You just drop fifteen-hundred-dollar gifts on each other as a sign of black solidarity! Is that who's going to be at this 'child's party'? The black and the buppified? Can you hand me a couple hundred dollars so I can buy a bag to puke in?! I'm feeling *sick*."

"That's fucked up, Noire." He slid his pupils into the left-hand corners of his eyes, glimpsed her face contorted in defiance, and was exasperated. Why was everything a goddamn black political statement with her? *If she wants to playa-hate, she might as well not play.*

They sat in difficult silence. Now riding along the city streets, they were greeted with the background sounds of an early spring Saturday evening in Harlem. Her face in the cab window, Noire watched as people claimed stoops and storefronts as congregation points. The streets were thick with good-natured activity and colorful conversation. As the taxi edged away from the neighborhood's nerve center toward its heart, more ornate architecture lined broader roadways and cleaner, less populous sidewalks. They were in Sugar Hill, historical home to the black glitterati and the so-called Black House. The area once was inhabited by icons of the Harlem Renaissance and now was peopled with old-money blacks and a new wave of home-owning buppies and adventurous yuppies. Single-family dwellings with the pose of urban castles lined both sides of the street, occasionally interrupted for a church where soft-skinned old ladies would carefully descend stair steps clutching Bibles and choir robes. This was the Harlem that everyone wished to claim for its un-self-conscious elegance, but black folks were especially happy to have it as such a public display of normalcy, race pride, and money.

"Dammit, Noire, will you just calm down. Everything will be *fine*. Marcus is a charmer and Lydia's the perfect hostess." He was sorry he had made the last statement before he could place a period at the end of the sentence.

"A 'charmer' and a 'hostess.'" She hissed his words back at him.

"Can't you just be open-minded? Is that so *hard* for you, Noire? I mean, you don't even *know* Marcus."

Noire felt herself losing their fight but threw another punch before she hit the mat. "And you don't know me. I'm not a charmer by nature."

Innocent grabbed her hand and looked at her with hard eyes.

"Noire, I'm *trying* to get to know you. Don't make it so difficult on me. OK?"

Noire glared back, her silence no sign of acquiescence. Innocent paid the cab driver, and they climbed the stairs of Marcus and Lydia's urban mansion.

Noire was struck by Lydia's conviviality. She was a larger woman than she had expected and she carried her proportions with the grace of good living. Her Byron Lars dress grazed her body as only a custom-made outfit could, and the ecru linen looked untouched by two-year-old hands. She took Noire's jacket—a vintage oilskin that was a bit incongruous with her prized Lola Faturoti antique silk dress.

"I'm so happy you both could come." Lydia's eyes danced between Noire's face and Innocent's profile that was turned toward an animated Marcus and another woman who looked to be his female incarnation. The woman stared Noire squarely in the face and addressed Innocent. "Is this your friend? Her hair is . . . cute. And I see she likes that, um, 'goth' look." She gave Noire an insincere smile and adjusted her own flawless James Moore creation.

"Desdemona, I'm sure Noire could tell you more about her sense of style than me, but I find it exciting." Innocent nodded apologetically at Noire and offered Desdemona a tight smile. Aggravated, Noire readied herself to respond but was cut off.

"It's been such a long time since I've seen Innocent." Lydia flashed unnaturally white teeth at the group, her gaze landing on Noire. "Please, Noire, come with me and I'll rest your jacket in the coatroom."

In the time it took for Noire to agree, Lydia had kissed Innocent's cheek and removed an invisible piece of lint from Marcus's back. He squeezed his wife's waist appreciatively. Noire received no introduction to Desdemona before Lydia turned to depart, cueing her to follow.

Ensconced in the crimson-colored coziness of a coatroom as large as her bedroom, Noire stood quietly and studied Lydia as she prepared to speak. She was a pleasing-looking woman; she seemed huggable and regal all at once. Deep dimples in both cheeks showed even when her face was at rest and her pupils twinkled like amber in her cherubic eyes.

"Desdemona is difficult." Lydia's words were delivered with low affect and no malice. "She's Marcus's sister."

Well, that explains a lot! Noire figured that a more dispassionate response would encourage more revelation. "I see."

"She wears her family's attainments like a mink stole around her neck, and likes to inspect those of others, hoping to find a skunk." Lydia sat upon a quilt-draped mahogany chest.

Noire found her words ironic. And why was she telling *her*? "I don't wear furs."

Lydia made her expression understanding.

Noire rolled back her shoulders.

"But she'll be impressed with your academic credentials. She doesn't have any of her own."

Noire smarted from the word "credentials" and the news that Desdemona lacked them. She sat down on a mirrored bench, her stomach swimming, as she read Lydia's knowledge of her in her assured posture. *It's gonna be a fucked-up night.* "I didn't come here to impress anyone."

"If I were on the road to a doctorate, I'd be pretty proud of myself." She smiled unreservedly. "I'm a social worker."

"Really?" Noire imagined her degree hanging in a gold-leaf frame on a velvet wall. "Do you practice?"

"I offer private counseling to children with emotional problems and learning disabilities."

"Wow." Noire smiled for the first time in an hour. "My younger brother has dyslexia."

"Really! I'm working with a dyslexic boy right now. He's a real charmer! Noire, we should go out and join the rest; they probably think we got lost." Lydia offered a comforting giggle. Noire had no time to ruminate on her pep talk. Their acquaintanceship sealed, the two made an unlikely alliance that would last the balance of the night.

Noire clung to the right corner of the Lincoln Continental that whisked her and Innocent away from Harlem.

"I'm sorry about all that, Noire."

"Mmm."

"I didn't think Desdemona . . . I mean—I've never seen her like that." He touched Noire's arm.

She turned to look at Innocent. "How can you be friends with people like that? Really."

"Marcus is not a bad guy, Noire. His sister has a negative effect on him." He shook his head. "She's insecure, Noire. You were an easy target."

"But it's not just her. It's all the goddamn pose, Innocent. When are folks going to get over themselves long enough to just be people, minus their expensive goodies and 'inside information'?"

"Are you including me in that?"

"You tell me." With her eyes, she asked him to say the right thing. Whatever that was.

"Noire, I like you. I do. I hope that's answer enough."

She searched his face, the passing streetlights spotting it with irregular light. "Thank you for saying that." She reached out and held his hand.

Noire had broken the three-date rule, Jayna informed her during their regular Saturday-morning conversation. "After three dates, I'm supposed to meet him."

"Girl, that's been dead since college."

"I'm reviving it. I want to meet him."

"I don't even know if I like him."

"You like him. Trust me."

The meet-'n'-greet happened thirteen hours later. The three stood in front of Dark Words Poetry Café in the East Village waiting for Jayna's latest Internet date, whom she had "met" on BlackPlanet.com. "Of all of the homeboys who responded to my ad," Jayna explained, "Dunbar really opened up. He's into sistas, thank God. He's a vegetarian." Jayna shook her head dramatically. She was giving Halle Berry tonight: all pixie hair and understated seduction.

Noire tapped her high-top leather Keds in a puddle of water. "Good for you, Jayna. You're expanding."

Jayna stuck out her tongue; Noire giggled. Innocent smiled, tottering on the brink between participant and observer. He compared Jayna's nou-veau glam to Noire's bohemia and wondered if they were as different as they appeared. Noire wore a red Les Nubians baby tee and a hip-hugging vintage jean skirt that brushed the tops of her sneakers. Her Afro-puffs stood on either side of her head behind a red, gold, and green crocheted scarf. Visualizing his own outfit—a body-conscious Charlie Allen ensemble of silk muscle shirt and gabardine stretch slacks—he imagined he looked more like Jayna's date than Noire's. He chuckled aloud.

"When a man chuckles, it's usually something scandalous!" Jayna snickered.

Noire held her cheeks in mock disapproval.

"Jayna?" A man with an inch-high Afro and holding two sticks of incense approached Noire and bowed in greeting. He floated in the perfume of frankincense and myrrh.

Noire liked him immediately. By the look on her face, Jayna did not. "No, this is Jayna." She pointed to her unsmiling friend.

"Peace, sista." He gave Jayna a hug.

Holding her body stiff, she managed to keep a distance between them big enough to wedge an unabridged dictionary. "Let's go in."

Noire looked at her in real disapproval this time. Innocent gave him a subdued black man's handshake.

They found a wobbly table with four mismatched chairs and sat. They ordered Red Stripe beer and cranberry juice for Dunbar.

"So what do you do?" Noire sipped her beer from the bottle and nodded in Dunbar's direction.

"Well, I work at a holistic wellness center, and I'm studying to be a nutritionist."

"I thought you owned a health food store." Jayna shot him a look.

"My uncle does. But I will inherit it from him when he crosses over." He smiled easily.

"Well, how old is he?" At that, Noire kicked Jayna sharply under the table. "I mean, does he require much help?" Jayna squinted at Noire.

"My father's brother did not always understand the necessity of living in harmony with nature and listening to his body rhythms." He sipped his cranberry juice. "He was among the unfortunate whose past intravenous drug use led to his HIV-positive status. But he has managed this challenge well by adopting a holistic lifestyle: he is a vegan and an herbalist. Uncle Africa is fifty-four years old."

Realizing that he had been silent, Innocent joined the conversation. "Thanks for sharing that. It must be difficult."

"The sun cannot rise and set without each of us making a contribution to the day."

Noire bobbed her head; Jayna sighed unappreciatively.

"Sisters, you are the embodiment of true African beauty. With my mouth I utter what my ancestral heart feels."

"Thank you, Dunbar. That's very kind." Noire smiled heartily for her and Jayna. "So . . . where do you live? Are you in the City?"

"Place is more a state of mind than an absolute reality. My soul sails across the African diaspora, living the lives my ancestors could not. I am free from the shackles of the oppressor, wherever my foot lands. I am an African . . . by way of the Bronx."

Jayna turned to Noire and rolled her eyes. Turning her face back to Dunbar, she proclaimed, "I don't call myself Panamanian just because my grandparents were born there seventy years ago!"

"There's no reason why you should not, Jayna." He looked at her compassionately.

Trying to break the tension with a new line of conversation, Innocent seized upon Dunbar's lyrical reflection. "So, where have you traveled in Africa? I'm from Côte d'Ivoire, myself."

"Countries are European constructions. Every land affected by the bondage of our people is Africa to me. Brother, do not limit yourself to a land parceled by those who sold our people into slavery and ripped our families apart."

"Dunbar, not arguing with you—understand that—but, we're all from *somewhere*. Embracing one thing doesn't discount another."

"If we embrace the Eurocentric definitions of our experiences, then we *are* discounting our truth."

"That's an interesting way of looking at it." Noire wrinkled her face and nodded.

Innocent bristled but made his face placid. "Saying I'm from Côte d'Ivoire has nothing to do with the white man, Dunbar, but everything to do with my family."

"You speak as you've been trained to." He shook his head.

"So where *have* you been, Mr. I-Am-Africa?" Jayna glared.

"Economic racism has crippled me, dear sister."

"So your trips to Africa have only included the five boroughs of New York City?" Jayna was incredulous and readily displayed it.

"Jayna, for godsakes! He's a conscious brotha—"

"He's a bullshittin' brotha, Noire. Why does it have to take a hundred sentences to answer a simple question?" She didn't even look at Dunbar.

"Sisters, please, let us not devolve into argument. This is what plagues our people now. I apologize if I've offended you. And brother"—he looked at Innocent—"I don't admonish you for adhering to Eurocentric models that require us to choose one identity over another. You, too, will grow. Self-definition is the first step to self-determination." Dunbar smiled at his silenced seatmates.

The lights in Dark Words Poetry Café dimmed further and the emcee announced that in addition to their regular Saturday-night open mic, they would have Mums and Jessica Care Moore as special guest artists. The crowd roared their appreciation. Dunbar lit another stick of incense and got up. Jayna raised her eyebrows, and Noire and Innocent looked at him in confusion. He walked over to the emcee—a thick man with a towering white head wrap—and embraced him heartily. They whispered for a moment before the emcee reapproached the mic.

"Family, Brother Dunbar is not on tonight's lineup, but we are happy that the spirit has moved him to speak." Whistles and snaps punctuated the air at the announcement. The emcee laughed. "That's right, give a hometown brotha some love." More sounds of appreciative anticipation filled the air. Dunbar handed his incense to the emcee and assumed a meditative position in front of the mic. The audience hushed. He looked up. "This is dedicated to Jayna, our beautiful Nubian Latina sister."

> To all the black girls named Juanita
> And the Latinas called Morena
> To all the girls who feel their Latin roots
> In their kinky roots

Who know that olive oil is yellow
Olive skin is tan
And olives can be red or green or brown or black
To the girls who tap out a 2-4 rhythm
Against a salsa beat
Whose gospel songs float up to Espíritu Santo
Whose plátanos taste best with their collard greens
To all the girls who know their diaspora
May not be politically correct
But it's still correct
To the girls who aren't "half" but "both"
To the girls who say "mira"
To all those who can roll their r's and those who can't
Who know that the people in Spanish Harlem aren't from Spain
And their own people come from Cuba, Alabama, Puerto Rico,
Brooklyn, Dominican Republic, Brazil, and Mississippi
To all those black girls named Juanita
And the Latinas called Morena
Who produce and reproduce a legacy
Who lay claim to a history
Who understand that the whole story is ours to tell.

Stomping accompanied the boisterous clapping of the audience. Dunbar crossed his arms over his chest and bowed, but kept his eyes cast on his night's companions. He returned to the table. Noire was the first to speak.

"That was a powerful poem." She looked at him apologetically.

"I offer my words to the world, sister. I am a vessel." He retrieved his well-worn jean jacket.

"Where are you going?" Jayna trained her embarrassed gaze over his shoulder.

"There is no reason for us to expend energy with people who don't affirm us. Peace and blessings, all."

Innocent stood up and offered him his hand. "Um, you take it easy, man."

"We are connected, you know."

"I know." Innocent looked down and locked his jaw.

Dunbar walked away and Innocent sat. His presence had vaguely unnerved him, and his abrupt departure further intensified his uneasiness. He knocked back his remaining half-bottle of beer and coughed. Then he squeezed Noire's thigh. Surprised, she flinched. "Sorry." He kissed her unprepared lips and found them hard against his. "Good guy," he offered, and bobbed his head on the end of his neck.

"Yeah." Feeling the tug from Innocent's odd energy on her left and Jayna's familiar postdate misery on her right, she felt out of sorts herself. She was more critical of Jayna's behavior than of Innocent's, but she didn't want to out her friend in front of him. So she remained silent.

"Please, don't say anything to me, Noire." Jayna rubbed her eyes.

"I think Dunbar said it all."

They sat quietly amid the din of an unofficial intermission.

"Noire!" Arikè squeaked her name and weaved her way through the overpopulated tables that crowded Dark Words's dull interior. A tall, grinning man followed behind her.

She kissed Noire on both cheeks. "When I heard Dunbar say 'Jayna' I remembered that you have a friend with that name, so I thought I'd look around. This is Dennis, my boyfriend."

They all traded hellos.

"You're good, Arikè. Well, this is Jayna . . . and this is Innocent." Repeated hellos.

She fixed her eyes on Innocent. "Well, Noire, now I see why the first date went so well!" She licked her lips, then giggled. Dennis kissed his girlfriend's cheek and Jayna rolled her eyes for the second time in ten minutes. "So, where's Dunbar? He was *great*!" Arikè looked at his empty chair.

"He had to leave." Jayna stared through Arikè.

"Hope no one scared him away!" She smiled sweetly and took a seat on the abandoned chair.

"Actually, *I* did. And I've gotten so good at it, that I think I'll make *myself* disappear. The four of you look cozy." She sprang out of her seat.

"Damn, Jayna!" Noire wrenched herself up as well. "We're going to the bathroom." She marched her to the women's rest room.

"OK, Jayna. Now you've truly flipped."

Silence.

"Dammit, Jay! What the fuck was all that drama?" She stared at her.

"Sometimes I'm not in the mood for being the odd woman out, OK?"

Noire sensed the haughtiness in her words and posture and was baffled. "*What?*"

"My date walked *out* on me, goddammit! Do I need to recount that for you?"

"Jayna, you *wanted* him to leave!"

"*No*, I wanted to *like* him, Noire. The way that you used to write to me about Cudjoe when you were in Ghana. The way that you like Innocent now. Noire, I want to *like* someone so that just *maybe* I can get beyond the first damn date!" Silent tears flowed out of her eyes, spoiling her careful makeup job. "I even bought this Anthony Liggins lookalike." She pulled at her blouse and whimpered quietly as Noire blotted her face.

"Hey, is everything OK?" Arikè stood by the door and looked on at the scene with visible horror.

Every trace of angst vanished from Jayna's face. She stared at Arikè with cold eyes. "Noire, can you please ask your friend to leave."

"Please, Arikè. It's been . . . a bad night." Noire's face was pained and pleading.

Arikè left silently.

"I'm going to go, Noire."

"I'll leave with you."

"Please don't. The last thing I need is one more incident to feel bad about. Go out there and enjoy your man and the rest of the poetry. And your *friends*. Innocent's a keeper." She smirked. Looking at herself in the mirror, she put on a fresh coat of lipstick and a pair of Maurice Malone sunglasses rescued from her tiny purse. "I'll leave you a message on your machine."

"OK." Noire watched Jayna perfect her game face and strut out of the rest room like the diva she so wanted to be. She was her oldest friend, and she loved her the way she imagined sisters would. But she didn't always like the woman she was forcing herself to become.

Noire returned to the laughing trio, making it a mellow quartet. The last words of Dunbar's poem echoed in her ears: . . . *the whole story is ours to tell.*

"Pokou here."

"I'm actually sorry that you are."

Noire's voice drizzled over Innocent's ears like warm maple syrup. "Yeah. The walls are closing in on me." He breathed audibly into the phone, his eyes pausing from their attention on his computer screen. His watch lay on the desk: 12:26 A.M. He massaged his pupils through his eyelids.

"What are you working on?"

"The usual stuff." His words were written in chalk, his nerves a fit of oversensitivity.

"Well, when do you think you can leave?"

"Four."

"Have you eaten?"

"*Yes.*" He grew impatient.

"I wish I could do something for you." Noire lay prone on her bed, the sheet wound around her naked form.

"To quote the Rolling Stones, 'You can't always get what you want.'"

"I'll think creatively . . ."

Innocent wallowed in work-induced delirium. "OK, Noire. Good night." Hanging up the phone, he gave a momentary glance to the remains of the day that had begun at seven-thirty in the morning and now lay in the corners of his office: a crumpled *Wall Street Journal*, printouts of stock quotes for his key clients, scribbled notes from meetings and conference calls, marked-up financial reports run by analysts nearly as overworked as he was.

It almost seemed fruitless to question whether it was worth it. After all, this was the life he had created for himself, the life he was trained for. In business school, he and his classmates vied for coveted positions like his that placed them at top financial services companies and promised the high intensity, high profile, and high compensation that fueled them through their all-nighters and arduous group projects. And he was one of the lucky ones: he had fast-tracked it to a vice presidency, and last year's tremendous bonus—which tripled his usual six-figure paycheck—put him at a neat half million. Innocent knew he didn't deserve anyone's sympathy and that he was sure not to get it. It was impossible to convince anyone that for every dollar he made, he earned the company many times that and that the opportunity cost of time spent away from the people, places, and things that he most cared about made him wonder if his success came at too high a price.

Innocent took a swig of his fourth Dr Pepper in three hours. He noticed a new e-mail.

> SUBJECT: A quick pick-me-up! ;-)
> DATE: April 7, 1999, 1:42 A.M.
> TO: lpokou@wright_richards.com
> FROM: Noire@nyu.edu
>
> My tongue is at your service.
> Let my tongue tickle your ears and explore the warm wetness of your mouth. Let me lick your nipples and feel them grow hard against the tip of my tongue. Let me travel south to your belly button, stopping for a fun-filled rest stop on my way downtown. Let me nibble you right where the tops of your thighs meet your groin, my nose nuzzling your hair, my breath hot against your skin. Let me ride my tongue lightly along the underside and then seal it with a kiss right at the head. Let me let you feel my whole face against you, my breath blowing through you. Let me draw all of you into my warm and wet mouth, slowly letting you fill me, and feel you pulsate with pleasure. Let my tongue tease him and taste him and tug at him ever so gently. You dangle at the precipice—ecstatic, frustrated, your muscles tense . . .

Innocent stared at the computer screen in disbelief. His throat was coated in sawdust and bile. A frustrated knot gathered in his pants. He fought to compose himself before calling Noire. Hearing her voice on the phone broke his cool. "Why did you send that message to my work account?!"

"*What?*" Noire's voice was hot with confusion and hurt.

"For godsakes, Noire! Our e-mail is screened—you know that!"

Noire hadn't even considered that; she had been caught up by her altruistic foray into cybersex. Unsure of how to respond, she remained quiet.

"Noire!"

"I know my name, Innocent!" She had no energy to back her defensiveness, so her next words dribbled out of her mouth. "I'm sorry. I didn't think about it. I'm sorry."

Innocent's anger melted into a sloppy mess on the surface of his mind. "Yeah. I just hope the guys in IT just jerk off and then forget about it." He sighed heavily. "Folks here play hardball and every day is a good day for a firing." Listening to his own words broke his spirit.

Noire heard the line drop. "I can't do this," she muttered into dead air. Perhaps she hadn't shown good judgment, but that was besides the point. Every twenty-four hours presented her with something new to deal with, or be sorry about, or get over. Innocent was a man whose motivations were his year-end bonus, brand-name friends, and pristine reputation. Status-conscious. Rigid. Calculating. Pensive. Noire tried to think of his character flaws. But he was far from terrible; she knew it. In fact, she *liked* him. She enjoyed his commanding gaze, his beauty, his confidence, his urbane intellect. But, what difference did any of that make if she didn't "get" him. Or couldn't. What if she just *couldn't*?

Pushing her phone off the bed, Noire cried soundless, shapeless tears until she fell asleep.

Dawn rested silently in Innocent's loft as he fumbled to pull his keys out of the door. His four-feet-wide clock, recovered from an old French mercantile exchange, commanded the far wall and announced his time of return as 5:29. The streets were quiet, save the occasional sanitation truck that rumbled along its early-morning route. Innocent viewed the amber glow of his apartment through a sleepy haze. The air was tinged with the freshness of springtime and the smells of old city streets. He opened his window, letting the chill circulate in the space.

He undressed in front of the window, allowing the crispness of the new day to arouse the nerve endings at the surface of his skin. It was Wednesday but in Innocent's mind, it was a day wedged into the workweek as a gift from God. He would stay at home today. Tuesday had stretched on until five-fifteen this morning, so he felt justified. He turned off the ringer of his phone and reduced the volume on his answering machine. Then he returned to the window, his bare chest pressed against the windowpane, the cool April air invigorating him. His mind was too agitated to allow him to rest his body, though he suspected his body would eventually win. But until then, he figured he would stand. Stand to greet the day that had been given him.

Noire hovered at the periphery of his thoughts; he brought her into sharper focus. The recollection of her e-mail made him flinch with momentary excitement until he remembered the tears in her voice. He hadn't meant to be harsh. But his fear of possible repercussions formed the words he spoke. Now that the day was his, he no longer had any fear and instead felt confused. He wasn't sure what he wanted personally or professionally, or whether Noire added to his uncertainty.

He walked over to his refrigerator that claimed a slice of the back wall of his long cavernous space. Together with a sink, cook range, and two cabinets sitting on a rectangle of gray slate tiles, it composed his industrial kitchen. He hesitated, testing his memory of what might be in there. Weeks went by in which he didn't even open the refrigerator door. Pulling it open, he found several half-full bags of gourmet coffee closed with paper clips. He had an onion and some moldy cheese but no eggs, so he killed his taste for an omelet and settled for coffee. Noire. She was like a favorite food to which he was allergic: too good to avoid, but with side effects.

His mouth watered, his thoughts fondling the image of Noire on the day they met. Just *looking* at her had awakened every carnal desire that had ever lived in him. He swallowed. But what did she want, and did he want it too? It scared him.

Innocent sat in one of his stainless steel high-backed stools and placed his elbows on the table flap that popped out of the wall in front of him. The cool metal chilled his flesh; he forced himself to remain still until he had sufficiently warmed it up. He drank his coffee black and without sugar, but measured out every teaspoonful before depositing it in his mouth until he no longer could. Then he turned the mug up to his lips and drained it of the balance, tasting the aftertaste, tasting Noire. He listened to the city wake up around him—the walls projecting the sounds of his neighbors' early-morning rituals into his own space. He coveted his stillness in the midst of their hurry.

It felt good to exit life. Nothing required his control or urgent attention. He strode over to his bed and sat cross-legged, looking at his flaccid penis hang against his leg like a curiously unnecessary appendage. He lifted it, holding it gingerly in his left hand, and examining its contours by new sunlight. He hadn't looked at his penis that hard since he was circumcised during his adolescent initiation ritual. Late to the experience of wet dreams and spontaneous erections, he remembered wondering why his penis was a symbol of manhood and why everyone seemed to have such a vested interest in what happened to this part of his anatomy.

Innocent smoothed his hands along the lines of his thighs, enjoying the hardness of his muscles as he flexed them for his own entertainment. His skin was the color of oxidized iron and had a patina of well-worn tools. *Can she ever be more of what I need her to be and less of what she is?* Maybe he didn't know what he needed. He lay down and stretched his body diagonally across the breadth of his bed. As sleep lay claim to his body, his mind continued its free fall through unexplored ideas, meandering in the detours without asking directions.

Chapter 8

Body Temperature

Noire made tax day a spiritual holiday; her bikini wax was her sacred ritual. Her Thursday-morning class a distant memory, she lay in The Home Spa exposed and unashamed, her glassy eyes blinking back tears of clarity. Barely a month shy of the completion of her first year of graduate school, she decided that she did, in fact, need Professor Fuentes as her ally. Sure, second semester was shaping up to be better than the first—last December's debilitating flu had forced her to get extensions on all of her term papers—but she knew that, without having someone in her corner, she would have an undistinguished grad school career in which she'd be putting in the same long hours with no accolades or special favors to show for it. She would christen their relationship by attending the American Comparative Literature Convention with Professor Fuentes as she had suggested.

Her mind drifting to Innocent, she decided to add a seaweed detox wrap to her ritual and prayed her credit card wouldn't burst into flame when it came time to pay for her holistic indulgence. Her naked body slathered in slippery green paste and marinating under tightly wrapped plastic thermal blankets, she imagined herself back in the womb. Soft orange light, the tang of essential oils in the warm air, and the eastern tones of Gigi playing in the background coaxed out every mixed emotion that was trapped under her skin. She sank into intense contemplation.

Innocent. They had had five dates in five weeks, dozens of phone conversations, and more e-mail exchanges than she could count. In that time, she had brought him into her world, talking about all of the important stuff: her parents, Jabari, Jayna, Professor Fuentes, school, even some of her money challenges. While she knew about Innocent's brother's death and a bit about his relationship with hateful Marcus, she hardly knew how he *felt* about anything outside of his designer tastes and his esteemed family name. Maybe her expectations were unreasonable so early in the game. But she felt unbalanced, and, she realized, uncomfortable.

Unwrapped from her cocoon, Noire stood in the shower and rinsed away her indecision. With her urban bravadista stance kicking into self-preservation mode, she decided that the last thing she needed was to get hurt, so she'd cut her losses with Innocent before he cut her.

Noire returned home just in time to accept a delivery of a bonsai tree. She read the note: *"It's been a long eight days, Noire . . . I want to see you. My treat, your plan. Say yes.—Innocent"* Her pounding heart drowning the voice in her head, she mouthed "yes" and walked upstairs.

Innocent shifted his weight from one leg to the other and waited for Noire to reemerge from the women's rest room. He counted the number of black men standing in the lobby of the Westside Theater after having seen *The Vagina Monologues*. Eight. There were at least two hundred women—most of them white—and maybe twenty white men. Of the black men, two were with black women, two were a couple, and the other four held the hands of white or Asian women. A group of twelve black women stood together. He wondered why the numbers were so skewed. Everything he knew about black women's experiences of their sexuality suggested that they should have outnumbered everyone else.

"So, what'd you think?" Noire returned and studied his poker face.

"Provocative."

"Good." His one-word answer felt loaded. She waited for more.

He walked toward the front door and held it open for Noire. "Did it make you uncomfortable, Noire?"

Walking hand-in-hand with Innocent along West 43rd Street, her heart remembered the flashes of physical insecurity that she felt when she walked down a dark street alone in an outfit that glorified her womanly attributes. Or the nervousness she experienced when another woman seemed to capture the imagination of a man she liked. She thought of all those pep talks her father gave her every night of seventh grade when she stopped being a good math student so that she would fit in, and the discouragement by her college adviser from applying to highly ranked colleges. She felt the unwanted hands that had grabbed at her in candy stores and on street corners, and the grown men who cat-called her once her breasts began to bud at twelve. The boys who cornered her in her middle school stairwell and grabbed her crotch, the ninth-grade biology teacher who explained the large genitals and voracious sex drive of black women, the college boyfriend who pushed her against a wall, the married college professor who offered to make her dinner at his "private" studio apartment. "Yeah, some of it. Especially as a black woman . . . it just hits close to home, you know."

"But so few black women were there?"

"I think that sometimes we don't have the luxury of looking at what it means to be a woman. Sometimes we feel we have to choose which struggle we most identify with: being black or being a woman. And sometimes it just hurts."

Innocent kissed her palm. "I had never thought so much about . . . vaginas."

Lightening the mood, "I bet you've thought quite a lot about them in your time." She flashed a devilish smile.

"I mean, what it means to have one. What the experience is like."

She turned to look at him. "Innocent, I'm happy you saw it with me. Thank you."

"Whatever it takes, Noire."

She looked at him and nodded her head. He was trying. He was really trying.

Innocent placed the 24-karat gold earrings into Noire's ears.

"You look beautiful, Mademoiselle. I am much obliged to have your company at such short notice." He brought her hand to his lips.

"And it is my distinct pleasure to have such a debonair man on my arm." She offered her most seductive smile in return.

They stood in Innocent's loft at seven P.M. on a Monday night. He pushed octagonal cufflinks through his double cuffs that set off his midnight blue Ozwald Boateng suit. Noire adjusted the sensuous Lawrence Steele dress that Innocent had delivered to his building for her only an hour before. Her overflowing bookbag lay abandoned on his bed. She strapped on her new Tony Valentine shoes.

"These are pretty, Innocent. Everything is . . . beautiful." She blushed and wiggled her toes in the delicate strips of leather that wound around her feet. "How did you know what to get?"

"I told Fadia, my shopper, that you were tall and stunning and she did the rest."

His shopper? Noire was sure her thoughts were etched into her forehead. She looked away. "But I don't have a bag, or even any makeup." She smiled sheepishly.

"Fadia thought of that too." He handed her a tiny purse that held lipstick, eyeliner, and blush. "I hope this is good enough."

"Innocent, I don't know what to say."

"I just want you to have a nice time, Noire. Dr. Rousseau is my dad's old friend from secondary school. Before independence."

She nodded.

"He's a bit of a character. He shuttles between here, home, and France. And apparently, wherever he happens to be, he throws a big black-tie affair in honor of the Bouaké carnival that occurs back home every March. He's a bit late this year. Bouaké is where he grew up when he wasn't at boarding school or backpacking across Africa. I think he just uses it as a good excuse to have a party." He snickered.

"Lucky us."

"Papa only called me at noon to tell me about it. Apparently, he wants to do some business with Dr. Rousseau and thought my presence tonight would warm him up to the idea."

"Oh."

"It was hell getting out of work early." Innocent bent down to give one more buff to his well-buffed shoes.

"I'm sure." Noire looked at herself in the mirror. She put on her makeup and stood in amazement. Innocent had dressed her from head to toe by describing her on the phone and had done an exceptional job of it. She would never have chosen this dress for herself, probably because she never would have seen it where she usually shops. It arrived without a price tag and she decided that it was best to remain ignorant. "Where's this jewelry from?" She turned around to face him.

He hesitated before responding, harmless arousal rumbling through his body. Noire was striking. Each feature was an invitation that he wanted to accept: her eyes the shape and color of toasted almonds, her lips a bow across her face, her regal collarbones a prelude to breasts that were well-placed teardrops he was sure he had cried himself . . . He cleared his throat. "The earrings are from Dr. Rousseau's hometown. It's a major center for the lost wax-casting method of goldsmithing. They make very intricate pieces."

"They're lovely."

"They're lovely on you."

Dr. Rousseau kissed Innocent on both cheeks and greeted him in warm-hearted French. Noire stared. He was white, a sunburned redhead of about sixty-five whose wiry frame was bundled in a sumptuous tradi-tional outfit. Madame Rousseau was a velvety black woman about ten years his junior. She was round but solid, and she wore the same fabric as her husband. She hugged Noire in greeting before Dr. Rousseau spoke to her with exaggerated diction. "Enchanting Mademoiselle, did you think I'd be black?" A guffaw leapt out of his skinny body. "Well, I try, but see what happens to me?" He pointed to his burnt skin. "Between the red hair and red skin, 'Rousseau' seemed like the most appropriate last name to choose!" He laughed again and squeezed his wife.

Noire stood in silence, a polite smile masking her dismay.

He glanced at Innocent knowingly before disclosing the mystery. "Once my family learned Madame was pregnant with our oldest"—he patted her permanently plump stomach—"my family gave me my inheritance and disowned me. So I disowned them right back and changed my last name."

"That's something." Noire nodded.

"But I've never looked back. Noire, you are scandalously beautiful. You must wear poor Innocent out!" He clapped Innocent on the back.

Noire slid her eyes over to Innocent. He seemed nonplussed.

"Well, come in. We've gotten such a nice turnout, despite the short notice."

A servant took their coats, and Innocent and Noire followed Dr. Rousseau into the main parlor of an expansive penthouse in a tony Upper East Side building. Several celebrities known to be interested in Africa were there along with a smattering of French models, Pan-African socialites, and every notable West African investor and government luminary who happened to be in New York City on the last Monday in April. Noire estimated a hundred people.

Their outfits were a montage of designers and styles that borrowed freely from African and European aesthetic sensibilities. A riot of colors, fragrances, and expensive tobacco rushed at Noire from every corner of the room. She noted Innocent's ease. Assuming the festive air, he mingled freely, chatting in French, English, and snatches of Baoule, Arabic, and Wolof. Listening to him chart histories and share recollections with their party-mates—mutual personal and professional acquaintances, recognition that he was the son of Jean and Marie Pokou or the boarding school chum of their children twenty years removed—Noire figured that Innocent had less than three degrees of separation with all present.

He took care to always introduce Noire, and he was patient with her rusty French, offering her the words that she struggled to find and fondling her bare back when she seemed frustrated. But she felt hopelessly uninitiated. And she didn't want to rely on Innocent to make her fun. So when a portly, square-jawed man in fine Malian cloth and carrying a carved staff deigned to speak to her, she was grateful.

"Happy you could join us. What brings you here?"

"My friend, Innocent Pokou." She pointed; he was now a distance away.

"Yes, I know his father. Business." He nodded sharply and Noire followed suit. "And you?"

Noire wasn't sure what he was asking, but she answered with, "I'm a graduate student."

"Where?"

"At NYU."

"Good. Do you know Manthia?"

Noire placed him into the category of demigod-scholar who she wanted to know, but didn't . . . yet. "Not well."

"I see."

Noire watched his feeble interest in her fade. He shifted his staff to his other hand and then waved at someone who hadn't waved at him. He walked off. She shrugged and grabbed a fuzzy navel off of a passing server's tray of drinks.

"I love your dress."

Noire turned around to see a six-feet-tall bald woman with polished skin and features drawn by God. Her French was unhurried and her smile broad. She had to be a supermodel. "Thank you."

"Lawrence Steele, right? I adore him. Maybe one day I'll get to do one of his shows." She wagged her head wistfully.

Noire basked in her compelling beauty. "I'm sure you will. What's your name?"

"Aminata. I'm from Senegal."

"Pleasure to meet you. Noire." She gave her an unrehearsed grin.

"Are you a model too?"

Noire laughed disbelievingly.

"Well, you are beautiful."

"Coming from you, that's an incredible compliment." She blushed.

"Believe me, I seldom say it to the other models I meet. Too many are ugly on the inside. Scared. Sad. You can't imagine the awful things some of them do to stay beautiful. It's all quite strange." She looked off.

Noire gazed at her, the corners of her mouth turned into a contemplative frown. "I'm sure."

"Well, Noire, I must leave. I have an early shoot tomorrow." She looked bashful.

"Good luck with it. Thanks for saying hi."

Aminata waved and departed.

Once again alone, and seeing that Innocent was in robust conversation with an ancient woman who reached up to pat his forehead every time he smiled, she wandered over to a middle-aged pencil-shaped woman. Her slim black dress jutted off of her shoulders without contacting any other part of her body all the way down to her ankles. She pulled violently on a fragile brown-papered cigarette and blew smoke through her nose. Noire imagined Fen-phen or laxatives, or perhaps even anorexia.

"*Bon soir, c'est* Noire." She extended her hand.

"Who are you, Noire?" She answered in labored English.

Noire didn't know how to respond to the question, so she wrinkled her face and made herself believe that the woman's meaning would soon be clear. Her hand hung in the air. She put it down.

"Dear, you must have a last name." She seemed annoyed in the way that people looked at parents who let their children misbehave on the subway: embarrassed for her and scolding at the same time.

"It's Demain."

"You're French?" Her tone suggested that she doubted it and would prove the lie if Noire tried to convince her otherwise. "I don't know that name!"

And you know everyone's name? "You haven't told me yours."

"Solange de Savoie. I'm French. From Martinique. I am descended from *la famille* Savoie in the Rhône region of France. My forefathers were winemakers. I'm *sure* you've heard of us."

Which "us" would that be, slaves or slave masters? "No, I haven't. So I suppose we're even." Noire gave her a steely grin and left.

Innocent saw Noire's determined stride across the room and extricated himself from his conversation. The party had become a kind of reunion for him, and he marveled at his own enjoyment of it. He walked toward Noire but was intercepted by Dr. Rousseau, who had a fresh vodka tonic in his hand. "Innocent, I tell you, I love your father. He was like an older brother to me—looking out for me, making sure I didn't get picked on by our other schoolmates who loved to beat the shit out of skinny little white boys like me." He kissed Innocent. Noire met them where they stood. "And tell him that your lovely lady friend has so charmed me that I would be happy to do anything I can for the Pokou family. Anything. Have him e-mail me and we'll arrange a time to talk."

Innocent gave Noire a peck on the cheek.

"You've chosen well, Noire!" Dr. Rousseau's declaration shook his body. He reached out and touched her back. She shrunk from his hand. "Oh, don't worry, love. I'm too old to make a woman like you happy. But you and I have the same idea. Africans are the best lovers. My dear Madame bore me seven children and still wears me out four nights a week." He shook his drink in the direction of his wife and gulped it down. "I can barely walk right now!"

Noire choked on her fuzzy navel. "Dr. Rousseau—"

"Darling, I became an African before you were born. Believe me, sex is hardly personal, especially not for a woman. Everyone knows if you please your lover, when you are pregnant, and how many men you've slept with. An African man cannot be fooled!"

Innocent winced and shrugged at Noire's scowl. But Dr. Rousseau's bloodshot eyes and swaying body told him that he was a mildly offensive drunk who was of more harm to himself than anyone around him. He tried to remember the last time he had seen Dr. Rousseau. Perhaps it was fifteen years ago. He remembered him as loud but good-natured. And with a perpetually full drink clutched to his chest. The distant memory turning over in his mind, he barely noticed Dr. Rousseau's body sinking slowly to the floor.

"Innocent!" Noire grabbed for Dr. Rousseau's arm. Innocent pulled him back to his feet and propped him onto his shoulder, where he sputtered bile-tinged alcohol and undigested food onto Innocent's jacket.

Madame Rousseau rushed over just in time to stand with Noire and watch Innocent drag Dr. Rousseau toward the bathroom. She sucked her teeth and inclined her head toward Noire. "My mother—God rest her soul—said, 'Adja, he is a fool, and a white fool at that!' But I have stopped seeing color long ago. After thirty-eight years of marriage, he is just *my* fool. My husband's problem is that, with all that he has, he has never felt comfortable being himself. But that's the man I love, blemishes and all." She clucked her tongue loudly. "Loving a man is impos-

sible if you insist on seeing his faults." Her expression was a mix of sad-
ness and contentment.

Innocent retrieved Noire's wrap, the front of his suit damp from the
hasty cleanup he had done in the rest room after holding Dr. Rousseau's
head over the toilet for a half hour. "I told you he was a character." He
hugged her. "I'm happy you came, Noire." With someone else, he might
have been embarrassed, but her kind eyes reassured him that she was
not put off.

"Me too," she whispered, and placed a featherweight kiss onto his
lips. He embraced her again, and she felt the desire that ran between
Innocent's body and hers. Innocent was a beautiful, confident, success-
ful, and compassionate black man who *liked* her. She couldn't imagine
anything else she wanted.

Professor Fuentes tailgated a speeding Greyhound bus and chatted
about the book she was trying to complete on Caribbean and Latin
American Spanish-language women writers. She and Noire were headed
to the three-day comp lit convention in Montreal. Her head was in a halo
of smoke, her mouth manipulating her cigarette; Noire tried to siphon
fresh air from the passenger window. "I refuse to do my writing at home
so I just end up staying in my office until all hours of the night."

"Where do you live?"

"The Bronx. Around the Bronx Zoo."

"Do you have children?" Noire figured that would be the reason she
would live there. She looked at the silver strands glistening in her black
hair and estimated her age to be about forty.

"I have a twenty-five-year-old son. Eduardo. He's back in D.R. with
his father. At this point I hardly know him. He has a child now, a girl.
I've never met her. She's three."

Noire could think of no good response.

"I got pregnant when I was seventeen. Eduardo's father was
thirty-five at the time. I was living with my grandmother. She made
me have the baby and give him to Rodolfo, his father. Then she sent me

to live with my parents here in New York. They lived in Washington Heights."

Noire had learned more than she expected. "My friend Jayna lives there. She's at Columbia's dental school. Where are your parents now?"

"They died about . . . sixteen years ago. I was around your age." She turned to look at Noire. "How old are you?"

"Twenty-eight."

"I was twenty-seven. They were killed in a car accident in the Dominican Republic. They had gone back for my grandmother's funeral."

Noire was flabbergasted by the tragedy and the flippant way in which she chose to tell it.

"Professor Fuentes, I'm so sorry."

"Bonita, please. I'm sorry too. Sorry that I never had a chance to say good-bye to my parents or my grandmother. I didn't go to her funeral because I hated her for sending me away after I had Eduardo. But none of that anger really made any sense after all. I just lost everybody."

Noire sighed.

"Sorry to burden you with all of that." Wrapping her left arm around the steering wheel, with her right she touched a new cigarette to the burning nub clenched between her teeth and adjusted it in her mouth. She pressed the nub into an overflowing ashtray. "So, do you have any children?"

"Oh no!" Noire laughed at the thought. "I'm just trying to date a guy."

"Mmm. What does he do?"

"He's an investment banker."

"Quaint. Where'd you meet him?"

"At a book signing."

"He reads?" Bonita sounded incredulous.

"The book was written by a friend of his. About black people and finance."

"Mmm. Well, that makes more sense."

Noire furrowed her brow and looked at Bonita, who squinted knowingly back at her. Noire turned away and bent her head toward the open window to take a deep breath.

"Just make sure you stay focused. Men like *that* have a way of taking us off our path. You're in this for the long haul."

Noire pursed her lips. *Men like what?* Bonita's words made her nervous. She hoped she wasn't so easily put off. She did not want to lose Bonita's good opinion of her even before it was established. Her right leg cramped from pressing it into the car's floor. She memorized the Greyhound's license plate number. They were only two hours into their seven-hour drive. Needing a break, she announced her desire to get some rest and turned her face away from her.

Bonita threw her cigarette out the window and turned up Celia Cruz's potent Afro-Cuban salsa on the radio. "I'll wake you up in about an hour. I'll be ready for you to take over driving by then."

Noire levitated as Bonita kissed the cheeks of colleagues and introduced her as the discipline's future star. She beamed, used one of Bonita's cigarettes as a prop, and chatted with a panoply of scholars in English, Spanish, French, and her rudimentary Papiamentu. She digested their brilliance, as they give birth to ideas that would one day become books, and realized that she was one of them. *She* would set the standard on scholarship in her field of interest and students would surround her in a semicircle, quoting her words back to her over wine and cheese.

Marveling that their bizarre car ride had become an induction into her chosen vocation, day after day Noire relayed animated stories about her conference adventures to Bonita, who would smile and nod, her eyes brimming with pride. And night after night—after intoxicating receptions, two-hour dinners with colleagues, and flirtation-filled nightcaps—she would look at Bonita with a powerful love that inadequately expressed her gratefulness for helping her to see her own possibilities.

"Read this!" Bonita plopped on Noire's double bed clutching sheets of hotel stationery. Shaken from her deepest predawn sleep, Noire breathed in the full strength of Bonita's cigarette and began to hack.

Dropping the papers in front of Noire, she retrieved her battery-powered smokeless ashtray and stood over her like an apparition.

Noire rubbed her eyes and conjured word pictures of her evaporating dream in Bonita's curly script. Bonita scooped up the papers back off the bed and proclaimed, "I'm finished!"

In response, Noire produced a hazy smile full of devotion but lacking in understanding.

"I've been struggling with the book's last chapter for months! Guess it was your good energy!" She took her last drag of her cigarette, stubbed it out, and kissed Noire on the forehead.

"Thank you, Bonita."

"We're good for each other." She patted Noire's cheek.

"I think you're right." Her voice was quiet and serious. She hugged Bonita. Then she fell back asleep.

"Pokou here."

"I'm back!" she squealed into the phone. She rolled her luggage into the bedroom and kicked off her boots.

"Happy you've returned safely." Innocent gulped his Dr Pepper and turned his chair to face the narrow rectangle of setting sun in his office window.

Noire retrieved her orange juice carton from the refrigerator and plopped on her couch. "It was *great*! Just *great*!"

"Good." He started to play a video game on his cell phone.

"Don't you want to hear about it?"

"I'm busy right now. But I should be finished by ten. Can I come over?" It was Sunday evening and he hadn't seen her in six days. He hoped she'd say yes and that she'd be generous.

"I'll be asleep."

"Can't I wake you?" He lost the first game and started another.

"Why don't you just stick your dick in a roll of spreadsheets and pump away!"

He turned off the game. "*That* was unnecessary."

"Turn down the volume on your goddamn video game next time, Innocent."

Innocent felt like leeches were robbing him of blood. He buckled. "I'm sorry."

"And I'm hurt." She hung up.

Innocent watched the black Bentley pull up to his curb. He opened the car door and helped Noire out.

"Fuck you, Innocent," she whispered. Her curiosity and insecurity were in a tense battle with her pride.

"Yes."

He called the elevator and they rode in silence.

Noire stepped into his apartment first and was met with the scents of lavender and sandalwood. Stubby candles lined all eight windowsills, their pale light flickering in the glass. Innocent pulled her sweatshirt over her head and removed her socks, sweatpants, and panties. He escorted her to the bed covered with yellow rose petals. She lay down and he massaged her body with luxuriant Urban Botanica oils. His hands slick, he glided over her every contour. He kneaded tension out of her muscles and controlled his want for her until she wanted him more. He watched her eyes, tried to dissipate their hurt. She was so beautiful, so dangerous. He shuddered.

She still held him within her. Internally, she fondled his loving thickness, drawing out all of the passion that was inside, though their climaxes had already played their duet. Perspiration gathered between her breasts and his, adhering him to her, creating a new scent and new feeling. Noire felt transformed.

"Oh, Innocent," she purred, embracing all of the meanings of his name as she traced the moist grooves of his back. She wanted to look into his eyes to complete their circle of emotion, but his eyelids lay quietly at full stretch. She listened to the deep regularity of his breathing and knew he was sleeping, restoring himself for her. Gingerly letting him exit her, she removed the condom in one clean motion and she stroked his back again, this time with the anticipation of another session of lovemaking.

Hearing his breathing become shallower, Noire rolled her body from Innocent's side. Replacing the condom on his still dozing form, Noire mounted Innocent, allowing for deep penetration immediately. Her groan was guttural as she took in all his size. Her body french-kissed his. In response, Innocent pulsed within Noire. Looking at her, he felt her urgency, experienced her nakedness viscerally. Stroking the roundness of her behind, he enjoyed the rippling of her muscles under his hands. Fitful concentration was etched on her face; Innocent sought to explore every crevice of Noire from the inside out. Tasting her salty-sweet nipples that danced before him, Innocent was a shaken bottle whose pressurized contents demanded release. He exploded into his lovely Noire.

Noire clawed at the fourth dimension, her groin clenching involuntarily, her toes splayed against the sky, her body snapping like a whiplash upon her lover. Bellowing the incarnation of her feelings as a love song for Innocent, Noire grabbed hold of his shoulders and pulled herself down to him. She felt like a waterfall upon him. She rushed and rushed and rushed, without end. Tears of ecstasy sprang out of her eyes as she moaned and cried, her physical and emotional beings a dance about her head and within her soul. Noire didn't want to know where she was and didn't want to be anywhere else.

Innocent stroked Noire's quivering body, overcome by her sheer beauty and unmitigated sensuality. He clutched the small of her now arched back and drew her hips into his own. But Noire's thoughts were elsewhere, everywhere. She saw her being bounce off the walls and splinter into a million points of light with every spasm in her groin. She was love and passion. Her all-encompassing emotion rewrote the story of the Middle Passage. She set all of the captives free with her groans and her shrieks, her moans and her cries.

Innocent held Noire's hand in the predawn. Studying the berry brownness of her skin, he wondered how he came to know a woman like Noire. Their meeting had become a metaphor for their relationship—strictly accidental. He reflected on the fearful delight of getting to know her, the quirky way her mind connected disparate thoughts, the power of her presence, the flames that leapt in her eyes. How was it that they became acquainted with each other?

Noire stirred from her sleep, interrupting Innocent's thoughts.

"Wow," she whispered, as if responding to the fleeting remnants of her dream. Propping herself up on her left elbow, Noire turned to face Innocent. "A penny for your thoughts."

"Oh, I don't know . . . I was just thinking about how beautiful your ass is!" he answered with a playful pinch of her behind.

"I thought you'd say something romantic like 'Noire I could fuck you all night.'" Her unarticulated feelings rioted inside her heart. She flushed hot before shivering.

Giving a nibble to her taut, dark nipple, Innocent murmured, "I could."

Noire sighed. Closing her eyes, she imagined herself as a fly on the wall of his brain, watching thoughts parade by, brazen and uncensored. "I want to know you. Innocent, let me know you." She thought she had said it aloud, but she wasn't sure.

Innocent hugged all of her into him as close as he could, his erection beating the rhythm of his heart. His body was a quiet storm of emotion that he suppressed by dint of will. Noire felt assured of his lust but not his affection; she turned away from him and prayed for dreamless sleep.

Noire watched Innocent's eyelids flutter against the new morning sun from her perch on his desk chair. A heavy banker's chair with cracked black leather on the seat and armrests, it was made for work and serious contemplation. It scratched the underside of her thighs as she shifted about. It squeaked and she saw Innocent's body flinch from across the room. "Talk." Her voice was a travel-weary command, her face creased with miles of thoughts, ideas, and fears. She prodded him over the precipice into wakefulness.

"What?" He peered at her in confusion.

"Talk. Tell me something. Anything."

"Noire, what's this about?" He sat up, his unclad body erect in the bed, his torso and legs forming two sides of a right angle.

"I want to know about you. Tell me a secret. Tell me something that scares you . . . that embarrasses you, confuses you. Share something with me."

"What do you think has been happening, Noire?"

"We've been getting to know me. I want to know you. And not the prepackaged version either." Noire's posture was rigid but her look was a flurry of activity. Her hair was a volcano recently erupted on her head and the points of her breasts asserted themselves against Innocent's gym shirt. She wore her cat-eye glasses slightly askew on her face and squinted concentration at Innocent from her seat eighteen feet away.

Innocent rubbed his eyes and pulled himself to the end of the bed. Recognizing his nakedness, he pulled the bedsheet loose and draped it across his lap. His feet—rough and slightly unkempt—peeked out from the black-and-white-striped sheet, making him look like he was dressed for work on the chain gang.

He looked at Noire and was convinced she could see the overturned hamper of thoughts carelessly strewn about his mind without rhyme or reason. "Noire—" He thought about seeking a reprieve from answering but surmised he wouldn't get it. She sat in silence.

"Noire, you scare me. *This* scares me. *We* scare me." Their eyes were wide, each of them shocked by what he had just said. Innocent glanced at the hurt in Noire's face.

"I mean, I care about you and I've been enjoying getting to know you and have fun with you these past couple months. But I have no idea where this is going."

"So I'm a diversion?"

"That's not what I mean." Innocent placed his hands as a triangle upon his lips and rested his elbows on his thighs. He had the appearance of a man in prayerful repose.

"Noire, you're not OK with who I am. I'm a type to you: arrogant, a beneficiary of colonialism and paternalism while my people suffered." Innocent frowned. He looked at Noire for a long time.

Emotion streaked her face but her thoughts were indiscernible.

"Noire, in a way, I am those things. But sometimes, having a life filled with choices hardens you in other ways. Your privilege becomes a barometer by which you're judged."

"This isn't just about *you*, Innocent. Lots of us have been considered 'black exceptions.' I mean, since my parents were newly baptized 'black is beautiful' converts who had broken the mold of what was expected of them, *my* whole life has been unprecedented. Innocent, I was one of only *four* black people at that conference." Noire was defensive, her arms and legs tightly wound together.

Innocent continued, unfazed by her last comment. "When I came here, I became classmates with the world's future business elite. I learned to be the one who everyone wanted on their team. I was a black man, an African, but I was still the exception, this time for a different reason. People didn't care about my family name. All they cared about was that I had an accent, a closet full of well-tailored suits, and no African American ax to grind. My presence didn't cause anyone to remember slavery because they never learned that those who were left behind were affected too. I presented no threat."

His expression called for a response Noire felt ill prepared to give. "Innocent, I can't say what you want me to."

"Say what you like. It's my life." He stared at her squarely. "That's what scares me about you. You seem to have spent all of your life just being who you are and feeling what you feel and not being afraid to let anyone know about it. But that way of living hasn't worked for me. In thirty-three years, I've become an expert at planning my life and fitting people into my plan.

"But here I am, looking at a woman whose very being is a glaring contrast to me. Noire, if things go wrong for you, your family and friends help you to correct and move on. But if I fuck up"—he scratched his head violently—"I'm completely out of luck. My nearest relative is a seven-hour plane ride away. As a black man—an African man—my choices have serious implications. The stakes are higher, Noire."

Innocent felt satisfied that he had at least made a point. He slouched on the end of the bed, his body spent from the effort of composing and unloading his thoughts.

Noire took off her glasses—holding them precariously by the stem—and rubbed her eyes deliberately. "Have I wronged you too? Am I supposed to feel bad for you?"

"You can accept me. It's like, I figured out how to do enough things right to win your affection, but you're still scrutinizing me. Fuck that, Noire. And fuck you for doing that to me. And because you do it to me, I do it to you."

"Don't make what you do my fault." Her voice cracked. She steadied it before continuing. "That's just wrong, Innocent."

"Well, then we're even."

Noire felt her internal organs collapsing in on themselves. The taste of bile sat at the back of her throat. "Why are we having this conversation?" She was an ant screaming in a cookie jar.

"This is the best conversation we've ever had."

Innocent rose from the bed, the sheet falling from his lap. Noire looked at him, seeing an irresistible naked stranger. He walked toward her and stood above her chair. Noire kept her gaze ahead of her, her eyes level with his waist. He kissed the top of her head, his face burrowed into her hair. "Noire?" His voice vibrated in her skull and shook her soul. He squatted down beside her. "Noire," he repeated, his tone new and caressing. He touched his right hand to her face and bestowed gentle kisses on her right and left cheek, placing them with all the care and deliberateness of a baby's first steps.

"I'm sorry." Noire felt the words flush her pores and free her heart. She kissed the palm of his hand.

In the time it took for her to see herself through his eyes, she saw the prospect of a real relationship and claimed it. She was afraid but would not succumb to her fear. So she called a truce and became Innocent's girlfriend.

The change was subtle. But her heart had shifted. She was off-road riding and didn't know where she was going anymore. Her sarcastic witticisms were replaced by an earnestness that left her standing naked at an intersection. She knew she would love Innocent because now she had to. Now that she had become that vulnerable, that truthful, that humbled, she had no choice.

Innocent read between the lines in her face, traveled through the tunnels that burrowed deep into her brain, let his tongue dance in the essence of her heart when he made love to her. She unnerved him, energized him, extended him into the rough territory beyond himself. But the minute he knew he had her he didn't know what to do with her. Was Noire the one all this had been leading up to?

Chapter 9

Visitations

The bass beat pounded a dull thud into the night air. Innocent and Noire walked in time to the music as they approached Dennis's neat brownstone on a tree-lined block of Stuyvesant Heights, Bed-Stuy's historic center.

"I think this is gonna be a funk-ta-fied Brooklyn groove tonight!" Noire did the bump with Innocent's unprepared behind.

"I guess they must have paid off all their neighbors so that they wouldn't call the police!"

"Knowing Dennis, he probably just invited all the neighbors. Everyone likes a good rump-shake every now and then. And if you're lucky you can launch your career as a calypso star!" Noire joked.

Innocent laughed. "How'd you know?"

"Nu-aaa-rah!" Dennis sang her name from the steps like the refrain from a carnival road march.

Tolu switched his hips in a furious soca dance, a Carib in each hand. At the bottom of the steps, Dennis grabbed Noire into his arms and then twirled her around in a West Indian mambo. Tolu sat the beers on a step. "How far now?" He greeted Innocent in Nigerian broken English and clasped his hand in a handshake and snap from back home.

"Looks like you two know each other!"

"Noire, he's my African brotha! I would know him a mile away!" Tolu and Innocent had another round of handshakes and snaps. Dennis gave him a black man's embrace.

"Hear what. You go on in, get yourself ah stout and just relax. Arikè's in there, feelin' good 'n ting. Enjoy yourself!" Dennis clapped Innocent on the shoulder, kissed Noire on the cheek, and he and Tolu resumed their dance.

"Good guys . . ."

They walked under a low-hanging sign that screamed YOU GO GIRL! HAPPY GRADUATION! and another that proclaimed WATCH OUT INS!

"What's up with that?" Innocent pointed to the second sign.

"She got a law fellowship."

"Seems like sleeping with the enemy."

"Yeah, well Arikè says she's gotta 'infiltrate before she can penetrate!'"

"I'd be happy if I never saw those three letters again in my life. The INS was my worst nightmare when I first came over here. It took me two months of going to their office every other day to convince them that I was here for school and not to engage in subversive activity while collecting welfare."

"Studying while black . . ."

Arikè planted rum-tinged kisses on both of their unsuspecting lips and asked Noire to help her adjust her halter top. She laughed, kissed them again, and danced away.

"Bubbly." Innocent watched her perky woman's form absorb into the crowd.

They loaded environmentally friendly paper plates with Trinidadian, Nigerian, and soul food as sustenance for a high-energy night.

"How'd they meet?"

"Arikè came on to Tolu at a Nigerian highlife party about a year and a half ago. She greeted him in Yoruba. He replied in English that because her intonation was off, she had inadvertently asked him to fuck her instead of asking how are you. Arikè said, 'How do you know it's a mistake?'"

Innocent wrinkled his face in confusion.

"His woman came over and Tolu said some lie about Arikè's father being from his village. Arikè took it as a challenge and left with his business card. They agreed to meet for drinks a few days later. Tolu brought Dennis with him.

"Arikè was pissed, but Dennis is a cool guy, so when Tolu left, she stayed. They dated but Arikè was noncommittal. On date number seven, Dennis proposed a toast. He said: 'To the possibility that you will eventually see how much I like you and respect you, how tremendously honored I am to be near you, how much I relish the sight of you, and how much I want to kiss you.'" Noire recounted it verbatim, recapturing Arikè's passion when she told her months ago. She sighed. "Anyway, Dennis tried to clink her glass but she kissed him instead!"

Caught up in the romance of the story even in its retelling, Noire asked, "Isn't that wonderful?"

"It's quite a story."

"It's completely romantic." Noire was overcome.

"Romance doesn't always make a relationship strong. But I'm happy for them."

"Romance keeps love *alive*." Noire shook her head.

"Ms. Demain." Innocent held out his half-eaten chicken leg with great ceremony and begged her to eat. He licked the chicken grease off of her fingers and then her mouth.

"This is a first . . ." She swallowed.

Noire spread a little more butter on her biscuit. Innocent's mouth was busy with his second rack of ribs. They were having a leisurely Saturday early-afternoon lunch at the Cajun Creole Café, Noire's favorite neighborhood haunt.

"So, my mom called this morning to tell me that Cousin Nandi called her last night. Remember I told you she's the one with the seafood restaurant franchise who lives in Baltimore?"

"Mmm."

"Anyway, Nandi said she wouldn't be using her summer house much this year because she just bought a vacation condo somewhere exotic. She's offering to rent it to the family for three hundred dollars. She asked Mom to ask me if I'd be interested in it. I was thinking about Fourth of July weekend."

"Where is it?"

Noire took another spoonful of jambalaya before responding. "Oh yeah, it's right outside of Charleston, South Carolina, on Edisto Island. It's one of the Sea Islands. That's actually where my family is from, on my mom's side."

Innocent raised his eyebrows to illustrate his interest as he cleaned the meat off of another rib bone. Noire dipped a deep-fried crawfish into a pool of creole sauce, then picked it up gingerly.

"Her house is really nice. We had a family reunion there about ten years ago. Come to think of it, that was the last one we had! Anyway, it's big; I think there are three large bedrooms and one small one and two kitchens, one on each floor. *And* it's right on the beach!"

"Sounds a little big for just the two of us." Innocent sopped up all of the assorted juices on his nearly empty plate with a soggy biscuit.

"Yeah. That's why I was thinking we could invite some other folks; make it a little holiday party!" Noire smiled, then looked at the lone rib on Innocent's plate and decided against taking it. She took a sip of lemonade.

"I mentioned it to Jayna but she can't go."

Laughing, Innocent asked, "When d'you speak to her?"

"This morning. Right after I got off the phone with my mom. Right before you called me."

"Oh. So Jayna can't come. Who else have you invited?"

"Nobody. I haven't had time to call folks. And besides, I wanted to see what you thought about the idea first." Noire saw no contradiction in her words.

"What if I can't go?"

"Where are you going?"

"Who knows; haven't set my July calendar yet." A sly grin peeked from the corner of his mouth.

"Oh, Innocent!"

"No seriously, sounds like a decent idea. Who else were you thinking of inviting?" Innocent finished off his iced tea and dipped his finger into Noire's plate.

"I don't know, maybe Arikè and Dennis."

"We'll be sure to have a rollicking ride if they come."

Noire chuckled. "Yeah, they really know how to bring the house down. What good-time folks do you have up your sleeve?"

His eyes narrowed as he thought. "Well, Marcus and Lydia are going to Chicago for a month. He said they're leaving in a few weeks, June 15 or something."

Noire rolled her eyes but kept her head down. "Mmm."

"Can you imagine, Marcus reads Nile stories from the *Wall Street Journal*?"

"I can imagine."

"Yeah." Innocent's cellular phone rang. "Pokou here . . . man, are you kidding me? . . . that's what I was saying this morning . . . mmm . . . OK . . . alright, I'll be there in"—Innocent checked his watch—"in like forty-five minutes . . . see, that's why you needed to negotiate the terms of this whole package before getting involved . . . OK, I'm sorry . . . I'm coming now. Easy."

Innocent pressed OFF on the phone and cursed under his breath.

Noire's expression was a question mark.

"That was Alexander. He's working on a deal and got stuck doing more than his fair share of the grunt work. Now he's freaking out because he has to have everything completed for a presentation on Monday."

"And that was his cry for help?"

"Yeah." His face was creased with annoyance. "Sorry, Noire."

"I'm sorry too." Noire frowned. She just finished the school year and hadn't seen Innocent in two weeks. "I was hoping we would have been able to spend a little 'quality time' before the gallery opening this evening."

"'Quality time' would have been nice, *ma cherie*." Bending over his empty plate, he kissed Noire's creole-flavored lips. "But duty calls, I guess."

"What's up with Alexander anyway? Seems like he's always in a jam."

"Part of it is his own hangup and part of it is some growing antagonism between him and a couple of the other first-year associates. Apparently Alexander doesn't fit into their clique."

"Why does his drama always come back to you?"

"Look, I'm just trying to look out for the brotha. Alexander is a talented and hardworking guy. He doesn't need to be eaten up by these turkeys."

"Well, how come everyone seems to like *you* so much?"

"My French accent. Makes people forget I'm black."

As they stood in front of the plate-glass windows of the restaurant, Innocent's heart operated at capacity. "I would have loved to spend some 'quality time' with my sweet, sweet Noire." His words sent a thrill through Noire's loins. She stroked his chest through his shirt and he squeezed her arms through the sweater she had hastily thrown around her shoulders.

"You'll make it up to me."

"Yes."

She made love to his spicy-sweet lips in the middle of Fulton Street.

Drawing a line along Noire's jawbone with his index finger, Innocent pulled away from her succulent lips. "I'll see you later on, Noire."

"See you." Noire's body was responding to the closeness of Innocent and she stood still to steady herself.

He stole one more kiss before they parted. Gym bag strapped diagonally across his body, Innocent walked jauntily along to the subway station and Noire floated back to her apartment.

Alexander's cubicle reeked of Doritos and a recently eaten pastrami sandwich. Clad in a golf shirt and Bermuda shorts, he looked like he had hoped for more leisurely plans for his Saturday afternoon.

"Thanks for comin' through, man," Alexander said without looking up.

"Tryin' to look out."

"What were you doin' when I called?"

Innocent shuffled through the marked-up copy of Alexander's presentation that was in a pile on the floor and gathered it in his hands. "Having lunch with Noire."

He peeked above his papers "Oh shit. I ruined your dessert!"

His eyes were an exclamation point.

Alexander put down his pen. "It's like *that*, Innocent?!"

"She's a special woman." His tone was serious.

"Mmm . . ." Alexander imagined what he didn't know. "So how's this stuff lookin' to you?"

Innocent reviewed graphs and models as well as Alexander's recommendations for the project. They discussed implementation strategies and scenarios of possible outcomes. He interrogated Alexander's assumptions and asked him clarifying questions. Cutting across him when he became wordy and vague, Innocent forced him to be succinct and precise.

Alexander's face was a collage of anxious expressions and suspicious looks. Innocent's face remained placid and his tone flat.

"What the fuck *is* all this?" Alexander asked.

"Do you plan to ask that on Monday?"

"No—"

"Then why are you asking me that now? Just answer the questions, Alexander. And don't wear all of your emotions on your face. Folks don't have to know you're shitting bricks."

Innocent continued to quiz Alexander on his methodology, the models he chose to present, and the means by which he arrived at his numbers. He made notes on Alexander's draft. Noticing the damp circles at Alexander's armpits, Innocent knew he had had the desired effect.

Finally he ceased with his questions. Alexander sat, edgy and anxious, behind his desk. He looked at Innocent.

"I suggest you wear an undershirt on Monday, man," Innocent chided. "Look, this is OK. I made some notes on the kinds of things you need to fill in. You make a few too many assumptions and don't show why you discarded certain models. But it's OK, man. Just work on pumping it up a bit more and you'll be good to go. And be confident. Know why you did what you did and be ready, willing, and able to explain it. Don't force anyone to pull it out of you. Nobody will be that patient. By the time you shuffle and scratch your ass, someone else is going to steal your thunder. And they'll get the credit for it. I'll be in my office for a bit in case you need me." Innocent got up and grabbed his gym bag from the floor.

"Thanks, Innocent." His look was genuine. Then, reclaiming some of his bravado, he added, "I was gonna beat your ass for a second!"

"But you were too scared to do it. I saw it in your face, Alexander. I'll be in my office."

As he fiddled with his keys, he heard the murmur of a Saturday afternoon at the firm. Turning on his computer, Innocent shook his head. What was wrong with a job that forced people to forgo a normal personal life so that they could put in the requisite face-time at the office? He knew all of the tricks: the strategically placed calls and e-mails sent to one's supervisor over the course of a weekday night or a Saturday or Sunday afternoon, the needless walks around to allow as many people as possible to see you. He dialed Alexander's extension.

"Alexander." He uttered his name like a command.

"Have you dropped a voice mail or e-mail to Renée today?"

"She's not here, man."

"So you didn't?"

"No."

"I suggest you do. Document you were here. Nobody gives a shit that I saw you."

"I can't take all this political bullshit."

"It's a game, Alexander. Play to win."

Innocent crunched on sunflower seeds. Checking tasks off of his Wednesday to-do list, he relished his momentary reprieve from the press of work needing his immediate attention. His 1:00 P.M. meeting had been canceled because Cliff's wife, Vera, had gone into labor. Throwing another handful of seeds into his mouth, he admired Mireille's recent photograph taken on her eighteenth birthday. Her mis-

chievous eyes brimming with youthful cheer, she stood in front of the
iroko tree that the family planted fifteen years ago, on the first anniver-
sary of Serge's death. Remembering his brother, he thought of
Charlotte, his twin. *How's her pregnancy progressing?* She was due in
less than three months, in mid-September. He typed her a quick e-mail
and pressed SEND. The phone rang.

"Pokou here."

"Hey man! It's Marcus." His voice boomed through the phone.

"You sound happy. What's up?" Innocent put his feet up on his desk.

"You won't believe who I had a meeting with. Lissette François!"
Marcus's smile was audible. "She's only in town for a day and a night
and she says that she hasn't seen you since b-school so she's headed to
your office now. She should be there in five or ten minutes."

"What?" Innocent felt excitement clutch his crotch and perspira-
tion spring out of his armpits. He wasn't ready to see her.

"Why is she here and why am I just learning about this now?" He
was suspicious.

"I didn't know she was here until I saw her this morning. My dad
asked me to go to a meeting regarding a resort property he's planning to
invest in and apparently Lissette works for the real estate development
company. It's a French outfit. They're doing something in St. Martin,
on the French side. It's fate, man!"

"What is that supposed to mean?"

"Look, you used to fuck her, and you bought her apartment. I think
you're in a better position to answer that than me."

"We're friends. But maybe you don't know anything about being
friends with a woman?" Innocent felt self-righteous.

Marcus deflected the question. "Well, she's gonna be there in a
minute so I suggest you put on some cologne and get rid of your hard-
on. Or are you really trying to tell me she has no effect on you?
Whatever you say, you'll be a liar when you see her. Damn, I don't know
why I never fucked her." His last statement was reflective.

"You are a son-of-a-bitch, Marcus."

"Don't be so tough, son. I could have let her catch you by surprise.
Sweeten yourself up and deflate your dick, black man. I'll speak to you
later."

Marcus hung up and Innocent collected his thoughts. He willed his growing excitement to retreat and grabbed his bottle of Creed from his desk drawer. Noticing the damp circles at his underarms, he closed his office door and hurriedly changed into the fresh Edwin Hall button-down that he kept for the occasional overnighter. *The shirt is fresh; no need to spray cologne everywhere,* he reasoned, not wanting to give himself away when she walked into his office.

The intercom buzzed as he pushed his cufflinks into his starch-stiff cuffs. *Too fresh for one-thirty P.M. She'll know.* He cursed himself. "Mr. Pokou, you have a guest. She says she's a classmate from business school."

"I'll be right out." Innocent crumpled his old shirt into his desk drawer and then waited for what seemed to be well over thirty seconds before sauntering out of his office. He adjusted his stride, taking care to seem neither too rushed nor too relaxed for work. Lissette stood at the end of the hallway, watching Innocent's uneven steps. She smiled broadly and deposited a noiseless kiss on his cheek that looked more businesslike than it felt.

"*Salut! Ça va?*" Her velvety French nuzzled against his ear as she pulled away from the side of his face.

He responded in kind, his words low and private, as if French was not appropriate for the office. "Lissette, this is certainly an unexpected pleasure."

"For both of us." She followed the path back to his office that he had directed with his hand. "You look wonderful. Did you know I was coming?"

"Marcus called me only a moment before."

"He spoiled my surprise."

"Not at all. He just called to make sure I was in the office, I guess."

"I had phoned to do the same. Didn't want for my visit to be in vain." She turned to face him, bracing herself against his office door. At five feet four in business pumps, Lissette cast her eyes up into his face at a steep angle.

Innocent ruminated over her words. "No waiting in vain . . ." He pushed open his door and announced, "Would you like to have lunch or coffee?"

Sweeping the office with one swivel of her head, Lissette digested its contents, her eyes resting on his cologne bottle atop a paper menagerie on his desk. "I don't want to take you away—"

Innocent winced at the sight of the Creed bottle. "I haven't eaten yet."

"Well, in that case, coffee is fine."

Sitting closer than colleagues but farther apart than lovers, Innocent and Lissette negotiated their mutual reserve, sharing tentative pleasantries and pregnant silences. By the time Innocent's sandwich arrived, his stomach was a knot of delight and confusion. The advancing afternoon encouraged them to settle into an intimacy of sentimental affection and current curiosity; they traded coffee-flavored tidbits from their lives.

Lissette told the severely edited story of her live-in boyfriend.

"I don't think I love him enough to marry him. I wish I did; we've been together for almost three years and it's disheartening to have to begin again at thirty-one years old. I have to break up with him but I don't have an apartment yet. I was renting a miserable flat in the heart of Paris when I first moved there but happily traded up to his duplex early into our relationship. He's French and Moroccan. He's an art dealer and his place is full of precious pieces from North Africa and all throughout the French world. I think I'll miss his artwork more than I'll miss him."

"Do you think you'd go back to Haiti?"

"Maybe." She peered into her coffee cup. "My parents don't know that I'm breaking up with Mounir; I think they were excited by the prospect of having a white son-in-law." She looked directly at Innocent and registered the question behind his silence. "I think you saw a picture of my family before. I'm the darkest. My father has always made it painfully obvious that he's uncomfortable about it."

Innocent stared at her jet-black hair, whose curls lay in lazy caresses against a cheek the color of buttered wheat toast. He strained to remember the family portrait that sat in the windowsill of her loft so many years ago—the off-white and barely sun-kissed complexions of her sisters, her mother's freckled face, and her father's aquamarine eyes and chestnut hair. He had always thought that Lissette was more beautiful than her sisters, but now he realized that perhaps his assessment was due in part to her striking difference. She shared her mother's upturned nose and widely set eyes; he couldn't recall if she looked like her father at all.

Lissette allowed Innocent his moment of reverie. She resumed her side of the conversation in the middle of a thought. "But I like being independent. There I couldn't even live on my own, unless I was married. I just don't want that."

"In Haiti? You don't want to be married?" Innocent hadn't followed her unvoiced thread.

"Oh no, I'd like to be married, but I don't want to *have to* be married, you know. But for me to live alone in Haiti when my parents have ample space and resources to accommodate me would be an affront to them. On the other hand, they're also concerned about their assets in France and would probably want for me to stay there because things are a bit unstable in Haiti right now." She sipped her coffee loudly to change the subject. "How about you? Tell me about Noire." She pronounced her name with a strong French flourish, one that Noire never used herself.

"She's a wonderful woman. Very smart. Active mind. Beautiful. And passionate. We've been together since we met in mid-March."

Lissette's eyes became devilish. "Ooh la la, Innocent. That's practically a record for you. She must really be something for her to have you hooked so well and so quickly! Do you love her?"

"Yes, I love her." His tone was defensive where hers had been playful.

"Innocent, I'm not suggesting that you don't." She widened her eyes as a form of chastisement.

"I know." He felt guilty about telling Lissette that he loved Noire before she knew herself, but he was certain that he wouldn't divulge his feelings to Noire for a long time. He couldn't risk telling her before he could accept the consequences of the disclosure. He had to be sure.

Innocent fell back into his chair, his chest concave and hollow. Lissette blotted her heart-shaped lips on her napkin and adjusted her posture to give and receive Innocent's full attention. She broke a corner of bread off of his sandwich and popped it into her mouth.

"It's just that . . . I love her but I don't always get her—or sometimes she doesn't get me. I don't . . . She doesn't always know how to access me."

"And do you know how to access *her*? Do you ask her the questions that she wants to answer and tell her the things she wants to hear?"

"I don't know."

"Don't you want to know?"

He didn't respond.

They sat in silence. Her hands once again in his plate, she broke off a larger piece of his sandwich. He watched her. Her lips pouted with every chew, the contents of her mouth dancing from side to side. She smiled and her face sprang to life: her nose became a child's playground amusement, her cheeks offered dimple-sized wading pools. Her heavy lashes drawn like peacock plumage, her gray-green eyes stood exposed to full appreciation. Innocent was incredulous. He hadn't spoken to, much less seen, Lissette in nearly four years, and now he could not account for the reason. But the softness of her gaze told him that they were still friends. They shared language, an expatriate's outlook, complementary professional aspirations . . .

Lissette guided Innocent's left hand to her lap with her right before deliberately bringing it up to her lips. "Innocent, you're a wonderful man and I'm sure you will do the right thing, both by Noire and, more importantly, by yourself."

They concluded the meal shrouded in melancholy. Lissette insisted on making lunch her treat. Innocent kissed a whisper on her lips in parting, wistful in the remembrance of what it was like to make love to her in the predawn light of the loft that used to be hers. He heard her French murmurings and felt her honey-dipped nipples heavy against his chest and saw her tearful smile at the conclusion of their lovemaking. Lissette's energy always calmed him, her voice always soothed him. They left each other promising to keep in touch.

Cassandra Wilson spilled thick Delta tales onto Noire's consciousness as she stood on her bed, in full sight of her body reflected in the dresser mirror. She fingered her nipples through her translucent camisole, studiously watching them rise to eager peaks against the fabric. Noire rolled them between her thumb and forefinger as though they were the nubs of a finely crafted cigar. Her movements methodical, she mimicked Innocent's reverent foreplay, her gaze transfixed to her reflection as his always was when he evoked the beginnings of her sexual response.

Releasing her breasts from behind the material, she noticed their buoyant independence. She wriggled out of her panties. Her naked form fully disclosed to the scrutiny of her own eyes, she surveyed her landscape. Noire's skin was the even brown of roasted chestnuts. She was statuesque. Her hips narrow, she had a satisfactory behind. She touched the unruly shock of hair between her legs and wondered if Innocent preferred it when she shaved. Kneading the lobes of her behind, she sought to enjoy their round suppleness that Innocent's insistent hands relished as he made love to her.

Noire wanted to untangle the contradictions of love that had become the archetype of her own relationships: lovers who could not love each other well, family who questioned blood ties. First it was her mother and father whose coparenting friendship grew in the wake of their romantic relationship. Then it was her childhood summers spent in New Orleans, which provided ample opportunity for her color-struck cousins to poke fun at her body—her long legs, brown skin, "nappy" hair, and throaty voice. Her father, then still a recent disciple of black pride, saw his brown-skinned daughter—her head a mass of unapologetically curly hair—as the ultimate statement of this pride and insisted that Noire represent the blackness that his family didn't readily acknowledge. He proudly sent her down to visit his family for a month every summer, where she stayed with her grandmother. Despite her shared features with her father, Noire's cousins insisted she was too black to be related to them. Grand-mère wasn't much better, offering by way of explanation that Noire couldn't help that her mother was a black woman. Noire was confused and hurt, wondering why her black family couldn't accept their own blackness.

She had put an end to the familial ridicule when, at thirteen, she announced that she would no longer be going down to New Orleans in the summer. But the taunts about her appearance lived on beyond mere teenage angst. Ever the progressive black woman, Noire had learned to hone her urban bravadista stance through many tortured encounters with bad boyfriends and competitive girlfriends. And so, the knowledge of Innocent's want for her adult body sometimes failed to quell the anxiety that seeped out of her in the form of tears or laced her words with a curious form of sarcasm. Why *her* and not the pressed and curled, six-figure Jenisa Washington disciples who could eat men like Innocent for lunch? At twenty-eight, Noire had an insecurity that had taken up residence, body and soul.

The phone rang, jarring her out of her contemplation. She stumbled off of the bed and ran into the living room, snatching the phone off the cradle on the third ring.

"I'm happy you're there." Innocent announced himself before Noire could say anything.

"Where are you?"

"In a car downstairs. Can I come up?"

"Sure."

They said the hasty good-byes of people about to see each other. Noire stood naked in the middle of her living room, deciding against putting on any clothes. She turned off all the lights in the apartment, letting the sunlight of an early summer evening send long shadows through the space, and lit a stick of incense before Innocent rang her doorbell. She buzzed him in and waited to hear him knock on her apartment's front door. She squirted a dollop of refrigerated chocolate syrup on her tongue before answering.

Innocent was greeted by a chocolate kiss, unwrapped and ready to be eaten. They exchanged no words, letting the strength of their thoughts dictate their urgent gestures. Noire couldn't imagine what had compelled him to leave work early to see her but she didn't want to know yet. She just wanted to feel him, to know that he was hers. She relished his driving need for her and let it soothe the open wounds she had exposed in the mirror only moments ago. Innocent drove Lissette to the back of his mind as he drank in Noire's passion and vulnerability. He drowned in the power of her love, reassuring himself that he was in the right relationship with the right woman. He serviced her generously, happy to taste her, to feel her stomach tense with pleasure, to hear her voice call his name.

Chapter 10

Different Stars, Different Stripes

July 1. Noire was anxious so she and Arikè made a list:

TONIGHT
pick up minivan
go food shopping (no pork!!)
buy batteries and bug spray
buy suntan lotion and K-Y gel (Arikè)
buy 200-speed film (Noire)

TOMORROW
call about tour packages
pick up Innocent, Dennis, and the rest from the
    airport—5:30 P.M.

That was the plan.

Noire felt dizzy watching the clouds rush past her window as they made their final descent into Charleston, South Carolina. She had never met Innocent's coworker

Alexander or his weekend "girlfriend," Dolores. And Mamadou had decided to fly in from Paris on a whim. Noire wondered if Innocent had even told Mamadou who she was; the second time Innocent mentioned him to her was at seven that morning from a taxicab. She could hear Mamadou in the background speaking Wolof with the cab driver. Innocent reminded her that he was the college friend he had described on their first date. The best friend who knew every West African in Paris. His painting hung in his apartment. Noire was sure to like him. Her nerves at war with her stomach, Noire downed her emergency stash of antacid and burped.

Massive oak trees dripping Spanish moss blanketed the Lowcountry, bringing a premature dusk to the ever-narrowing Edisto Island roads that burrowed through the lush green canopy. Noire negotiated their silver van through the dense greenery dotted by shacks that could only be called quaint if they had been on a movie set. Giving Arikè a skeletal history of the Sea Islands, she explained the stark contrasts between the poverty of many Gullah people who traced their ancestry through generations that had tumbled in and out of slavery, and the seasonal white migrations to choice beachfront resorts on Kiawah, Seabrook, and Hilton Head Islands. Edisto Island had resisted the most commercial development efforts, and she took an uneasy pride in the foresight of her family for not selling all of their land on the island. Though many had sought escape from the site of their former enslavement decades before, Cousin Nandi, the resident family futurist, had managed to retain twenty-five acres. Her own sagacity made her the sole owner of the remaining Williamson family property; she built nine houses on the land and never missed an opportunity to fuss about the hundreds of acres that shortsighted Williamsons had abandoned, lost, or sold for less than the price of freedom.

Arikè reflected on her status as a new American; she had been born in the U.S. to an English mother and a Nigerian father. Rather than stay in the country that had brought them together, they decided to pioneer a joint life where neither had the advantage of citizenship or family ties.

Their plan worked; they enjoyed a happy marriage that reinvented itself continually against the backdrop of a respectable home in a New York City suburb, three sons, and a daughter.

The smell of saltwater announced their arrival on the skinny finger of land called Edisto Beach that butted up against the ocean. Cousin Nandi's house—a sturdy colonial sitting atop squat wooden legs—seemed perpetually outfitted for the July Fourth holiday: blue clapboards, a white picket fence, and a red mailbox. The front yard was a shaggy muff dusted with sand. Noire and Arikè explored the interior—scouting out the best bedrooms for themselves—before bringing in their luggage and the groceries. They threw open windows, trying to air out the unused smell that stood in corners and closets before the others arrived tomorrow. Noire fished around for incense sticks in her backpack and lit one in every room.

By nine o'clock, dusk had given way to a sultry evening.

"So we're here!" Arikè let out an excited giggle in the kitchen. "This is going to be so nice, Noire. Thanks so much for inviting Dennis and me."

Noire made her smile look genuine to mask the apprehension lurking in the shadows of her mind. She didn't know Alexander or Dolores, and she was especially worried about Mamadou. There was no saying they'd have a nice time.

"You know, it's cool to hang with you like this. I mean, before everyone else comes down. We really haven't had this kind of time before."

Arikè julienned zucchini in a professional food processor while Noire chopped onions by hand. The purr of the motor and Noire's onion-induced sniffling accented the quiet of the house. They enjoyed the silence as they cooked.

The meal prepared, Arikè led them to a perch on the steps outside and balanced her plate on her knees. Taking a forkful of their aromatic creation, she set it down again and kissed an unsuspecting Noire on the neck. She jumped.

The outline of Arikè's lips lingered. "What was that for?"

"I'm just happy, Noire." Arikè's unmitigated glee shined through her voice.

"Just *happy*?"

"Yes." Then looking at Noire, she saw the question marks raised in her eyebrows. "Noire, I just wanted to share it with you." Her voice became quieter, more atmospheric. "You know, sometimes you don't realize how much you need to get away until you do. Just to let yourself hear what quiet is." She began to eat her food. "Sometimes I feel like my life is a mishmash of subway rides from hell, busywork, and black bourgie parties, you know. It's much. It's good to just be comfortable with not being 'where the party is at.' It's the way most people live."

Noire realized that she never really thought about how Arikè processed the world or what was on her mind. She nodded her agreement. "We take the trash heaps, cramped quarters, and take-out Chinese for granted. It's part of what it means to be a New Yorker. And most of the time I like it. Most of the time it's exactly the kind of life I think I want. But sometimes it really doesn't live up to the hype."

They chewed their food deliberately, trading smiles between mouthfuls.

"Noire, what *do* you want? I mean, really?"

She knew Arikè expected a reply more candid than she was willing to offer. "I don't know. Love, like everyone else. A career that pays my bills and also gives me a sense of accomplishment." She hunched her shoulders.

Arikè stared at Noire until she had to look up. "I want to have children who will have a relationship with my parents. I want to feel really loved and respected by a man I really love and respect. I want to feel free to know all of the happiness and vulnerability and raw passion that I can stand!" She forked more food into her mouth but kept her gaze straight ahead.

Noire wanted her to stop looking at her, at least for a minute. "Um, yeah, I want those things too. I mean, especially the last two."

"You don't want children?" Arikè was incredulous.

"I don't know. I mean . . ." Noire didn't want to explain what she meant.

"Noire, you're twenty-eight years old. It seems like you should have a pretty clear sense by now."

She felt her heartbeat in her throat. "Arikè, I'm not like you. My parents have never been together; it's like, at ten months old, I drove them apart forever. Sometimes the love of baby making gets lost in the child rearing."

"Noire, any child would be lucky to know all of your love and beauty and passion."

Tears bathed her eyes and her body grew warm from the inside out; Arikè had soothed her in a place that most people couldn't reach. She remembered the day when she was nine years old and her teacher wrote a note for her mother, writing on the outside "Mrs. Demain."

"But her name is Williamson. My mom and dad aren't married."

"Well, then they're divorced." The teacher nodded her head in confirmation and changed the "Mrs." to "Ms."

Again, Noire corrected her. "No, it's Ms. Williamson."

Her teacher, a self-styled reformed hippie, patted Noire's plump cheek. "That's so sad that even *you* couldn't bring your parents together. Ever." She hugged Noire's unwilling body, seemingly using her protestation to justify prolonging the forced affection. Noire wasn't starved for love. But in her statement as Noire heard it, her teacher had made a causal link between her parents' lack of marital union and a deficient love for her.

For many years after, Noire wondered what she could do to make her parents love each other enough to want to become an official family, with Noire as the focal point. But she never asked the question, fearing the answer would implicate her. So instead she persisted in being a good student and exemplary daughter. Her parents were pleased but seemingly no closer to marriage, so Noire became resigned to the permanent state of affairs. But when her father married Celine at one month into her pregnancy with Jabari, Noire concluded that her brother had something that she lacked.

Her sensitivities coating her skin, Noire tingled as Arikè's hand swept across her jawbone. Her kind eyes peered into Noire's soul. Inclining her head toward Arikè, she was surprised that her lips were met so readily by her receptive mouth. It was a shy kiss, more affectionate than sensual, but it felt special and different. Suddenly self-conscious, Noire tried to disappear into the floorboards.

Despite her best supernatural efforts, she remained where she was. Arikè ran the tips of her fingers over Noire's knuckles. "You're a beautiful woman, Noire. And in these past few months, I've grown to really appreciate that. It's all good."

Noire's perplexity churned the food recently arrived in her stomach. Staring at Arikè's placid face, she tried unsuccessfully to scan her own emotions. She felt like her eleven-year-old self getting her period for the first time: vulnerable, embarrassed, chosen. Older but not wiser. Preparing to speak, Noire listened to herself intently, unsure of what she would say. "I've never done that before." She still knew nothing; she frowned.

"And maybe you never will again. But do yourself a favor and let yourself be OK with it."

Dennis and Arikè claimed the backseat of the minivan for the hour drive back from Charleston International Airport. They filled the time with heavy petting. Noire drove. Innocent sat beside her, and the odd trio of Alexander, Dolores, and Mamadou took the middle row. Bob Marley sang from the speakers of the van, muffling the sounds of Dennis, Arikè, and the highway. Innocent glanced over his left shoulder to catch Mamadou's serene face turned toward Mecca, his eyes closed in his fifth set of prayers for the day, and Alexander tangling his fingers into Dolores's hair.

"*Mira*, stop!" She lit a cigarette and pulled away. Innocent winced, wondering why she had accepted the airplane ticket that Alexander offered her only one night before.

"Um, can you take that outside?" Arikè's voice emerged from the back of the minivan.

"This is bothering you?" Dolores whipped around to face Arikè.

"Yes."

Noire screeched to the side of the road dangerously close to a gas station. Alexander flung open the door and jumped out. Dolores clenched her cigarette between her teeth and detached herself from the chair. Her miniskirt, damp with the moisture that had gathered on the underside of her well-formed thighs, clung to the crevices of her quivering behind. Innocent saw no sign of underwear. Alexander slipped his hand underneath and made the necessary adjustments. She gave a slight smile and puffed her cigarette.

"Noire, do we have any Hennessy at the house?" Alexander put his arm around Dolores's waist. She removed it.

"Good idea!" Arikè and Dennis's voices made the declaration in stereo. Dennis peeled off three twenties and handed them out the window to Alexander. "Add this to the liquor fund."

Alexander and Dolores said that they would walk to the Liquor Heaven that hugged the far side of Dixie Fuel. Innocent watched the face of the praying Mamadou for any signs of distress as Noire drove slowly through the station and parked in front of the store, waiting for them.

Mamadou slid to the end of the seat and opened the door. "*Venez avec moi!*" he ordered Innocent, and jumped out.

Innocent shot Noire a helpless look and climbed out of the van behind his friend. Noire looked away.

"What in the hell is going on?" Arikè's voice traveled across the middle row and landed at Noire.

She closed her eyes and made "Redemption Song" a passionate duet. Bob didn't complain.

Dolores and Alexander returned, their arms full of brown paper bags and each other. They all clamored back into the van.

"Shit is cheap down here. We got Hennessy, Guinness, Bailey's, two kinds of rum, some mixers, and even a little tequila, just in case!" Alexander's hearty laugh was met by Dennis's declaration to "let the party begin."

"Guys." Innocent turned to face the rest of his temporary housemates. "Mamadou asked me to tell you—since he doesn't speak good English—that he doesn't drink. He's an observant Muslim," he added by way of explanation.

"More for me, I guess!" Alexander kissed Dolores.

"Mamadou thought it would be important to make that clear."

"Thanks for telling us." Noire smiled at Mamadou, then turned the key in the ignition. "*Exodus! Movement of jah people . . .*"

Noire found Mamadou sitting on the stairs of the porch. The sun was still new in the sky. "I thought I'd be the only early riser." Noire spoke self-conscious French before taking a seat beside him.

He smiled broadly, the appreciation of her effort written across his face. "I didn't see any coffee in there or I would have made some."

"Oh, Innocent brought some down. It's still in his bag. We figured it would be better than anything we could find here." She got up to retrieve it.

"Don't worry, there's plenty of time for coffee. Enjoy this morning with me."

They sat watching the rising sun draw vivid colors across the surface of the ocean and into the sky. "I am an artist, you know. I work in watercolors mostly, though I've recently become interested in pastels. The sky is my inspiration." He still faced the water but reached out to squeeze Noire's upper arm. "That, and the energy that comes from people. I am very sensitive to people's moods. I like your energy, Noire."

"Thank you." She felt bashful.

"You know, you show me something about Innocent that I didn't know he would do. You have a fire that I've never known him to seek out in . . . a companion." Mamadou seemed to choose his words carefully.

Noire tried to imagine what Mamadou might have seen in her in the twelve hours since they first became acquainted. "What kind of women does he usually go for?"

Mamadou laughed. "When we were at university, I usually went for the more bohemian women—the artists, the writers. Innocent was more content with women who appreciated the arts but who were not artists themselves."

"But I'm not an artist."

"But you are. You speak in three dimensions. Your voice is a Coltrane song. Your look is an adventure."

Noire was flattered and curious. "So I'm more fascinating than his past girlfriends?"

"Everyone has a story. But with some people, the story is more visceral. You make people feel things." He paused, seeming to consider his next statement. "I'm happy he's with you, Noire. I think you are helping him to access the part of himself that is like you. I think that this is why he and I are friends—the same thing. I am the part of himself that he can't wholly accept. But you are helping him to love it because he loves you."

"Sitting on these stairs seems to make me cry," Noire stated quietly. Mamadou had told her Innocent loved her, but she would have to hear it from him to believe it. She looked at Mamadou through glassy eyes. "There's just so much I wonder about with Innocent. I guess that's what a relationship is: you make it up as you go along . . ."

"But there's always the preface. And of course, there's never an objective point of view, is there?"

"There isn't." Noire dried her eyes with the back of her hand and blinked back the new tears that threatened to replace the old. She got up, figuring that a stretch would help her to recenter her thoughts. "Why don't we make some coffee? It's sure to get people to wake up; we have a lot to do today."

Mamadou thrust his legs out from under him and pulled himself to standing. He squeezed Noire's upper arms with his commanding hands. "Yes. But we have already witnessed the best part of the day."

The tour bus was full of black and Japanese tourists. Gullah Tours advertised itself as highlighting all of the historic locales in and around black Charleston. The tour guide, a forty-something native of Wadmalaw Island named Lutie, spoke with what seemed an indistinct West Indian accent and a West African cadence. She was fudge colored, and her words sounded sweet and soothing despite the harsh story they told. She shepherded her flock of tourists through the sites of former slave markets, taking care to note how the so-called slaves were cleaned and oiled before being put on display for purchase. As they walked toward the water at the heart of downtown, Lutie pointed out where the central whipping post once stood and explained how pregnant women were sometimes made to lie barebacked on the ground, a semicircle of earth dug out to protect their distended stomachs, as they received their forty lashes. It was not an act of mercy but cheap insurance that the valuable cargo they carried would one day make it to the selling block. Stopping at Emanuel African Methodist Episcopal Church—the oldest A.M.E. church in the South— they learned the plight of Denmark Vesey, whose elaborate slave rebellion in 1822 would have likely succeeded in crippling the slave economy in the Lowcountry had it not been foiled at the last minute by a few enslaved

Africans who used betrayal as a desperate attempt to curry favor with their white slave masters. The news prompted the hanging of Vesey and five others, and mass hysteria among whites that further terrorized both free and enslaved black people.

Driving out of the city, Lutie escorted her somber group through the grounds of Boone Hall Plantation, contrasting the opulence of the main houses with the slave quarters. She told them about how the many plantations that produced sugar, cotton, and indigo, and especially "Carolina gold"—rice—drove the economy that demanded the trade in Africans as their primary source of labor. She noted that the Gullah people traced their line of descent largely from the Guinea Coast and Congo River Basin. Their distinct Creole was an English-based language with syntax, word borrowings, and formations from a variety of Bantu and Akan languages that hugged the African coast from present-day Senegal, down through Sierra Leone and Côte d'Ivoire, east into Nigeria, and south into the Congo. When the group returned to their own vehicle in Charleston, they were oppressed by the humidity and the burden of knowledge they now shared. The air hit their faces in hot gasps as they rode along.

Innocent reflected on the irony of witnessing this part of America's legacy on the eve of its birthday. "How does it feel to be an American knowing that this is your history?" he asked of anyone qualified to answer.

"Man, I feel jacked. There's no other way to feel." Alexander seized upon the inquiry. "But it doesn't make me feel any less an American. I mean, I'll keep my passport. Maybe I would have felt different back then, but . . ." He hunched his shoulders.

"For me, it's kind of someone else's history. I mean, I'm American—I was born here—but because my parents aren't, I'm removed from it in terms of tracing my own lineage." Arikè made her statement while navigating the minivan back to Edisto Island. "But of course some of my ancestors were sold into slavery too."

Noire pulled herself into her own thoughts and eyed the others suspiciously.

"This is where your mother is from. Doesn't it feel personal?" Innocent forced Noire's response but kept his distance.

"When I first visited Edisto Island at six, my mom told me that we had been field slaves on rice plantations. And my great-aunts and -cousins and -uncles had the complexions and African features to prove it. But my mom grew up mostly in Baltimore and felt ashamed of her Gullah background until she studied them in college. She taught me to feel proud of being from this place. And I am proud. We're the ultimate survivors. What we saw today makes me know that black people are survivors. That's my legacy." She turned toward Innocent, trying to register his reaction.

"But how do you reconcile your pride in being black with being American?"

"There's nothing to reconcile. I'm black and I'm American. I'm black American . . . African American. My history is American history too." She felt defensive. "The Fourth of July is just like any other holiday. You make it what it needs to be for you. That's why some non-Americans and even Native Americans can celebrate Thanksgiving despite this country's history of exploitation and genocide of Indians."

"Mmm." Innocent willed the tension out of his face. He took Noire's hand in his and closed his eyes.

"So?" Her voice was agitated.

Innocent popped his eyes open and stared at her. "What, Noire?" He looked at her with mock ignorance. He didn't want to say what he thought, but her eyes, and the looks of the others, told him that he had to respond. He chose his words carefully. "It seems silly to celebrate the liberation of a country that never recognized your people's independence. At least in Africa, we are celebrating our freedom from colonial rule. That makes more sense."

Noire ruminated on all of the African countries that had gained independence only to fall into vicious cycles of forced military rule, crushing economic policies, and seemingly irreconcilable ethnic clashes. Unsure that she should give voice to the thoughts that crashed into her head, she remained quiet.

"But you're missing something, Innocent." Alexander jumped in. "My ancestors *fought* for this goddamn country—"

"Well, that doesn't make sense either. What's the logic: that if enough black people die in battle, white people will somehow realize your humanity? Look at the millions of Africans who died during slavery. That didn't convince anyone that our lives were worth anything." Innocent shook his head.

Dennis lowered the volume of the David Rudder CD and turned to face the back of the minivan. "With all of the civil strife in Africa—and factionalism in the Caribbean too—as well as black-on-black crime *right here,* seem like the black man don't even value his own life *now!* Listen to what this righteous man is sayin'!" He restored the music's volume and pointed at the car radio. He sucked his teeth and turned back around.

Alexander shot his arms above his head. "Internalized racism! White folks taught us how to hate ourselves! *That's* the straight-up problem!" He affirmed his declaration with a sharp nod of the head.

"It's not as simple as that, Alexander." Arikè drove aggressively. "I mean, you're not wrong, but my mother doesn't hate my dad, and she didn't teach my brothers and me to hate ourselves."

Wading through the multiprongs of the conversation, Noire tried to steer it back to the original topic. "The bottom line is that I have *claims* on this land. I mean, I'm the descendent of Africans, but my great-grandparents *made* this land. Their blood is here. That's mine; that's my heritage."

Arikè's voice rose again. "As a black woman who's family is both from the land of 'the oppressor' *and* 'the oppressed'"—she paused dramatically—"my bottom line is that we have to choose what we hold on to and what we discard. That pertains to our culture *and* our family upbringing. Not everything deserves to be retained."

"So the U.S. should just throw out the Fourth of July?" Dennis guffawed.

"No, we just need to own up to what's negative about it so that we can denounce those things. But we can still hold on to the good stuff: life, liberty, and the pursuit of happiness, the Bill of Rights, Constitutional representation."

"Tell that to the Puerto Ricans!" Dolores's voice—which no one had heard beyond a few three-word phrases in two days—boomed louder than everyone's. "As a U.S. commonwealth, we have a governor but no voting representative in the Congress or electoral votes for president, and our language and culture are under attack. It's like we're a colony of the U.S. And don't get me started on the Indian reservations in *this* country. So much for 'the land of the free and the home of the brave' recognizing the humanity of its citizens!" She crossed her arms on her chest and heaved.

"Well, the U.S. has a long way to go." Noire's statement was a weary anticlimax. The seven brooded quietly. Innocent looked at their puckered lips and furrowed brows and closed his eyes. He had a headache.

Humidity hung in the air, making bathing suits reasonable clothing for an evening on the beach. The porch stairs looked like the top shelf of a cheap bar. Mamadou nursed his cranberry juice while the others quelled the day's potent emotions by pushing their limits of tolerance. Dinner had been pizza and leftovers, so the free-flowing alcohol soon took effect, slurring words and slouching backs.

"Man, you been so fuckin' quiet this whole trip. You need to loosen your ass up!" Alexander pushed his filled cup at Mamadou's chest.

Flustered, Mamadou responded quickly with *"Non, merci, j'ai déjà une boisson."*

"Man, what the fuck? Speak some goddamn English for a change. Loosen the fuck up!"

Dolores grabbed the cup out of Alexander's hand and poured it onto the sand. It splattered on his bare feet. "You didn't seem to mind that I was speaking Spanish when you fucked me last night!"

Arikè ran to the water's edge, screaming as the cold froth met her ankles in a rush. "Isn't anyone going to join me?" She plunged herself into the ocean just as the moon grew higher in the sky. "The water is freezing!" The others watched her as she splashed around for a moment, making her own fun. "Noire, come on in!" she squealed over the sound of high tide.

"But you just said the water is freezing!" Noire yelled from where she knelt, her knees buried in the sand.

Arikè ran back out of the water, chased by a wave rapidly advancing on the shoreline. She stood in front of the group, goose pimples rising on her flesh. Reaching behind her back, she unfastened her skimpy bandeau top, revealing wet breasts that stood at complete attention.

"Woo woo!" Arikè screamed as she spun her top around in her left hand, her breasts alive with motion.

Noire bounded to her feet. "What the *fuck* is your problem? This is *not* the French Riviera and not every homeboy is your goddamn man. Folks don't have to know what you got!"

Mamadou walked toward the house and Dolores burst out laughing. Innocent cast his eyes downward but remained sitting where he was. Alexander ventured to speak, his refilled cup raised high: "It's the Fourth of July. If an American woman wants to show her titties to her friends, who are *we* to judge?!" Dolores snorted.

"Shut the fuck up, Alexander." Innocent's voice was measured.

Dennis stepped in front of Arikè and whispered into her ear. He helped her to put on her top and then walked her back into the house. Alexander and Dolores wandered further down the shore.

Noire collapsed to the sand as she felt tears well up in her for the second time that day. She held up her head with her right hand and supported the weight with an elbow chunked into her right thigh. Innocent reached out and touched her knee.

"She was having fun, Noire. That's all." His voice was calm.

"She shouldn't have done it." Tears caught in her throat, preventing her from saying more. *Was our kiss just another "fun" thing for Arikè to do too? Did she mean any of it?*

Scooting closer to her, Innocent let Noire spill water onto his chest. He held her hand and let her cry.

Chapter 11

Show versus Tell

"We want all the gory details." Jayna kissed Noire's sweaty cheek in greeting and kicked her apartment door closed. She mopped her underarms with the back of her hands and wiped them on her cut-offs. "Feels like back home!" Jayna did a restrained cha-cha to the clave rhythms that bounced from her boom box to the four pieces of furniture in her stifling studio. Alan clapped accompaniment.

"Hey, Nate. Alan." Noire stepped out of her sandals and stood in front of the fan, trying unsuccessfully to dry the semicircles of perspiration that outlined her breasts against her T-shirt. "Well, the subway station smelled of hot urine and ineffective deodorant. And the rats were playing dodge ball on the tracks, girl! When are you gonna break down and get AC?" Noire needed an ice bath.

"Girl, we heard that your homegirl Arikè got naked in front of your man!" Alan held his lemonade to his bare chest and punctuated his statement with a death-defying snap. Noire plopped down on the cushion next to him.

"That is just *so* horrible." Nate offered his condolences.

"She didn't get *naked!*" Noire rolled her eyes at Jayna. "She took off her bikini top."

"But wasn't she wearing a thong? Look, thongs don't cover much last time I checked. Especially when you're bare breasted!" Alan shook his sculpted physique at Noire. She thought of the video from Miami Sound Machine's "Conga."

"Alan, can't you see you're making her uncomfortable. Let her tell her own story." At that, Nate crossed his legs in the armchair he occupied. Perspiration glued his undershirt to his slight frame, making him look like the "before" to Alan's "after." Jayna handed Noire a glassful of ice and a can of lemonade. Then they settled in to listen.

Newly distressed, Noire described Arikè's actions with more venom than she had originally felt, insisting that she herself was horrified, shocked, *and* embarrassed by Arikè's flagrant display in front of "not only my man, but Alexander and Mamadou as well." She lowered her eyes, ashamed of her sensationalism.

"She just doesn't care," Jayna huffed. "Noire, I'm sorry to tell you, but your girl's a ho."

"Can I get a witness?!" Alan held up his hand and swayed to the gospel music that lived in his head only for the purpose of telling folks about themselves.

"Was she raised around white people?" Nate looked concerned.

Jayna gulped her second can of lemonade and stared at Noire. Noire cut her eyes around the room. Since she would not mention her confusion over the intimate kiss and kind words that Arikè had also shared that weekend, she couldn't say anything more. Alan wanted drama, Nate pathology, and Jayna vindication.

"Well, Noire, better to know now than later. Chick can't be trusted." Jayna gave an unsympathetic grimace.

Noire shrugged her shoulders, then got up and grabbed another can of lemonade from Jayna's fridge. If she and Jayna had been alone, perhaps she would have tried to talk to her about Arikè . . . without telling her everything. But with Alan and Nate there, she didn't dare. Her feelings were not their business. She collapsed back onto the cushion and guzzled her drink.

Alan instigated a new line of conversation: the love lives of every black person connected to Columbia's health sciences campus. Noire shrunk back from the conversation; the three of them had enough fuel to go on without her. Once they had examined every permutation of every "scandal" they collectively knew about—with Arikè as a ready punch line for mediocre jokes—they fell quiet.

Alan tried again. "So, I ran into Mr. 'Down-home' Houston in the boys' bathroom last week. I'm telling you, Jayna, they don't grow 'em like that in the North. You *really* need to hit that before some white girl does!" He sucked on an ice cube expressively.

Noire's laugh was boisterous; finally Alan turned his attention to Jayna, who looked mortified. Nate excused himself to the bathroom.

"Girl, you just need to calm down." Alan leaned toward Jayna. "Don't think homeboys aren't talking about your ass whenever they get a notion. I say you need to party like it's 1999, because honey, it is!"

His tongue sunk into her delicate folds. She balanced on the edge of his desk, his computer monitor steadying her weakening frame as he plunged deeper within her. She poured her love into his thirsty mouth and he drank readily. Noire splayed her legs open further, high from her own pleasure and in love with the sight of his head between her legs.

She groaned loudly. Were all of his coworkers really gone? Innocent had assured her that even investment bankers went home on a Friday night in August. Noire ached from the intensity of his loving and brought his face up to meet hers. She kissed him powerfully, tasting herself on his tongue. Their eyes remained open. Noire wrote volumes of love sonnets with hers. Innocent stopped kissing her but continued to stare. He was transfixed, his heart threatening to overflow with emotion.

Black love, he mouthed, eyeing her new tattoo at the base of her spine that peeked from under her fragile Indian cotton top. An elegant red heart with BLACK etched inside, it punctuated the erotic exclamation point at the seam of her back. As she fastened her sandals, he imagined his tongue anointing the heart, then gliding over the curve of flesh rounding out the silk gauze of the Moshood wrapper skirt that hugged her figure. She righted herself and he was in full view of her skimpy blouse outlined by the molten chocolate of her skin. She applied a slick of tint to her lips and he felt lust claim the core of his body.

"I'm ready!" Noire flung her arms out behind her like a starlet.

She ignited every erogenous zone on his body. He stepped closer to her and slid his hands under her blouse. Her pliant breasts spilled through his fingers. He was engorged, and Noire kneaded the length of him, focusing him on an attainable goal. His toes curled and body flexed, he gushed liquid energy from every inch of his being. Exhilarated, he kissed her lipstick onto his lips and changed into a fresh shirt. They had dinner plans.

The décor of the main dining room signified its old-white-money past but was populated by its new clientele of inherited wealth. The maitre d' scowled at Noire and greeted Innocent by name. Noire raised her eyebrow and followed Innocent as he tunneled through the tables of quartets and duos making polite conversation over apple martinis and top-shelf cosmopolitans. The air-conditioning accommodated the dinner jackets and imported summer wraps of the restaurant's August patrons. Innocent handed Noire his blazer. They sat.

"Thank you." She stared first at the rows of silverware in front of her and then into the pale sea of trust fund–sponsored affluence.

"You're welcome." He watched her beautiful breasts disappear behind his lapels. "Do you want to leave?"

"The maitre d' knows you."

"Renée comes here with clients. For work."

Noire wrinkled her face.

"I wanted a nice place."

"You know *lots* of nice places, Innocent."

"For our fifth-month anniversary." He gave an uneasy smile.

Noire gasped. "Today's Friday the Thirteenth."

"Then I'm a day off."

Noire patted his hand.

"Do you want to leave?"

"No."

. . .

They sipped red wine and made small talk about the last few months: Noire had finished her first year of grad school in May. Innocent had brought on a new client in June and was hopeful that he had secured the business of yet another potential client by month's end. And they had managed to enjoy their first vacation together last month, their motley crew of travelmates notwithstanding.

"It's been an eventful five months." Noire felt a pang. She hadn't spoken to Arikè since the holiday weekend and she missed her. Jayna counseled Noire to confront her, but Noire had nothing to say. Her feelings had been hurt, but she still felt too sensitive about their exchange for her to risk hearing something she wasn't ready for.

"It has been." He looked into Noire's soft brown eyes and felt bad that he had been critical about her in front of Lissette. Noire was the most beautiful woman he had ever seen. "I stopped past the African Burial Ground this morning. On the way to work. Have you ever been?"

"Once. My dad and I went over there shortly after they discovered the site in June of '91." She noticed his hands shaking. "Why? Did you get a funny feeling about something?"

"It's hallowed ground, you know."

"I know." She searched his face.

"It made me think about what you said when we were in South Carolina. About the blood of your ancestors being here."

"They're *our* ancestors, Innocent."

He sat quietly.

"Are you OK, sweetie?"

"It's just—I love you, Noire."

"Oh, Innocent." Her voice was hushed. Nuzzling her lips into his cheek, she murmured "I love you, too" against his ear. As she rested her face against his, her breathing was deep and slow. He held her right hand with his; she raised a toast with the other. "To many more anniversaries . . ." She clinked his glass and took a sip.

"Yes," Innocent whispered. His vision blurred and he spilled red wine onto his white shirt.

Part II

Dénouement

Chapter 12

Closing the Deal

Innocent stared at the September 28 headline in the *Wall Street Journal*: WRIGHT RICHARDS ACQUIRED BY CALHOUN & MASTERS FOR UNDISCLOSED AMOUNT. Yesterday's internal memo had previewed the article's salient information: his company's CEO would step down and assume a position on the board of directors. The new company, now awkwardly named Calhoun Masters Wright Richards, would consolidate operations in the Calhoun buildings and relinquish 60 percent of Wright Richards's offices in the World Trade Center. Layoffs would begin to be announced immediately.

Massaging the serenity prayer into his temples, Innocent actively slowed his breath. The news wasn't new, but its declaration from the front cover of America's foremost financial daily made it irrevocable. And there was no comparison between the 65-million-dollar business of Wright Richards's 20-person Media, Entertainment, and Telecom group, and Calhoun's 225-person outfit that generated nearly 800 million dollars in revenue last year. He grabbed for his ice-cold coffee and knocked it over. It spread like liquid brown fingers across the newspaper's lead story, making the headline one big blurry word and coloring in the sketch of Calhoun's smiling CEO. His feet dodged the rest that rained onto the floor.

"Life's a bitch and then you die, son." Alexander slid through the open door and plopped into a seat.

"What happened?" Innocent wiped up the mess with old balance sheets.

"Jefferson, McRae, A. J. Peters, and Sabrina got canned a few minutes ago. A. J.'s wife is expecting a baby."

"Shit." Innocent's mouth turned to sawdust; that was his whole team. He noticed a confidential envelope from Renée's office sitting among his coffee-splattered mail and ripped it open. He digested every word in one pass. "At least you were spared." He pointed to Alexander with his chin.

"For the time being. I might be selling the *Wall Street Journal* in a second, yo. Don't sleep . . ." Alexander's voice was exhausted.

"Right now ignorance is muthafuckin' bliss . . ." Innocent shook his head.

Renée appeared in the doorway looking mournful. Innocent and Alexander shot up out of their seats involuntarily.

"Alright then—" Alexander sidled out of the room.

Renée pushed the door closed. "You saw my memo?"

Innocent remained motionless and wordless, letting her create her own entry point for conversation.

She nodded for him, sat down, and gave herself permission to continue. She cleared her throat. "Well, as you've likely surmised"—she flailed her left hand toward the memo without looking at it or at him—"we've had to make some hard decisions. We—Wright Richards—didn't have the upper hand in negotiations. Not at all." She tempered her voice. "It was determined that Calhoun's MET group is stronger than ours, and so we've cut your team as well as Nadia's and Connor's. The decision just came so quick . . ."

Innocent didn't blink. He watched her mouth move in slow motion, her lips forming words he didn't want to hear. He compared her erratic body movements to his stoic reserve. His stillness contained his anger. His silence hid his hurt. Restoring his sense of sound, he waited for the last sentences he knew were coming.

" . . . You'll be asked to report to Human Resources within the hour. They'll discuss your severance package with you. And of course we'll do what we can to help you find a suitable position elsewhere. I just wanted to give you some forewarning." She scoffed at her own words. "Innocent, I'm so sorry."

"Thank you for coming to tell me." He knew that she could have left the grisly task to Human Resources. She wouldn't have been the first.

Renée's cheeks flushed, and her hair was suddenly misplaced. "I've so enjoyed working with you." She gave a desperate smile. "This is almost as hard for those of us who stay."

Innocent's eyes turned to black ice. "There's no need for overstatement. Thank you, Renée." He offered her his hand.

She grabbed it for support. "Of course. I'm sorry." She rose, hovering above her seat as if unsure of her role in all of this. She awaited a sign from Innocent that she was free to go.

"I'll be fine." He stood up and inclined his head. Renée disappeared, leaving the door ajar.

Innocent started to gather the few personal effects he had in his office—his undergraduate and graduate degrees; his picture of Mireille; two starched and pressed shirts; and cologne, deodorant, and a toothbrush. He turned a tiny pewter pebble from Noire that said DREAM around and around in his hand, then dropped it into his pants pocket. He printed a few e-mails and forwarded his computer-based address book to his personal e-mail account. He jotted down the phone numbers that were in his Blackberry handheld wireless, knowing he would have to return that to HR, and programmed them into his cell phone. Then he looked out the window, rediscovering the view of the Statue of Liberty and New Jersey that had been situated behind him for the year and a half that he had this office since his promotion to VP. It was a nice view that he seldom enjoyed. With the street noise eighty-five stories below, this was the best of all city perches; he had a view that was serene and picturesque.

• • •

Innocent studied the midafternoon sunlight that polished his apartment to a high gloss. He clutched his two shopping bags of displaced office possessions and sat on the corner of his bed. The crooning baritone of the building superintendent issued a Russian dirge as incomprehensible as his feelings. Releasing the bags, he seized upon his thoughts.

He knew he had made the right decision not to prolong his departure from Wright Richards over a series of weeks. *Worse than losing your job is losing it and still coming back*, he reasoned. He didn't want to see his former secretary and former colleagues. Didn't want to be subjected to countless repetitions of the same battery of questions by all who felt newly empowered to pry into his life.

"What are you going to do now?"

"Will you be OK financially?"

"What kind of severance package did you get?"

"Do you have any family depending on your paycheck back home?"

"Will you go back to Africa?"

He didn't want anyone to feel like they could be critical of the black VP, wondering aloud whether he lived a life that was too extravagant for his own good and waiting to see him crumble under the weight of his own professional uncertainty. His pride was hurt, but he didn't need for everyone to be a witness to it. Better to walk out with his dignity preserved.

He thought to call Noire but figured she'd probably be at school. He could e-mail her, but what could she do except come over, look sullen, and hypothesize about issues she knew little about. He hadn't the energy to explain.

His cell phone vibrated on his hip. "Pokou here."

"I called the office but they said you left." Marcus's voice fought the sounds of the city streets.

"I got dropped, man."

"Hey, I'm sorry."

"Yeah." He loosened his tie and kicked off his shoes, listening to the silence between them.

"Look, what are you doing?"

"Rethinking my apartment's color scheme." His words bit into the phone line.

"Shit. I know. Hey, can I buy you a drink? I'm up on 23rd. Why don't we meet in the middle in like a half hour." Marcus was declarative.

"Not feeling social."

"But I don't want you to get into a funk about this."

"Too late."

"This could be an opportunity for you."

"Divorces are opportunities for second marriages." His voice crackled with sarcasm.

"Innocent, I'm tryin' to help you out."

"I'm feeling fucked up, Marcus. Can't a man feel fucked up on the day he gets fired?"

"I'm coming over."

"I might not be here."

"I thought you said you weren't going anywhere?"

Innocent tried to make his tone conciliatory. "Marcus, now is not the time. Not *now*."

"I'll leave you to lick your wounds, but we've got work to do. I'm on your side, black man. Don't forget it."

Noire called at six-thirty. "Innocent?" She whispered his name as though it would break from forceful articulation.

"Hey." His voice cracked so he decided not to say more.

"I'm watching the news and heard about the merger. I called your office and they said you left hours ago." Her words were streaked with unasked questions and hurt feelings that he didn't try to contact her about it.

He remained silent.

"Innocent?"

"Yeah."

"Do you want me to come over?"

"If you want to."

"That's not what I asked you."

"Noire, I'm being an ass. You can ask Marcus. If you come over, I can't promise that I'll act any better."

"I'm coming over." She hung up the phone feeling upset. He had spoken to Marcus and not to her. She called in an order to the Cajun Creole Café, took a quick shower, put on matching underwear, and redressed.

Arriving at his loft, Noire gave a momentary sweep to Innocent's ear with her tongue. She smelled of sweet oils and came bearing gifts. She spooned the food out of its take-out containers onto Innocent's nicest square plates and laid it out on his sliver of a table. She poured white wine and then summoned him to come and eat. As he lumbered across the floor, she inserted her CDs into his player and pressed RANDOM and PLAY. She looked at him and registered a smile on his face. Only then did she smile as well.

They ate to the penetrating voice of Oumou Sangare, the wailing trombone of Wycliffe Gordon, and the lush phrasing of Dianne Reeves. Noire watched Innocent's shoulders slacken and his eyes soften as he looked up at her.

"Thank you, Noire."

She smiled in response and let her toes wander up his pant leg. "I brought the peppermint foot cream."

Innocent's eyebrows created double arches across his forehead. "What have I done to deserve this?"

"Nothing, sweetie. I love you. That's all."

Innocent stood over a smoking frying pan in pajama bottoms and a sleeveless undershirt. They were two weeks into their new routine: Innocent made dinner on Mondays, Tuesdays, and Fridays, and Noire readily offered her unconditional love, willing body, and uncritical support.

"Hey."

"Hey, you!" Noire pushed the front door closed and approached Innocent from behind, planting a noisy kiss at the nape of his neck.

"I'm making lamb chops. Can you wash the tomatoes and slice them up for the salad?"

"I brought champagne!" Her voice was expectant.

"I already have wine."

Noire stared at the back of his tilted head. She counted minutes in groups of three.

Innocent switched off the flame and turned toward Noire's crumpled face. "What's wrong?" He frowned at her.

"Innocent, I brought champagne to celebrate my good news." Tears were beginning to draw slow lines down her face.

"What good news, Noire?"

She remained silent, suddenly unwilling to share what she had been brimming to tell him only moments before.

"Noire, what good news?" Still holding the spatula in his right hand, he motioned and flicked fried onions onto the floor. He stooped to pick them up.

"I won a fellowship. To study in Curaçao next summer." Her voice was quiet and unemotional. She sounded like a recording.

"I didn't know you had applied for that."

"I hadn't told anyone."

His stomach tightened. "Does Jayna know?"

She shook her head.

Recognizing the incongruence between the disappointment in Noire's face and her news, he added, "Congratulations."

She stared at him.

"Should we have the champagne now?" He diverted his eyes and invented busywork.

"With the meal is fine."

"It's practically ready. I just need to finish the salad. Do you want salad?"

"If that's what's on the menu."

"Noire, it's been a fucked-up day. It took everything I had to get up and start cooking."

"I'm sorry about that, Innocent. But it had been a good day for me . . . a really good day—"

"Until now . . ." He finished her thought.

Noire walked into the bathroom and splashed water on her face. She cursed the tears that seemed to well up in her eyes more easily nowadays than she had ever remembered. She was becoming an emotional woman in the way that she had always hated. She hated the tears, the ups and downs, the melodrama of it all. She looked at her face in the mirror—a face that was nearly twenty-nine—and willed it to act its age.

She flushed the toilet to explain her time in the bathroom and rejoined Innocent at the dining table. He had served each of them a lamb chop and a simple salad. A loaf of French bread lay on the table between the champagne and two empty flutes.

"Would you like to open it?" Innocent picked up the bottle and held it out to her.

She popped the cork without ceremony and poured it. They toasted, the only noise being the soft clink of their glasses and their first gulp. She picked at her salad while Innocent cut up his lamb chop and took rapid mouthfuls.

Innocent finished before Noire and cleared away his plate. He walked over to his CD player and put on Teddy Pendergrass's greatest hits. He looked at Noire—who watched him from her seat at the table—as he removed first his undershirt and then his pajama bottoms. He stood naked in the center of the apartment, staring at Noire.

She planted herself in her chair, unsure of what to do. She looked at Innocent exposed before her. She wanted him so badly, but she needed him to want her more, so she waited. He walked over to her, taking her hand and leading her toward the center of the room. He swayed in time to the music, his hips leading hers in a slow grind. Her hands traveled the length of his body, sending shivers down his spine. She groped for the fullness of his cheeks, her hands insistent and unashamed. Innocent buried his face into Noire's bushy Afro. He let her hair caress his face as he guided her body. He whispered what Teddy pleaded: "Let me make sweet love to you, baby!" his breath moist in Noire's ear.

Noire stepped back. She slipped out of her blouse, unfastened her bra, and wriggled out of her jeans and panties. Innocent looked; Teddy sang. They were bare before each other, together and apart.

"I love you." He threw her the lifeline she wanted.

She reached out and traced his lips, imprinting his words onto her fingertips.

"Noire, I love you . . . so much," he whispered into the space between them and stepped in to fill it.

She took him into her arms.

"Good morning." Innocent croaked his first words of the day into the phone.

"*C'est* Lissette."

"Lissette?" He peered at the hole in the bed that Noire had left only a few hours earlier.

"*Oui.*" She chattered into the silence Innocent left by his confusion. "I am in New York City. I will be traveling between here and Paris for a while. I have left Mounir, you know, but I am still working with *Développement du Tropics*. They will relocate me here or to Miami."

"Mmm."

"Aren't you happy to hear from me?"

"Of course."

"I am sorry about your job, but it really is only a momentary setback."

Silence.

"Marcus told me that he's been trying to talk to you about some business deals."

"You spoke to Marcus?" He threw his legs off the side of the bed and marched over to his coffeepot.

"He's the one who told me about your situation. He gave me your home number. So I think he might be a good resource for you, Innocent."

"I just need some downtime."

"That's reasonable. So, how's Noire?"

"She's great."

"What are you doing on Sunday afternoon?"

"I don't know."

"Let's have coffee. The three of us. I'll come over."

"I'll need to check with Noire."

"If she can't make it, I understand. But I'd certainly love to meet her. Let me give you my mobile phone number. I don't have a real phone yet."

Innocent scrambled for a piece of paper and wrote the number down as directed. Lissette confirmed the plan for the two of them; he'd report back on Noire's availability once he knew. She blew a good-natured kiss into the phone and hung up.

Innocent counted the coffee drops that dripped into the machine. 486. He drank three cups straight, then flossed his teeth for fifteen minutes. His gums throbbed. The phone rang.

"*Bonjour*, beautiful."

"You just made the morning good."

"My powers are far-reaching." Noire chuckled to herself. "So, what's shakin' at the love palace?"

Innocent swished mouthwash in his mouth and cringed as it hit raw flesh. He spit out. "I just got a call from Lissette. She's a friend from b-school. The one I bought my loft from. We used to date. Anyway, she's back in town for a bit—she lives in Paris but may be moving to the States—and was hoping that the three of us could have coffee on Sunday afternoon. I told her that I would check with you."

Noire decompressed what he had stated before responding. "So you bought the apartment from your ex-girlfriend and now she wants to meet me?"

"She'd like to have coffee with us, yes."

"And you said yes?"

"I told her I'd speak to you."

Noire weighed her options: she could join them and make it three, or opt out and make it two. She chose the lesser of the two evils but remained noncommittal. "When and where?"

"Four P.M. Here."

"Your *apartment*?!"

"She's a nice person, Noire. She'll probably be interested in hearing about your trip to Curaçao. She's from Haiti."

"Innocent, I should go." His neutral tone irked her. She needed to end the call before she said something that would ruin her day.

"I'll talk to you later, then."

"I'm having dinner with Arikè."

"Really?" Innocent stopped short of sending his regards. "Well, have a good day, Noire."

"Bye."

Innocent rubbed his eyes. Squinting into the morning sunlight that streamed into his windows, he decided to go rollerblading. He wanted the wind to air out his mind, and the remnants of rush-hour traffic to keep his reaction time quick and thoughts short.

Arikè's knee rested against Noire's leg. Her eyes were closed as she hummed loudly to the soulful moaning of Phyllis Hyman. Noire tried to latch on to the loose threads of conversation that rose from the clusters of wrapped heads and manicured dreadlocks seated around them at the Cajun Creole Café. She hadn't seen Arikè since July. The song ended and Arikè opened her eyes. Noire saw tears in them.

"I love her so much." Arikè pulled her napkin from her lap and dabbed. "When she died I thought I had lost my soulmate."

Noire admired the neat french manicure on Arikè's tiny hands and her not-quite-corporate vintage Patrick Kelly suit that paid homage to every curve of her petite frame. When Noire had hugged her in greeting, she didn't want to let go, so soft and delicately scented was the midnight blue fabric. They had already exchanged opening pleasantries and had tacitly forgiven each other their former indiscretions, thankful that absence had made their hearts grow fonder.

Noire's emotions were a mishmash. When she talked to Arikè on their own, she got the kind of adrenaline rush one gets when a person really likes and affirms someone. She made Noire feel loved and fun and funny. She liked to feel that way. And, more than with any of her other female friends, Noire was always aware of how attractive she was. Arikè was like a sensuous fabric on her naked skin. She wasn't in love with the fabric, but she liked how it felt when it touched her.

Arikè giggled as she shared the news of her recent move into Dennis's house nearly three months ago after she took the New York State Bar Exam at the end of July.

"My dad isn't too happy about it. He says that I'm going to make things unbalanced between the two of us because it's his house. But the thing is, I don't own a house and I was being kicked out of NYU housing and I don't have any money on my fellowship's salary. I'm poorer than I was after I finished Spelman. And we've been together for a year and a half already. It just made sense."

"But if you could have gotten an apartment, would you still have made this decision?"

"I guess so . . . I don't know. But what's the point in imagining scenarios that aren't real?"

"Because they can help you to be clear."

"I am clear. Dennis is my lover and my friend. He makes me feel safe and special and he doesn't think I'm weird or a freak or whatever."

"Who thinks you're a freak?" Noire's eyes grew large with concern.

"Do you know what Dennis whispered to me that night on the beach?"

She winced, unprepared for Arikè to bring it up.

"He said, 'Baby, don't give folks more than they can handle.' And when we went back to our room he undressed me and gave me a bath. He even washed my hair." Arikè's eyes grew soft with the memory.

Noire saw the conviction in Arikè as she stared at her. Her mind filled up with all the harsh thoughts she had had during that same incident on the beach. But in all those thoughts, she had never wondered what Dennis said to Arikè. Not once. Noire dropped her eyes and piled rice onto her fork.

"How's Innocent?"

"He's having sort of a rough time these days . . . after the merger. He got canned."

"Oh no," she cooed.

"Yeah." Noire crunched on her blackened catfish. "And, one of Innocent's b-school classmates—a woman who he dated—is back in town and wants to meet me."

"What's that all about?"

"I don't know. But apparently she's the one he bought the apartment from."

"Yuck."

The anxiety in her face demanded a longer answer.

"I guess I'm just always skeptical of these 'friendships' that folks have with their exes. I mean, they broke up for a reason, right. Friendships between former fuck-buddies present challenges." She pushed too many green beans into her mouth. "And the fact that he lives in her space too! It's like he can't get away from her memory." Arikè shook her head and proceeded to finish her meal.

Noire lost her appetite. Her imagination ran amuck; she imagined Lissette contaminating Innocent's thoughts as he made love to her in his apartment. How often did he fantasize about her? Would he forget and call out her name one day?

"What do you think I should do?"

"About what?"

"About Lissette? She's coming over to Innocent's place to have coffee with us on Sunday."

"Meet her. But look beautiful and make it clear that her relationship with Innocent is black history. Be gracious but not too friendly. And after an hour and a half, see her to the door. Then fuck Innocent's brains out."

Noire laughed.

"I'm serious. Make sure that he's clear that you're the better woman—you look better, you have more grace, and you can turn him out. You don't need him making any comparisons."

Intimidation painted her thoughts green and her heart yellow. Noire feared she couldn't offer him the cosmopolitan business savvy and designer tastes that she supposed Lissette possessed. "I've already done the work for him."

"Well then, Noire, you have three days to get yourself together. Remember, he's with you, not with her. Don't psyche yourself out. OK?" She reached out and grabbed Noire's hand that lay at the edge of the table, pulling it to her lips. "I love you, Noire. You'll be fine."

When Noire arrived at Innocent's apartment at three-thirty, he was just stepping out of the shower. This was only the second time she had used her keys to his apartment. The loft smelled of Ajax and eucalyptus and sparkled like new money. She offered to oil him down.

"To what do I owe the pleasure?" was his response, spoken from the bathroom.

She remained quiet, wanting him to see her before she said any more. As she thought he would, he peeked out the door. She arranged the sunflowers that she had brought with her in a vase of handblown aqua glass.

"Noire. You look exquisite." He visually fondled the softness of her GiGi Hunter cashmere sleeveless cowl-neck that hugged her buoyant breasts and then tapered against her stomach. Burnt sienna, the color made her skin glow and complemented the white-and-brown hound-stooth check wool skirt that flirted with her knees. His eyes traveled down the length of her legs, stopping to appreciate her chocolate brown square-toe lace-ups, the heels of which were unnamable geometric figures. He walked over to her and planted a kiss lightly on lips that glistened with understated color. He removed her wire-rimmed glasses and traced her arched eyebrows with his fingers. He replaced her glasses carefully. "Thank you for the flowers. They're lovely."

Noire blushed under the weight of his commanding gaze. "You're welcome." She retrieved his Urban Botanica body oil from the bathroom and Innocent sat on his bed. Standing over his form, she began rubbing his back and chest. She loved to touch his skin, loved the sheer beauty of his complexion. She rubbed him skillfully, adding a bit of heft to her strokes to offer a hint of a massage as a bonus. She removed his towel and adorned his lower body with oil, using the same knowledgeable touch. He now stood above her and she sat on his bed. Her hands were at work, her mind on the task at hand. She sought not to titillate Innocent but to assure them both of the rightness of their love for each other. Noire finished the exercise with a pat on his behind.

"Noire, you're too much."

"And you're naked, love. It's three forty-five."

He smiled and went about the apartment gathering up boxer shorts, jeans, and his favorite T-Michael aubergine boiled wool sweater. He dressed and sprayed himself with Creed. "Shoes." He fished out brown leather mules.

"Those are nice."

"Thanks. I got them in London a few years ago but hardly find occasion to wear them."

"Mmm."

He began to brew some coffee and placed a crumb cake into the oven to warm, and Miles Davis's *Kind of Blue* in his CD player. At 4:05 the doorbell rang.

"Who is it?"

"*C'est moi*, Lissette."

Hearing her silky French gave Noire a moment of panic. *Why the fuck is this woman here anyway?!* Protestations echoed in her mind by the dozen. She beat them into submission by the time she heard the knock on the door. Noire stood by Innocent, wanting to minimize any unsupervised contact between him and Lissette.

He opened the door and Lissette handed him a white box apparently laden with pastries. "*Bon soir*, Innocent!" She kissed him lightly on both cheeks and stepped inside the room. "Noire!" Her smile was broad and sugarcoated. She stuck her head forward for the requisite double kiss. Noire obliged, making her smile only a little less enthusiastic. "I brought some sweets, Noire. Hazelnut croissants. Innocent always used to like them." She smiled as if on a toothpaste commercial, her English sounding like a French lullaby.

"You're too kind," Noire said through partially clenched teeth. She took in her look: her honey-colored skin, doe eyes with the lightest hint of makeup, red pouty lips, and heavy black hair that lay demurely against the collar of her sage Stephen Burrows silk shirt dress. She had already unwound herself from her enormous camel-colored pashmina wrap. Barely three inches of exposed leg asserted itself between her hemline and the top of her fragile black boots, which added three and a half inches to her exceedingly well proportioned frame.

Innocent placed the box on the table across the room and returned to where Lissette and Noire stood. "I don't have many chairs," he apologized, "but why don't we sit over here."

Noire claimed a seat on the bed and watched Innocent walk over toward his desk chair.

"I wouldn't mind if we sat in the dining area. I always used to love to look out this window as I took my morning coffee." Lissette strode across the floor with authority. Noire left her perch and accelerated toward the choicest seat at the table. She hesitated near it and watched Lissette take the seat facing away from the window. It was a minor victory. Innocent pulled his desk chair to the edge of the table. He waited for both Noire and Lissette to climb onto their high chairs. He sat in his desk chair and grew small by comparison.

Noire got up to get coffee mugs from the kitchen and Innocent joined her to find three matching dessert plates. They arranged the plates, cups, and silverware on the table. Innocent filled three-fourths of Lissette's mug, two-thirds of a cup for Noire, and a full cup for himself. He sat the coffee down and spooned out the correct amount of sugar for both Lissette and Noire before filling Lissette's cup with cream and Noire's with skim milk. Noire noted his ease. He didn't ask questions to which he already knew the answer; how she took her coffee was just one of the many things that Innocent knew about Lissette.

He opened the pastry box that Lissette had brought and sat down. "We also have crumb cake warming in the oven."

"Thank you, sweetie." Noire smiled gratefully at Innocent.

"So, Noire, you're more beautiful than Innocent even said you were."

"Innocent said little about you." Noire made her face benign and recrossed her legs.

"I was telling Noire that you're from Haiti. She's going to Curaçao to study Papiamentu this summer."

"How exotic! You know, I'm working on some business deals in St. Martin—on the French side though. But people on the Dutch side of the island speak Papiamentu as well."

"Yes, I know." Noire sipped her coffee. "I've also become interested in Haitian Kreyòl." She pronounced it with as authentic a Haitian accent as she could.

"What about it?"

"Well," she cleared her throat, "just that it exists as a real language in Haiti. The fact that books are written in it and that the upper classes don't often speak it openly."

"I didn't grow up speaking it, but the house help taught it to us— my sisters and me—when we were little. I think Maman knows it too."

"But you don't speak it to each other or to other Haitians?"

"No."

Noire stared at Lissette, incredulous that her family refused to use the language that 90 percent of Haitians spoke, most as their native tongue.

"In Curaçao, as well as the other Netherlands Antillean Islands, it seems that all socioeconomic and racial categories speak Papiamentu."

"Not so in Haiti." Lissette's voice struck a note of finality to that part of the conversation. She chatted a bit about work, the joys of France, and her transition back to the States. Innocent offered fond remembrances of his time in Paris. He and Lissette traded innocuous bits of gossip about their classmates in Europe. Noire drank her coffee.

"So, where are you staying now?" Noire rejoined the conversation.

Lissette didn't bother to look at her. "Well, Innocent, you know I still have a fondness for this neighborhood"—her smile was pregnant with inside information—"so I'm at a long-term hotel just a few blocks away."

Noire shot a look at Innocent.

"I think I was telling you before, Noire, that Lissette sold me this place a little while after she moved to France. I was lucky to get it. It's almost impossible to hear about lofts in SoHo, especially if you're not tapped in. And I wasn't in '97!" He laughed, though nothing was funny.

"But I miss the place. This apartment was good to me . . ." Lissette looked wistful.

"What's past is past." Noire pelted pin-sized daggers into Lissette's eyes with her own. She watched her skin grow hot pink under her silent attack.

Innocent refreshed his coffee. "I've never known you to be sentimental, Lissette."

She forced a chuckle up from the hollow of her chest. Noire looked at the clock on the wall. Within forty-five minutes, Lissette would be gone. She would make sure of it.

"I visited Marcus and Lydia on Friday. Little Nile is just a dream. Makes me think that I'll want children soon. And their house is just lovely." This was said directly to Innocent.

"Yes, Noire and I have been up to visit. Marcus has certainly done nicely for himself."

"Lydia's a social worker," Noire interjected. "She works with children with learning disabilities, including one dyslexic boy; my little brother has it too. We've talked several times."

"Oh, is that right?" Her brow furrowed. "Does he attend New York City public schools?"

"He actually lives in New Orleans with his mother. He's my half-brother."

"I see."

"I saw him in March and he's coming up here to spend Thanksgiving with our dad. He gets extra tutoring and is doing quite well. Thanks for your concern." Noire watched the confusion dance across Lissette's face before she replied, "Of course, of course."

Innocent offered more coffee all around. They made perfunctory conversation, with Noire leading and Lissette following, her mouth set in a well-crafted smile. Innocent ran interference without success. When Noire bit into another croissant, he changed the subject.

"Mireille wants to study at Howard. She's eighteen, you know."

"Time flies." Lissette's smile was genuine.

"She just e-mailed me to say that Maman and Papa are letting her come over here to visit." He looked at Noire and added, "I just got the e-mail this morning."

"Well, I can't wait to meet her!" Noire masked her surprise with a look of happiness.

"Travel with her down to D.C. She shouldn't be alone." Lissette creased her brow.

"Since I have extra time on my hands these days, I'll be sure to. She's been corresponding with a Senegalese girl at the school."

"*C'est magnifique!*" Lissette sparkled.

"She'll probably stay with the girl in her dorm room and I'll just get a hotel nearby."

"Radu and Meeta just bought a nineteen-room home there. He's at the World Bank."

"I didn't know."

"You should get together." Lissette retrieved her Palm handheld from her black clutch. "Let me beam his information to you."

"Just write it down for me if you don't mind."

Noire fidgeted in her seat and then escaped to the bathroom.

Lissette handed him Radu's address. "Sweet girl." She switched into whisper-soft French.

"She's a great woman." Innocent was equally quiet.

"I'm sure . . . She looked distant when I mentioned Marcus and Radu." Her pursed lips overstated her concern.

"She knows Marcus."

"Mmm." Pulling closer to Innocent, she took him into her confidence. "Perhaps you need to make an *extra effort* to make her feel included."

Noire emerged from the bathroom.

"That's a good idea!" Lissette returned to her singsongy English and popped out of her seat, her little feet clicking briskly on the floor as she walked toward the bathroom.

Noire sat down beside Innocent. He kissed her cheek. "Thanks for meeting Lissette."

"She's your friend."

Freshly lipsticked, Lissette announced her intention to leave. She was twenty minutes ahead of schedule. Noire concluded that Lissette was a bona fide professional. She made her round of double kisses and flitted out the door with great ceremony.

Innocent kicked off his shoes and flopped on his bed. A headache wedged itself between the two halves of his brain. He turned his head weakly to the left and peered at Noire on the other side of the loft. Her back was to him, her body bent into the oven. He thought he should say something, but nothing seemed right: *Sorry? Thank you? I love you? Are we doing the right thing?* The only emotion he could pin down was anxiety. Seeing Noire and Lissette together made him anxious, like a schizophrenic trying to appease two dueling personalities. Which one was really him?

Noire kept her back to Innocent as she took the crumb cake out of the oven. She hovered between anger and fear. She felt she had been tested for no good reason, and she wasn't sure how she scored. But didn't Innocent love *her*? Wasn't he in a relationship with *her*? Her heart beating loudly in her chest, she ate a piece of crumb cake standing up.

Chapter 13

Hardball

Innocent pulled the hood of his windbreaker closer around his head. The early November sun that morning had been deceptive; he hadn't dressed warmly enough and now the sky was blanketed with clouds. "I'm reevaluating," he scowled at Marcus, knowing his answer was unsatisfactory.

Marcus clapped caked mud out of the spikes of his Footjoys and began to change from his sneakers into the golf shoes. They were in the parking lot of Pelham Golf Course at the northern edge of the Bronx. "You've got a goddamn M.B.A. What are you trying to figure out?"

"Fuck you, Marcus."

"Yeah, fuck you, Marcus!" Returning from the bathroom, Khalib came alongside Innocent and gave him a playful grin.

"Aren't you a twist on Mr. Rogers!" Alexander laughed at Marcus as he walked up to the trio. "We're all set."

Marcus stood up, grimaced, and sat back down to

adjust his shoes. "Alexander, you've worked with the brotha. You know he's a deal-maker. Tell him to get off his ass and make some deals!"

"All I know is that we better make our tee time. We *could* be watchin' basketball at Ballers and Shotcallers!"

"But you forget, we're high-falutin' Negroes!" Khalib stretched to warm up his back and arms. "Marcus is trying to join the ranks of Tiger Woods."

"I can't; he's Cablanasian . . ." Marcus got up and slapped his friend on the back.

Alexander guffawed. "You ain't right!"

"Look, I'm not mad at the brotha. If I could get paid like he does, I'd be whatever the fuck I feel like!"

"Don't say that too loud, Marcus. The incognegro police wear plain clothes!" Innocent snickered, picked up his golf bag, and started walking toward the course.

They paired themselves up according to ability: Marcus, with a handicap of four, partnered with Alexander because his was a fifteen. Innocent's six handicap balanced out Khalib's eleven. Innocent teed off, sending the ball far out into the distance.

Marcus nodded his head. "Looks like you've been practicing your game in your newfound spare time."

"I've always been good."

They moved from hole to hole, the conversation following as circuitous a route as their game. Bringing the basketball pastime of trash talking squarely into the golf arena, they chided one another on their skills. By the time Alexander stood to take his first shot at the ninth hole, Khalib had built a complete lexicon of jokes about his game. "Don't stress, Alexander. You've got at least seven more shots till you get it in. Plenty of time!"

"Last time I checked, eleven wasn't nothin' to write home about. Maybe you need some softer grips so you won't get so shocked by the ball. I've got some Silly Putty in my car!"

Running out of jokes, their conversation fell into the well-worn standby: sex and women.

"Khalib, I heard through the grapevine that your shit's on lock-down. What happened?" Marcus took a swing and watched the ball puncture the sky.

"Who'd you hear that from?"

"From all the homegirls whose pussy been hittin' the ground ever since you stopped catchin' it!"

"I'm dating Delphina."

"Delphina. She sounds Egyptian or some shit!" Alexander offered commentary without understanding.

"Believe me, Delphina's as homegrown as they come." Marcus returned to Khalib. "Why?"

"She's a beautiful, together sista. That's reason enough I would think." His tone was defensive.

"Look, I'm just tryin' to look out. There's a *lot* of beautiful sistas out here."

Innocent stepped into it. "Marcus, why are you always 'lookin' out' and your ass is married?"

Marcus looked at Innocent with disdain.

"How's Noire, by the way?" Alexander's voice was buoyant. "Now she's a beautiful sista!" He blinked heavily.

Innocent flinched. "She's good. Just won a fellowship to go to Curaçao next summer."

"Man, shit!" Marcus shook his head.

"What's wrong with you?"

"That's what I want to ask you! She's about to pack off for the summer and then what? She's a waste of your time."

"Marcus, why the fuck do you have such an issue with Noire?"

The four men stood at the twelfth hole like soldiers at attention.

"She needs to be dating some leisure suit–wearin' muthafucka who looks like Maxwell and thinks feeding the homeless is a job instead of a tax write-off. She's not your flow, Innocent. I mean, what do you think the future of your relationship is with her? Really? And you got women like Lissette and Naomi and even that South African chick who would hook you up in a heartbeat."

"This is a fucked-up conversation. I can't believe this shit."

"Believe it. Look, if we were twenty-five years old, I'd say fuck her for as long as she amuses you. But you're pushin' thirty-four and you've got shit to do. Noire's a distraction. She's probably the reason you can't make up your mind about shit!"

"You're a fucking mercenary, Marcus. You know, you never asked my opinion of Lydia and I never gave it to you. She was your choice. Let me make my own goddamn choices."

"Brothas"—Khalib cleared his throat—"let's just play this fucking game." He sunk the ball into the hole.

It was five P.M. and completely dark. Innocent opened the door, perched his clubs in the corner closest to his bed, and called in an order of more sushi than he could reasonably eat, thinking that he could fill up the hollow that kept shifting all around his body. He gave his credit card number and hung up.

Peeling off his clothes, he decided to take a shower. Near-scalding water pummeled his back. He took it like a well-earned punishment. Noire's image floated in the pool of water that gathered at his feet and coated his skin as he swiped the bar of soap across his chest. He heaved, feeling a physical heaviness from the thought of her. Marcus's words scorched his ears: *You're pushin' thirty-four and you've got shit to do. Noire's a distraction. She's probably the reason you can't make up your mind about shit!*

A distraction. "What the *fuck* am I doing?" Innocent whispered his words. Hot water ricocheted off of his head and drizzled into his mouth. His skin began to sting. He turned off the water and stood still, trying to recover by force of will.

The bell rang. He slopped out of the bathroom and across the floor to the buzzer and pressed it. Timing how long it would take for the delivery person to make it up to his floor, he dried off and slipped into fresh boxers and a T-shirt. Opening the front door, he confronted Noire's smiling face.

"Surprise!" She held his order in her hand. "The guy came up just as I got to the building. Nothing like a personal delivery!" Her jubilation was dead on arrival.

"Mmm."

"I was shopping in the area and thought I'd pop by. See if you got back. How was it?"

"It's been better."

"Who won?"

"We did."

"Great! By how much?"

"Noire, I don't want to talk about it."

"OK. Well, can I at least take off my coat?"

Kicking the door closed, he took her coat and threw it across the bed. Then he dropped down next to it. Noire sat on the floor, gathering her purchases between her outstretched legs.

"Please, eat. But let me show you what I got. Can you believe it? Lafayette 148 had a sample sale!"

She held up a clingy baby blue turtleneck, a brown suede skirt, and an assortment of textured tights. Innocent was quiet. She excused his silence as a by-product of eating. But when she noticed his hands and mouth motionless in front of his half-full platter of sushi, she narrowed her eyes at him.

"What?" His voice was a whispered roar.

"Why the bad attitude?"

"Noire, what if I told you that you were wasting time on me?"

Her lungs deflated.

"What if I told you that your love—our love—is just a passing thing?"

She felt as if he had thrown a bowling ball at her chest. *"Passing?!"*

"Noire, lasting relationships aren't built just on love. There's compatibility, having similar goals and complementary dispositions, having the will to see it through—"

"The 'will' and the 'love' come first. I have them both and I'm *willing* to work on the rest! What about you?!"

"Noire, that's unfair—"

"What's unfair about it? You started this fucking conversation."

"Noire—" Innocent cupped his head in his hands. He had no energy for the exchange he had just begun, but he felt driven to pick a fight with her.

"Look, just because I love you doesn't mean I'm supposed to be with you. I mean, you're immersed in the Ph.D. program, planning to travel. I've got to wonder, where does that leave me and our relationship? Noire, this is your life and you love it, but it's not mine, and I don't know how I'll ever fit into it. You're not even sure that you want kids. Where does that leave me?"

Noire was incredulous. Where did it leave *her*? "Innocent, you just outlined my life without even consulting me. Is this why you're sulking? Because of all the stuff you *think* you know? Innocent, living is an organic process. You're in my life and I love you. I love you harder and stronger than anyone else *ever*. That means a lot to me. I know that we have life aspirations that aren't a perfect match, but *life* isn't perfect!"

"Noire, you make me sound like some sort of a mercenary."

"That's your word."

"Life is about more than just romantic love."

"Is this supposed to be news to me?"

"Can't you just listen to me?!" He squeezed his eyes closed and forced the words to line up on his tongue. "Look, if the millions of Americans who are divorced from the 'loves of their lives' are any indication, love cannot always conquer all. Sometimes longevity rests in compatibility of temperament and goals." He nodded, affirming his own statement, and then added, "Before my grandfather died seven years ago, his fifty-four-year marriage with my grandmother was a perfect example of that."

Noire was silent. She hated when Innocent presented examples that she couldn't contest. How could she argue with the relationship of his eighty-year-old grandmother in Africa?

"Innocent, look, I have nothing to say about the relationship between your grandparents or anyone else. You know why? Because I wasn't there and don't know if they were miserable or not. In fact, I don't give a *shit* about how anybody else chooses to go about their marriage or sex life *or* career. I'm talking about you and me, period. That is the *only* relationship I care about!"

"Noire, I care about it too, but we're not sealed off from the heartache and headache of the rest of the world."

Noire pulled her fingers through her hair. "I shouldn't have come over and we shouldn't have had this conversation. I'm sorry I disturbed your evening." She silently repacked her bags and tried to beat back the water that threatened to spill out of her eyes. She couldn't look at Innocent, so she didn't know that pools stood in his own eyes. She reached past him and grabbed her coat. Slinging it over her shoulder, she carted herself out of the door and down the stairs before she allowed herself to stop and wipe her tears away.

Jayna and Noire settled into two graying overstuffed chairs, a sliver of a coffee table nestled snuggly by their knees. Careful not to kick the table over, Noire put down her chamomile tea and biscotti.

"Look, girl, I just don't know what to say. I mean, I haven't been in anything this deep before." Jayna concentrated as she measured four level teaspoons of nondairy creamer into her decaf coffee.

Noire drained her tea ball and fished out the few wayward leaves that had escaped. She looked up to meet her friend's eyes but they were cast downward. She slurped her tea.

Have you talked to little Miss Soft Porn?" Jayna smirked.

"That's harsh, Jayna."

"Getting naked in front of your friend's man is *harsh*."

"Anyway . . . In answer to your question, not really." Remembering her biscotti, Noire dipped it into her teacup.

"How about your mom?" Jayna took a baby sip of her coffee and added more cream.

"I haven't told her all the recent developments," she said through a mouthful of stale biscotti.

"Maybe you should. Not all the sex stuff, but . . . ."

Noire rinsed her mouth of biscotti and polished off the rest of her tepid tea in one gulp. "Yeah. I've just been sort of reluctant to say all kinds of bad stuff about Innocent because then she'd just tell me to leave him or something."

Jayna stirred the nearly white coffee before her. "That's better than what Mama would say: 'If you got a man with cash, you better hang on tight until you say I do!' Maybe you *should* leave him." She took another sip. "But your mom is really thoughtful about stuff."

Noire took a sip of Jayna's coffee, made a face, and sat it back down on the coffee ledge. "How do you know all that?"

Putting another teaspoon of brown sugar into her half-filled coffee cup, Jayna responded with, "Noire, you've been telling me what she's said to you for the last fifteen years! Her advice has been pretty on point all the way through."

"Except regarding sex!"

"True." They both laughed, remembering the conversation Noire had with her mom when she realized that Noire was sexually active. She was in college, and while they discussed Noire's boyfriend at the time, her mom advised her to wait a year before making such a serious decision. After she hung up the phone, Noire had walked across the hall to Jayna's room to tell her about it.

"Wait a year? A *year*! Shit, even the most understanding homeboys are not gonna want to *just* make out for more than six months."

"If *even*!" Noire agreed.

"I'd like to see what our love lives would be like if we heeded *that* advice."

"Well, we *don't* heed that advice and our love lives are still nothing to scream about."

"Yeah, but . . . maybe I need to get back to you on that point tomorrow. But tonight, I have my *fifth* date with fine Mr. Kwabena Reed!"

"Well, I'm scared of you!"

"Yes, be scared of me!"

"Crazy! Don't do anything Mom wouldn't do!"

"I can make no promises."

"Well, damn."

As Jayna and Noire laughed over that memory, Noire decided to stop by the house later so she could talk to her mom.

Noire sulked as she rode to Queens on the subway. How could Innocent just dismiss their relationship as "wasted time"? Frustrated all over again, she glanced around the subway car. So many faces full of unreadable emotion. What issues were most important to *them*? Nothing connected her life to theirs except for their common train ride together. If the trip were uneventful, they would disappear from each other's lives, perhaps forever, once they reached their destination.

But if something went wrong—say a mechanical problem or power failure—their vacant stares would become looks of panic and anger. They would be forced to confront one another; their lives would clash up against each other as they lamented missed job interviews or dates or pickups from the baby-sitter. The subway was a curious place where bodies touched even when lives did not. Was this a metaphor for life? Were people more comfortable keeping their inner selves a secret even as they accumulated bedfellows?

Noire struggled with that thought as the train pulled into the station. Stepping onto the platform, she said a silent good-bye to the people with whom she had shared thirty minutes of her life. Thirty minutes and then they were gone. You don't feel bad when it's only been thirty minutes, but what if you leave after almost a year?

"Whatever the crisis, I'm happy to see you." Flora looked up to see the smile in her daughter's eyes. She was spread out across the floor, old record albums scattered about her awaiting placement in their new home: a floor-to-ceiling storage unit that Noire's father had come over to assemble the night before.

Noire tied herself into a knot on the reupholstered sectional sofa. She was always surprised at how large the apartment seemed, now that it only held Mom's belongings. Her eyes swept the expanse of windows that made up the fourth wall of the living room and framed the dusk-covered Queens street six stories below. A long hallway ran north to south and led to two bedrooms unseen from where she sat. It was a stark contrast from her own segmented rectangle of an apartment.

She didn't want to betray her sole purpose for visiting, so she chatted for nearly an hour, delighting in her mother's stories from work.

"Marsha was suggesting that we try this new line of clothing, but I told her, 'Those pants don't have space for a real woman's behind! Send that catalog down to petites!' Being a small woman herself, she was almost offended. But I nipped that one in the bud too. I said, 'If you want to be large and lovely, you're more than welcome to join us. But until then, you just need to take my word on this one!'"

"Mom, you are too much!"

"Not too much; I'm just right! It took me fifty years for my hips to be ripe. I'm not mad at them!"

They giggled through several more stories until Noire made her entrance. "Innocent is questioning our relationship."

"How?" She turned her gaze to her cataloging.

Noire was grateful for the privacy. "He says love isn't always enough—"

"You both love each other?"

"Yes." She marveled at how easy it was to say that to her mother. "He says that we have competing goals."

"Do you?"

"I don't even know, Mom. He thinks we do. I mean, I don't know what my goals are."

"Yes you do, baby." She looked up to find Noire's surprised stare.

"I mean, I just don't see all this incompatibility."

"What are his examples?"

"That's the thing. They're not real examples. He keeps on talking about other people—his grandparents, parents, friends. But that's not *us*."

"Well, if it's him, maybe it *is* you. He's half of the relationship."

Noire puzzled over her mother's words.

"There's something to be said for not forcing a situation. No matter what you may think personally, you've got to believe that the other person's viewpoint is also valid. That's what it means to be in a relationship. If you can't do that, you might as well just walk away." She got up and stuffed her feet into her slippers. "Just a minute." She left the room.

Noire stared at the album covers full of gaudy writing and psychedelic colors. It was hard to believe that that music was current when she was a baby.

"Here." Mom walked toward her with a folded paper in her hand.

Noire opened it and looked it over, noticing the handwriting. "This is from Dad."

ETHEREAL

*I began to see
the we in me
when I stopped fearing
the you in you*

*Your words were no longer
misunderstood
because I didn't understand them
I learned to learn
your meaning*

*Your you morphed into
A we in me
My me joined your you
to make the we
my me never knew with you*

*Disagreements meant
no more than
not agreeing
Agreement is not affirmation
nor must affirmation be agreement
a-me-ment?
We know word play all too well,
to read metaphors literally*

*The unknown is sometimes knowable
But even when it's not
it's not bad for the not knowing
the we in me knows
not knowing is knowledge too
more obtuse, but also
more profound,
it is faith.*

On the occasion of our daughter's third birthday—Love, Paul

"But you weren't together?" She looked up from the paper and across to her mother.

"We were raising you. And that's a kind of togetherness that has to be selfless if it's to be successful. We had finally come to realize that. Being jointly responsible for another life that you can't control is the ultimate act of faith."

"Mmm."

Flora stared into her daughter's face. "Why are you looking like that?"

"Because I don't get it."

"There's nothing to get, Noire."

She frowned.

"Noire, the whole point is that relationships are not things that you figure out. You don't win anybody over by advocating for your viewpoint."

"I know that. That's Innocent's problem, not mine."

"I think it's yours too. You think that you love him enough, or that you're compatible *enough*. But time is the best judge of that. Allow yourself to be in a relationship with him. And take note of what feels good and bad about it. Stop managing the relationship."

Noire's body clenched up and her mind became heavy. She looked at her mother and wondered if she had been helpful when she made her feel bad. "I suppose I should say thank you for your words of wisdom."

"Don't say what you don't mean, baby. But it's always good to see you." She pulled herself up from the floor and kissed her daughter's forehead.

Chapter 14

Bang

A parade of Ivoirians processed through the arrivals gate at JFK Airport in a steady stream. Innocent scanned face after face looking for Mireille. Her Air Afrique flight had landed nearly an hour earlier and still she hadn't emerged. He watched his compatriots, their anxious expressions bursting into wide grins full of anticipation once they alighted on the faces of loved ones. Then they would yank their cumbersome luggage to the end of the passageway, their family members clapping and clucking their tongues in recognition and love.

At ten minutes into his second hour of waiting, Innocent saw his sister emerge, a woman dressed in traditional clothing for her debut in the States.

"Mireille!" His hand shot up into the air and flailed about.

"Ah! Innocent!" She clutched her floor-length wrapper skirt with her left hand and maneuvered her laden luggage carrier with careless swiftness.

"*Attention!*" He cautioned her to be careful of the

elderly woman whom she had gained on and who now stopped to rest right in Mireille's path.

Arriving at the end of the walkway, Mireille was greeted by Innocent with a hug and multiple kisses that bounced from cheek to cheek. He flushed with emotion as he embraced her, overcome with his own happiness. Her face held all of the wonder he remembered of the boisterous sixteen-year-old he had seen two years ago, but the time had sharpened its angles and her eyes held stories of young adulthood and first love.

"My brother has missed me!"

Innocent laughed, momentarily embarrassed by his display. "Didn't you miss me just as much?"

"Of course." She looked around. "Are you here alone?"

"Yes."

"I thought that Noire would have joined you to meet me."

He thought about the invitation that he failed to extend. "You'll get a chance to meet her in a few days." He commandeered her luggage carrier, negotiating it with care through the bustling airport. "Why did it take you so long to clear customs?"

"It wasn't customs. Immigration questioned me for a long time about my travel itinerary. They didn't like the multiple stops and open return dates for my trips to Washington, D.C., and Paris and home. They said that an eighteen-year-old who has never left Africa shouldn't have so much to do all of a sudden." She sucked her teeth in annoyance.

Innocent's sigh was barely audible. *Did being black always make you a menace to society in this country?* "I'm sorry about all that."

They jumped into their hired car that had been circling the airport for over a half hour waiting for them.

"I wanted to take a New York City taxi!" Mireille's eyes filled with romance.

Innocent pointed to the line that slithered along the perimeter of the arrivals building. "Tomorrow. But if we wait for one now, it'll be tomorrow by the time we get to the front of the line." He watched his sister's eyes widen. "Did you know that there are nearly eight million people who live in this city?"

Mireille frowned at the cold November morning sun and wound

Innocent's extra scarf and oversized trench coat tighter around her body.

"We'll buy you a coat tomorrow."

"Why not today?"

"Sleep today, shop tomorrow."

Given that Innocent and Noire hadn't spoken since their fight days earlier, he sent her an e-mail:

SUBJECT: Mireille is here

DATE: November 11, 1999, 7:33 A.M.

TO: Noire@nyu.edu

FROM: theINNOCENTone@mymail.com

Noire,

Mireille arrived yesterday. She wants to make your acquaintance, and I recall you being interested in meeting her as well. I'd really appreciate it if you'd agree to brunch on Sunday. We'll be going to church in the morning, I think, so maybe after 11:00. We'll be around 23rd Street.

Thanks, Noire,

Innocent

Innocent dawdled in front of his computer for a half hour and watched his inbox. But Mireille was eager to begin her first day of sight-seeing: the Statue of Liberty and World Trade Center before an early lunch with Alexander, power shopping at Saks, an afternoon stroll through Harlem, and dinner at Marcus and Lydia's, his suggestion of a peace offering.

At Mireille's insistence, they took a yellow cab to the foot of Manhattan, and then stood in a seventy-five-person line waiting to board the boat that would take them to the Statue of Liberty and Ellis Island. Innocent looked at the tourists as they ogled the skyscrapers that rose before them like beanstalks in a concrete field. Wearing "I♥NY" scarves and hats, they basked in the bone-chilling temperatures that made their windburned noses run and that pushed cold air up coat

sleeves and around exposed ankles. Mireille's own inexperience with
cold weather made her no less enthusiastic. She clapped her New York
Yankees mittens to her face as she craned her neck up to see the World
Trade Center's 110th floor.

"We'll be over there in a little while. The observation deck is on the
104th floor. It might be too windy to go outside, but hopefully they'll
let us out."

"What floor were you on?"

"The eighty-fifth."

"Of which one?"

He pointed to the first tower. "The one with the antenna. Alexander
is still there. We'll stop by briefly." Innocent wasn't looking forward to
seeing his ex-coworkers but thought he could be gracious for the ten
minutes it would take for him to say a few selective hellos and collect
Alexander.

Mireille huddled against her brother as they sat on the outdoor deck
of the Statue of Liberty Ferry. Allowing himself to be more tourist than
tour guide, Innocent marveled at the cityscape seen from the back of the
boat and the views of the Statue, Staten Island, and New Jersey to the
front. This was the city that he had called home since September 1993.
His first knowledge of New York had been JFK and visits to the INS office
to clear up his immigration status. Then his New York became West
110th to 120th Streets. It consisted of cheap and filling West African cui-
sine found along Harlem's main thoroughfares, male bonding of the
highest order during study groups and Thursday happy hours in Uris
Hall, and a refined identity shaped by meetings of the Black Business
Students Association and social events at International House.

He met Lissette at the latter, and his world expanded to include
SoHo. The early part of their relationship gave him ample opportunity
to feel the pulse of the eclectic downtown neighborhood—to visit the
art galleries and funky European boutiques and clandestine lounges
tucked along the cobblestone streets where supermodels and struggling
artists re-created themselves amid soft hues and expensive drinks. But
their time together eventually devolved into late nights and early morn-
ings with him struggling above Lissette's naked form. At the time, he
thought that they had settled into a pattern of relationship that was no

longer new but was comforting. Lissette did comfort him. But when graduation day came, they could not figure out what would hold them together a continent away now that Lissette was moving to Paris and they couldn't seek each other's bodies in the quiet hours of the day. They parted and called themselves friends. But he seldom talked to her. Their relationship lived through third-party b-school contacts or early-morning remembrances when his bed was dampened with his release from titillating dreams.

His work life post business school had worn down his creativity, suppressed his wanderlust. He had become a cog in the wheel. But then he laughed to himself, *Isn't that what I wanted? Wasn't I striving toward the prestige of a good title and a fat paycheck?* And now that he had neither, what was next for him? He hardly knew. Before, New York had been ready-made, but he would now have to remold it in his own image if he planned to stay.

Mireille had dozed off, jet lag still toying with her internal clock. Innocent shook her as the boat approached its first stop. Her eyes were full of alarm for the twenty seconds it took for her to remember where she was. Then she reclaimed her role as the enthusiastic New York tourist.

The little Buddhas and conga drums that lined the wall behind Innocent and Mireille distracted Noire. Elevator-music renditions of American standards spilled from tiny speakers that hovered above them at the Asian and Nuevo Latino fusion restaurant. Her body was riddled with nervous tics: she twirled her hair, tapped her feet, played with her chopsticks, and popped olives like sleeping pills. Innocent sat like a Buddha, his smile molded onto his face, his words benevolent and patronizing. Shy to speak in her textbook English, Mireille sheepishly answered Noire's questions with the least possible words. Looking at Mireille slunk back in her chair, Noire gave in to her own insecurity and announced, "French it is!"

Mireille was a dam released; she chatted about her time in New York City and her study plans. She told Noire about her impressions of the New York skyline, her visit to Alexander's office, and her walking tour of Harlem.

"It is a beautiful neighborhood. Some parts at least."

Noire nodded.

"And Marcus's house is just incredible. He and Lydia told me about the history of the house and the neighborhood. I would never have guessed; you never hear good things about black America except for the music. Lissette seemed equally surprised even though she lived here for several years."

Noire choked on an olive. "*Lissette* was there?" She said this in English and glared at Innocent.

"Marcus invited her."

"So he figured it would be nice to have the three of you over for dinner!"

"Noire—"

"I'm still waiting for my second invitation. Actually, my *first*! I just came along for the ride with you last time. I could have been anyone!"

"It all just kind of happened. Marcus invited me up to apologize and because he knew Mireille was in town."

"Apologize for what?"

Innocent felt a knot form in his stomach. He shouldn't have said anything.

"For *what*, Innocent?"

"We had an argument the other week."

"If I recall, you had an argument with *me* last week too. Were they related?" Noire's eyes gleamed fear and hurt.

"Noire, please." He beckoned toward his sister, who had been concentrating on the rapid-fire English, hearing the brusque tones even when she may have missed the meaning.

"No, Innocent." She sighed. "It seems that you can have an *impromptu* dinner with your sister and friends and ex-lovers, but with me you have to make a special appointment. And then you take me to some cheesy restaurant where we're sure not to be spotted by anyone we know."

"That's crazy!"

"What is? After eight months I still haven't made the cut! Have I?"

"Please, Noire." Mireille's eyes pleaded with her. "I am sorry." Limited by language, she repeated, "I am sorry."

"I'm sorry too." She smiled sadly at Mireille, then looked at Innocent. "Seems that I keep on feeling sorry for my actions these days!"

"Noire, we were having a nice brunch—"

"No, we weren't. It was *fake*, Innocent."

He was defeated.

"Mireille, I hope you enjoy the balance of your stay. I need to leave."

Mireille got up as Noire put on her coat and wrapped her scarf around her neck. She kissed Noire on both cheeks, whispering into her left ear, "I don't want you to feel bad. I like you. You are very pretty."

"*Merci*, Mireille. *Adieu.*" Noire walked out the door without looking back.

Still wet and wrapped in a towel, Innocent sat on the edge of the hotel bed and called Heritage Access, his travel agent. He had to meet Mireille in a half hour at the main gate of Howard University's campus, but he knew he had to book his trip before he had a chance to think about it further. He had the time, he figured, and the money. A few weeks in Paris before heading home for the Christmas holidays were probably just what he needed. As he confirmed Mireille's flight to France for Tuesday the 23rd and booked a flight for himself, he felt momentarily bad for depriving Mireille of her opportunity to experience Thanksgiving but reasoned that she had no expectation of the holiday and wouldn't miss what she didn't know.

He dressed, bought a cup of coffee and the *Washington Post* in the hotel lobby, and stood at the taxi stand. He arrived at the campus just in time to see his sister stroll up to the gate. Clad in her new coat, jeans, and boots, she already looked like a college coed. He shook his head, amazed that his baby sister was a woman. She waved when she saw him emerge from the cab. Her smile was radiant. As he walked up to her, she proclaimed, "I love this school, Innocent! I love it! I can't wait to be here!"

Mireille led the way to the Visitor's Center. Her stride was assured. She told him about her night on campus—the Senegalese woman with whom she stayed, the African Students Association meeting she attended, the food at the dining hall. One very tall fellow in richly embroidered West African traditional dress inclined his head and greeted Mireille with a respectful *"Bonjour, mademoiselle"* as he walked by. Mireille's face was a placid smile in response to his words, but once she and Innocent passed him, she turned toward her brother and showcased all of her teeth in a broad smile. "Seems that you met quite a few people yesterday!" Innocent ribbed her, touched by her exhilaration.

Joining six others, Innocent and Mireille toured the place that they hoped would guide her along her path to womanhood.

Innocent arose silently from his air mattress that straddled the side of his desk in his loft. He glanced across the room to confirm that he hadn't disturbed his sister asleep on the bed. Casting his eyes out the windows that faced northeast and surrounded his bed, he saw the promise of a new day at the bottom of the sky. The windows closest to him remained coated in midnight blue. He clicked on his computer and sat down at his desk, the screen reflecting multicolors onto his face. His mind was full by the time he began his e-mail to Noire. He birthed thoughts through his fingertips with great effort and urgency; they arrived on the screen in bursts and gasps. His eyes blurred but his hands remained true to task, resting on the keypad between ideas. The sky grew brighter, bathing his mind in the cold light of a clear morning. His words were earnest, his meaning arresting. He felt a lump rise into his throat as he pressed SEND and released it to Noire.

It was six-thirty in the morning and Innocent already felt emotionally depleted. He stretched his body prone, his legs shooting out straight from his hips and meeting the floor at an angle, his neck braced by the back of the chair, and his behind pushed to the end of the seat. He felt as though he might fall off, his body collapsing into itself and then spilling onto the floor. But he remained rigid, fighting gravity and fatigue to hold his position.

Finally folding under his bodyweight, he crumpled into the chair and awakened Mireille with the screech of the wooden castors on his broad plank floors. "Sorry," he whispered, then disappeared into the bathroom to get dressed for a spontaneous rollerblading excursion.

The sun was new to the sky when Innocent made it to the cycling and skating path that curved along the outer periphery of the West Side Highway along the Hudson River. Frosty air assailed his nostrils and rushed into his lungs, forcing him to exhale in strong bursts that formed a cloud before his face. The cold bit into his cheeks even as his body grew warm. He skated north. He shared the path with the few others who chose to greet the heatless Sunday morning sunrise with physical exertion. His legs drew large arcs diagonally across the ground; he raced to keep up with his thoughts.

Innocent came close to flying. He felt the displaced air as oncoming cars rushed past him on his right. His arms and legs coordinated to propel him forward making a *whoosh, whoosh* noise that sounded to him like wings flapping. His lungs burned from the air that fueled his prolonged sprint. He began his descent on the western edge of Harlem that became Washington Heights and decided to push east at 145th Street and turn left onto Broadway. The wide thoroughfare was alive with the swirl of city debris and early-morning bodega runs for newspapers, *plátanos*, *salchichón*, and *queso frito* for hearty Dominican breakfasts. Innocent decelerated and hugged the right-hand corridor of the street, the heels of his hands pressed into his thighs as he heaved in an effort to slow his breathing. He didn't know what time it was, but the small packs of children clutching Sunday School catechisms and rosaries in gloved hands, or being escorted by grandparents and older siblings, suggested that at least the first wave of churchgoing New York was off to their standing appointments with God.

He thought of Mireille. She was probably awake and dressed, wondering where he had gone. Stopping at the corner of 150th and Broadway, he pulled his cell phone from the breast pocket of his anorak and called his home number.

"*Bonjour. Allô?*"

"*C'est* Innocent." He apologized in advance of her questions about his whereabouts and encouraged her to take a taxi to church without him.

"But I made breakfast."

"I'm sorry, Mireille. I'm nearly twenty kilometers away from you; it'll take me at least an hour and a half to get home."

"I'll put it in the refrigerator then."

"That would be great."

"You know, I don't have to go."

"Please, go on ahead. Take some money off of my desk and make sure you carry both my phone numbers with you."

"Can I get a manicure afterward?"

"If you'd like."

"I noticed a place last time."

"OK. Take fifty dollars. Don't put it all in one place though."

"I know."

"You'll need to tip the manicurist."

"I know, Innocent. I'm a woman. We know these things."

He chuckled at her use of the word "we." "OK, OK. I'll see you I guess around noon, twelve-thirty."

"See you then!"

"And take the extra set of keys off of my dresser and lock the door."

"OK . . . Good-bye."

"Good-bye." He tapped END and snapped the phone shut. Then he began his return trip at a more leisurely pace.

Noire shook sleep out of her work-weary body. She had been up until three in the morning trying to complete a paper prospectus that was due on Monday. Her alarm clock screamed 10:00 A.M. from across the bedroom. She screamed back and wrapped her pillow around her head, holding it to her ears until the clock stopped its aural assault. She dozed, releasing her ears and hugging the pillow to her cheek. She lay right below consciousness, content to prolong the inevitability of the day.

The phone rang, jarring reality back into her head. She stumbled out of bed, her bare feet walking the cold floor reluctantly.

"Hello." Her voice strained to reach the minimum threshold of audibility.

"Girl, you still asleep?"

"Yes, dammit. What do you want?"

"You're not gonna keep friends like that!" Jayna laughed.

"I haven't succeeded in losing you yet!" Noire cackled.

"She's got a quick wit even when she's tired . . ."

"I was up late doing schoolwork. What's up?"

"That's what I was calling to ask you. You've been ghost. Didn't know if you were depressed or something."

"I'm too busy to be depressed."

"So you're in denial?"

"I deny that." She now stood barefoot in her living room.

"When's the last time you spoke to Negro?"

"Last week. Last Sunday. When I met Mireille."

"He hasn't called you?"

"No."

"He's fucked up, Noire. I'm sorry to tell you."

"I haven't called him either."

"I hope you're not apologizing."

"I'm not."

"He's the one who needs to come correct."

"Yeah, I guess."

"Noire, please don't sound so weak!"

"This isn't a fucking wrestling match, Jayna!"

"Look, I'm just telling you to watch your back."

"Mmm." Noire retrieved her nearly empty carton of orange juice from the fridge and turned it to her face.

"You've got to look out for number one."

"That's almost funny, coming from you." She boosted herself up onto her kitchen counter.

"What's that supposed to mean?"

"I mean that you've not made too many good decisions on the man front in a minute! Or are you holding back on me?"

"What do you want to know?"

"What's going on, basically."

"Nothing."

"Jayna, are you trying to tell me that you haven't been up close and personal with a homeboy in like eight months?"

"Noire, ask the question you want answered."

"Why are you being cagey, Jayna? Do I have to say 'Jayna, are you sleeping with anyone?' just for you to tell something to your best friend?" She chewed on cold pita bread.

"I thought Arikè was vying for that title."

"What the *fuck* is going on?"

"Noire, you haven't asked me a sincere question about myself in like forever. That's why you don't know shit. 'Cause you don't want to know shit."

Noire was speechless.

"See what I mean. You can't even make an honest inquiry."

Noire smarted with the remembrance of their last few conversations. She became defensive. "Girl, I *have* tried to ask you stuff but you don't say jack shit. You nearly shouted me down when I suggested you think about therapy."

"That's because I didn't want a suggestion. I just wanted to talk. Be heard."

"Damn, Jayna." Noire shook her head at the suddenly complex conversation. "Why didn't you tell me that instead of just clamming up?"

"Noire, when you call me it's to talk about Innocent and to tell me what Arikè already said to you. I am tired of trying to figure out where I can fit my stuff in."

The straight line between Noire's ears constricted, pulling her eyes closer together. She shut them, willing her tension headache not to take hold. "I didn't know that's how you felt. My mom said—"

"Your *mom*?! Why are you bringing her in to *my* business?"

"I just . . . when you told me about Spencer—your white-boy confusion—"

"So I'm *confused*?"

"What would *you* call it, Jayna?" Noire was flabbergasted.

"Why ask *me* when you could ask your mother!"

"Dammit, Jay, there's just no good way to help you!"

"See, that's your problem, Noire. You're trying to be my goddamn therapist. Save that shit for Arikè!"

She counted to ten. Slowly. "Look, I'm sorry, Jayna. Really."

"You've been thoughtless before." Her air of victory did not prompt her to be gracious.

"So?" She tried passive concern.

"What?"

"I'm all ears."

"Noire, I don't know what to tell you. I avoided Spencer like the plague for a few months. It wasn't hard since we had finished the rotation. But he saw me in the hallway like three weeks ago and confronted me. It was quiet but ugly."

"My God, Jayna! So what happened?"

"Nothing. He accused me of being cold and I told him that I did what white boys have been doing for centuries—fucking on the run—and that it shouldn't be new to him."

"You said that?!"

"Of course I did!"

"But why?"

"I sure as hell wasn't gonna tell him the truth so he can psychoanalyze me like you keep trying to do. Damn, Noire, he's over it. Don't *you* trip!"

"Just doesn't seem like you should have said that to him."

"Well, I did."

"And what about that first year that Alan was raving about?"

"It's not working out. He ain't ready."

"So you got together?"

"Yeah. He's got some skills but he just isn't coming correct."

"What's he doing wrong?"

"He just isn't doing it right. He doesn't make me feel special."

"Do you make him feel special?"

"Whose side are you on?"

"Can't I ask a question?"

Noire tried to formulate an appropriate comment when Jayna broke into her thoughts. "Look, I don't need to test the waters with a Negro for months and months before I know that shit is wrong. I can see it a mile away."

The insinuation of her statement edged into Noire's mind as the pause in their conversation lengthened. "I hope that wasn't for my benefit."

"Hope what you need to. All I'm saying is that Negroes need to respect the queen they have or we need to step. I'm not trying for a repeat of Mama's past, present, and future bullshit."

"Look, I'm sorry I didn't ask about how you were doing. I've been caught up."

"I accept your apology. Listen, Noire, I need to head out. We'll talk later."

"OK."

"Bye."

"Bye."

Noire's headache grew to a grapefruit-sized pain lodged at the base of her neck. She entered the bathroom, splashed cold water on her face, and brushed her teeth. She ran her wet hand through her hair and fingered it into a respectable Afro. Then she walked into the living room and plopped onto her desk chair, hitting the computer's ON button. She logged on to her e-mail.

SUBJECT: traveling

DATE: November 21, 1999, 6:21 A.M.

TO: Noire@nyu.edu

FROM: theINNOCENTone@mymail.com

Noire,

It was this time last year when I first told my mother that I wouldn't make it home for Christmas. I told her that work was tight and that the days off could prove detrimental at year-end. I had just made VP so my story was plausible, I thought, but Maman didn't think so. She made me feel miserable, but I still didn't go home because I didn't want to. I didn't want to break my flow . . . didn't want to lure myself away from the life that I have become comfortable with in New York. Going home was a tease for me—and a source of stress. At the time, I felt that going home made it hard to come back. And so I conducted an experiment. I just didn't go home.

A year later, I see just how unnecessary my experiment had been. The life that I thought I had doesn't even exist anymore. And, seeing Mireille, I realize how much I missed out on since I was last home in '97. Not going home didn't make me miss it any less. In fact, it's been exactly the opposite. My decision cost me celebrating my grandmother's 80th birthday and Mireille's 18th and the weddings of family and friends. It's curious what you do to create a life in a place that's not home. The concessions you make for the lifestyle that you've chosen out of want or necessity are immeasurable. And two weeks of vacation a year isn't enough. It doesn't make up for the other fifty weeks.

I'm going home this year. Mireille and I leave for Paris on Tuesday. We'll stay with our sister Charlotte and her family for a few weeks before heading home in mid-December. I don't know how long I'll stay but it'll be at least through the first of the year. I haven't been home for more than two weeks since secondary school. The trip is overdue.

Noire, I don't know what to say about what's going on with us. Maybe the time apart will make it clearer. I've never loved someone like you, Noire. Don't know what that says about me.

I hope that you have a Happy Thanksgiving and that your semester ends well. I'll call you when I arrive in Côte d'Ivoire. You can e-mail me or call me on my cell phone if you need to reach me.

Take good care,
Innocent

He was going away for at least a month . . . leaving in two days. Noire's headache spread to her heart. She slumped over her computer as if shot in the back. Ironically, the only thing she could think to do was call Innocent. She picked up the phone and dialed his number. Listening to it ring two and a half times, she had a change of heart and hung up. *Maybe I do need for him to just appreciate me,* she paraphrased Jayna's words. She stared at the phone, unconvinced.

"*Bonjour, l'etranger.*"

Lissette greeted Innocent as he rolled up to his apartment building. He was sweaty, exhausted, and stunned.

"Let's go in. It's cold. Mireille told me you went blading. She said you'd be back around ten-thirty. I got here at ten-fifteen. I didn't want to miss you."

They rode the elevator in silence and arrived at his door just as the phone began to ring. He fumbled around for his keys. It rang two and a half times, then stopped when they got inside.

"Guess I missed it."

"Oh well." She smiled.

"I'm a bit of a mess, Lissette."

"Why don't you take a shower? I'll make coffee."

Her suggestion was reasonable. He peeled off his outer layers of clothing and took off the in-line skates. Lissette stared at him from her seat on his bed. She had already taken off her coat and hung it on the corner of his closet door. When she bounced onto his unmade bed, her breasts giggled through her silk pajama top. Her dance tights clung to her figure; she sat with her legs carelessly thrown open.

"Mireille's been sleeping there."

"Um-hum."

Stripped down to his boxers, Innocent walked into the bathroom and pulled the door closed without shutting it completely. He lathered himself up, his erection pronounced and not about to disappear any-time soon. He rested his forehead against the wall and let the water run down his back. He knew Lissette was behind him a second before he turned to see her. She pressed him into the corner. Her mouth was insis-tent, her hands commanding as she reached for him and began to stroke him with her right hand. He felt her coat him with something, slip on a condom, and rub him again. "It's silicone based," she explained. He nodded just as she took him into her with a gasp. Innocent's body was on autopilot, his actions reactions. His hands danced across her breasts. Grabbing them, he suckled her right breast, hot water funneling into his mouth as he tugged at her nipple.

He felt all the blood drain from his extremities and into his core; his knees buckled. Lissette turned off the water and together they slipped into the base of the bathtub. She positioned herself above him in a primal squat. His hands stroked and fondled her blooming lips as she rode him. Reentering her, he propelled himself vigorously; he was flushed with readiness. Her scream broke out of her chest just in time to meet his. Their voices chased each other up the tile walls, echoing in upon themselves and falling back into the tub with their wet, limp bodies.

•   •   •

Lissette chatted with Mireille about Paris and fashion and all the "in" Francophone African haunts as Innocent packed. Their conversation was white noise that drowned out his thoughts. He laid out summer clothing alongside his heavy winter sweaters and wool pants. He put his whole attention on the task before him: setting aside a summer and a winter suit to put into the cleaners in time to be ready for their Tuesday-evening departure.

"Mireille?" He interrupted their conversation. "We need to go shopping for Charlotte and the baby. And we need gifts for Maman and Papa too."

"We should get something for Nasima's children."

"Nasima?"

"She helps Maman."

"Can you make a list of all the people we need things for?"

"OK."

Innocent continued his packing, his body as raw as his emotions. He hated his vulnerability before Lissette; he couldn't let her know just how confused and weak he felt, because once she knew, she could make him beholden to her. He didn't know what she would do with that power. He doubted she felt anything other than triumphant—her competitive spirit only a little bit stronger than her sense of entitlement—but feared being drawn into any of her gentler feelings. So he studiously avoided a head-on collision with her penetrating stare that bore holes into the side of his head.

Chapter 15

In Touch

Noire stood next to her father in the serving line. He placed a scoop of stuffing on every plate that passed him before Noire asked if they wanted ham as well as turkey. She and her father spent Thanksgiving morning as volunteers for the Resurrection Church Soup Kitchen in Harlem. Her father wasn't particularly religious, but he had developed a brand of secular humanism that incorporated elements of Christianity, Black Nationalism, Garveyism, and socialism consonant with the way he lived his life. His commitment to the soup kitchen was weekly, but on special occasions Noire joined him. Jabari, up visiting for the holiday, bobbed and weaved through the crowd, delivering glasses of lemonade and iced tea.

By noon they had already served a full Thanksgiving dinner to five groups in four hours. Watching the Resurrection clientele eat what would be the only meal of the day for many, Noire ruminated over the assortment of friends and family whom she would join at her mother's table full of smoked turkey, smothered beef ribs, and

Southern fried chicken in a few hours. This year Jabari, who had taken to calling her mother "Auntie Flo," made her family complete. There was cruel irony in watching people who were strangers to one another celebrate Thanksgiving as a midmorning meal in a soup kitchen.

Paul grabbed Noire's hand for the fifth Thanksgiving prayer of the day and whispered, "When you lose sight in one eye, be thankful to have it in the other. Life can be more happy than sad if you remember to smile."

She squeezed her father's hand and gave him a fragile smile before bowing her head.

Standing on the subway platform, Noire listened to Paul tell the newest story of his life:

"I remember hating my family for all of its neuroses. My mother loved the white blood that ran through her veins more than she loved her black ancestors who endured the repeated rapes and beatings that gained her her coveted complexion. When I left New Orleans, I felt I had left that self-hating crap behind. Your mother represented everything that I wanted to be: an unapologetically black person. When I first saw her, I was sure I could stand on her Afro and reach heaven. And in a way I did." He gave Noire's head an affectionate squeeze. "But my time with Celine forced me to love what I used to hate. Celine was from where I'm from, and so I had to accept that our background wasn't just bad; good things could come out of it too, like my love for Celine and Jabari." He cast his eyes in the direction of his son, who sat on a bench grimacing at a comic book.

Noire was surprised to hear him say he loved Celine and wondered if he still did. "Of course. She's trying to be the best mother to our son that she knows how to be. I just couldn't love her in the way she needed me to. Not over the long haul."

"But you and Mom are still friends and you never got married."

"I don't think I've ever understood your mother and me. She is the oldest and dearest friend that I have. I don't know if I could have been the husband she needed, though."

"But why not?"

"Because it never happened."

"What does that mean?"

"It didn't happen, Noire. Maybe we were so caught up in how our lives may have been different—"

"If you didn't have me?"

"No, honey. Believe me, we have never regretted having you. Never."

Noire stared at her father, waiting for him to say the right thing.

"Noire, hindsight is always 20/20. You know that. But it doesn't mean that the road not taken would have been the better road." He cleared his throat and continued, his voice stronger. "It's like, you didn't get into that specialized high school you applied to. You didn't get in. But that's where you wanted to go. I'm sure you were smart enough, and of course you could have done well. But you didn't get in. I can't say whether being there would have given you a better education or outlook on life. It's impossible to know. But you turned out alright in my book!" He laughed, his eyes soft reflections of his daughter's.

"Thanks for the endorsement."

"That's what dads are for!" He grabbed her hand. "So how's that guy you're dating?"

Jabari popped out of his seat and tackled his father with a ten-year-old bear hug. "What guy?"

"I don't know."

"Do you have a boyfriend, Noire?" He blushed for his sister.

She gave his head a momentary squeeze.

"You don't want to talk about it?"

"I guess not."

"Well, I'm always here, you know."

"I know."

December began like a bad dream. Noire was worn out from the semester, and her emotions were frayed cloth wrapped clumsily around her mind. Her life had become miserable, she concluded in a moment of clarity. She was a poor graduate student who did nothing but read foreign-language books that most people didn't know existed and the rest didn't even care. Her man was an ocean away and maybe wasn't her man anymore, it was Friday night, and she had PMS.

Noire decided against calling Jayna. She still reeled from her indictment that she was a thoughtless friend. She knew a fresh dose of self-centered anguish might have unpleasant repercussions months later. She flipped through her Filofax, glancing at the names of her classmates and a host of fair-weather friends. She needed to fill her head with the voice of someone she actually cared about. She called Arikè, who answered on the first ring and kissed her hello through the phone.

"I'm making chocolate pudding and I rented this sort of erotic movie. Dennis is away on business. Come over! We'll have a slumber party!"

Noire agreed before she understood what Arikè had said. They jumped off the phone and Noire collected her toothbrush, clean underwear, a big T-shirt, and a bottle of gin. Feeling suddenly extravagant, she took the six-dollar taxi ride over to the house, arriving in record time.

Arikè came to the door in Dennis's rugby shirt and booties. Her face was scrubbed clean and her hair a curly tumble across her head. Her hug made Noire feel special and loved.

"I brought gin!"

"Well, it's on now!" Arikè giggled.

Leaving her coat, shoes, jeans, and bra in a heap, Noire joined Arikè in the kitchen as she took the chilled pudding out of the refrigerator. She drew smiley faces on each with whipped cream and handed Noire a spoon.

They settled into the avalanche of pillows and cushions that lined the far wall of the living room and Arikè pressed PLAY on the VCR remote control. "Have you seen this? It's about two Indian women who fall in love."

Noire raised her eyebrows.

"It didn't get great reviews"—she began eating her pudding as she stared at the opening credits—"but I always wanted to see it."

"Arikè, are you bi?"

She faced Noire squarely. "I can find women beautiful and sexy. Does that make me bi?"

"I don't know."

"I don't know and I don't really care." She poured her glass halfway with gin. It sizzled on the pile of ice cubes that rose up from the bottom. Then she began filling Noire's cup. "Tell me when to stop."

An hour into the film, Noire felt warm, her body moist with desire. She reached out to the nape of Arikè's neck, her fingers sinking into her hair as she massaged the base of her head. Arikè let an appreciative groan escape her lips. She closed her eyes and Noire took it as a sign to continue her exploration. She traced Arikè's lips with her fingertip. Arikè eased herself into a fully prone position, giving Noire a better vantage point from which to look at her beauty. Arikè's face was a work of perfection as Noire beheld it. She wanted to see if she found the rest of her body to be equally as perfect.

With her hands, she pushed Arikè's rugby shirt up from the bottom, revealing first her pierced navel and then her golden breasts. She stared at her with new eyes. Noire gasped along with Arikè as she realized her breasts fit perfectly into her hands. Arikè pulled her shirt over her head. Pink lace panties were her only modesty.

"You're beautiful," Noire whispered, her fingers fluttering across skin that felt like silk and smelled of vanilla.

Arikè opened her eyes and smiled. She rose up onto her elbows. "Can I see you?"

Noire pulled her shirt off and cradled her elbows in opposite hands. Arikè removed Noire's arms with a gentle movement of her hand.

"You have the most amazing breasts I've ever seen." She bent her head to them, brushing them with her lips. Her tongue met Noire's nipple like a wet feather. Noire held Arikè's head in her hands, enjoying the feeling of her face nuzzling her chest, her warm breath issuing from her nose. She felt like they were in a two-person cocoon, removed from the questions of the rest of the world.

Using the tip of her tongue, Arikè traced a continuous line from the peaks of either breast up along the underside of her chin and landing in a wispy graze of her lips. Noire let her introduce her tongue into her mouth, tasting it, feeling the velvet of her tongue meeting hers. They kissed languidly at first, then gathered intensity as Arikè's playful touch visited delights along her belly and at the small of her back. Noire followed her gentle lead; she continued to fondle Arikè's breasts and nibble on her earlobes, lips, and neck, their softness exciting new sensitivities in her. Their legs entwined, she relished the novelty of her petite perfection in communion with her. Noire felt her loins tighten. Arikè responded in kind, her hands clutching at pillows to steady herself as she sank into an orgasmic haze. Noire didn't know when hers began or ended. She just felt a warm glow encircle her body and send her off to sleep in Arikè's arms.

Noire stared at the sight of Arikè—asleep and unclad—in amazement. She glowed like uncut diamonds in the fragile sunlight. Noire moved, knowing she would wake her.

"Hey." Arikè rubbed her eyes and gave Noire an early morning smile.

"Morning." Her voice was tentative. She reached for her T-shirt, trying to cover up her freedom with something more familiar.

Arikè stopped her with her hand. "Thank you for sharing yourself with me. I needed you in more ways than you can know."

Noire hugged Arikè to her. She had also needed the intimate touch of a caring soul, the sensual affirmation without qualification or explanation. She pulled her shirt on, knowing that she was covering up her body but not her spirit.

Innocent spent his second week in Paris with his oldest and most sincere friend, Mamadou. As an unsophisticated nineteen-year-old first-year at the Sorbonne, Innocent had followed the comparatively world-wise Mamadou everywhere he went, learning the city through the eyes of the seventeen-year-old Senegalese painter. Even now, fourteen years later, Innocent felt the thrill of spending time with Mamadou; he desired his good opinion of him.

Mireille still stayed part-time with their sister, Charlotte, husband Michel, and fourteen-week-old Bibi, and made the rounds with two other girlfriends from secondary school who were beginning university in France. Innocent had instantly fallen in love with his brand-new niece—the latest addition to the Pokou family—and was in awe of her facial expressions and sounds and even her peculiar baby smells. But after a week, he knew that their cramped two-bedroom apartment in the 19th arrondissement was taxed to the limit. Charlotte still slept on Bibi's schedule and sank into deep and fitful naps at four-hour intervals.

He was happy to see Charlotte, though he felt he hardly knew her. She was three years his junior, and at thirty-three, he hadn't lived on the same continent with his thirty-year-old sister for nearly half her life, having left Côte d'Ivoire for university when he was nineteen and she sixteen. He could not link his knowledge of her then with her life now. His teenage years had been filled with boarding school and academic holidays spent in pursuit of juvenile pleasures, which did not often include socializing with Charlotte.

Serge's death when Innocent was seventeen had irreparably damaged their tenuous relationship: Charlotte had blamed Innocent for the loss of her twin, and Innocent internalized her accusation. He and Serge were traveling to Innocent's girlfriend's Sweet Sixteen party. Fourteen-year-old Charlotte was home sick with malaria. How could Innocent have let Serge—then a five-feet-four, bony, ninety-five-pounder—ride on the back of their neighbor's motorcycle? The backseat of the car in which Innocent rode held only his girlfriend's birthday presents. Innocent hadn't caused the accident; the motorcycle slipped on loose gravel and Serge's lightweight body was thrown into oncoming traffic. But Innocent was the *eldest*, Charlotte screamed; he should have known better. The only Pokou sons, Innocent and Serge had a relationship that extended far beyond that of brothers, but to Charlotte, no one suffered as great a loss as she did. She never let Innocent mourn with her.

Five years ago—when twenty-five-year-old Charlotte brought then-fiancé Michel home to meet the family over the Christmas holidays—was the first time that she and Innocent talked about Serge's death.

"Inno, Serge was the other part of me that's been missing for eleven years."

"He was my brother too. My *only* brother. And my friend."

"When you share your mother's womb with your brother for nine months, the bond goes deeper than blood. He's in my spirit, Innocent. We knew each other before we knew ourselves, before *anyone* knew us."

Innocent wiped tears from his eyes. He didn't know Charlotte. He told her that. Not since she was fourteen. But oh, how he cherished her when she was little—his precious baby sister—before boarding school took him out of her day-to-day life when he was just ten. Serge joined Innocent at their boy's boarding school two years later, so their relationship grew. The one with Charlotte stagnated.

"Charlotte, I can only say I'm sorry."

"I'm sorry, too."

Their embrace awkward, they knew that they could never make up for lost time. Innocent would never be the older brother he wanted to be to her. But at least he had Mireille. In the years following Serge's death, Innocent had developed a strong bond with his baby sister, whose fifteen-year age difference offered him a big-brother ego boost minus the guilt.

Innocent met Mamadou in the Latin Quarter at an outdoor café in the student-filled *place de la Sorbonne* blocks away from the Seine River. It was seasonable December weather, but, though Mamadou was African by birth, he had long since grown accustomed to the curious French pastime of drinking hot beverages while sitting in the cold. His gloved hands brought his second latte to his lips as Innocent approached.

"Innocent!" Mamadou rose from his seat and embraced him heartily. Innocent felt him scan his face, knowing that soon he'd ask him what was wrong. They sat down and Innocent wondered aloud when they had last passed time together in a Paris café. He calculated at least five years, right after his first year of business school. Innocent had been rushed in subsequent trips or else they missed each other entirely.

"I've found a space!" Mamadou sounded triumphant.

"Where?" He sipped his recently arrived coffee.

"In Montmartre. It's wonderful. Right at street level and near the metro stop. There are four bright studios above a cavernous gallery and a bit of office space on the main floor. I can see Sacré-Coeur from my studio."

"You've moved in already?" Innocent laughed at his friend's eagerness.

"I started bringing canvases over. It's going to take a while." He smiled in return and sipped his latte.

"Where are you with securing funding?"

"This is a bit harder. I have one very rich Moroccan art dealer who put up seed money so that we could lease the space. But other serious investors have been less forthcoming. My partner hasn't been able to raise—"

"Is his name Mounir?"

"The dealer? Yes. How did you know?"

"He's my ex-girlfriend's ex-boyfriend."

"Ooh la la!" He pursed his lips in perplexity. "Not Noire? You haven't broken up with her, have you?"

"No, not her. And I don't know if we're still together or not."

"Who then?"

"Lissette. Remember, I dated her when I was at Columbia. She worked here for a few years."

"Mmm." He nodded. "And Noire. What of her?"

"It's complex."

Mamadou's eyes went soft. Seeing this, Innocent averted his own; he couldn't watch Mamadou look at him like that. It was the look that said, *Have patience.* He didn't want for this to be his fault.

"I don't know what to say, Mamadou. We don't think about things the same way."

"But her spirit is right for you, Innocent. And she loves you."

"You've met her only once."

"It is evident. The way that she looks at you, looks out for you. She has power and passion."

Innocent shook his head violently. "Sometimes it's overwhelming. She wants me to share deep secrets with her and just let the power of our love drive the relationship."

"Sounds like she has the right idea."

"Mamadou, when have you known me to just go with the flow?"

"I've never agreed with your rigidity."

"It's not being rigid. It's being practical. It's not always having your head in the clouds and your heart on a platter."

"If you didn't love her, Innocent, I'd say forget about her. But you do. You said so. Noire is a real woman who lives in the real world. If you open yourself up to her, maybe you'll find that she's just what you need."

"I don't know."

"Allow yourself to be OK with not knowing. And keep on loving her all the while."

Innocent called the waiter out from the warmth of the café. He reluctantly appeared with a coffeepot in his hand. He refreshed his coffee and ducked back inside before he was asked to do anything else.

"So tell me more about this artists' collective." Innocent chose not to utter another word about Noire; her name burdened him. He queried Mamadou on the collective, asking him how much money he still needed to open it and whether he had a business plan in place.

Mamadou explained that he'd have to amend it if his partner did pull out as he had threatened. "But maybe it would be a good thing. Right now he's slowing things down; he's not helping at all. Some potential investors have been scared off. They see him as dead weight."

"Maybe he is."

"But I've known him since my first group exhibition twelve years ago."

"But he may not want it as much as you."

"You're right."

"This is your dream."

"I just felt that I needed a partner."

"Only if he adds value."

Mamadou drained his cup and signaled that he wanted another.

"How many can you drink?"

"As many as it takes to keep me from freezing out here!"

Innocent laughed, then became serious again. "I'd like to see your business plan, including a spreadsheet of the numbers."

"Are you interested in investing?"

"I could be . . . I could be."

Noire decided to take up jogging. Just like that. In the middle of December. She donned her cross-trainers, layered on all the athletic clothing she owned, and set off for Fort Greene Park on Tuesday morning at seven-thirty. The air was raw and filled her lungs to capacity.

Unaccustomed to the rigors of her new sport, she felt her chest would explode after a half mile of effort. The park taunted her from where she stood, arms akimbo, at the corner of Cumberland and DeKalb Avenues. She reconsidered her athletic resolve as a cramp made a knot of her left calf. She started to stretch her unprepared muscles belatedly, muttering self-deprecating obscenities into cold puffs of air.

"This is a surprise!" Alexander was standing on top of Noire, kissing her cheek before she had a chance to respond.

"Hey," she eked out between pants.

"Do you always jog around this time? I've never seen you."

"No."

"Where do you live?"

"Ten blocks . . . Cambridge."

"Yeah." He nodded with recognition. "Innocent told me you were around here. How is he, by the way?"

"In France. Then home. Christmas . . . New Year's." Her chest was aflame.

"Right . . . He mentioned he was doing some traveling when he and Mireille came up to the office."

"Mmm."

"So how's Arikè?"

Noire missed the shift in topic. "Fine. She and Dennis . . . living together. Bed-Stuy."

"OK. Good stuff. Black love and all."

She nodded and attempted to breathe through her nose. Quietly.

"Look, I should jet. Workin' for the man, you know."

"How are things . . . after the merger?"

"It's tough. Innocent really looked out."

"Yeah. Well, have a good day. Happy holidays."

"Actually, I'm planning on having a little Kwanzaa–New Year's thing. Here's my card. Send me your e-mail address so I can invite you. And Arikè too. I mean, I'd like to invite them both. You can bring . . . a girlfriend or someone."

"OK. Thanks. Take care, Alexander."

"Later, then."

Noire turned to walk home. Her jogging career ended, she claimed defeat gracefully and stopped by the Cajun Creole Café for chicken and waffles before returning to the term papers that hung over her head.

Noire lifted her water-shrunken toes out of the bathtub and imagined the life of a grape destined to become a raisin. Submerging them back in the tepid water, she calculated that Innocent had been in Côte d'Ivoire for about ten hours. It was minutes to nine o'clock on Saturday evening and nearly two A.M. there, exactly a week before Christmas. His morning flight from Paris landed him in Abidjan at about four P.M. local time.

His e-mail sent early that morning had been a reporter's missive. After reading it the eighth time, she determined that she and Innocent were still in some semblance of a relationship, then she kicked herself for giving him so much power. He had drawn a thumbnail sketch of his time in Paris, mentioning how wonderful his new little niece was and sending Mamadou's regards. He said he was about to leave Mamadou's and pick up Mireille from Charlotte's apartment.

Noire watched the flickering light of her votive candles create warped pictures on the oily film of the lavender-scented bathwater. She thought about their conversation when he called a couple of hours ago. The delay in satellite transmission had made him sound physically and emotionally distant, but he said that he was happy to hear her voice. He supplied a two-minute summary of the flight and his reunion with his family, describing form instead of substance. She solicited no extra information and neither seemed to mind. Her most passionate words were good-bye.

Noire was chilly sitting in the tub but she wasn't ready to leave it. She scooped down further and the water grazed her ears and hairline. Her knees broke through the surface and rose like a small brown mountain range. She closed her eyes and forced her mind to rid itself of extraneous thoughts.

Her brain dormant, Noire let her hands wander across her cool, wet body aimlessly. The pure tactile sensations made her body soft and sensitive. Her hands continued their roaming, stopping first at her breasts, where she felt their weight and fullness. Her nipples were the only part that danced in and out of the water and the shock of the cool air against them kept them firm and eager under her fingers. She continued her journey and dawdled at her stomach. Caressing the taut skin, she admired the muscles that were struggling to assert themselves. Fondling her underbelly, she almost re-created Innocent's nibbling on the lip of skin under her navel. Noire's body responded with a tremor that caused the water to splash playfully against her legs.

Her hands traced their way down further and met in the warm V of her legs. Her fingers reacquainted themselves with her intimate terrain, sending spasms through her. They came lightly at first, then intensified, the contractions causing her to move involuntarily. Waves of her building orgasm crashed against the sides of the tub. Seconds chased minutes with urgency. The sounds she made were low but audible. Noire felt her anxiety exit her being and float out upon the water. She bore down and warmth radiated out from her body's core. The muscles of her stomach were still active with exertion as she slowed the motion of her fingers.

Resting her head against the cool porcelain of the tub, Noire breathed deep quick breaths and experienced all of the residual pleasure emanating from her body. Her eyes remained closed, their lids relaxed against the eyeballs. Noire thought of nothing but felt everything.

As the minutes crept by, Noire became aware of the cool water around her. Using her toes to break the suction of the bathtub stopper, she felt the water drain slowly away from her. Once she sat in a shallow pool, she lifted herself out of the tub. The ring of her phone butted up against her reemerging thoughts.

Hastening her ascent back to reality, Noire bounced out of the bathroom and into the bedroom, where the phone rang for the third time.

"Hello." Her voice was dusky and unused.

"Noire, can you hear me?"

"Innocent?" Her vocal cords awoke in confusion. She couldn't imagine that he would call twice in the same night. It had to be after two in the morning there.

"No, it's Cudjoe!"

"Oh my God!" Her body flushed and a smile kissed her lips. "Hi! How are you? Where are you calling from?"

"I'm in London for the holiday. My mother has been here on busi-
ness for the last couple months, so my father, Ama, and I decided to
join her for Christmas."

"And your fiancée?"

"That's a long story . . . we broke up—"

"What?!"

"I'll e-mail you about it once I figure out what the hell happened.
That's partly why we're here too."

"Oh."

"But I wanted to wish my favorite American a happy Christmas!"

"Christ-mas . . ." She said it like it was a novelty.

"Well, it's two A.M. here and I'm standing outside in the bloody cold
at a pay phone. I didn't want to wake anyone. I won't make this long."

"I'm just happy you called."

"I'm happy I called too. And that you were home!" He cleared his
throat. "You're a . . . a great woman, Noire."

His words sent an unexpected thrill through her damp body. She
smiled loudly enough for him to hear it. "Cudjoe, please give my love
to your family."

"I will and you do the same. Stay sweet, Noire. I'll e-mail soon as I
can find a computer! Happy Christmas!"

"Yes. Merry Christmas." Noire heard the phone click on her last syl-
lable. She returned the handset to its cradle and sat on her bed, savor-
ing the voice she hadn't actually heard in over a year but that she still
treasured. Noire's mind easily tumbled back to her junior semester
abroad almost eight years ago. The other students on the trip had
teased her that Cudjoe was just her "African experience," but Noire
resisted the narrow description. Sure, prior to him she hadn't dated a
man from the continent, but she and Cudjoe had connected on more
than just mutual exotification.

Cudjoe was brilliant. It was like he had another level of conscious-
ness that Noire had survived without for the first twenty-one years of
her life. She struggled to read all of the daily newspapers just so she
could have intelligent conversations with him. They debated everything
with the passion of intellectual foreplay. She couldn't get enough of
Cudjoe.

He had been equally fascinated with Noire. He was well traveled—
the son of a development banker mother from Jamaica and an econo-
mist–political activist father from Ghana—but he had never come
upon a woman more irreverent than Noire. Her lack of pretense
unnerved his sensibilities. She seemed ignorant of class and social order,
and sought out professors and petty merchants alike for conversation.
He marveled at the way she gave them her equal attention and carefully
considered their opinions even as she prepared to disagree with them.

"Noire, where does your 'attitude' come from?"

"My attitude? I guess I could say, 'I got it from my mama,' but that
would be cliché. I don't know what you mean anyway."

"What I mean is"—he measured his words—"why do you treat
everybody the same way? It's as though you don't recognize the differ-
ences between a janitor and a politician."

"I guess I don't think of people in terms of their jobs, Cudjoe. I
mean, a job can change. But your humanity doesn't."

He contemplated her words before he continued. "Of course, Noire.
But there are social conventions nevertheless—"

"You know what's funny about social conventions? They're
premised on what people think they know about other people. But so
often the knowledge they think they know is wrong, or at least relative.

"When I first got here, lots of people thought I was rich because of
my clothes, and some even mistook me for a 'dark white person'
because I talk like an American and have dollars in my pocket. People
revered me for things that aren't true about me. Fact is, many folks at
this university are a lot more well off and well traveled than me.

"But do I deserve any more or less respect based on these external
markers that change meaning from place to place? Believe me, in New
York City, nobody cares that I'm a book-smart black girl from Flushing,
Queens."

"When I first met you, I assumed you were 'like me' and I wonder
how much that affected my reception of you. Of course, I also thought
you were beautiful."

Noire rolled her eyes at Cudjoe.

"I never questioned where you might fit into the social hierarchy."

"Three things, Cudjoe: I *don't* fit into the social hierarchy. I *resist* hierarchy. Secondly, haven't you traveled enough to know better? And third, one man's chief is another man's slave. Isn't that slavery's miserable lesson?"

Cudjoe was singed by the flames that leapt out of Noire. "Fine that you choose to 'resist hierarchy,' but that doesn't mean it doesn't exist. And in terms of slavery, it *reinforced* social distinctions."

"To whose benefit? Not black folks!"

"Stop living in a fantasy world, Noire! You know, I've always been treated as a son of the professional elite, no matter where I went. By *black people*, Noire. Since I always went to school in Africa and the Caribbean, I wasn't subjected to the taunts about being black that I guess children in the States experience—"

"Black countries don't count!"

He ignored her statement; it didn't warrant an answer. He continued, "And so I didn't bother to question anything. It was only upon entering university that I began to examine the extreme classism that governs this society. I mean, my parents talk about these issues all the time, but it's all academic somehow . . . But still, I continue to be—my family is—upper class."

Noire balked. "So you probably wouldn't even talk to me in the States. I'd just be one of those 'kids on financial aid' to you. You'd be off enjoying sun, sea, and sand for spring break while I schlepped it back to Queens to catch up on my MTV."

"Noire, I can't even respond to that. You've got a lot to learn."

"Maybe I have, Cudjoe. But I'm supposed to be learning new things on this trip. So you can teach me the man you *really* are!" Her eyes twinkled with desire.

Cudjoe spent their succeeding four months together showing Noire many things about himself, Ghana, and life. As she sat naked on her bed, she relished reliving that time with him.

It was one A.M. Noire sat amid the sea of paper that was a roadmap of her exhilarating five-month relationship with Cudjoe: the poems written during class, the letters stained with palm wine and his own tears, the sexy notes he slipped under her dorm-room door. She read them all

in sequence, reliving the moment she received them, recalling the new-
ness of love and self-exploration.

She remembered when she fell in love. Two months after meeting
him, Cudjoe had borrowed his mother's car; they drove three hours
west along the Ghanaian coastline. Arriving at the fishing town of
Elmina, they watched the bustle of activity as the fishing canoes came
into the harbor after a night out catching herring and sardines, and the
self-possessed women who controlled the fish trade orchestrated the
complicated though equitable system for buying and reselling fish.
Elmina Castle stood in the background, its massive whitewashed façade
belying a history of war, colonial rule, and the warehousing of Africans
during the slave trade. Cudjoe and Noire walked inside. Rather than
take the official tour led by a guide, Cudjoe gave her a private tour of
the castle that incorporated a history of his family members who had
been sold, raped, born, and killed there.

His voice a rough whisper, he explained that his mother's people—
the Trelawny Maroons of Jamaica—had kept the memory of their
Ashanti roots alive through their aggressive resistance to British slavery
on the stolen land across the Atlantic. He described the misery of living
in windowless dungeons that housed as many as two hundred women
or men at a time, the sick, dying, and dead coexisting with their heartier
brothers and sisters who hailed from the African interior as well as the
coast.

Cudjoe dipped his fingers into Noire's tears and traced them onto
his own face. "Your sadness is my own, Noire. But we are survivors. And
your name proclaims the resilient beauty of our people. When I see
you, I see myself."

Her eyes wet from the memory, Noire read Cudjoe's eight-page let-
ter that marked the end of their relationship. It was full of affirmations
and love, but also concerns that it was not possible to grow a love that
couldn't live in the present but only relied on the powerful experiences
of their past. Noire felt melancholy but fortunate. She couldn't imagine
the woman she'd be if she hadn't loved Cudjoe. He had opened her up
in more ways than one.

Chapter 16

Alterations

Innocent left the family room with little fanfare. His father shuffled about the ground floor locking up the house. It was not quite ten P.M. and Mireille had already gone up to bed. He entered his childhood bedroom and looked around. The room had undergone a coat of fresh paint, and a woven bedspread that he was sure his mother had purchased for this homecoming covered his narrow bed. He dropped the tape that Noire had given him on their three-month anniversary into the tabletop boom box on his dresser. Nina Simone's adult tales spilled out into the nighttime quiet as he flopped onto the bed and closed his eyes.

" . . . *and she makes love just like a woman, yes she does . . .*" Nina interpreted Bob Dylan's words with throaty irony. Her third-person narrative had the authority of the feminine voice of God. Her words were thick, sweet, and sharp like licorice in a mouth hungry for food. Innocent pressed their meaning to the back of his head and let his thoughts roll across his body.

The day had been an hour shorter than usual, but its many nodes and barbs overloaded his senses. Seeing his father was a shock. Innocent had stooped over to hug his fallow frame; at sixty-seven he had been robbed of his broad-chested stance and was no longer as tall as his son. He was pensive amid the buzz of holiday-season reunions around them.

"Where's Maman?"

"Home cooking. Marie said seeing her firstborn is cause for celebration." His eyes were gray from old age and moist with emotion.

"It's good to see you, Papa."

"It's been too long."

"I know."

They sped along the main thoroughfare that cut through Abidjan's active Marcory and Treichville neighborhoods en route to his parents' cushy Cocody. The city, at nearly four million inhabitants, was fully engaged in the activities of a Saturday afternoon. Street hawkers plastered gadgets and foodstuffs against closed car windows whenever a traffic light or other delay made them idle for more than a moment. They skirted the east side of the skyscraper-riddled business district of Le Plateau before rounding the lagoon toward Cocody. Pulling into the circular driveway of his parents' home, Innocent saw Maman open the huge carved front door and hold the pose of a mother welcoming home her wayward son.

He knew that some people stayed away for a good deal longer than two years. But this was different. Whereas many of them had gone to find opportunity and success, he already had it and everyone knew it. His parents' pride made them quick to broadcast his professional accomplishments to family and friends who in turn stuck their chests out with pride of association, or else waited to hear about a change in his fate for the worse.

Such was the peculiar situation of those who traveled abroad for work and school. Had their parents' sacrifice been worth it: paying many more times the domestic school fees in foreign currency, waiting anxiously to see if they would remember their roots when it was time to fall in love and have children, wondering how the sacrifice of making one's child a world citizen would benefit all who remained in their country of birth.

As soon as he walked into his parents' home, Innocent felt the weight of his father's hopes for a continuation of his textile import and whole-saling business, and his mother's expectation of grandchildren that she wouldn't have to board a plane to visit. When he and Mireille arrived, they were greeted with a welcoming party of his father's assistant and two daughters of a prominent local family who Maman said "just happened to pass through" en route to home. He had noticed their driver sound asleep in the family's car parked in the driveway of his parents' house.

Outwardly, the mood was light. Celebratory. Mireille gave out the gifts that they had brought with great ceremony—perfume for Maman, golf accessories for Papa, Innocent's good secondhand jeans and barely worn shoes for Nasima's husband and growing sons, American logo-emblazoned T-shirts and American feminine toiletries for Nasima and her daughters. Tubourg beer, Youki soda, and fresh *bandji* palm wine fueled conversation as a hearty home-cooked meal filled stomachs, endearing one to the other. "Ona and Chi-Chi made the *foutou* and *attiéké*," his mother announced as the group indulged in the pounded yam, cassava, and plantain-based mixtures. Innocent knew that her statement was especially for him. She didn't care that she had just directly contradicted herself about the accidental nature of their visit. It didn't matter. All knew what was at stake so all played the game.

Noire's mixed tape lulled Innocent to sleep. Tomorrow the questions would begin.

In his first seventy-two hours there, Innocent got a crash course on the most political instability Côte d'Ivoire had known in its thirty-nine years of statehood since independence from France. A protégé of President Felix Houphouet-Boigny—the country's only president from 1960 until his death in 1993—President Henri Konan Bedie had become increasingly unpopular for his scurrilous economic policies and his nationalistic political strategy of "Ivoirité," which many believed to be antagonistic to immigrant groups and ethnic minorities. Ethnic and regional tensions throughout the country flared to a fever pitch, and many forecasted an outbreak of civil strife. At thirty-three, Innocent felt a disquiet that he had never known in his home country; he took to heart his father's para-noid entreaties to remain close to home and to stay off the roadways after nightfall. His unease softened the blow of not being able to take up temporary residence in the "boys' quarters"—obsolete servants' living areas beside the main house—because of his father's security concerns.

Innocent spent his days running errands for Papa across Abidjan and into nearby Grand Bassam. In his downtime, he examined the wares of roadside artisans and textile vendors, speaking in his rudimentary Dioula as market women chided him on his attempts to haggle prices in a language he hardly knew. Occasionally he slipped in a visit to one of the few secondary school friends with whom his twenty-year-old friendships still had enough nostalgia to warrant a couple of hours meeting their wives and toddlers. In the evenings, he would steal a half hour right before dinner to walk around Cocody and watch the setting sun glint off of the copper-colored towers of the Cité Administrative across the lagoon in the distance as his neighbors made preparations for the encroaching night. Returning, he was greeted by elaborate meals presided over by his mother and with a daily menu of hand-picked "guests": young women whose carriage, looks, and family background Maman thought fitting as a possible mate for her only surviving son. Some of them had been Charlotte's schoolmates who had managed not to get married either due to academic study abroad or somewhat plainer features and simpler manners than their contemporaries. But most were younger, newly emergent on the scene as eligible women who had the perfect combination of cosmopolitan orientations and Ivoirian sensibilities. Since his parents' marriage was an interethnic one, Innocent's mother was more liberal than some about ethnic heritage, but she still preferred Baoule or Abure women for him.

His first few days were full of inner conflict. Silently he raged against his parents' personal and professional plans for him, knowing that they saw his job loss as a sign from God that now was the time for him to return home, settle down, and head his father's business. But he soon learned that there was no need for protest . . . yet. He had nothing else to do and had articulated no plans to stay or leave.

As Papa constructed complex verbal assaults against President Bedie and reminisced on the early days of the Boigny era over the dinner table, Mireille shot sidelong glances at her brother, wordlessly rating the young women who sat across from him and next to her. Mireille seemed more entertained than annoyed by her mother's insistence to marry her brother off, but occasionally she made a point to unsettle a woman if she especially disliked her:

"Aïcha, you're so quiet this evening. Is that because you have no opinion on what's going on in our country? Do you even understand it?"

Though Innocent thought some of his sister's attacks to be brutal, he admired Mireille's ability to stand up for herself. She patently ignored Maman's admonitions and in so doing registered her own discontent with her tactics at landing a trophy wife for Innocent.

After five days of multiple female visitors for Innocent, she was fed up and planted herself at the bottom of his bed in the nighttime quiet of the house.

"Do you like any of these women Maman keeps inviting?"

"I don't like them or dislike them. I have no sense of them."

"So ask her to stop. Tell her you have a girlfriend! Tell her you have two!"

He looked up from his book. "Two?"

"Did you think I didn't know? I'm a woman; I know these things."

"What things?"

"That Lissette wants to be your girlfriend again. I know something happened between the two of you."

He remained silent, unwilling to admit anything to his sister that he would not encourage her to do herself.

"So, who do you like?" She smirked.

"What do you mean?"

"Inno, please don't play dumb. I stayed with you for two weeks!" She shook her head in mock castigation. "They are both very pretty."

"Who do *you* like?" He raised his eyebrows at Mireille, suddenly curious to know her thoughts.

"I like them both. Lissette speaks beautiful French and seems very refined. Maman would like her even though she's not from here. Noire was so upset when I met her that it's hard to know her personality. But she seems to really love you. I don't think that Lissette could love you like Noire can. But maybe you wouldn't mind that."

She pressed her mouth together, signaling the end of her assessment.

Her words bothered him, but he made his face slack. "You're perceptive."

"So you think I'm right?" She smiled broadly for her accomplishment.

"I think that you take the time to think through things for yourself. It's a good quality to have. But sometimes it's hard to act on what you know."

"I'm not going to let Maman marry me off to some big man she thinks has enough money and a good family name. *I'll* become a millionaire and then I can pick whoever I want."

"If only it were so simple."

It was the morning of Christmas Eve. Innocent sat up in bed and clicked on the radio. RTI, the state-owned national radio station, interspersed local and world news with an assortment of music formats, making the broadcast remind him of a potluck supper. He looked at his morning excitement rising from between his legs and contemplated whether he would go the route of relief or dismissal when the newscast was disrupted. Then, an unnamed military official announced that this and other media outlets throughout the country had been seized by the military and that Côte d'Ivoire was undergoing a coup d'etat.

"Innocent!" His sister's voice broke against the wood of his door.

"I heard! I'll be right down."

Noire sat amid holiday wrapping paper on her couch. She sang along with hip-hop and R&B Christmas carols on the radio as she struggled to create inspired designs from ribbons and bows. It was barely nine in the morning when the phone rang.

"Noire, have you heard?" Her father's voice was too gloomy for the day before Christmas.

"What happened?"

"There was a coup in Côte d'Ivoire. A few hours ago."

"Oh my God."

"I just heard it on BBC. It was breaking news. The newscaster explained that a military general named Robert Guei headed it. He said he would impose a curfew in Abidjan beginning at six P.M. in order to prevent looting and the likelihood of casualties."

Noire scrambled to tune her short-wave radio to the British broadcast. She listened as the report went on to state that many Ivoirians were critical of Bedie's presidency and generally supported his ouster. However, the Organization of African Unity and European Union both issued statements expressing their grave concern at the use of military force to unseat a democratically elected leader and entreated Guei to return the country to civilian rule at once.

She and her father had been silent on the phone as they listened. "I should call Innocent."

"OK, honey. I hope he's OK."

"Me too." She pressed FLASH and then dialed his international cell phone number.

"All circuits are busy now. Will you please try your call again later?"

She slammed down the phone. Logging on to the Internet, she scoured the CNN, All Africa, and Le Monde websites for information but was met with only a few articles that stated even less than she had just heard on the radio. She drafted six hysterical e-mails before sending a more sedate seventh to Innocent.

SUBJECT: ARE YOU OK??
DATE: December 24, 1999, 10:23 A.M.
TO: theINNOCENTone@mymail.com
FROM: Noire@nyu.edu

Innocent,
My dad told me about the coup. ARE YOU OK?? They didn't say anything about violence but mentioned the imposed curfew. This is terrible! A coup on Christmas Eve! I tried calling you but can't get through. PLEASE call or e-mail me and let me know you and your family are fine.

I'm concerned,
Noire

She hit SEND and jumped off-line just in case Innocent tried to call.

By nightfall, internal and external news reports confirmed what Ivoirians had already surmised: the coup had been successful. All who lived in the Pokou compound sat in the family's living room to watch the address to the nation on state television by their former army chief turned military leader General Guei. Stating that he had dissolved the country's constitution, parliament, and court system and replaced it with a nine-officer National Committee of Public Salvation with him as the president, he advised all to remain calm.

"I will take care of everybody," he announced through the airwaves to the captive audience of Ivoirians. "You should not be worried."

"Of course we're worried! How can we not be?" Papa responded with authority. "This country has never seen such barbarism in all these years."

"But, Mr. Pokou, you agree that Bedie had to go. He was ruining our country." Nasima spoke meekly, eyeing the others for support.

Her husband came to her aid. "Yes. The IMF was probably going to force another devaluation of the CFA. Things are hard enough as it is."

"That may be true"—he paused and assumed a statelier posture—"but no constitution! No courts or parliament! How can a 'committee of public salvation' replace all of that?"

Maman spoke up. "But, Jean, this is only temporary. It was a drastic measure to get rid of that corrupt Bedie."

"So you get rid of corruption through corrupt means?! This is the start of turmoil for us. The world will laugh at us for being yet another African country that resorted to a military coup as our so-called salvation . . ."

Innocent was somber. "What do you think it will mean to our economy? No matter whether we think the action was necessary or extreme, I'm sure that foreign investment will dry up and countries like the U.S. will freeze their foreign aid."

"Then let them!" Mireille piped up. "Why must Africa always worry about what the U.S. or Europe thinks about what we do?"

"We worry because we have to worry, Mireille." Papa turned

toward his daughter. "I don't like it either, but that's the way it is."

"It's almost the twenty-first century! We talk as though we were still under colonial rule. I'm sure there are enough educated Ivoirians here and around the world who could help us to change our fate. That is, unless we want to always be beholden to France, the U.S., and the IMF!"

Innocent saw the flames of passion leap from his sister's eyes. She believed what most had long since abandoned. "What do you think we should do, Mireille?"

"Become committed to start with. So many of us are indifferent to the plight of our own country, our own continent. Once we've created the collective will to change things, we can figure out a way to remedy our problems."

He dropped his head, his own inaction resting heavily upon his shoulders. "You're right. This is about more than another African coup. It's about having structures that are sustainable."

The phone rang, startling everyone. The lines had been overloaded all day. Mireille ran to get it. Conversation swirled around the room about the leadership skills and military background of Guei and the ineptitude of Bedie during his second term, but Innocent thought about his sister's stinging indictment.

"Innocent, it's for you. It's Noire." Her face was plastered with a smile as he jumped up. She handed him the phone.

He removed himself to the hallway. "Noire!" His voice was high with surprise.

"I'm happy to hear your voice. I've been worried about you all day. I couldn't get through on your cell."

"Thanks for your concern."

Noire ignored his statement, thinking it bizarre that he could expect anything less. "Are things really bad there?" Her voice was quiet as she braced herself for his response.

"No. I mean, I haven't been outside of the compound all day so I really don't know. The streets have been pretty clear, I'd imagine. But the military has been driving around. Shooting into the air."

"But people haven't been killed?"

"Not as far as I know."

"That's good. So you didn't get my e-mail?"

"Our phone lines have been pretty much down all day. We were surprised to hear the phone ring just now."

"Well, I called like two dozen times."

"Thanks, Noire. Really. I'll tell my family you called. They'll appreciate your concern."

Noire blushed. She interpreted his words to mean that she was known to the family and reveled in the feeling. "Well, my dad was the one who called me about it."

"Yeah."

"I hope you can have a Merry Christmas after all this."

"We'll muddle through somehow, I'm sure. Hey, but you have a wonderful Christmas. Because of the phone situation, I probably won't be able to call. But Merry Christmas, Noire. To you and your family."

"Thanks . . . I'll tell them." She felt giddy in anticipation of her report. "Bye, Innocent. Merry Christmas."

"Merry Christmas. And thank you."

They hung up. Innocent stuck his head into the living room before heading upstairs. "That was a friend from the States. She called to make sure we were all OK."

"That was nice." His mother was the only one to acknowledge him.

"OK, good night."

"Good night, Innocent. Sleep well." She turned away from her son and back to the conversations that boomed around her.

Noire stood at the main entrance to The Greater Allen Cathedral in Jamaica, Queens, clasping a bag full of her parents' gifts. Her mother sometimes felt moved to call the Reverend Floyd Flake's church her spiritual home and shared the diamond-shaped superstructure with eighteen thousand other followers who attended one of three Sunday services. Young people whose church clothes consisted of a blazer added to last night's club outfit comfortably coexisted with professionals in well-appointed suits pushing baby strollers and stately older women who strode in wearing their best winter renditions of Easter bonnets as an outward sign of their inner devotion. Her mother walked up in a tailored burgundy wool coat and a hat that made her head look like a rabbit-hair pencil eraser. She kissed Noire's chilly cheek. "Merry Christmas, baby."

"Merry Christmas, Mom."

They walked into the church and took seats in the balcony next to a couple with two fidgety children. Not a regular churchgoer herself, Noire had a list of intentions that was considerably long. She struggled to stay prayerful rather than lamenting past slip-ups and cutting deals with God if things worked out as she hoped.

Reverend Flake stepped into center stage first to make announcements about Bible study, celebrity sightings, and investment clubs before preparing the congregation to receive the word by the offering. Reiterating the mantras of tithing and home ownership, he smoothed the road between material prosperity and spiritual readiness. Checks and bills of every denomination tumbled into scores of collection plates, filling them to capacity. Encouraged by their own generosity toward God's home and plans to acquire their own, the congregation elevated their minds and hearts to the word as delivered by Reverend Flake. He was a preacher in the best African American tradition: drawing verbal pictures, telling parables, mopping his brow of perspiration that poured out of his head from the effort of preaching the Gospel. The most outwardly righteous shook handkerchiefs high above their heads or sprang up as if commanded. Others raised words of encouragement, agreement, and submission. "Well . . . preacher preach . . . tell the truth . . ." became incantations that gained momentum during the sermon like a wave at a baseball stadium. Her heart full, Noire generously added to the collective voice of the congregation, her eyes bathed in wetness and her spirit anxious and hopeful.

Service let out at one P.M. She and her mother took the F train to her father's apartment on Roosevelt Island. A strip of land barely three miles long, the island was nestled between the exclusivity and bustle of Manhattan's Upper East Side across the water to its west and the Queens neighborhood of Long Island City that shared the Roosevelt Island Bridge to the east. Since childhood, Noire had loved the whimsy of this self-sufficient village right in the middle of New York City that was her part-time home. Exiting the subway station, she and her mother made their way along the cobblestone street—the only actual street through "town"—toward his apartment building, walking past the island's one bank and library before turning left at the grocery store onto a footpath leading to his complex.

Once inside, Noire presented her parents with their gifts. For her father, she had the CD-ROM version of *Encarta Africana 2000*, a framed map of the transatlantic slave trade routes, and a subscription to *Doubly Conscious* magazine. Her mother received an oversized, framed black-and-white photograph that she had taken of her on the beach at Fire Island last summer and a ticket to the opening night of August Wilson's play *Jitney*. "We'll go together," Noire explained. Her parents bestowed rounds of hugs and kisses on her before proceeding.

"This is from us." Dad handed her a tiny gift-wrapped box and a bulky manila envelope.

"Open the box first," Mom directed.

Noire was puzzled. She had never received a joint gift from her parents in her memory. Unwrapping the box, she found a plain silver band.

"Paul gave that to me the Christmas right before you were born. It was our only Christmas together. We agreed that you should have it."

Noire was speechless, unsure that she should have the only gift that they had shared as a couple. She said as much.

"It's not the only gift, Noire. We got you two months later." Dad's smile was heartfelt.

"Thank you." She darted her eyes between their two faces.

"Don't thank us yet. Open the envelope!" Their voices were one.

She slipped her finger into the corner and ran it along the top. She pulled out a folder and opened it to find a bound booklet with her name at the top followed by the words "Flexible Premium Deferred Variable Annuity."

"Do you know what it is?" Mom smiled and frowned at the same time.

"I'm not sure." Noire flipped through the pages.

"It's your first investments. Flora and I put five thousand dollars into it to start you off, and we'll add a thousand dollars to it every Christmas until you finish graduate school. Then you can continue to grow it."

"Wow." She stared at the paper that represented more money than she had ever possessed all at once.

"We had always wanted to do this for you, baby—to give you a little nest egg—and finally this year it all came together for us." Mom's words were hushed.

Tears rolled down to the corners of Noire's lips, drawing a smile that reached up to her eyes.

"It was a bit of a stretch, but . . . well, we just thought it was important." Dad's face harbored an emotion Noire could not identify.

"You took this out through Wright Richards."

"We got in touch with Innocent before he left the firm. He chose the portfolio; it's all socially responsible."

Noire blinked damp eyelashes. "Thanks, Mom and Dad. For everything." She fit the ring to her middle finger on her left hand.

It was minutes to midnight. Noire sat in Dennis and Arikè's living room watching replays of the year 2000 as it greeted Australia, Japan, Egypt, England, and France. As the clock counted down the final minute before the new year, Arikè handed Dennis and Noire each a glass of champagne. They stood up and counted the final seconds.

" . . . five . . . four . . . three . . . two . . . one . . . Happy New Year!"

Arikè kissed Dennis first, a percussive kiss that inspired in him an alcohol-induced snigger. She turned to Noire and their kiss was decidedly softer. Noire froze, consumed with her own shock at Arikè when Dennis followed his girlfriend's lead and planted a wet kiss on Noire's mouth.

"2000, baby!" Dennis raised his glass and gulped his champagne in one shot.

Arriving at Alexander's condo at twelve forty-five, the three were greeted by live African drumming and freestyle dance by a woman and man hired for the purpose. Occupying the third and fourth floors of an ample townhouse, Alexander's place was a profusion of African American art and memorabilia of slavery and Jim Crow segregation. Lit only by flickering candlelight, the pieces had a portentous quality that emphasized the insidious purposes for which they had been used.

"Welcome and Happy New Millennium." Alexander approached

the trio, planting socially acceptable kisses on Noire and Arikè's lips before giving Dennis a hearty black man's embrace.

Arikè looked at Alexander playfully. "Well, you know, the millennium doesn't really start till 2001. But we'll let you slide this year!"

"Slipping and sliding is what I do best!" He shot her a sly grin, which she answered with a giggle and wink.

Noire looked quizzically at their playful banter and then glanced at Dennis to see if he noticed. He was looking around the room.

"This is a great spot, man! The artwork and all." Dennis grinned at Alexander.

"Thanks. Tryin' to support, you know."

"Looks like there are quite a few artists who should feel well supported."

"My mom went back to school at Morgan State a couple of years ago. She's studying African American art. She kinda got me into it."

Noire looked at Alexander with new eyes. "That's great." Many of her Baltimore cousins went to Morgan State. She reminded herself to talk shop with him at another point.

Alexander took their coats to his bedroom and Arikè followed him. Noire stood cautiously beside Dennis.

"Thanks for hippin' us to this party."

"Oh yeah. Alexander wanted to invite you."

"It's a good time to reconnect. Seems like I haven't seen you since that weekend."

"Yeah."

"But Arikè told me you spent the night a few weeks ago."

She turned to look at him.

"I'm happy you two are friends," he said wistfully, and kissed her cheek.

Her body tensed.

"It's all good, Noire. You're a beautiful woman. No playa-hatin' here." His laugh bellowed into the room.

Noire blushed. They stood still in the momentary quiet as the deejay prepared to take over for the drummers who were moving their equipment upstairs.

"Let's get this party started!" Arikè danced up to them and whisked Dennis away.

Innocent viewed the approaching dawn with awe. His eyes were heavy with sleep since he had kept watch with his mother throughout the night to usher in the New Year. But he stood in the still morning air behind the house, his body facing east, and let the sun blanket him with warmth as he used to when he was a boy. Even when he was sick, he would pull himself out of bed to witness the sunrise. It was the time he felt closest to God.

When the clock stroked midnight six hours before, he was holding his mother's hand in the haze of the living room. Grand-mère had struggled out of her bedroom and stood across from him, leading the family in a series of prayers spoken in her native Abure. What Innocent did not comprehend in literal meaning he understood in context. She thanked God for granting all of them the blessing of seeing a new year in this lifetime, a new decade, a new century, a new millennium. She talked about the life that she has lived, the changes she has witnessed in her people and in the world. She asked for forgiveness on behalf of all who were shortsighted and lived only for what they knew and didn't strive for the glories that they could not see. She closed by asking for strength for her family for any of the trials that they may experience in the weeks and months ahead.

Her creased eyelids held back tears that Innocent had never seen. His chest was full with the feelings of his heart. He was happy to be home to see this woman with whom he could never communicate well. Finally, in her fervent Abure, he understood what he never did when she would manipulate her tongue into ill-formed French sentences and struggle to extract local meaning out of foreign words. The prayer over, he hugged her, knowing that he might never hug her again. He felt humble as she reached up to place her hand on his head and glided her leathery palm down the length of his face.

His grandmother returned to her room in a security-gated section of the main floor, insisting that she go alone. Her steps were short but brisk.

Chapter 17

Fresh

"Grand-mère is dead." Innocent whispered the statement to Mireille. They stood at the beginning of the hallway that led to her room. "I felt something this morning as I watched the sunrise so I came in to check on her." Innocent reached out to his sister, comprehension creeping across her face in the form of silent tears.

"Does Maman know?"

"No one else has come down yet." He stroked Mireille's head, her silken braids running through his fingers.

"I want to see her." She clutched her brother's hand, leading the way back to Grand-mère's room.

She lay on her back. Her face was at peace, the corners of her mouth suggesting a smile. Her eyes closed, she looked as though she were enjoying a sentimental dream.

"She looks happy, Innocent."

"She is." Innocent smiled back at his grandmother through his own tears.

"She made it to see 2000 . . ." Mireille turned to Innocent. "We should tell Maman."

"OK." He remembered his mother's eyes when he told her about Serge's death and let Mireille walk ahead.

SUBJECT: recent developments
DATE: January 7, 2000, 5:32 P.M.
TO: Noire@nyu.edu
FROM: theINNOCENTone@mymail.com

Noire,

I hope that you had a good New Year's. Mine was quiet; I spent it here with my family. My grandmother brought the year in by praying in Abure. It really moved me. And at dawn I went to stand outside and greet the day.

Grand-mère passed away that same day, right before dawn. She's now lying in state in her room. Since so many family members had already come back home for the holidays, we will be able to have the funeral rites on the 10th. Charlotte, Michel, and Bibi will be flying in on the 8th. It's a bit overwhelming, but Maman is doing OK though; she's very prayerful.

I think I'll be here a few more weeks. This trip has given me lots to think about, and of course I've been able to spend time with people I love, so it's been very important for me. Hopefully we'll be able to talk more about that when I return.

Noire, I'm sorry that I've hurt you. I don't know what you've been thinking about us, but I would look forward to talking to you. I hope I have the opportunity.

Take good care,
Innocent

Noire didn't respond. She knew she should be supportive and sympathetic, but somehow, she didn't have it in her emotional reserve. Not right then. Her body felt anxious, her mind focused on her own present. Bonita Fuentes had invited her to an intimate dinner party in honor of her birthday. She didn't know who would be there but assumed it would be mostly faculty, advanced graduate students, and personal friends. Noire knew it was yet another test of her mettle; Bonita believed in the sink-or-swim method of mentoring. Noire didn't want to sink.

Her home was colorful and had a dainty quality to it that Noire had never seen reflected in her manner or minimal office adornments. The air in the apartment was full of the sticky-sweet smell of freshly made Dominican pastries. Bonita twirled around in a body-skimming red dress with a fluted skirt. Her hair pulled back into a low-slung bun with wispy curls at her temples, she had the look of a flamenco dancer and the carriage of a dominatrix. Kissing men and women powerfully on the lips whenever the mood struck her, she made everyone submit to her commanding presence. She presented Noire to the assemblage of eighteen with a flourish. "Noire is my most recent inspiration. I love her like a daughter!" She kissed her, depositing red lipstick on her mouth.

"More like a girlfriend, Bonita!" The speaker chuckled; Noire recognized him to be from another NYU department, perhaps French.

"Love is love! And tonight I love everyone!" With that she strode away from Noire, leaving her to fend for herself.

Noire felt timid, unaccustomed to socializing with the professors with whom she had taken classes. She made her way to the punch bowl of sangria sitting on an ornately carved wooden server with what she figured to be a big pink crocheted doily.

"Hello, Noire." A man the color of baked apple pie—and looking as sweet—walked up to her.

"Hi."

"I've seen you around the department. I'm Nácio." He extended his hand. Noire met his with hers, and he brought it to his lips. "It's very nice to meet you."

"I've seen you too. Are you a grad student?" His penetrating brown eyes framed by heavy lashes made her blush. His upturned top lip held the promise of cool drinks of water on hot days. She felt hot.

"Unfortunately, yes. I've been at it for nine years."

Nine years! "Why so long?" She made her voice calm.

"After my oral exams, I took some time off. I needed to clear my head. I spent my days in therapy and my nights jerking off just so I could remember that I was a person beyond this fucking Ph.D."

His gentle voice made the crudest words sound caressing.

"Wow."

"It's just so intense, so monotonous sometimes. It's like training for the marathon alone . . . but you don't know how far you have to run." He sat down his beer and poured himself a glass of sangria. "*Salud!*" He clinked his glass to Noire's. "So, how are you faring?"

"So far so good. I'm a second-year so I'm still doing coursework. But Prof—Bonita has been very encouraging." She smiled.

"Bonita is an amazing woman." He picked up a napkin. "May I?" he asked before Noire knew what he was doing. He blotted her lips. "Her lipstick was still on you. If I knew you better, I would have asked if I could lick it off. But I'm a gentleman."

Noire felt her leg muscles begin to malfunction. "Why don't we sit down?"

"Let me just run to the bathroom. Here, hold my drink." He handed it to her and skipped off down the hall.

Noire made her way to the cherry red antique sofa that was pushed into a corner of the room. She drank her sangria without tasting it, her mouth needing something to do.

"I'm back."

"You're quick."

"I had to be. Didn't know if there'd be another gentleman sitting down next to you by the time I came back."

Unnerved by his boldness, Noire decided to be bold herself. "So why didn't you approach me when you saw me in the department?"

"I was afraid you were spoken for."

"And you're not afraid of that now?"

"It's my New Year's resolution: to do what I feel and worry about the consequences later. So far so good; you're still talking to me."

"That's because you're charming. But you already knew that."

"Charm is in the heart of the beholder. I'm flattered to know you find me charming."

Noire giggled to herself. She couldn't believe this.

"May I have a better whiff of your perfume?" He ran his left hand behind her ear and down the line of her jawbone before bringing his hand to his nose. His eyes remained trained on Noire's open stare. "Delicious."

"*¡Dios mio!*" Noire exclaimed, half in jest, to her Latin suitor.

"And she speaks Spanish too! God is smiling down on me!" Nácio grasped her bare shoulder. "I would like to spend some time getting to know you, Noire. You tell me when." He kissed her lightly on the cheek and got up.

Noire spent the balance of the night in vibrant conversation with everyone. She had been initiated. And she basked in Nácio's glow that he bestowed upon her so openly and generously.

Surprised that he hadn't received a call from Noire, Innocent anxiously checked his e-mail to find a message from her.

SUBJECT: Re: recent developments
DATE: January 9, 2000, 10:45 P.M.
TO: theINNOCENTone@mymail.com
FROM: Noire@nyu.edu

Innocent,

I'm really sorry to hear about your grandmother, but I'm happy that she made it to see 2000 and that you were there to spend time with her. My thoughts and prayers are with you and your family, especially your mom.

Things here have been good, busy actually. I brought in the New Year with Arikè and Dennis and then we went to a party that Alexander had. Jayna got there at about five in the morning. He has a really nice place. Great artwork. He sends his regards.

Bonita has been a tremendous advocate for me. Because of her, I'll be volunteering at the American Comparative Literature Association conference. It's at Yale this year, February 25th through 27th.

Again, please give my condolences to your family.
Noire

Innocent read and reread her message. She sounded distant, preoccupied. In the third reading, he noticed that she hadn't asked when he would be back, though he had been gone for seven weeks. Nausea claimed the pit of Innocent's stomach. Family members streamed past him, preparing to leave for the funeral. When Charlotte walked by with Bibi to tell him it was time to go, he made a quick trip to the bathroom and tried to restore order to his body.

That night, as relatives milled around in what was now a family reunion, Innocent made plans to return to New York. Though his mother's arranged dinner dates had ended after Grand-mère died, he still was tired of the constant questioning about his marital plans and the name dropping that followed as aunts and cousins joined in a robust discussion of his need for a wife and children. He had become a gopher for his father, ferrying messages across Abidjan to his business associates and clients. The more he did it, the less he liked it. He tried to suggest Lamar, his younger cousin on his father's side, as a good choice. Lamar was bright, eager, and trustworthy. And he wanted very much to become a part of things. Innocent brought him on his errand runs and watched Lamar placate disgruntled clients and gently acquiesce to the will of his uncle's associates even as he did just the opposite of what they wanted. When he and his cousin arrived back at the house, it was Lamar who reported to Papa the events of the day. Innocent knew that Lamar could make his father happy in a way that he never could. So he slowly broke Papa into the idea with the hope that by the time he finally said something, the decision would be a foregone conclusion.

At two and a half weeks since the coup, it was clear to everyone that it had been successful. The likelihood of future unrest was high, and Innocent knew that if he got stuck in Côte d'Ivoire for an extended period of time without his own plan, Papa would compel him to succeed him in the business and Maman would then insist that he become engaged to either Aïcha, Ona, Chi-Chi, Paulette, Awa, or Nayanka.

Grand-mère's death had opened his eyes to the promise that his own life held: he had a woman whom he loved, an enviable education that could land him another job if he wanted it, and enough liquid assets to live comfortably for at least two years. And he had his family. Counting his blessings made him ashamed at how seldom he showed gratitude for any of them. He never questioned his good fortune as though he could never lose it. But on New Year's Day he lost the grandmother he never bothered to know and there was nothing he could do about it. He couldn't afford to make that mistake again.

He called his travel agent in New York and got booked on a nighttime flight that would leave Abidjan close to midnight on the 15th and arrive back in the U.S. the morning of January 16. His plans set, he felt lighter and determined to repair and rebuild his life.

Nácio met Noire at her apartment. She set the African violets he brought her on her mantle and gave him a wispy kiss on the lips before they departed hand in hand. They chose Liquors, the darkest and quietest of the trendy restaurants littering Fort Greene's DeKalb Avenue, and sat in a tight booth that assured frequent body contact.

Noire felt special, beautiful, and confident. She didn't hurry her life story into three hours nor did she try to make an impression. She just allowed herself to do what came naturally and Nácio was outwardly appreciative.

"Have you been to Puerto Rico?" Nácio sipped his espresso and looked at her eagerly.

"Yes. I loved it. I've never met nicer people than in Puerto Rico!" She spoke sincerely.

Nácio glowed. "I grew up in Ponce, the big city right in the center of the island. Everyone likes Old San Juan, but that's because they haven't been to Ponce."

"I like Ponce."

"You've been?"

"No, but I like you!" Noire felt playful and saucy.

"Be still my heart! Noire, have mercy on a little *jíbaro* boy like me!"

"*Bueno. Tendré la misericordia en tu.*" She wooed him with her plush Spanish.

Nácio gulped air as though faint and then tantalized Noire's willing lips with naughty pleasures.

• • •

Nácio deposited Noire on her front stoop and sent heat waves through her body with his unqualified adoration. He stared at her, his hands resting in the curve of her waist. "Noire, a woman like you cannot be single. It's impossible. Tell me the truth so I can come back down to earth and get on with my life."

Her heart skipped in her chest. "I actually was in a serious relationship. I mean, I still am, I guess. He went away for a while but I think he'll be back soon. We left things a little up in the air."

Nácio dropped his eyes lower. "Well, even that is more hopeful than I had expected. He is a lucky man. You're too beautiful a woman for anyone to have you wait for long." He kissed her lips wistfully, then ran his hand through her wonderfully thick and carefree curls. "Thank you for this date. No matter what happens, I'll always have this. I'll look forward to seeing you around the department and would be honored to be your friend. And if things don't work out with your man, I'd be happy to do the best I can to make you happy."

This time Noire kissed him. She relished his feelings for her, though she convinced herself it was based on little more than playful conversation and sexual attraction.

"Thank you, Nácio." Her smile was unreserved.

"The pleasure is all mine."

Noire floated up the four flights of stairs to her apartment. She sat in the dark on her couch and stared at her shadowy walls. Noticing the flickering light of her answering machine, she got up to listen to her messages. There was only one.

"*Noire, I'm calling from the airport in France. I have a two-hour layover here and should make it back into New York at about nine o'clock in the morning. I hope you're well; I'll call when I get in. I miss you.*"

Innocent came over Sunday morning bearing gifts. Noire had ordered brunch from the Cajun Creole Café and kept it warm in her oven while Innocent busied himself with presenting Baoule and Dan masks, small Senoufo divination statues, and an Angy Bell designer Ivoirian woman's outfit made of richly embroidered Côte d'Ivoire wax textiles. Noire modeled it at his insistence, enjoying his appreciative gaze as she did so. Innocent was all smiles and kind words; he seemed to be making an effort to be conciliatory. But Noire had no intention of letting him off so easy.

"So, Innocent, I appreciate all the love, but I must say I don't know how to take it."

He lowered his head, striking a posture of humility. "I'd like for you to take it as a sincere expression of my love and commitment to you."

Noire was incredulous. "Just like that?"

"No, Noire. I respect you too much to expect you to just swallow the hard feelings from before. But through all of that, my love for you didn't diminish. Not at all. To my mind, that stands for something."

She pursed her lips, heartened by his words, but unsure of their meaning.

"The trip was good for me. It forced me to think about a lot of things. I'd like to tell you about it. But before I do, please tell me you are willing to listen." His face was cleansed of any false modesty or ego. He just sat there, awaiting her words.

"I'm willing to listen."

He got up to hug her, clutching her into him, rocking her body from side to side. Noire ran her hands up and down his back, finally resting on his taut behind that she realized she had been craving. She felt woozy and overcome.

She let go. "I got brunch."

"OK, and I have dessert."

Noire smiled despite herself. She retrieved food from the kitchen and they broke bread. Turning to face her on the couch, he fast-forwarded through the balance of Mireille's visit, deleted his encounter with Lissette, and ruminated on his time in France and Côte d'Ivoire. Distilling his conversations with Mamadou to a benign reference that "he thinks you're pretty great; you made quite an impression on him," he sidestepped any mention of his chaperoned dinner dates and his mother's explicit desire to see him married, preferably to an Ivoirian woman. His story was full of his reunions with family and friends and his experience of the coup. Noire listened actively, enjoying the sound of his voice as he spun his tales. She hardly cared about half of what he talked about and just loved the fact that he was saying it to her.

When it was her time to speak, Noire painted her world in broad brushstrokes. She chose not to describe the nature of her sleepover with Arikè or the quality of her New Year's kisses from her and Dennis. She hinted at her date with Nácio just to gage his reaction but remained vague. Though she saw the effort he made to freeze his face into a pleasant smile, she noticed his jaw tighten and a vein jump at his temple.

"I guess I came back just in time." Innocent breathed deeply, forcing calm into his body.

"Are you sure about that?" Noire wanted to see Innocent sweat, wanted to feel his fear.

Reading her game, he tried to extract himself from his discomfort. "I suppose I should keep from saying something arrogant or just plain wrong."

"Innocent, if ever silence were prescribed, this is *not* the time." She narrowed her eyes. He didn't deserve to feel so comfortable.

He acquiesced. "Noire, I just hope I can be a better boyfriend to you than I have been. You're a wonderful woman and I'd be crazy if I didn't put up a fight. I miss you, Noire. I want to once again know that your wonderful smile is for me, and to listen to you speak all those languages that live inside your thrilling and quirky brain. I want to see you wear those crazy cat-eye glasses and talk to you about your family, and hang out in Brooklyn with you. Please, let me do those things."

Her mouth stretched into a deliberate, yet optimistic, smile. She sat her plate down on the floor and eased back onto her couch. Her posture open, she welcomed Innocent to kiss her. His approach was meek. Respectful. He kissed her face, taking care not to touch her below the neck until she asked him to. He ran his tongue along her hairline, dipping it into each ear until she giggled with glee. He explored the mysteries of her mouth, enjoying the new games and sensations she offered him. He breathed along her neck, nuzzling his head into the crook of her jawbone and sucking her delicate skin. She felt different to him but he didn't question why.

She brought his hand to her breast and he cupped it, kneading it in preparation for more erotic delights. He let his eyes momentarily sweep across her body. Her nipples were firm against the fabric of the outfit he bought her, and her legs hung open as if on broken hinges. He ran his right hand along the top of her wrapper skirt, unwinding it from the front of her body. Her legs exposed, he found her dewy at the meeting of her thighs. He rose up, retrieved a condom from his wallet, and pulled off his shoes, pants, and boxers in a few quick bursts of motion. He concentrated his attention on trying to time his orgasm to hers but he felt himself welling up faster than he could counter. As soon as he entered her, he exploded uncontrollably.

"Oh, Noire, I'm sorry," he whispered, his ego tarnished.

"It's OK, honey. Just means you missed me." Noire's look was triumphant.

"I did. I did."

Chapter 18

Black Love

Not only did the month of February stoke the flames of love and encourage a particular reflection on black history, but it also became the backdrop for rediscovery between Innocent and Noire. The month of both their birthdays, they enjoyed the novelty of celebrating them as a couple for the first time. Innocent's came first, on the 10th, with hers on the 25th. Noire prepared to usher in his thirty-fourth year with dinner at an Ivoirian restaurant, Meshell Ndegéocello live at Sophisticated Crib, and her very own striptease that Arikè helped her to perfect.

Noire was happy to have Innocent back and willingly juggled the two priorities that claimed all of her emotional energy—school and her lover. Where one faltered, the other stepped in to fill the void. In this way she remained full to the brim and a bundle of mental, physical, and emotional activity. Innocent was grateful for Noire's powerful loving and relished his uncomplicated life that allowed him to fully reap the benefits of it.

Lissette was shuttling between Miami and St. Martin at least until June, Marcus and Lydia were traveling throughout Brazil scouting out new family investment opportunities, and Alexander was immersed in the rigors of work and finally seeming confident enough to handle it on his own.

They became protective of their anonymity even as they attended as many art exhibits, concerts, and cultural events that they could cram into their schedules. They also coveted the quiet times, the times when they were together alone, clad in T-shirts and boxer shorts. In those moments, Noire was convinced that life could be perfect.

"Noire?"

"Um-hum." She kept her head down, though she had paused her reading.

"Can you check your e-mail? I seem to have lost my connection or something. I'm trying to figure out if it's my DSL line or just my e-mail account."

"OK." She didn't stop to process whether his request made sense and walked over to where he sat at his desk. She logged on successfully. "I'm on," she announced. He had gone to get a drink from the refrigerator.

"Might as well check your e-mail while you're there."

"I guess." She opened up her account and saw three messages. She decided to open the one from Nácio once she was home. Bonita had forwarded her some information that she was expecting about next week's comp lit conference. "You sent me one!" Nothing was in the subject line. She opened it up:

SUBJECT: (no subject)
DATE: February 17, 2000, 8:03 P.M.
TO: Noire@nyu.edu
FROM: theINNOCENTone@mymail.com

Noire,

In honor of our one-year anniversary, I would like to celebrate by taking a trip to Jamaica with you. I have taken the liberty of reserving two airline tickets and hotel rooms in Kingston and Port Antonio for your

spring break, from March 9th to the 19th. I must book the trip before ten
P.M. tonight, so you have about an hour and forty-five minutes to think
about the merits of my offer.

I hope you say yes.
Innocent

"Yes! Yes!" She screamed and tackled him at the refrigerator. Jarred,
his orange juice crashed in a wave onto Noire's shirt. She howled as
Innocent showed mock disapproval.

"Tsk, tsk, mademoiselle. Now I'll have to clean all of that off of
you." He pulled her shirt over her head. "That's what happens when
young girls act rowdy." He licked orange juice off of her breasts dutifully.
Squatting on the floor, he traced the juice that had streamed down her
stomach with his tongue, blotting her navel dry. He pushed his hands
up the legs of her boxers and searched for her crotch. "You seem to be
damp there too. Let me see what I can do about that." He licked her
dry, but not before he made her wet.

"Happy birthday, Noire!" Jayna's voice boomed into her sleepy ear.

"Hey, thanks. What time is it?"

"Time for you to be up, Ms. Thang. It's six-thirty. Twenty-nine-year-
olds need to start their beauty regimen just a little earlier!" She chuck-
led into the phone.

Noire sat up in her bed. Innocent's hand kneaded her belly.

"I really do have to get up, too. I have that conference up at Yale."

"See, I'm your alarm clock! Look, I have a present for you but I just
haven't bought it yet. But it's coming."

"I know. Thank you, Jayna."

"That's what friends are for. Well, let me let you get your morning
freak on before you really have to get up. I know homeboy's there."

"That's what I love; you're understanding."

"Exactamundo! OK, I'll catch you later. Enjoy your conference . . .
and everything that comes before. No pun intended!"

"Crazy!"

Noire stood by the front doors of Yale's Hall of Graduate Studies, where she handed out surveys for the annual Comparative Literature Convention.

Bonita bolted through the door looking harried and placed a careless kiss on Noire's cheek. "*Querida mia*, I'm actually shocked to be here. But I figured, rather than stay home and slit my wrists, I should come and support Nácio. He's presenting a paper."

"Bonita, are you OK?!"

"When you've had the kind of life I've had, you're never OK. Some days are harder than others. Today is my son's twenty-sixth birthday."

"Oh." Noire didn't mention that it was hers as well.

"Do you know where Nácio is speaking?" She thumbed through the program.

"I didn't know he was even going to be here." Noire remembered his e-mail that she never opened last week and cursed.

"You should come and hear him. He'll be happy you did." She kissed Noire on the cheek again and left.

Noire stood a few more minutes, then determined that her presence would not be missed. She traced Bonita's steps down the hallway.

Nácio delivered his paper in a Spanish that caressed the senses. His voice coated her thoughts with memories of her travels throughout the Caribbean and Latin America and reminded her why she loved that language most of all. He crackled with passion and even those whose mastery of Spanish was minimal grasped his meaning. Noire was consumed with his presence, in love with his sound, and entranced with his convictions. His ideas leapt up and captured the imagination of all who sat within range of his voice.

He concluded his talk to rousing applause, none more vigorous than Noire's. Walking back to his seat in the middle of the auditorium, he was enveloped by a kiss and hug from Bonita. Noire looked upon the scene longingly, wishing that she could have been the one to congratulate him. Nácio shared her passion; he understood the critical importance of "their" role in the field as people of color bringing the voices and languages of black and brown people into the academy. Noire returned to her post at the entrance to the Hall of Graduate Studies, her emotions picking up where her intellectual appreciation left off. She was moved.

Noire arrived back in Brooklyn late Sunday afternoon and went straight to see Arikè. She was preparing a traditional Yoruba meal of *iyan* and *egusi*—pounded yam and melon-seed soup—for her parents, who, realizing that their daughter was in a very serious relationship with Dennis, thought that a trip down from New Rochelle to have dinner was in order.

Arikè shuttled around the kitchen. "I got the pounded yam from a Yoruba woman in Staten Island. Can you imagine, she actually pounds it from scratch? She's like seventy years old and she has arms like Arnold Schwarzenegger!" She tittered and fussed over her stew and soup that boiled in separate pots.

"Do your parents like Dennis?"

"Everybody likes Dennis."

"I mean, are you worried that they'll point something out to you that you didn't realize? Something bad?"

"I doubt that there's too much they'll see in three hours that I haven't seen in two years."

"It's just the perspective they have, being married such a long time."

"Yeah, I guess."

"How long has it been for them?"

"Um." She seemed to calculate in her head. "They've known each other for thirty-six years, I think. But they've been married for thirty-three."

"Wow."

"It's kind of a record these days. I feel blessed, really. They've been good role models for me. Their marriage, I mean. It kind of gives me hope."

"Do you think it's impossible for folks like me to have a happy marriage because we have no role models?" Noire projected her own thoughts onto Arikè's words and felt hurt.

"Oh God no! Did I say that? No, Noire, that's not what I meant at all. I just mean that . . . I don't know. There are all different types of successful love relationships. I'm just happy to have witnessed one of them. I guess that's what I mean."

"Do you love Dennis with your head or your heart?"

"I'd like to think both." She tasted her stew and added a pinch of salt.

"I mean, does living together feel like a rational choice or an emotional one?" Noire nodded, satisfied that her question finally came out right.

"Mmm." She considered the question for a moment. "I think that the best kind of love takes account of your whole being. You can't compartmentalize it. I mean, it's not a job that you put in hours at and then the rest of the day you think about something else. I think it's got to feel right on a lot of levels."

Dennis's keys rattled in the front door. He walked into the kitchen with fresh tropical flowers. "I had to go to this high-price spot in Brooklyn Heights for these." He kissed Noire on the cheek and Arikè on the lips.

"Tell Noire what you love about me."

"Her righteous ass . . . no doubt!" He pinched her behind and blurted out "Dat bumsee lookin' good, boy! Arse fuh days!" in his deep Trini accent.

Arikè laughed. "See what I mean. It's nothing and everything all at once!"

Noire smiled to cover her somberness. "Look, I know you guys are still getting ready, so I'm going to head home."

"Oh, stay. There's plenty of food." Dennis tasted the stew and coughed. "Hot!"

Arikè looked at Dennis. "Get bread."

"Thanks, but I'd just as soon push out. It's been a long weekend."

Arikè dried her hands on a dish towel. "How was that conference, by the way?"

"Terrific. A guy that I know from the department presented. He was great."

"That will be you in a year or two, Noire. You're our next great scholar!"

Noire grabbed her coat from a kitchen chair, said her good-byes, and walked toward the bus stop. The approaching dusk made the cold air colder.

Innocent spent his third week in the New York Public Library's business division on 34th Street and Madison Avenue. There he outlined the progression of research he would need to follow to identify what kind of business he could set up between West Africa and the U.S. He would begin by using the traditional channels—the World Bank and International Monetary Fund—to carefully cull records of foreign investment in Côte d'Ivoire and its neighboring countries. He would also read up on the private funds that invested in Africa and other emerging markets to help him determine what markets seemed profitable. But even as he conducted his research in the comfort of the library a block from the Empire State Building, he knew that the real work would begin once he was back on the continent, talking to people, amassing a local knowledge of the landscape, and sniffing out opportunities. He had been able to fit in only a fraction of the preliminary legwork in between the errands he had run for his father. But his efforts were cursory attempts to separate the wheat from the chaff. He kept his plans quiet, superstitious about revealing them when they were still so early in their development. He didn't want to be questioned or dissuaded by anyone.

Every day he left the library at five o'clock and joined the afternoon crush of people on the subways. In all of his years in New York City, he had never been a part of this aspect of city living. His days had begun before sunrise and ended with a chauffeured car home after most couples had watched the early news and made love. He didn't know what it meant to be in the thick of it. So while other straphangers hung limp from stainless steel poles, he was energized. He felt as if he had become an authentic New Yorker, that he could claim an intimate knowledge that only those whose days began and ended with iron chariot rides from one purgatory to another could claim.

In the evenings, he would dissect pieces of Mamadou's business plan and e-mail his comments and suggestions. Noire came over two to three times a week, and he spent the night every Monday. When they were together, they talked, worked, watched TV, and made love. He could rely on their lovemaking to fatigue his muscles and drain his mind enough to ensure a good night's sleep. And in the morning, if he awoke before her, he would savor the sight of Noire as she lay still, her hands clutching the end of the bed. He would pull back the covers just enough so that he could look at her "black love" tattoo on her delicate back and her luscious behind. She had the appearance of a bud vase and her head was the rose. His love for her was uncomplicated and complete in those early-morning ruminations. He wanted to reach out and touch her but didn't because he knew he would lose sight of her simple perfection as soon as she moved.

It was a year and a day since they first met. Innocent held Noire's hand as their taxi snaked through Kingston, Jamaica's Thursday-afternoon streets. Men toting cages of live chickens, and women toting children, darted across the roads that were lined with newspaper hawkers and street purveyors of oranges, plantain chips, and warm fruit juice. The rhythms of street commerce conducted in Jamaican Patois and the press of warm brown bodies claimed them heart and soul. "It looks like home," Innocent whispered to Noire, kissing her on the cheek. Her mind fastened on the Sea Islands of her mother's ancestors, she replied, "Yes, it does."

Entering the stylish New Kingston neighborhood that was their destination, they turned onto Hope Road. They drove past Devon House, built by Jamaica's first black millionaire in 1881, and the Bob Marley Museum, which had once been his home and that of Tuff Gong recording studio. Tucked right behind these two historic houses, their hotel was a sherbet-colored guesthouse with views of the Blue Mountains.

After whisking New York City's grime down the drain, they lay down, the windows blowing tropical winds across their clean, unclad bodies.

"If we're lucky, we may be invited to dinner tonight." Noire sounded bubbly.

"How's that?"

"Cudjoe's e-mail."

"Mmm. Who is he to you?"

"A friend. We used to date in Ghana." Her tone was casual.

"He's Ghanaian?"

"Yeah. His mom's Jamaican though." Recalling her first introduction to his historic name, she added, "You know he was named after a Jamaican warrior—a Maroon who led a standoff between the runaway slaves and the British. His mom is descended from the Trelawny Maroons who trace their roots to the Ashanti and other West African ethnic groups. Isn't that fascinating?" Noire's face wore her admiration.

Interesting though his ancestry was, Noire's ex-boyfriend did not figure into Innocent's idea of an anniversary trip, but he couldn't see a way around it. "Uh-huh."

"I'd like for you to meet him, Innocent. He used to be very important to me."

"Is he still?"

"I guess . . . I don't know. Not in the same way of course. That was eight years ago." She pulled herself to the edge of the bed and started dialing.

"You remember his number?"

"It's seven digits, Innocent."

He slid his right hand around her waist and fondled her belly as she spoke on the phone. Her voice was buoyant, he noticed. Almost jubilant. She gave the hotel address and Innocent's international cell phone number to Cudjoe. Her smile echoed through the room.

Noire hung up and turned toward Innocent. "Are you jealous?"

"No."

"Are you nervous?"

"No, Noire."

"Good. He'll pick us up in two hours; we're invited to his aunt's house for dinner. That gives me just enough time to fuck your brains out. Is that a deal?"

Innocent pulled her onto him and complied with all her wishes.

• • •

Innocent saw lust drench Cudjoe's features at the sight of Noire. He pulled her up into his arms and hugged every crevice of her body. Noire's hands fondled the nape of his neck for the duration of their embrace. Pulling away, she kissed him just shy of his lips.

"Meet Innocent," she said breathlessly.

Innocent unwillingly gave Cudjoe the handshake and snap of West African male bonding. He had already gotten enough love from Noire.

"It's great to meet you, mon. Noire looks so good, must be a testament to you. Thanks for looking out." Cudjoe's accent was inflected with the best West African intonations and Caribbean rhythms. His smile was broad.

Innocent looked askance at him. "She's a great woman."

"That's for sure." He paused, as if in reflection. "So, should we head out?" Cudjoe opened the hotel's front gate for Noire, then walked through himself.

Standing at the car, Noire hesitated before jumping into the passenger seat beside Cudjoe. She threw Innocent an apologetic look that morphed into a smile by the time her behind touched the chair. Innocent was a pretzel in the backseat of the hatchback.

Cudjoe explained that he had been staying in Jamaica with family for the last month. He had applied to Jamaica's branch of the University of the West Indies for a teaching job and was hopeful that it would come through. With a master's degree in economics from Cambridge University, he thought he'd try his hand at academia while he decided on what was next.

"I still haven't been to the States. But now that I'm here, it's a stone's throw away."

Dinner was a tortured affair. Noire enchanted Cudjoe's family with her sincere though faulty attempts at Patois. They were enraptured by her course of study, her travel experiences, and her language mastery. Innocent grew small in the glare of her spotlight. Cudjoe, on the other hand, took pride in her as a reflection of his own ambitions.

Noticing Innocent's silence at last, Noire included him at the periphery of conversation. "Innocent's from Côte d'Ivoire. He's quite a world traveler himself." Her smile was mediocre.

"We're celebrating our one-year anniversary." His declaration had an air of unintended melancholy.

"Congratulations." Cudjoe's aunt was gracious.

The bammy became slabs of soap in his mouth, the jerk chicken congealed fire. "I'm afraid I'm not feeling well. Perhaps the flying . . ." Innocent made an effort to sound rational.

"Let me fix you some tea." Cudjoe's aunt directed Innocent to the living room sofa and disappeared into the kitchen.

Out of earshot of the dining-table conversation, Innocent caught sight of Noire's pitying eyes and the back of Cudjoe's head which moved in time with his animated hands.

Noire peered over Cudjoe's shoulder to Innocent slouched on the sofa. She considered going over to sit beside him but enjoyed her robust discussion with Cudjoe too much to leave it. Seeing him reinforced the bond of love and admiration that had sealed him to her heart eight years ago. The planes of his face more mature and pleasing, he was the best representation of an ideal man she had ever dreamt before Innocent. Cudjoe's mind was a storybook that Noire was free to roam through, now as much as ever. Seeing Innocent's eyes close, she exonerated herself of the responsibility of entertaining him and focused on entertaining herself.

"Noire." Cudjoe's voice dropped in volume, forcing her to pull in even closer. "Where did you find him? I can't believe you like him." His voice flat, his meaning bared its teeth.

"I love him, Cudjoe."

"He's cardboard compared to you."

"I haven't seen you since you broke up with me and you criticize my boyfriend?"

"Maybe I'm being unfair, but that doesn't change the truth. What do you two have in common?"

"Cudjoe, I came down here to be with him. To celebrate our anniversary, for godsakes."

"Well, I hope it's a good time for you." He sounded insincere.

"It will be."

Innocent opened his eyes to witness a conversation that had grown in intensity and intimacy. His eyes tightened. He knew he couldn't stay; he felt unwell.

"Noire, I'm sorry but can we leave? I'm not myself." He raised his voice enough to bridge their distance.

"I was thinking that we should get you back to the hotel." She was equally loud.

"I'll take you." Cudjoe shot out of his seat and fished the car keys out of his pants pocket.

"Thanks." Noire's look was tepid. She rushed into the kitchen to offer a hurried thank-you to Cudjoe's aunt, then reappeared.

They drove home in silence. Depositing them at the hotel's wrought-iron front gate, Cudjoe mournfully shook Innocent's hand. He turned to Noire. "Take good care of yourself." He kissed her cheek and squeezed her hands in his.

"You too," rasped in her throat. She and Innocent walked inside and went to sleep.

Their first full day in Jamaica's most populous city was a riot of arts appreciation—the Craft Market, National Museum, National Gallery, African-Caribbean Heritage Centre, and Parade area for a view of Edna Manley's noted sculpture *Negro Aroused*. They visited the Institute of Jamaica, the Bob Marley Museum, and Devon House before stopping for a long-overdue lunch. Laden with purchases of souvenirs and artwork marking every stop, Innocent and Noire became a part of the Friday congestion that choked the streets. The day ended with dinner at a homespun establishment with a loyal local following, where they learned about a comedy show at the Little Theatre that they later attended.

The major tourist attractions covered, they spent the balance of their brief Kingston stay soaking up the city's unself-conscious pageantry. They hired a car and driver to take them through its many faces and moods, contrasting the expansive University of the West Indies campus in the lush Mona neighborhood with Trench Town which oozed an insolence that was a response to poverty and neglect as well as pride of place and a distinctly Jamaican sensibility.

With no others to distract them, Innocent and Noire relied on their own bonds and became each other's special friends. Together they shared experiences that no one else knew, and they felt drawn to each other in a way that nothing before then had afforded them. So, by the time they climbed into their rented SUV for the second leg of the trip, they were intimate companions.

More confident of her abilities to drive on the left side of the road despite her inexperience, Noire appointed herself the designated driver. Innocent was her navigator. They were a half hour east of the city, stopping for an abbreviated breakfast along the pockmarked road of Gordon Town's center as churchgoers sauntered off to church. They picked up bite-sized reinforcements for the rest of the three-hour trip to Port Antonio at the northeastern edge of the Portland parish. Climbing into the Blue Mountains, she turned the car off of Route B1 and onto a road lined by moss-covered trees and small shacks improbably clinging to rock formations. Noire crept around the hairpin turns as buses and trucks dared to overtake her, unperturbed by their blocked view of the lane of oncoming traffic.

The sunroof of their four-wheel-drive vehicle open, Innocent reached up to grab the clouds that cascaded down the mountainside as they ascended still further into this scantly populated country. The land claimed by the Maroons who had escaped the bondage of slavery and successfully resisted British aggression was dotted with small patches of growing bananas, vegetables, and coffee. Mavis Bank Coffee Factory, known for processing Blue Mountain coffee beans, sat quiet in observance of the Sabbath. But Innocent and Noire found some enterprising Jamaicans willing to sell them the prized beans and who offered local lore and a complimentary cup of brewed coffee to go to supplement their purchase.

They cut through poorly paved roads and dense vegetation up to Silver Hill Coffee Farm, where they rejoined the main road that pushed through the heart of Portland. At Buff Bay the road at last met the Caribbean Sea. Noire stopped to stretch her legs and flex her hands.

Innocent's gaze followed the interminable green that drenched everything behind him and the blue that stood before him. "Do you want me to take over?"

"Please."

They switched places. The sun crept toward the top of the Jamaican world; they had already been driving for nearly three hours, though they had another hour and a half still ahead of them. "I suppose the guide-books were written by people who took these roads at sixty miles per hour!" Noire observed, incredulous.

They wended their way east along the coast, the silence a comfort-able reinforcement of their love. Noire let her thoughts float over the breathtaking scenery that made a wide arc around her head. It was Sunday afternoon and she was driving in the most beautiful place in the world with her lover and friend. Things finally felt right.

"Noire?" He cast his eyes over at her.

She offered a dreamy smile in return.

"Today's the actual year anniversary of our first date."

"Happy anniversary." Her voice was a song.

He let his memories roll back to that day, to the conversation and what they did. But mostly he thought about the way he felt: giddy and alive, out of sorts, surprised at himself.

Pulling into the town of Port Antonio along West Street, they were greeted by a clock tower that, together with a redbrick courthouse, composed the city center. Musgrave Market chattered melodiously below, and West Harbour and East Harbour stretched out into the sea. Riding past Christ Church, the town's most prominent place of wor-ship, Innocent slammed on the brakes and crossed himself.

"What happened?" Noire gasped.

"My grandmother. That woman looks just like her."

Noire watched an elderly woman struggle along the narrow sidewalk just beside the church, her back to the car. She didn't know what to say and instead watched Innocent's lips mouth a silent prayer before moving the car. Turning right at the church, he drove up a half-mile incline to Bonnie View Hotel. Boasting a long history and spectacular views over-looking all of Port Antonio, Bonnie View had the pose of a gracefully aging woman who still wore spotless white gloves in the summertime.

Innocent and Noire threw open their windows and admired the late-day sun twinkling gold light in the blue sea. They settled into their home of the next six days.

Full of faded elegance, Port Antonio was a place that sauntered on its most hurried day and sighed in appreciation of the approaching evening. They ambled through the market and ate bananas while Noire shared secrets about the pain of her childhood summertimes in New Orleans and Innocent talked about his brother, Serge, and his boarding school experiences. Returning to the Bonnie View, they refreshed themselves for an evening of fine dining at Mille Fleurs.

Over appetizers of smoked marlin on honeydew and ackee soufflé, Innocent began to share his professional plans with Noire.

"When I was in Paris I went to see the space that Mamadou has secured for an artists' collective. I've reviewed his business plan—suggested some revisions—and I've decided to become a silent investor."

Noire's eyes lit up, her body language attentive to his words.

"He has one big investor already and I've talked to Dr. Rousseau and another contact of my father's about fronting some money. That should be up and running sometime this summer. I'll probably go back around then."

"That's great. How long will you stay?"

"A week or so I guess. I don't know yet."

Noire thought about her summer in Curaçao and figured he was entitled to that much.

"Mamadou has a stable of very talented artists at his reach—including himself. It should be a tremendous offering. I think it'll be lucrative."

She bobbed her head, unclear how it all would work but sure she could ask at another time. "I really like Mamadou. That should be great, working with him like that."

Innocent nodded his agreement. "Yeah. I think so." He nibbled at the nearly finished appetizers. "So, how's Bonita Fuentes?" He said her name with an exaggerated Spanish accent.

Noire laughed. "She's fine. I have a big meeting with her the Monday we return."

"About what?"

"My academic progress, research plans. Stuff like that." She shrugged her shoulders.

"You always seem to be so worried about those meetings."

"Mmm . . . I wouldn't say 'worried,' but they're important. Bonita is . . . my ally."

"You make it sound like a war."

"She looks out for me. There are a lot of egos floating around the ivory tower."

Their dinner came: spiced fish with tamarind and coconut sauce for Noire, and chicken in June plum sauce for Innocent.

As the sun fell lower in the sky and spread out like an orange Popsicle melting onto the surface of the water, Innocent lost interest in humdrum conversation. His eyes lascivious, he savored her breasts, which danced behind the diaphanous veil of her Epperson Studio dress that had been his birthday present. "You look delicious. I could throw this plate over the balcony and eat you all up!"

"Then I'd be all gone." Noire was coy in return.

"Well, perhaps you'll give me the pleasure of one dip as a nightcap."

"I'd be happy to make that wish come true."

"You're too good to me."

They watched the day close the book on itself and the serenity of the evening settle over the town.

The days ambled along at a measured gait. Noire would have been happy if time had stood still. She piled up nuggets of perfection and reveled in waking up beside Innocent day after day. If her relationship with Innocent were an experiment, then Port Antonio was the ideal conditions for positive results. They ventured beyond the town into the neighboring coves and bays, making themselves regulars in the laid-back good times of eating jerk meat straight from the grill on the beach at Boston Bay and splashing around in the frothy waves of Long Bay. Caressed by the sun during the day, they made fervent love at night.

Their time growing short, they planned an excursion to Moore Town, the place where the Winward Maroons had resettled their head-quarters after Nanny Town was demolished. The celebrated Nanny Town was the point from which Nanny of the Maroons led a guerilla war against the British during the First Maroon War, from 1720 to 1739.

Moore Town carried on the tradition of resistance to the encroaching British soldiers who sought to subjugate these brazen ex-slaves or, barring that, merely obliterate them. But the Maroons—who had settlements on both the east and west of the island—had the advantage of knowing the terrain that became their battlefield. Even as they renegotiated the terms of their relationship with the British, they had earned their autonomy from British rule that has its successor in a partly autonomous state from the Jamaican nation.

Negotiating uncooperative dirt roads, they arrived at the town exhausted. Noire wasn't sure what she had expected but found herself disappointed by the sight of a modest sign marking the existence of this historic place.

Innocent was already leaning against the car. Noire got out, took a picture of Bump Grave, a monument to Nanny and her legendary resting-place, and shrugged. "Just seems like there'd be more, you know."

"The spirits of our ancestors whisper in the wind." Innocent stared across the distance, the power of the place palpable to him. He reached out to Noire and transmitted the knowledge that coursed through his body. She became limp at his touch; it imparted understanding of all that she could not see.

Finally at an end, their anniversary vacation had become a living being with whom they had built a codependent relationship. In their last night, as the wash of love still clung to their skin and warmed their hearts, they each began to be afraid to leave their friend. Noire thought it was her reluctance to rejoin the New York City winter. Innocent rationalized that he felt anxious about his uncharted professional landscape. But they thought it better to leave those concerns unarticulated, as though speaking them would make them more real than they were. On Sunday morning, as they drove down the steep street that rolled out in front of their hotel, Innocent once again stopped short in front of the church. This time he got out and Noire followed him into the imposing edifice. Wearing clothes too casual for the Sunday worship services set to begin, they nevertheless were the most reverent of all who milled around. They sat in the last pew until the first notes of the opening hymn. Then they left and Noire climbed into the driver's seat.

"Noire, I do love you."

"I love you too." Their voices quiet, they steeled themselves for their return.

Noire decorated the pages of her book with yellow highlighter markings. The seven A.M. sunlight streamed into Innocent's unadorned windows where she sat, her feet upon his desk. Innocent stirred from sleep. He walked across the length of the loft to where Noire sat facing the window. Circling her chair to face him, he used his mouth to retrieve the highlighter cap from between Noire's teeth. Blowing it artfully to the floor, he returned to Noire's lips and sought her tongue with his own. His eyes were closed and his mouth wet with excitement. Removing the pen from her right hand, he placed it in the book and let book and pen fall neatly to the floor. He straddled Noire's sitting form and his naked body displayed his want for her as he caressed her breasts through her T-shirt.

Noire held his firm behind in her hands, squeezing the vibrant cheeks that moved beneath her fingers. Licking Noire's lips, Innocent opened his eyes and saw the sunlight glowing in the soft brownness of her stare.

"*Bonjour*, Mademoiselle Noire." He murmured it like a mating call.

"Morning, beautiful." Her body felt excited and compliant.

"*Voulez vous couché avec moi?*" he sang.

She laughed at his allusion to the hit 1970s song by LaBelle. "I was trying to finish reading this book so I'd be prepared to talk to Bonita after class this evening."

"Well, you can feel free to *think* about the book as you make hot, passionate love to me. I promise not to take offense."

She kissed him in response and massaged his inner thighs.

Removing her shirt, Innocent appreciated her unique beauty revealed once more to his loving sight. He placed the shirt on the floor and laid Noire upon it. Innocent's body cast a shadow over her form and caught them in a curious picture framed by the sun. He lowered himself onto her and cupped her breasts in his hands. Taking her nipples into his mouth, Innocent heard a sigh escape Noire's lips.

Noire directed him into her. He entered slowly, each of them overcome with the experience of their union. Their perspiration and tears commingled as they synchronized themselves. Noire felt Innocent's mouth go cold as he accelerated their rhythm. Balancing his weight on his arms, he pulled himself up over Noire. French words rushed out of his mouth as he tottered at the brink of inevitability. Innocent climbed inside of Noire and his entire being moved within her body. Noire pulsated for them both and then she felt Innocent flood her. The two of them, one within the other, were suspended in the moment, ecstasy etched on their faces.

Innocent brought her hand up to his lips. Noire stared at him through wet eyelashes. Her body was a bowl of jelly in an earthquake. Her muscles danced to separate tunes, creating a frenetic harmony of motion. Innocent rested his head on her quivering belly. His feelings were on the surface of his skin and the heat of his body imparted his love. Sucking on the lip of skin below Noire's navel like a pacifier, Innocent fell into a twilight sleep.

His mind was full. His body and his heart had joined Noire in a twosome and yet his thoughts were in conflict. He felt himself ache for her, need her. He was giddy and afraid.

Noire's mind created chaos out of her thoughts. Carelessly tossed back and forth, they had lost their order and relative importance. She and Innocent seemed to complete each other but her excitement was prone to devolving into disquiet unexpectedly. Noire actively pushed her cacophonous thoughts to a little-used corner of her mind. She felt the soothing warmth of Innocent's breathing on her stomach and told herself that she was lucky to be in love with such a wonderful man.

Chapter 19

Choose One

Bonita Fuentes paced the length of her office, her right hand absentmindedly flicking ashes to the floor. Noire watched her churn thoughts through a sieve before giving them voice.

"You have a unique opportunity in front of you, Noire. You are a young black woman who has the potential to take this field by storm. At thirty-five you will have published your first book; you'll be hitting your stride. You'll be where I am now at forty-three. Noire, I hope you want these things for yourself as much as I want them for you. You have to. Everyone has to. And if they don't, I hope you give them no more than a passing glance. Our field needs what you have to offer it. I'd like to see you apply for this one-year fellowship in Haiti. You'll be finished with coursework by first semester of next year; this could be an incredible opportunity for you to set up your comparative look at Papiamentu and Kreyòl." She cursed at the cigarette stub that now burned her fingers, threw it into her overflowing ashtray, and lit another.

Noire knew she was right. And she knew that Bonita had enough fire in her belly to see Noire successfully through the process. But Haiti for a year? She made her concerns vague and watched Bonita fidget through her lies.

"Noire, there is no good reason for you to even question this! When I was your age, I had a twelve-year-old son I didn't know who was being raised by a man I no longer loved. I had a *million* reasons why I should not have pursued my dream. But I did it. I stuck with it. But you have *nothing* to hold you back." She peered into Noire's eyes through a plume of smoke. "And please don't tell me that your ambivalence has anything to do with that man you're sleeping with. You are a beautiful woman. I'm sure you have men begging to know you and who would travel with you if that's what it took to keep you. If he makes the trip, great. But if not—" She blew smoke into Noire's stunned face.

She winced. "Bonita, I'm not *fucking* Innocent; he's my boyfriend! And since when are highly educated black women in such great demand?" She stood up and towered over Bonita, who promptly walked away and glowered from across the room.

"I will write a recommendation for you and the chair of the department will do the same once I speak to him." Her cheeks hollow from the effort, she pulled on the cigarette, almost turning it inside out.

Why was Bonita so sure that the perpetually inaccessible Dalinger Dolan would be accommodating? Noire had barely seen him four times since starting the program, twice during orientation. Noire sat back down.

Bonita followed suit. "But we must take care of this before you leave for Curaçao. And Dalinger is going on paternity leave in a couple of weeks. At the end of April."

Noire raised her eyebrows.

"So look over the application, and then let's get going on it in the next day or two." Bonita dismissed Noire with a wave. Her face creased in inexplicable annoyance, she seemed to turn her thoughts to issues that ran deeper than Noire's academic and professional career.

Since Mireille had used her brother's mailing address in her Howard University application, he had the unique pleasure of receiving her acceptance letter. It was actually a package, complete with several personalized letters from deans and students alike, as well as student orientation information. Innocent's heart swelled with pride at his sister's accomplishment. Mireille would have the experience that he had always imagined. He glanced up at his clock—6:15. This being daylight savings in the States, it was 10:15 in Côte d'Ivoire. He called Mireille and got through on the third try.

"*Bon soir. Allô?*" Mireille's voice had the silky quality of an expectant lover.

"It's your brother."

"Oh!" She sounded like his sister again. "I didn't expect that you'd call on a Monday," she apologized.

"I know. Guess what I got in the mail today?" He gave her five seconds to think before he answered his own question.

"Oh wow . . ." Her voice was mystical, far away.

"Aren't you excited?"

"I can't believe it. I sort of wasn't counting on getting in."

"Why not?" Innocent felt confused. "Well, but you got in, Mireille. You got in!"

"Do Maman and Papa know yet?"

"No! I wouldn't tell them before you. Why are you acting strange? Aren't you happy?"

"I guess I just had—so much has happened since December."

"Like what?"

"Just things. Life."

"Mireille, please cut the bullshit!" Innocent heard her gasp but he couldn't help it.

"Innocent, I'm a woman. So many things happen in the life of a woman."

"Is this about Abdul?"

"Sort of." Her voice was tiny even as she tried to sound big.

"Please don't tell me you'd consider passing up this opportunity because of him!"

"I *love* him!" Mireille's indignation became palpable.

"Are you sleeping with him?"

Mireille's silence expressed her hurt at her brother's breach of her privacy.

"I'm sorry. Look, Mireille. I'm sure you're in love and everything, but you're not even nineteen years old. How can you make a decision about your whole life at this age?"

"People do it all the time. College, marriage, babies. Grand-mère was eighteen when she had Uncle Issa."

"There's no comparison."

"Times change but people stay the same."

He felt desperate. His own desire to see her at Howard encompassed everything he invested in Mireille's success and happiness after he failed to safeguard his brother Serge's life and was shut out of Charlotte's for so many years. Mireille was his only hope to do right by his siblings as the eldest. She had to let him do it.

"You know, Mireille, I'm not going to argue this point. But don't lose sight of what you want. You *want* to go to Howard. I saw it in your eyes when we visited. You *owned* that campus. And if I recall, you even had an admirer."

"I don't need admirers. I have a man!"

"Abdul is twenty-three years old. He's not a man!"

"Is that how you felt when you were running around Paris after college? Like you weren't a man?"

Innocent was dumbfounded. "Mireille, just please think about it. This is a great opportunity. Abdul should want it for you. If he loves you, he will want you to do what you really want. And if it's meant to be, he'll be there for you."

"I'll think about it . . ."

"I love you, Mireille . . . most of all."

"I know. Good night, Innocent."

He heard the phone click in his ear. He was spent, his happiness broken shards of glass on the floor of his heart.

Noire's Tuesday afternoon class had been canceled. She sat in the computer lab at school instant-messaging Jayna:

BLACK TOMORROW: Time is getting pretty tight. What's the plan?

PEARLY32: I told Alan that I'd let him know by Friday. He needs the money by the 15th.

BLACK TOMORROW: Do you have it?

PEARLY32: Not really. But Mama said she'd give me a couple hundred dollars toward the trip. Nate's been before. He said that once you're there it's really cheap.

BLACK TOMORROW: So he's going too? I thought it was just fourth-years.

PEARLY32: Not enough black folk here to be exclusionary! ;-)

BLACK TOMORROW: True. Are you going to invite homeboy? What's his name?

PEARLY32: Yeah. Phineas.

BLACK TOMORROW: What?! What kind of name is that?

PEARLY32: He's Phineas the third or some shit. It was some sort of tribute to the family's benevolent slave master.

BLACK TOMORROW: That's crazy.

PEARLY32: He's trying to go by his middle name now.

BLACK TOMORROW: What's that?

PEARLY32: Jerome.

BLACK TOMORROW: LOL!!!

PEARLY32: I know, don't laugh. Only black folks would name their child Phineas Jerome Houston III. It's all good though.

BLACK TOMORROW: So things are getting better?

PEARLY32: He likes me. And girl he's got some real skills that I'm not mad at. So . . .

BLACK TOMORROW: He's the hookup.

PEARLY32: Basically.

BLACK TOMORROW: Multitasking homeboys can't be taken lightly! ;-)

PEARLY32: I'm sayin' though. So, what's up w/ Innocent? You hardly talk about him.

BLACK TOMORROW: Hard to IM about that. It's complex.

PEARLY32: How?

BLACK TOMORROW: We're just not . . .

PEARLY32: What?

BLACK TOMORROW: I just feel a little pressed about school and everything. It's hard. I don't really discuss it with him. School, I mean.

PEARLY32: You should.

BLACK TOMORROW: It just feels like wasted energy, like I'm taking him away from stuff.

PEARLY32: Girl, Negro ain't even got a job!

BLACK TOMORROW: I mean that what's important to me doesn't always feel important to him. And vice versa, sometimes. I mean, he listens, but he doesn't understand.

PEARLY32: I don't even understand half the shit you say. But so what. You're my friend.

BLACK TOMORROW: It's not the same.

PEARLY32: I don't know what to tell you.

BLACK TOMORROW: I know.

PEARLY32: Damn, Noire.

BLACK TOMORROW: I don't even know. It's funky.

PEARLY32: Well, if you want to talk more, give me a call. I'll be in late, but . . .

BLACK TOMORROW: Thanks. I'm cool.

PEARLY32: Look, I have to go. Take it easy, OK?

BLACK TOMORROW: Yeah. Wait—

PEARLY32: What?

BLACK TOMORROW: When's graduation? Tryin' to figure out when to book my Curaçao trip.

PEARLY32: May 17. Alan and I are gonna throw a little party. You'll get an invite. Gotta fly!

BLACK TOMORROW: OK, bye . . .

Noire closed the instant-messaging window and clicked onto her e-mail. She had one.

SUBJECT: food and drink!
DATE: April 11, 2000, 3:33 P.M.
TO: undisclosed recipients
FROM: Arike@mymail.com

Fabulous friends and lively loved ones,
Dennis and I thought we'd spice up Tax Day by celebrating our second

anniversary a few days early. We'd love it if you could come through for a little dinner party on Saturday the 15th at 7:30 (Jaime, that does not mean midnight!) and just enjoy some good music, food, and drink. And if we can get Dennis to drink enough rum, he'll be sure to demonstrate the latest winin' straight from Trinidad Carnival 2000!

> We hope to see you!
> Arikè (Dennis's other half . . . we won't say which)

She forwarded the message to Innocent with the added lines, "I hope you'll join me; it should be fun. BTW, I'll be over a little later than anticipated. I have to meet with Bonita," and then closed her e-mail account.

Noire sat down to Jamaican take-out. Innocent hadn't bothered to take the food out of the containers but he helped himself to Noire's red snapper that he had ordered for her. She decided to pass on the oxtails he had for himself. They fed their hunger before launching into anything beyond small talk.

"I spoke to Mireille yesterday."

"How is she?"

"She got into Howard." His voice was flat.

"That's great." She looked up from her food. "But you don't seem to think so."

"No. I'm happy. She's just talking about her change of heart." His face was a grimace.

"Why?"

"She's in love. Apparently her boyfriend doesn't want her to leave."

"She said that?"

"No, she's making it sound like it's her decision."

"So she definitely said no."

"She said she'd think about it."

"Maybe she just needs to come to her own decision."

"Just as long as it's the right one. If she turns it down, it'll only be because of him."

Noire nodded. Her stomach clenched up and threatened to discharge all she had eaten.

"So what do you think?"

"I think she has to do what's right for her."

"What do *you* think is right for her?"

"I don't know, Innocent. I hardly know Mireille."

They ate in silence as Noire worked up her courage to make her own announcement. "So, I met with Bonita earlier."

"Right, how was that?"

"It was good. I agreed to apply for a one-year fellowship to Haiti. She just told me about it yesterday." Noire watched Innocent's jaw tense. He had stopped chewing and sat the half-clean piece of oxtail back in its aluminum container.

He bounced his head on the end of his neck in a misplaced nod before speaking. "So, what's it all about? The fellowship?" He forced tension out of his eyes.

"It's for predoctoral research. Bonita says that she can almost guarantee I'll get it."

"How's that?"

"Because I'm good, for one. And because I have good support. She and the chair of the department will highly recommend me."

Innocent knew he was supposed to be excited for her. "When will you know?"

"Late August. I finish my coursework the fall semester of this coming school year."

"Of course. Right." His head resumed its bouncing. He pushed his plate away from him. "So I take it that Bonita encouraged you to do this."

"She said I'd be crazy not to."

Innocent rubbed his eyes and then looked at Noire. "I think I told you I'd be going to France for a couple of weeks this summer."

Noire nodded, trying to trace the shift in conversation.

"So I'll be there for a portion of June and maybe into July."

"That's great."

"The main investor in the project is a guy named Mounir Assad. He's Lissette's ex-boyfriend."

Lissette's name punched Noire in the stomach. "So I guess she proved helpful in this little arrangement."

"She had nothing to do with it. Mere coincidence. Like you going to Haiti."

"Why are you being mean?"

"I'm just talking. Telling you shit. Being straight-up about shit."

"I don't understand where this is going." Her voice was as thin as tissue paper.

"Noire, I don't understand it either. Sometimes I just don't." His left hand held up his head that swam with cruel intentions. He didn't know why he wanted to hurt Noire, but he did know that he was hurting himself.

They stared at each other, flames in Noire's eyes and ice in Innocent's.

Noire arrived at Arikè and Dennis's party alone. She had made herself look the part of a congratulatory friend, but her heart fought back the envy that grew like a vine around the corners of her being. Dennis greeted her at the door, rum punch in his hand, and hugged her with the vigor of an old friend. "Hey, where's Innocent?"

"It's unlikely he'll make it."

"Well, hey, we're happy to have you. We know it was short notice!"

She smiled appreciatively. Dennis knew how not to ask too many questions.

He walked her into the front room, his arm draped around her shoulder. "Everyone, this is Noire. She's Arikè's buddy and I love her like an auntie!" Garnering the requisite laughter, he continued. "I'll let you mix an' mingle an ting."

Arikè came down the stairs wearing a flesh-colored b. Michael dress that clung to her figure. Sleeveless, the neck was a large oval-shaped cutout that revealed her unadorned neck and the tops of her breasts. She clicked along the wooden floor over to Noire and kissed her in greeting. Noire's forlorn look at Arikè's appearance made her hug Noire as well. "Hey, it's good to see you. You look great. I see you still have your tan!" Arikè pinched the cheek she had just kissed. "Thanks for coming. Really."

One of Dennis's friends refreshed the drinks of the twenty-five people present and then Dennis and Arikè took center stage. Dennis began.

"When I met Arikè, it was sort of as a favor to my boy Tolu here"—he pointed and Tolu raised his hand—"but I couldn't have known that she would be so beautiful and yet so mean! It took seven dates before she would even sit close to me, but when she did, she kissed me. I've been hooked ever since. And so, to make sure that I never lose this amazing woman, I've asked her to marry me—"

"And I said yes!" Arikè squeaked, her eyes gleaming with happy tears. She sniffled and caught the tears with her fingers. "We just wanted to share this very special time with all of you because you mean so much to us. Thank you so much for coming. We love you!"

The assemblage hooted, clapped, and ogled Arikè's chunk of an engagement ring now installed on her finger.

"Now, let's get this party started!" Dennis bounced around like a child on a sugar high.

Noire blotted her own tears with the palms of her hands. Realizing that her stinging tears seemed inappropriate to the occasion, she found the bathroom and sat on top of the toilet, trying to collect herself. India.Arie sang "Brown Skin" from a transistor radio. There was a knock on the door.

"Somebody's in here." Noire's voice was weak.

"It's me," Arikè announced from the other side of the door.

She stood up to unlatch the door and Arikè slid in.

"Hey, sweetie. Look at you." Her voice was cooing.

"I'm sorry. Congratulations. I'm so happy for you." The words stirred up unshed tears that caught in her throat.

Arikè hugged Noire, absorbing the vibrations of Noire's trembling body. When her silent wheezing began to subside, Arikè said, "Why don't you wash your face with some cold water."

Noire did as she was directed and Arikè opened up the toilet seat and sat.

"I'm sorry, Noire. I just really needed to go to the bathroom." Her face was reflective. "My stomach has been a little off these past few days. I guess the engagement and all."

"Do you need me to leave you alone in here?"

"Oh no! I'm fine now. I'm just saying . . ." She wiped, got up, and flushed. Washing her hands at the sink, she said, "OK, let's see you. You need just a little makeup on your eyes. I have something right here." She pulled out a compact from the medicine cabinet and dabbed lightly iridescent powder over Noire's eyes and on her cheeks. "You look beautiful. You just need a hint of lipstick." She kissed her dutifully on the lips, then took her finger and spread the newly deposited color around.

"Thanks." Her smile genuine, she gave Arikè a hug and opened the bathroom door.

"The man is back!" Marcus was a neon light flashing through Innocent's cell phone.

"*Bienvenue,*" Innocent whispered as he walked into the vestibule of the business library.

"I should say the same to you. Didn't you just get back from somewhere?"

"Noire and I had gone to Jamaica. But that was over a month ago."

"I can't keep track of you globetrotting folks."

"I heard they named a city after you in South America."

Marcus laughed. "Almost, man. It was a good trip." He told Innocent about the major deal he closed in Brazil and the project he scouted out in Argentina. "And Lydia and I made a baby too!"

"Hey, there you go!"

"I still got it."

"When's she due?"

"We don't quite know—I was too excited to understand a thing the doctor was saying in Brazil—but she's going to her OB/GYN this week."

"Well, congratulations."

"Yeah, thanks." Marcus blushed through the phone. "So how're things on your end?"

"Things are things. I'd like to talk to you soon about some of my professional plans."

"No doubt. I've been waiting to hear you say that for months."

"I just needed some time to clear my head."

"Fair enough."

"But now I'm ready to dive in headfirst."

"That's my man!" Marcus's pleasure was evident. "And on the personal front?"

"Tryin' to do a reassess."

"Was Jamaica jacked up?"

"No, that was great. But when we returned, reality slapped me in the face. I don't know, man. We'll see . . ." Innocent had already said more than he meant to. He hurriedly changed the subject. "Mireille got into Howard."

"That's great!"

"But she's acting confused because of the guy she's dating."

"There will be plenty of Howard men who will let a beautiful woman suck his dick."

"Man, we're talking about my *sister*."

"Oh, my bad! Sorry, man . . ."

"Yeah." Innocent shifted on the stone bench, uncomfortable by the remark.

"She'll see the light. She just needs to do it in the next week. When are decisions due?"

"May first."

"Just lay on her a little. She'll do the right thing."

"I hope so."

"She will."

"So, I should get off the phone."

"When am I gonna see you?"

"Soon. When do you have time?"

"Give me a week, week and a half, to wade through my mail. Let's try the end of April."

"Sounds good. We'll touch base before then."

"Of course. You take it light."

"Alright."

"Oh. Where's Lissette?"

"In Miami."

"You need to think about that."

"Later, Marcus."

"OK, son. Later."

The end of the semester unraveled Noire's frayed nerves. She could not contain all the thoughts that pushed against the walls of her brain while also tending to the demands of her heart. She knew she had to bear down and finish her work—two term papers, independent research for Bonita, her Papiamentu proficiency exam, and now the fellowship application. She found it hard to prioritize, not merely because her workload was taxing, but because her academic obligations had tremendous professional implications.

Adding insult to injury, her emotional capacity was saturated. She had no more space for the steady diet of insecurity and angst that her relationship with Innocent fed her. In her daydreams, she regularly sought the uncomplicated content of those Jamaican afternoons when she would exchange simple Patois phrases with the guys who sold jerk chicken and pork at Boston Bay while Innocent stood at the water's edge, the turquoise water lapping at his ankles. She would rejoin him and they would talk about all of the small things that were the threads that formed the fabric of intimacy. No agenda, no assumptions. They had allowed each other to love their unspectacular selves, uncomplicated by motives and the scrutiny of friends and loved ones.

But now Innocent punctuated her most negative thoughts about herself. Calling upon all the things she thought she valued, she felt disloyal and ugly, unable to reconcile her personal politics with her present state of affairs. So she became critical of Innocent. She resented the lifestyle that he was able to afford for himself even despite the fact that he hadn't worked since September of last year. She questioned his political and social leanings, pointing to friends like Lissette and Marcus as people who have never struggled for anything, thought that historically black colleges were cool experiences en route to Ivy League graduate degrees, and traveled business class to everywhere their minds could imagine. What did Innocent care about, beside his friends, his business, and his sister? Noire was convinced she fit into none of those categories.

Was Innocent her *friend*? She wondered how he really felt about her upcoming trip to Curaçao and her probable year in Haiti. Was he happy for her? Did he want for her to have the academic career that she desired, the way that he encouraged Mireille to pursue *her* own dreams? To her mind, his professional aspirations could be realized anywhere he had a laptop and a mobile phone. Was he willing to travel with her?

And suppose he asked her to stay. Would she? What would it mean if he asked and she agreed? Noire could think of no satisfactory answer to any of it. She felt like a child hopelessly pounding a round peg into a square hole, her frustration made all the more palpable by her lack of understanding. She struggled with why she persisted in her relationship with Innocent. Was she mistaking her own driving need to be loved with the love she tried to believe she had for him?

Or maybe it was her ego that couldn't let her say good-bye without branding herself a failure. Noire gave a cheerless snicker. She had always prided herself with being smart and being right. But at the end of the day, love wasn't about pride. It was about being humble and honest, whatever that looked like. Her stomach clenched in fear.

Noire clued into her surroundings in time to get off the A train at West 4th Street. She traced her daily walk to the comp lit department, sure that she could see her footprints on the pavement. That walk was her life. It was a part of who she was at twenty-nine years old and would be the bedrock of all she hoped to become. Noire felt suddenly protective of it. Cutting diagonally across Washington Square Park, she looked at all the nameless faces that held claim to the world they had in common. She stared into those faces and none of them belonged to Innocent.

Innocent carefully eased his color-printed pie graphs into plastic sleeves. He inserted them into the portfolio binder that represented the first three months of his research on possible business ventures he could develop between the U.S. and Côte d'Ivoire. The binder assembled and labeled, he flipped through his handiwork and thought about what he would say to Marcus. He felt pleased with his creation—which exemplified his own interests and not business school requirements or an employer's needs—but was disillusioned by how remarkably little he had been able to unearth using the traditional research methods.

Africa, as an aggregate of business locations, products and services, and innumerable investment opportunities, remained the proverbial dark continent to every "respected" multinational business index. With the small exceptions of pockets of oil-rich land and the minerals and raw materials that were extracted from countries, refined, and then sold back to their inhabitants at retail price, no one knew or seemed to care about the true potential the continent had to offer. Africa, both as a continent and as its individual countries, was analyzed using a deficit model. The world lens viewed it as a drain on the agricultural, health, and financial resources of richer nations who funded charity work and so-called international development schemes that paid their European and American employees in their home currency while mourning the persistent underdevelopment that seemed to plague the "good-hearted but shortsighted" Africans. No popular economic analysis drew parallels between underdevelopment and colonialism, slavery, unfavorable trade relationships, educational disparity, and ethnic factionalism.

Innocent was careful not to place wholesale blame on everyone else for the problems that African nations faced. He recognized that political instability and economic discontinuity resulted from leaders' greed, nepotism, and lack of leadership. He was keen to the persistent corruption that crippled infrastructure development and siphoned money back into foreign markets through private bank accounts. But the internal vices were born from, and nurtured by, the external mechanisms that maintained the status quo.

He knew that his ideas would not change the course of things. He was one man with only limited access to capital. But he felt that if he could tap into the network of resources that a person like Marcus Gordon could garner through his family's power, wealth, and prestige, eventually he could go far toward building one tiny piece of the plan that would help to create a more financially and politically viable continent.

As he showered, Innocent imagined all the ways in which Marcus might react. The most he could hope for was guarded interest and a slew of questions that he would have to do added research on to answer. But either way, Innocent knew that he needed to move forward with his plan to define and grow his business, even if it took him five years to do it.

• • •

He met Marcus at his home office. With Lydia out meeting with a girl for her twice-weekly therapy, and Nile out with his nanny, the house stood still except for Marcus's laughter that shook the walls. He was tan and fit; his travel had treated him well. Flipping through the pictures from the trip, he recounted anecdotes about their adventures through Bahia and the Amazon.

Staring at the self-assured smile that three-year-old Nile readily displayed for the camera, Innocent felt emboldened to ask Marcus what he wanted for his growing family.

"I want what everyone wants—for my children to grow up to be whoever they want to be in whatever way they want to do it. Nothing more, nothing less."

"But how would you feel if Nile"—he struggled to make his statement palatable to his friend—"wanted something totally different. Let's say he decided to subsist on a commune."

"Why would he do that?"

"I don't know why, Marcus. I'm just asking how you'd feel."

"Given the caviar tastes that this little boy has, I doubt that would ever happen."

"But you're expecting another child."

"Innocent, if you're asking if I have expectations of my children, the answer is yes. I want them to have a good life and part of what that means is having money. I make no bones about that. If I ever had a child who rejected that . . . well, I suppose that I would've seen it coming. But I can't worry about that. Right now, I just want this new baby to be born healthy because you can't buy health. Then, I hope that my children never feel limited for being black."

"How could they? They're rich and they don't even know it."

"Innocent, there's no escaping American racism. Even at the chi-chi prep schools I attended till college, white kids knew how to be mean to black kids."

Innocent digested his friend's thoughts.

"But that's not what you came here for, to ask me my philosophy on child rearing."

"No. But it's related, because my professional interests reflect my own dreams for the children I hope to be blessed to have." Innocent launched into his commercial for his business research with his pitch book as his only prop.

They returned to Marcus's office and fell into intense exchange that matched Innocent's expectations. Marcus was interested in the noble ambitions he outlined, but he was more concerned about the bottom line. He grilled Innocent with questions that he could answer only inadequately. Jotting notes feverishly, Innocent calculated an arduous road ahead of him. Marcus made no commitments and was clear that it would be a long time before he did. He wanted to see that Innocent had some "skin in the game," that he had invested his own money as well as time into making his ideas a viable business. They ended their two-hour-long meeting with Innocent ringing sweat out of his undershirt. But he left feeling grateful for the cross-examination and hopeful that Marcus's scrutiny would morph into interest and ultimately financial backing.

Noire pressed PLAY and her answering machine responded. *"It's Arikè. I sent you an e-mail. Hope you read it soon. Oh, it's three-thirty. Bye."* Fresh from her latest procrastination technique—giving away clothing to a nearby church—Noire returned to her apartment with the intention of finishing her last two papers. She had met success with most of her outlined projects but had only ten days before the rest was due. Arikè's message, however, created another diversion.

She awoke her computer screen from its slumber—the fourth in as many hours—and logged onto her e-mail account.

SUBJECT: Where love resides
DATE: May 1, 2000, 3:12 P.M.
TO: Noire@nyu.edu
FROM: Arike@mymail.com

Noire,
I've been thinking about the questions you asked me a while ago about how I love Dennis and "where." I was a little caught up when we were talking

that day, but it really did hang with me. And as Dennis and I got closer to deciding to make our relationship permanent, I thought about it even more.

In all of my dating life (which has been considerable! ☺) I've felt like I had to be Ms. Diva or Sex Goddess or Exotic or whatever. I couldn't just be me—the quirky, intelligent, sensual, or vulnerable side of myself. Even after Tolu introduced me to Dennis, I still had designs on Tolu, like I was going to "win" him or something and then have the last laugh. But Dennis had the patience to just get to know me, to see me minus my bravado and drama. And when he did that, I felt free to love him because I was free to love me too. So, in terms of where my love for Dennis resides, it lives in my spirit.

Dennis is a great guy for so many reasons. I know that some folks look at him and figure that I must have decided to hang in with him for his house and because I can meet the musicians he represents or whatever. And those things are nice. But at the end of the day, nobody cares about that. Dennis loves me for myself even as he inspires me to be a nicer, more generous person. When I see how he stays in contact with his family in Trinidad, I feel more committed to my own family. And when I watch him get upset at all the tragedies we digest on the evening news along with supper, I remember to be more compassionate toward everyone.

Not everybody wants or needs the same thing in a partner, and so it's hard to say what should take precedence as you go about meeting people and falling in love. But if you know what's really important to you in your heart of hearts, and what your own strengths and weaknesses are, then you're more apt to recognize the person who's your complement when you meet him.

Noire, I don't know what will happen between you and Innocent, but I can say that in you I see a woman whose passions drive her to commit to things. That's why you're going to be such a great scholar or whatever you want to be—because you know how to dig in for the long haul. You need someone who respects that about you. It's also a quality you should definitely examine as you think about what drives your feelings about Innocent. Do you love him for who he is and what you two are together, or do you feel driven to succeed in this relationship just like you do in other aspects of your life?

Noire, in the nearly two years I've known you, I always liked your energy and enthusiasm for life. And in these last six months you've come to be a friend who I genuinely love. You are a beautiful woman, both on the inside and the outside. I want so much for you to be happy.

Love,
Arikè

Noire's heart felt physically full. She called Arikè's work number and was greeted by her voice mail. She hung up the phone, retrieved the orange juice carton from the refrigerator, and planted herself in front of her computer.

Pleased with her two-hour stretch of continuous writing, Noire decided to take a break.

"Innocent!" She said it like a hushed command, preempting his statement of it.

"Noire?" He no longer took her calls for granted. They had traded a few terse e-mails in the two weeks since they last had dinner together. "How are you?"

"I'm mostly OK. Tired. I've pulled a few all-nighters."

"I hope you're taking care of yourself."

"Thanks."

"How's your family?" Innocent asked.

"Fine. Yours?"

"Good, thanks. Mireille accepted Howard's offer."

"I'm sure you're happy."

"Relieved, yes. I think she realized that she had this golden opportunity to live away from our parents and took it." He snickered.

"Mmm."

"Yeah."

They breathed into the phone, watching the silence multiply like a virus.

"So, you called—" Innocent pushed a cough out of his chest.

"Yeah, I just wanted to . . . touch base. Two weeks until I leave."

"Time flies."

"It does."

"We should probably get together soon. I mean—"

"I wanted to suggest that." She threw a dried apricot into her mouth and choked.

Innocent sipped stale coffee patiently until she recovered.

"That's the other reason why I called."

"I can make myself available."

"Monday?"

"The eighth? OK. When?"

"I want to go where we can talk."

He shook his head, the phone rubbing against his ear like a dull knife.

"How about three P.M. at Prospect Park. By the benches near the arch."

"Oh, in Brooklyn?"

"I'm still studying."

"No, that's fine."

"Have a good weekend."

"Good luck with your schoolwork."

"Thanks."

Clicking the receiver, Noire called in her standard order from the Cajun Creole Café. Studiously avoiding any thoughts of Innocent, she put on her sneakers in slow motion and took five minutes to scavenge the $7.04 she knew she needed to pay for her food from the corners of her couch, her jacket and pant pockets, and, finally, her wallet. As she dragged toward the front door her phone rang.

"Hey, Arikè. I tried calling you earlier. Thank you so much for that e-mail. Really. Look, I just called in an order that I need to pick up. Can I call you back in like ten minutes?" Noire's words came out in a rush.

"Noire, I'm pregnant."

Noire collapsed to the floor where she had stood. "Oh my God."

"Yeah, that was my response."

"Are you happy?"

"Yes! And scared shitless. I can't believe it. We were being careful."

"Does Dennis know?"

"No. I tried him at work and on the cell but he must be in the subway or something."

"Does anyone else know?"

"You're the first."

"Oh my God."

"I wanted to tell Dennis first but I just couldn't wait! But don't tell him I told you."

Noire wondered when she would even have an opportunity to do something like that. "Of course."

"I'm going to be a mother."

Noire was silent.

"You didn't think I'd do anything else, did you?"

"I don't know what I think, Arikè." She told her the truth. "It's just a shock. I bet you weren't planning things this way."

"It's a blessing . . . Dennis will be speechless."

"Arikè, wow." She groped for words. "I know that you really want children."

"I'm due January 2!" she squealed.

"Oh my God."

"Yeah, I know. Guess I wasn't keeping on top of things. My period has never been really regular though. But . . . I just kinda didn't know what was happening in April . . ."

"Yeah. Wow." Noire's thoughts were in cartoon bubbles above her head. She tried to decide what to say. "Well, wait till you tell Dennis before you tell anyone else."

"Oh, I will now. I just had to say it, to make it real first. But I'll wait."

"Hey, I'm sure the two of you will be great parents, even if it *is* coming a bit early!"

"Thanks for being such an awesome friend, Noire! I love you."

"I love you too, Arikè." The words brought tears to her eyes.

"OK, so I'll let you go and get your food!"

"Oh yeah."

"Well, bye!" Arikè was gleeful.

"Congratulations . . ."

Chapter 20

Come to the River

Innocent watched Noire nervously. A beautiful brown miniature, she advanced through multilanes of traffic on her bike. Cars competed for first place behind the ambulance that parted the sea of vehicles rounding the Grand Army Plaza arch. She attempted unsuccessfully to weave through the cars, then, as a city bus gained on her, she retreated to her place at the periphery of the outer lane. She was winded when she arrived.

"I'm really sorry I'm late." Noire dismounted her bike and unstrapped her helmet.

"I would have preferred if you were later and hadn't run that light." He kissed her awkwardly on the cheek and she missed his face altogether.

"You weren't supposed to see that."

They walked into the park littered with the after-school crowd—teenage sweethearts seeking an unchaperoned backdrop for their urgent make-out sessions—as well as stay-at-home parents with toddlers and golden retrievers. Finding a vacant park bench, they claimed it,

Noire using her bicycle as a barricade to deter others from trying to share it with them.

"It's good to see you." Innocent stared into her face.

"I look like shit. I haven't gotten any sleep."

"You look like you're busy. That's all." He reached out and touched her hair cautiously, unsure whether he still had the privilege.

"It's dry."

"It's longer."

"I guess." Noire reached down and seized her water bottle from her bike, happy to have something in her hands. She fondled the bottle, forgetting that it had any other purpose.

Innocent sat stock-still. Ever since he was a child, he would amaze himself with his ability to create external calm from internal chaos. But Noire's fidgeting made him nervous. He reached out to silence her hands and ended up holding one. She sat her water bottle in her lap.

"So . . ." Noire looked off.

"Noire—" his voice broke before he could utter another syllable. He cleared his throat. "Um. You know, when I was in Paris, Mamadou said that your spirit was right for me. And even Mireille said that you really love me. And I really love you too. And so, you know, I've wanted to have this relationship work because you are such a wonderful woman." His lips stretched into a momentary smile. "But I just, I don't know if I am able to accept it. The love. I feel overwhelmed." He shook his head.

Noire's face was clouded as she fought to understand his meaning.

"Noire, I just, I don't think I even know how to love you well. I don't know if I can make you feel bubbly and complete the way that you were with Cudjoe. I had never seen that in you—that side of you—until I saw you talking to him. I spent the rest of the trip trying to make you feel comfortable to be yourself. But it was such a conscious decision on my part."

She struggled with his words, choked on them. She wanted to see his face, to know what he was feeling on the inside, but he cast his gaze on their linked hands.

"Innocent?"

He looked up and she saw her face reflected in his glistening eyes. She felt a tidal wave crash within her. She closed her eyes and concentrated on her breathing, begging her most dangerous emotions to retreat. "I didn't know that's how you felt about Jamaica. I had thought that it was perfect, that we had finally figured out how to be good to each other."

"Noire, it *was* perfect."

"But it wasn't a natural state of being for you, for us really."

He remained silent.

Her heart filled her chest. "You know, I thought that all we had to do was iron out some kinks and we'd be OK. We have our love."

"We do."

"But I've begun to wonder what was driving the love. I was beginning to get caught up in identifying our motivations—my motivations—and trying to determine if they were good enough." She wiped an escaped tear from the corner of her eye. "I think it's good to think about those kinds of things. But it had become a preoccupation with me. I started to identify all the things about you that I didn't know or couldn't readily appreciate. I regressed back to where I was when I first met you. I don't know what that says about me . . ."

Innocent felt wounded, though he could see in her face that she hadn't meant to. His jaw tightened.

"Maybe your success just made me feel hypersensitive about my own lack of it."

"You're going to get your Ph.D. and I've lost my job." Innocent was incredulous.

"The fact that you could even be out of work and still travel to Paris and home and then finance our anniversary in Jamaica and invest in Mamadou's gallery is like, totally outside of my realm of consciousness, Innocent. Before our relationship, I didn't think I'd ever experience that kind of comfort up close and personal. It kind of blows me away. I mean, I'm happy about it for you—and I've benefited from it—but it's something I'll probably never have for myself. And mostly I'm OK with that. I mean, I didn't decide to pursue academia for the money." She spat out a pithy laugh. "And *that's* such an uphill battle. From day to day I don't know if Bonita is pleased or disgusted with me. I feel like my whole academic and professional career hinges on my ability to strike the balance between friend, therapist, and protégée with her. It's bizarre." Noire stopped herself short, feeling as though she had veered very far off course.

Losing control of his enforced cool, Innocent bobbed his head up and down. "OK . . . OK . . . ," he muttered to himself as Noire looked on. "So . . . maybe we're not going to make it." His words exited his body in a low hiss.

"Yeah." Her own voice floated on an emotional torrent. "Maybe not."

They sat surprised at themselves, wondering if there was a way to take back what they had just said. But there wasn't. Noire got up first, her water bottle dropping off of her lap onto the grass-splotched dirt below the bench. She was jarred by the noise. Innocent picked it up and handed it to her.

"So, I'm going home." Noire put the bottle back in its holder.

"Are you OK to bike?" He looked at her body that swayed in the spring afternoon breeze.

"I'll take side streets." She contorted her face to produce the slightest of smiles.

"Please be careful." He alternated between wiping his left and right eyes.

"I will." Her face flushed maroon.

Innocent placed a shadow of a kiss on the crevice between her cheek and her lips. She strapped her helmet on and mounted her bike. "Bye."

"Noire?"

She aborted the momentum she tried to gain to climb up the hill.

"Maybe we can see each other before you leave?"

"Maybe." She pressed down on her bike pedals as hard as she could and lifted herself out of the park.

The chilly evening air dried saltwater rivers onto her face. Already wracked with shed tears, Noire felt her shudders exaggerate her own pain. She walked along, her black long-sleeve FIGHT THE POWER T-shirt fighting to keep her warm, her flip-flops slapping the pavement in a premature summer rhythm. She grabbed for the change she knew was in her pants pocket and cleaned her face with the back of her hand before entering the bodega. The boy behind the counter called upon all the wisdom and compassion of his seventeen years as he asked, "Damn, are you OK, Mami?" He never made any secret of his fondness for Noire during her many late-night runs for junk-food sustenance, but now he was outdone.

"No."

"Well, I'll kick his ass for you."

"No need." She sat the tub of Häagen-Dazs Dulce de Leche ice cream on the counter and counted out $2.99.

"It's $3.29 now. Price went up last week. Sorry," he added.

"I have $3.06." Her voice was withered.

The boy pulled some stray change from his own pockets and put it into the register. "It's OK, Mami. Feel better." He packed her purchase in a paper bag and placed it in her hands with all the reverence of a minister imparting a benediction.

"Thanks." Noire dragged her feet along the store's cracked linoleum floor.

She let herself feel all of the self-pity that an independent black woman was never supposed to allow herself to feel. Her tears were quiet now, almost righteous. She felt too bad to be strong and too sad to be angry.

Noire woke up surprised that she was alive. Thinking that she would have dehydrated herself from crying and drowned herself in a pool of misery, she sat up on the couch and composed herself. Though she felt the cricks in her neck and pinches in her waist, she forced herself to remain still.

Her mind was suddenly full of a conversation she and her mother had had five years ago, on the third anniversary of Big Mama's death.

"You know, after Mama died, I knew I would die too. I was sure I would wake up dead, that the grief would have driven me to it. But I was alive. And I noticed that the sun was shining and then was shocked that I could recognize anything that was beautiful. And then you came into the bedroom and, as I looked at you, tears filled my eyes. You hugged me because you thought I was crying because Mama was dead. But I was crying because I still had many reasons to be alive. I looked at my lovely twenty-one-year-old daughter and realized that neither of us was ready for me to leave. And mostly, God wasn't.

"It was in that moment that I understood what the old folks meant when they said, 'Well at least nobody died.' Because when someone dies, you know it. And even then, you have to keep living until it's your time to go."

"Nobody died." Noire whispered it to herself now. She sat there, feeling all the anguish her heart could feel, and remembered that neither she nor Innocent had died. And for that matter, neither had their love.

So what had she lost if not love? What happened to make this very beautiful thing that they shared become something unusable and destructive?

She rubbed dried tears from her cheeks and eyes. Her mouth was thick with the essence of too much Dulce de Leche and she tried vainly to cleanse her palate with her own saliva.

Noire went to the bathroom and brushed her teeth and washed her face. She studied her wet face in the mirror, looking for signs of added wisdom that often showed up as character lines on a woman's face. She saw none.

Innocent watched the sunrise from where he sat in the middle of his bed. The new yellow light drenched his face in false warmth. He threw his head forward, letting its weight pull his spine taut. He felt curiously out of step; his body rhythms convulsed as if he were a record being played backward. He reflected on yesterday's conversation and wondered if he had meant what he said. Could he really not love Noire well and receive the love she had for him or was he just scared to let himself do it? Was it the same thing?

He pulled his arms up from the sockets. His joints cracked. His body groaned. Fully awake, he became aware of his growing nausea and tore himself from the bed just in time to release his stomach sickness into the toilet. He flushed and rinsed his sour mouth with water, afraid to ingest even one drop for fear of a rapid reversal.

Tired from the violent activity that claimed hold of his digestive tract, he poured himself back into bed and drifted into unconscious numbness for four more hours.

Figuring that Mamadou was the best person he could reach out to, Innocent began to compose an e-mail to him.

SUBJECT: Noire
DATE: May 9, 2000, 10:13 A.M.
TO: pan-african_painter@france.com
FROM: theINNOCENTone@mymail.com

Mamadou,

Noire and I broke up yesterday. I feel fucked up about it, but it was the right thing. She felt it too. I was trying to just let things unfold but it became too hard somehow. And she was questioning whether my value system lines up with hers. I don't know if we've shot ourselves in the foot, getting caught up in such things. I mean, isn't happiness about enjoying the process of finding "the answers" rather than being paralyzed by the questions? Perhaps our obsession with both is the problem.

I think you've given me more credit than I deserve in rooting for this relationship with Noire. Her kind of loving is just so intense. Her LIFE is so intense in ways that I can barely touch.

I don't know if I'm making a bit of sense right now. I just broke up with the most selflessly devoted woman I've ever dated in my life. I think I must be crazy.

Innocent

Sending the message into cyberspace, he felt momentarily purged. He popped open a warm Dr Pepper and tried to continue with his life.

Noire's printer spit out twenty-six pages of mediocrity; it was the last thing that stood between her and the completion of her second year of graduate school. The realization mostly joyless, she reminded herself that she could now focus her attention on preparing to leave for Curaçao. The trip took on the flavor of a great escape and she was thankful for it. Her father had already rounded up a friend who would stay in her apartment and, importantly, pay her rent for the three months she was away. All she was responsible for was getting herself on the plane in seven days.

But before that there was Jayna's graduation to be celebrated. She called her friend. Jayna prattled noisily for a few minutes, her chatter covering up the awkwardness they both felt about Noire's recent turn of events. Noire tried to pick up her own spirits.

"I finished my last paper."

"Congratulations, Noire! That's a big accomplishment." She sounded like a motivational speaker.

"Just need to close up shop for the summer."

"Well, I know you can do it! You've always been great at that kind of stuff."

"So are you and Alan all ready for your big party?"

"Girl, so much drama. Nate has given him fever about inviting his ex-boyfriend."

"Oh Lord."

"Yeah. But he did it anyway. He said that he's his friend."

"Mmm."

"He also invited Marcus."

Noire was silent.

"I mean, maybe he won't even come. But they're like, frat brothers or something."

"Maybe they used to fuck too."

"I'm sorry, Noire."

"He knows to keep his distance."

"Exactly. Besides, Nana and Papi are threatening to lead the Macarena!" She giggled at the thought.

"*That's* worth seeing!" She forced a chuckle.

Firmly on the footing of shared family knowledge, Jayna made more conversation about her mother's latest boyfriend and the uncle that she was afraid would get drunk and embarrass everyone. Jayna was a sister to Noire, their friendship dating back to training bras and first periods and embarrassing french kisses with boys. Listening to Jayna's happiness, Noire felt happy for herself.

Jayna finished the family gossip, and her voice became more sedate. "Yeah. Holler if you need anything. Even if that's just someone to listen to you breathe. Whatever I can do . . ."

"Thanks, Jay. I can't wait till the seventeenth. I'll feel like a proud parent!"

"You've been there through it all! She smiled through the phone. "Take care, OK?"

"OK."

Innocent drummed his fingers wildly to A *Love Supreme*. John Coltrane's supplicant saxophone cried like an unfed child in his loft as he listened to Mamadou's answering machine message. He began to speak when Mamadou picked up the phone, his voice sounding soupy.

"Sorry, I was painting. Catching the sunset."

"I was just going to leave you my travel dates."

"I actually want to talk to you. Just not to everyone else."

"OK. Well, first, I arrive on June twelfth at 9:55 A.M. your time. And my return is booked for July fourth. But I can change it if necessary."

"Last July fourth I was in South Carolina with you and Noire." He sounded reflective.

"What a difference a year makes."

"Thanks for the e-mail."

"Yeah."

"Anyway, life is a peculiar game. And it is always interesting to watch how things unfold and blossom."

"True."

"Hey, Innocent, I'm going to catch the end of the sunset. But hang in there."

"Definitely."

Arikè had become an icon for prenatal health. At almost seven weeks, she was a resident expert on yoga, Kegel exercises, and diet, and downed a thick, green spirulina-and-wheatgrass shake every day. Today she shared the experience with Noire. Quizzing Noire on her emotional state since the breakup, Arikè kissed her emphatically on both cheeks. "I wonder if this baby will have the hots for her auntie when she's born just like her mommy does!"

She was effective in eliciting heartfelt laughter from Noire. "You are a crazy woman!"

"On the contrary . . . I have good taste! Smarts, looks, well-decorated passport to exotic locales!" She pursed her lips and opened her eyes wide in mock amazement.

Noire was warmed by Arikè's glow. She sipped her banana-carrot-apple-ginger smoothie. "So you're sure it's a girl already, huh?"

"Dennis and I have a bet. I figure that since I'm carrying the child, she hears my voice more often and so I'll win!"

"How are your parents about things?"

"They're happy to see this huge engagement ring on my finger! But seriously, they're excited. She'll be their first grandchild." She patted her barely rounded tummy that revealed nothing. "But Dennis and I are going to get married on Sunday, September tenth. It'll be at their house."

"Wow."

"Yeah, Mom wanted it earlier so that I wouldn't have to wear a maternity dress but I told her to just give it up!" Arikè laughed. "I'll be pleasantly plump!"

"You look happy." Her words were an affirmation.

"I am happy. I really am happy. And so is Dennis."

Kissing Innocent good-bye at the airport, Noire knew why she loved him. She stared at him, memorizing the face in front of her, the man who had indulged her, challenged her, exposed her to herself with compassion. She touched him, fondling the sweetness of his lips, hoping they'd make a permanent impression on her hand. She made love to his eyes one last time, marveling at their wet shininess.

His tears fell silently onto her palm as he kissed her hand extended toward his face. Then, clasping that hand within both of his own, he brought the entangled trio to his chest and rested it there. He wanted to tell her he loved her in his most sensitive places. But the words caught in his throat. With their hands on his chest, he whispered, "Noire . . . my heart."

Her cheeks were covered with the drizzle of a hot summer rain. Bringing her hand down to her side, she planted butterfly kisses on Innocent's wet eyelashes. Pulling her to him, Innocent wanted to hug Noire forever but she cut it short. There would be no forever. But she cherished the memory of forever.

Turning to go, Noire only uttered a plaintive good-bye.

"I want this to be a good trip for you."

She would only be gone for three months, but they were officially bidding farewell to their relationship. Here it was May 19, only a year and two months since they first met, but they had signed their secret names in each other's hearts using indelible ink.

Noire walked to the gate with measured steps. Stopping, she pivoted slightly on her heels. Innocent was a few yards away from where she had originally left him, but he still hovered as if expecting her to turn around. She waved and mouthed her mother's words: "Nobody died."

Grace

Willemstad was eye-candy. Noire wended her way through the city's Dutch-named streets lined with lemon-yellow, bubble-gum-pink, and baby-blue-colored seventeenth-century European-style buildings that gleamed with fresh coats of paint. A main port of call during the Dutch slave trade, the island was populated by a brown rainbow of people who spoke Papiamentu and hailed from Curaçao and other points in the Caribbean. And Venezuela's nearness assured a steady stream of Latin American music, food, and people.

Only 171 square miles from end to end, the island was bathed in northeasterly trade winds and dry 80-degree days and 60-degree nights. A part of the Kingdom of the Netherlands through its membership in the nation of the Netherlands Antilles along with Bonaire, Saba, St. Eustatius, and Sint Maarten, Curaçao was the official seat of the country's central government. And as the primary conduit for drilling and refining Venezuela's oil, the island held sway over the country's economy and interests. But Curaçaoans, like all people of the Netherlands Antilles, had Dutch citizenship and carried Dutch passports.

Her rented room was a modest affair in the private home of a schoolteacher on a street tucked behind the Curaçao Museum in the Otrobanda section of Willemstad. Connected to the Punda side of the city—the capital's governmental and commercial center—by Queen Juliana Bridge and the long Queen Emma footbridge that opened once or twice an hour, Otrobanda was full of the part of daily life that was residential, familial, and social.

Getting her bearings, Noire made a trip to her friendly neighborhood Internet café—more of a hastily assembled computer room with only a water fountain and gumdrop machine to count toward its "café" offerings. A brisk five-minute walk from her transitory home, the café hugged the neighborhood's commercial district. She paid for thirty minutes and sat down at a computer facing the pane-glass storefront. Her NYU account announced thirteen new messages, most with subject headings like "Made it?" or "I just wanted to make sure you got in OK; e-mail ASAP." She opened the message titled "you." It was from Innocent.

SUBJECT: you
DATE: May 20, 2000, 4:31 P.M.
TO: Noire@nyu.edu
FROM: theINNOCENTone@mymail.com

Noire,
I called the airline yesterday and learned of your safe arrival in Curaçao. I hope that this trip is a wonderful one. This poem is for you.

I love you,
Innocent

She double-clicked on the attachment:

GRACE

The bedtime prayers I uttered as a child
Requested that God take my soul if I died.
I didn't deserve it.

It wasn't what He owed me.
It was grace.
Grace—the space for mercy and unconditional love
For compassion and beauty that rises out of pain.
It respects what it can't immediately understand,
It seeks to accept, without fear of reprisals,
All that makes a person himself.
Grace gives us the strength to know
The potential and limits of love
And to be unselfish,
Letting go of what we cannot affirm.
I ask God to take my soul when I die,
But in the meantime, I pray for the gift of grace.

It had come to this: grace. Noire smiled, her eyelashes wet and heavy. She looked up from the computer screen and into the street that paved a path to a country she did not know. She logged off of her account, leaving messages temporarily unread and unanswered, comfortable with all of the questions that awaited her outside.

Reading Group Guide

Noire Demain, a Ph.D. candidate at New York University, is a twenty-something bohemian with an appetite for intellectual stimulation and eclectic fashions. And she's looking for her own brand of social consciousness in a delectable black man's package. So when she finds herself an "Afro in a sea of perms" at Brown Betty Books, she's not happy about it. Her best girlfriend, Jayna, stands her up and leaves her to fend for herself in a room full of black urbanites with six-figure salaries and summer homes on Martha's Vineyard. This is not Noire's idea of a good time.

But rising above the coiffed and coffee-colored faces is a particularly compelling example of black manhood—Innocent Pokou, a velvety dark, tall, and gorgeous Côte d'Ivoirean. Innocent is instantly attracted to Noire's energy and beauty. And he's available. An investment banker who belongs to an African elite of wealth and privilege, Innocent is cosmopolitan, ambitious, and intrigued with Noire. Noire's own desire-filled intrigue wins out over her disdain for the Buppie set, and she surprises both herself and Innocent by giving him her contact information.

They may be in love. They also may be totally wrong for each other. Their ideologies—as well as their closest friends—are at opposite ends of the spectrum. Their cultures are equally dissimilar. And with his family in Côte d'Ivoire pressuring him to find an "appropriate" wife, is Innocent willing to get serious with Noire? Then, as they say, "stuff" happens. A Fourth of July weekend at a beach house with a mix of his friends and hers will lead to emotional fireworks and a bonfire of unexpected attractions. Add the return of a former lover and a journey for both Innocent and Noire, and suddenly bedroom promises seem made to be broken . . . unless these two extraordinary people can discover what matters most, what touches deepest, and what fulfills the needs of both heart and soul.

A Love Noire tolls the bell for the black urban professional. It presents clashing ideologies at every turn through the lives of Innocent, Noire, and their friends and family. It is upon their collective stage that we confront diverse and incongruent black identities, romantic expectations, and social and financial aspirations. Their hearts entangled in a powerful love burdened by the weight of competing interests and fragile chosen identities, Innocent and Noire fight to sustain a relationship that successfully incorporates the best of both worlds.

QUESTIONS FOR DISCUSSION

1. Noire observes that Innocent "knew a life that most Americans didn't experience and fewer realized exists in Africa. He made no apologies and felt no contradictions about who he was." Does Noire feel contradictions about who she is? If so, what are her conflicts about her identity?

2. Compare the parents of Noire with those of Innocent. How much do you feel that family influences a person's choice of a partner? Why did Noire choose Innocent? Why does Innocent choose Noire?

3. Now look at Grand-mere Demain. What has been her influence in Noire's life, both positive and negative?

4. Why is Noire affected by skin color and hairstyle? Do you feel that a light skin tone and so-called good hair are still given preference in the African American community? If so, why? Do you see this changing in the next decade?

5. Innocent thinks this about Noire: "She unnerved him, energized him, extended him into the rough territory beyond himself. But the minute he knew he had her he didn't know what to do with her." Discuss Innocent's character. Why does he not "know what to do with her"?

6. Several characters raise provocative issues about being black and American and still celebrating the Fourth of July. What are the arguments? What is Innocent's viewpoint? What is Noire's?

7. What do you make of Noire's sexual experimentation with Arikè? Do you feel it is believable in the context of the story? What about her relationship with Professor Fuentes, her NYU mentor? Is there a sexual element?

8. Compare these relationships with Noire's longtime friendship with Jayna. What forms the basis of their bond? At this stage in Noire's life, do you think she shares more in common with Jayna or Arikè?

9. Innocent says to Noire, "Lasting relationships aren't built on love. There's compatibility, having similar goals and complementary dispositions, having the will to see it through . . ." Do you agree or disagree? Do you believe Innocent really thinks that, or is he just having second thoughts about Noire?

10. What is the significance of Noire's name? What about Innocent's? Are their names symbolic? Ironic? Think about the book's title. In what ways does it foretell the story?

11. Discuss the other young couples in the book—Arikè/Dennis and Marcus/Lydia. Why do their relationships seem to work? What

about Jayna? Why does she have difficulty with a long-term relationship?

12. When Noire goes to Jayna for advice about her relationship with Innocent, they reminisce over the advice Noire's mother had given her when she was an undergraduate: to wait a year before becoming physically intimate with a man. At the time, both she and Jayna balked at the suggestion as unrealistic, and they still don't follow it now. How do you think physical intimacy affects the pacing and intensity of a relationship? Does it have unintended outcomes? What advice would you give Noire or Jayna as they pursue love?

13. What are the overarching lessons about love in this story? Who learns them? What kinds of love relationships—romantic, familial—do we witness and how do these relationships grow? How do the characters grow in their understanding of love?

14. What do you predict for Noire's and Innocent's futures?

15. Have you had an intimate relationship with someone of a different cultural or financial background than your own? How did you deal with any conflicts concerning your differences? Did those differences strengthen or disturb your relationship?

16. How did your family or friends react to your cross-cultural, -faith, -generational, or -financial relationship? Did you accept or reject their feedback or let it affect your relationship?